"AND I SUPPOSE YOU HANDCUFFED ME TO THE BED AND SEDUCED ME JUST TO BE HOSPITABLE."

Her eyes widened, and then suddenly she was laughing. Not a soft chuckle, but a full-out laugh that brought tears to her eyes.

"You think that's funny, do you?"

She stopped laughing, but her eyes behind the glasses still twinkled with humor. "If you knew me, Mr. Cates, you'd think it was funny too. I've never seduced a man in my life."

"So what were you doing in my bed last night?"

Elizabeth's mouth opened, but nothing came out. She closed it and swallowed hard. Before she could try again, a gunshot rang out.

Praise for the
DEEP IN THE HEART OF TEXAS Series

CATCH ME A COWBOY

"4½ stars! A heartwarming return to Bramble, Texas, with many familiar faces. This is an emotional story that will bring the reader to laughter as well as tears and spark a desire to see more of the characters, both new and old, who live here."
                                              —*RT Book Reviews*

"An absolute hoot!...*Catch Me a Cowboy* is home to a plethora of wacky characters who make this a fun story... A winner!"   —RomRevToday.com

"Rewarding...Perfect for a lazy summer afternoon."
                                              —*Publishers Weekly*

"This series continues to be a riot of fun. I was laughing out loud and loved the children."   —SingleTitles.com

MAKE MINE A BAD BOY

"A delightful continuation of *Going Cowboy Crazy*. There's plenty of humor to entertain the reader, and the people of the town will seem like old friends by the end of this entertaining story."   —*RT Book Reviews*

"Funny, entertaining, and a sit-back-and-enjoy-yourself kind of tale."   —RomRevToday.com

"If you're looking for a romance true to its Texas setting, this is the one for you. I simply couldn't put it down."
                                              —TheSeasonforRomance.com

"I absolutely loved Colt! I mean, who doesn't like a bad boy? Katie Lane is truly a breath of fresh air. Her stories are unique and wonderfully written...Lane, you have me hooked."
                                              —LushBookReviews.blogspot.com

"Another fun read and just as good as [*Going Cowboy Crazy*]... a perfect example of small town living and the strange charm it has. I really enjoyed reading this one and hope that Katie Lane is writing a third." —SaveySpender.com

"It will make you laugh, and then make you sigh contentedly. *Make Mine a Bad Boy* is a highly entertaining ride." —RomanceNovelNews.com

GOING COWBOY CRAZY

"Romance, heated exchanges, and misunderstandings, combined with the secondary characters (the whole town of Bramble), who are hilarious...This is the perfect summer read. Katie Lane has a winner on her hands; she is now my new favorite author!" —TheRomanceReadersConnection.com

"Entertaining...[with] a likable and strong heroine." —*RT Book Reviews*

"Ah, I want my own cowboy, tall, dark, and handsome, but alas he is only between the pages of the book, a good book at that. Katie Lane knows how to heat the pages and keep you burning for more. Romance, steamy love scenes, humor, witty conversation with a twang, all help the pages keep turning. I'm looking forward to reading other books written by Katie Lane." —BookLoons.com

"An enjoyable romp...a fun, down-home read." —*All About Romance* (LikesBooks.com)

"I enjoyed this book quite a bit. It really reminded me of an early Rachel Gibson...or early Susan Elizabeth Phillips. Faith became a sassy, intriguing heroine...The chemistry between these two ratchets up to white-hot in no time." —TheSeasonforRomance.com

"Frequently amusing...The lead couple is a wonderful pairing while the third wheel hopefully gets her own tale." —*Midwest Book Review*

Also by Katie Lane

Trouble in Texas

KATIE LANE

FOREVER

NEW YORK   BOSTON

Forever
Hachette Book Group
237 Park Avenue
New York, NY 10017

www.HachetteBookGroup.com

Printed in the United States of America

OPM

First Edition: December 2012
10 9 8 7 6 5 4 3 2 1

Forever is an imprint of Grand Central Publishing.
The Forever name and logo are trademarks of Hachette Book Group, Inc.

The Hachette Speakers Bureau provides a wide range of authors for speaking events. To find out more, go to www.hachettespeakersbureau.com or call (866) 376-6591.

The publisher is not responsible for websites (or their content) that are not owned by the publisher.

ATTENTION CORPORATIONS AND ORGANIZATIONS:
Most HACHETTE BOOK GROUP books are available at quantity discounts with bulk purchase for educational, business, or sales promotional use. For information, please call or write:

Special Markets Department, Hachette Book Group
237 Park Avenue, New York, NY 10017
Telephone: 1-800-222-6747 Fax: 1-800-477-5925

*To two of my favorite hens, my sisters,
Christy Poling and Sandi Frentzel*

Acknowledgments

I'm so fortunate to be surrounded by a gaggle of amazing "hens" who keep me sane in this crazy chicken coop of life:

My loving daughters, Aubrey and Tiffany,
Most precious granddaughters, Gabby and Sienna,
Sweet sisters, Christy Poling and Sandi Frentzel,
Supportive mom-in-law, Kay Smith,
Longtime L-peeps: Lori Tillery, Lu Loomis, and Linda Chambers,
Fun Harley Mama, Annie Sevieri,
Hilarious writer and texter, Tammy Baumann,
Therapeutic walking buddy, Charlene Kennedy,
Best neighbors, Tina Wolf and Mrs. Chavez,
Fabulous Double-D's: Arlene, Becky, Cathy, Dorothy, Jill, Sandie, and Sue,
Lovely Ladies of LERA, too numerous to list,
Business-savvy agent, Laura Bradford,
Book-polishing editor, Alex Logan,
And my wonderful readers.
To you, and all the beautiful women who touch my life and make it richer, a BIG HEN HUG!!!

Trouble in
Texas

Prologue

THE GLOW FROM THE WINDOWS beckoned like a campfire on a cold wintry night, rivaling even the brilliant canopy of stars that hung overhead. With his journey almost at its end, William Frances Cates nudged his horse into a gallop. It had been a long, hard ride, and he was cold, tired, and hungry. However, it wasn't these needs that spurred him on as much as the need for a woman.

And not just any woman.

His woman.

The stable boy was there to take the reins as soon as William swung down from the saddle. He took the porch steps in two strides, completely ignoring the couple that sat on the swing, giggling. The uppity English butler greeted him at the door.

"Good evening, sir," he said as he took William's hat and duster. "She's been waiting for you."

The news almost had William smiling. Instead, he nodded at the man and followed him to a room just off the foyer. A wall of smoke rolled out as the door was opened, and William squinted in at the group of people who sat at the poker table. The men paid him little attention, their gazes riveted on their cards and the woman who dealt them. The dealer glanced up, and her ruby red lips tipped in a seductive smile.

"Game's over, boys," she said in a husky voice that warmed William more than the fire that burned in the hearth.

One man started to argue, but all it took was a delicate arch of an eyebrow to get his mouth to snap shut. The room cleared, and William was left with the most beautiful woman he'd ever seen in his life.

He had never been the type of man to let his emotions run wild. In fact, he had been described as cold and aloof. But there was something about this woman that broke through his wall of restraint. Something that had him ignoring the rules he'd lived by all of his life. Something that had him crossing the room and sweeping her into his arms.

He kissed her, and all the loneliness of a lifetime melted away. This was what he'd come for. This was what he needed. More than food, water, or air. Just this woman. Forever this woman.

The kiss was more than just lips touching. It was the anthem of love reunited. The merging of two halves into a whole. The confirmation that there was hope for all lost souls.

William was so consumed with the kiss that he didn't even glance up when the door opened. It took the resounding gunshot to pull him away. He whirled around just in time for the second bullet to hit him square in the chest. The impact threw him back against the wall, and he placed a hand over the wound as he slid down to the floor.

His assailant stood in the doorway with the gun still smoking. William should've been shocked. But as his life bled out between his fingers, all he cared about was the woman who knelt down beside him. The woman whose soft sobs hurt more than the hole in his heart.

"I love you," she whispered. She cradled him close, surrounding him in the scent of lilacs. "I'll always love you."

Suddenly, death had no power. And he smiled.

Chapter One

Henhouse Rule #1: Always give a man the kind of welcome he won't forget.

BRANSTON WILLIAM CATES WAS LOST.

He had been traveling the same dirt road for a solid hour and had yet to see any signs of civilization. Just miles of mesquite and sagebrush, the occasional lizard that streaked in front of his half-ton pickup, and the large black vulture that had been circling overhead since he'd entered west Texas.

West Texas.

Who in their right mind would want to live here? Of course, who in their right mind would take off on a road trip when there was plenty of work to be done back at his office in Dogwood? Time was money, and five hours spent on a highway a foolish waste of both. There was just one thing that trumped the almighty dollar in Brant's book, and the only reason he was driving on a dirt road in the middle of nowhere.

Family.

He glanced down at the navigational system, but it seemed to be as lost as he was. The green arrow sat in the middle of an empty screen inching toward nothing.

Patience not exactly his strong suit, Brant had just decided to turn around when a house took shape on the flat horizon. It grew larger and larger until it became a huge monstrosity of a building with two stories and a red, steeply pitched roof that, with its missing shingles, resembled a checkerboard on the tablecloth of the bright blue sky.

As he got closer to the house, he realized that the roof wasn't the only thing that needed repair. White paint bubbled and peeled on the siding. Half the shutters hung by only one hinge. And the front porch drooped worse than his grandmother's gardening hat.

To the left of the house sat a faded red barn, bookended by two gnarled-trunked cottonwoods. Another cottonwood shaded the front yard—a yard filled with waist-high weeds and a large wooden sign.

Trespassers Will Be Prostituted.

Brant had never been much of a smiler. His daddy claimed he came out of the womb frowning, and Doc Connelly got a real kick out of confirming the fact. But as Brant stared at the sign with the faded green letters, the corners of his mouth curved up—briefly.

So this was Miss Hattie's Henhouse, the infamous Texas bordello that had brought politicians to their knees and outlaws to their deaths. It seemed inconceivable. Brant hadn't expected to find the grand mansion he'd read about, but he certainly hadn't expected to find a pile of sticks that looked as if a stiff wind would topple it like a house of cards.

He was surprised by the disappointment that settled deep inside him. He had never been a dreamer. He preferred to deal with hard, cold facts. But the legends and stories about Miss Hattie's had seeped into his subconscious, filling his mind with images of the legendary whorehouse and the ladies who worked there. Ladies with names like Sassy Kate, Sweet Starlet, Daring Delilah, and the pièce de résistance, Hattie Ladue—the larger than life madam who had started the house of ill repute over a hundred years earlier.

It was Miss Hattie who had occupied most of Brant's thoughts in the last month. Miss Hattie who had spawned sensual dreams that had him waking up in a sweaty state of arousal. Maybe that was why he felt so disappointed. The dreams had replaced the nightmares that had plagued him since the tornado. If the dreams stopped, there would be no reprieve from the memories that lurked in the corner of his mind waiting to consume him when he least expected it.

He drove up a deeply rutted road and parked in what was left of a brick, circular drive. After the humidity of east Texas, the late September air felt hot and dry. He tugged his cowboy hat lower as he got out of the truck, then maneuvered through the weeds that almost obscured the pathway.

A flash of black pulled his attention up to the sky. The vulture still circled directly overhead, its long-feathered wings spread wide, its beady eyes searching for death. Some would take it as a bad omen. But Brant didn't believe in omens, just curses and revenge.

"You here on business or pleasure?" A raspy, feminine voice stopped him in his tracks.

His gaze narrowed in on the shadowy form in one corner of the porch. After seeing the condition of the house, he had assumed that Miss Hattie's was vacant, so it took him a moment to get over his surprise and pull off his hat.

"Is there a difference?"

A husky cackle was followed by a soft hum as a battery-operated wheelchair rolled out of the shadows. Brant had learned the importance of a poker face a long time ago, but it took real effort to keep his shock in check. The pictures in the history books of a blond temptress were nothing like the nightmarish creature who squinted back at him. A huge magenta wig surrounded a face with more makeup than a circus performer. If the wig and makeup weren't scary enough, the scanty negligee was downright terrifying. Or maybe it was the bits of wrinkled skin displayed.

Or possibly the gun that was pointed at Brant's heart.

"I've always liked my men with a smart mouth," the old woman said. The lit cigarette that was stuck to her upper lip waggled with each word. "You lost, honey?"

Brant kept his gaze locked on the bony hand that shook more than a leaf in a hailstorm. "I guess that would depend on whether or not this is Miss Hattie's?"

Her eyes narrowed. "And who wants to know?"

Given the events of the last few months, he figured his name wasn't exactly on the list of most beloved men in west Texas. Still, Brant wasn't one to hide behind an alias. He was who he was and rarely regretted a decision.

"Branston—"

The woman started to cough, not a delicate cough covered with a hand, but a deep, chesty cough that sent the cigarette flying into the weeds and shook her entire frail body—including the hand that held the gun. Brant barely had time to duck before a bullet whizzed over his head. The next one didn't miss. A blaze of fire streaked across his arm, causing him to drop his hat and grab the wound just below his shoulder.

It was funny. As much as he wouldn't have minded

dying in the last couple years, now that he had the opportunity, some unknown will to live kicked in. He took the steps in one leap and pulled the gun from the woman's hand.

It wasn't difficult. Her coughing had stopped, and she stared at the blood that seeped through his fingers. She took the sight better than Brant did. He could stare down the fiercest business competitors and three headstrong little brothers, but blood had always made him a little light-headed. A wave of dizziness washed over him, and he reached out and steadied himself on one of the porch posts.

"Minnie!" A woman's voice filtered out of the screen door only seconds before it was shoved open by a petite bleach-blonde who could've won a Marilyn Monroe look-alike contest if not for the wrinkled skin and glasses so thick her eyes looked like they were staring through a goldfish bowl. When she saw Brant, she stumbled to a stop, her high-heeled shoes clicking against the cement of the porch.

"Goodness, Minnie," she said in a breathy, Monroe voice. "You didn't tell me we had company." She jerked off her glasses and batted her long, fake eyelashes.

"For the love of Pete, Baby," Minnie said, "we don't have time for your shenanigans." She waved a crooked red nail at Brant. "Can't you see that the man is bleedin'?"

Baby placed her glasses back on and sucked in a breath. "Oh no, Minnie, not again. Last time you shot someone we got in loads of trouble with Sheriff Hicks."

Last time? Brant had just started to process this new piece of information when the front door opened and a tall, slender woman stepped out on the porch.

She was as old as the other two, but not as blatantly painted or dressed. This woman wore no makeup and looked like a throwback from the sixties in her bell bottom jeans, floral blouse, and leather sandals. Her hair was long and gray and held back with a chain of dandelions that she took off, then walked over and placed on Brant's head.

A wistful smile slipped over her face. "Can I have him, Minnie? After all, you got the last one."

"Jesus, Sunshine," Minnie huffed, "that was over thirty years ago."

Sunshine looked confused for only a second, and then she laughed. "Oh, Minnie, you're such a tease."

"For the love of Pete, will you two quit fawning over him and get him a chair before he passes out." Minnie pressed her fingertips to her temples. "I need to think."

"I'm not going to pass out," Brant said. "All I need is a towel and the cell phone from my truck so I can call the sheriff." He wasn't planning on pressing charges, but he did think the sheriff needed to confiscate any guns Minnie might still have. Next time the crazy old broad could very easily blow a hole in herself.

"But you can't do that," Baby said. "We can't have the sheriff coming out here. Not when we're just getting the business started back—"

"Of course we need to call the sheriff," Minnie cut Baby off. "But first we need to get Branston's wound cleaned up. Sunshine, go get the stuff Doc Mathers gave us when you cut your finger. And Baby, why don't you make us a drink? I'll take a double, and fix our guest here a Wild Rooster."

If possible, Baby's eyes got even bigger. "A Wild Rooster?"

Minnie's eyes hardened. "You heard me. After being shot, I think that's exactly what a man needs."

"I-if you say so, Minnie."

Baby hurried back inside with a staccato click of heels while Sunshine offered him one more airy smile before she followed. When they were gone, Brant walked over and sat down in one of the wicker chairs.

Why he had stopped by the house on the way to his brother's wedding was beyond him. He should've known that he wouldn't find any answers here. Of course, if he was truthful with himself, he would admit that his desire to stop by Miss Hattie's didn't have as much to do with his family's history as it did with the vivid dreams he'd been having. Dreams of sultry eyes that held a promise no man could refuse.

But Miss Hattie was long gone. The only thing left was a dilapidated mansion and a bunch of crazy old ladies. Which Minnie only confirmed when she rolled over to him, hooked her long nails into the hole that she'd blasted into his shirt, and almost ripped his sleeve in two.

She leaned closer. "Well, I think you'll live. I have bunions that are bigger than that."

Brant examined the wound and had to agree. Despite the blood, the gash was no more than a couple inches long and not very deep. Although the loony old gal had ruined his favorite tailored shirt.

"You should consider yourself lucky." She sat back in the wheelchair and took a long drag of her cigarette, then released the smoke through her mouth and nose.

"Luck isn't something I count on," Brant said.

Minnie studied him through the smoke. "Then I guess we're two peas in a pod because I don't put much store in it, either."

Baby came hustling back out with two glasses of amber liquid that sloshed over the rims and onto the porch. She gave one to Minnie and then offered one to him. He went to take it and realized he still held the gun. Being a bit of an antique buff, Brant had no problems recognizing it. It was a Remington derringer, more than likely made in the late eighteen hundreds. Since the gun only had twin barrels and both shots had been used on him, he felt comfortable setting it on the table before accepting the drink.

"Bottoms up," Minnie said. She downed her drink in one gulp.

Brant took his time. A Wild Rooster turned out to be nothing more than an expensive brandy that slid easily down his throat and took the tension from his shoulders and the sting from his arm. While he sipped the drink, Baby stood over him looking anxious. Figuring it had to do with him calling the sheriff, he started to tell her that he had no intention of pressing charges when Sunshine came back out with an armload of bottles, tape, and bandages. For being a little loopy, she seemed to know a lot about first aid. While she expertly cleaned his wound and bandaged it, he set the empty glass down and got to the point of his visit.

"Have you ever heard of a man named William Cates?"

Minnie lifted one penciled-in eyebrow. "Name sounds familiar. Who is he?"

After Sunshine secured the last piece of tape, Brant leaned forward. "My great-grandfather. Supposedly he was shot here."

Baby sucked in her breath. "You shot his grandfather, Minnie?"

Minnie held up her hands, the cigarette dangling from her lip. "Don't look at me. I've only shot three men in my life—that sneaky bastard who took off with our best silver, that writer who stole our stories and never gave us a cent, and Branston here." She looked at Brant. "When did this shootin' take place?"

"1892."

She snorted. "Lots of folks got shot back then—thus the name the Wild West." She took another drag of her cigarette. "Is that what you're doing here? Searching for a bit of family history?" Her eyes narrowed. "Or is it revenge that you're after?"

The woman was perceptive. He'd give her that. Brant wanted revenge. He wanted someone or something to blame for the death that followed him like the vulture that still circled the sky. Except looking at the three old women, he realized that he wouldn't find it here.

And maybe he wouldn't find it at all. But that didn't mean he would stop trying. Looking for answers about the Cates Curse was the only thing that kept him from insanity.

That and his family.

The thought of his family reminded him about his brother's wedding. He started to get to his feet, but a wave of dizziness had him falling back in the chair.

"Feelin' a little light-headed, are you, honey?" Minnie asked. At least, he thought it was Minnie. He was having trouble focusing. In fact, everything suddenly seemed a little fuzzy and surreal.

A hand slipped over his pectoral muscle. "So are we going to keep him, Minnie?"

Keep him? Brant pushed himself up from the chair. The ground rocked more than the deck of the fishing boat he and his brothers had rented earlier that summer.

There was a husky chuckle. "It looks like it, Sunshine. Now quit mauling him and help Baby get him upstairs."

Brant started to say that he wasn't staying, but his mouth wouldn't form the words. He took a step forward and stumbled. Two arms slipped around his waist and steadied him before he was guided through the front door. From that point on, everything became a jumbled blur. A ride in an elevator. A long hallway. A soft bed with slick sheets that smelled of lilacs.

When he hit the bed, he rolled to his back and tried to focus. A woman appeared. A woman with amber eyes and piles of wavy blond hair. She floated above him, the hint of a smile on her lips.

Brant recognized her immediately, and his eyes closed. *Miss Hattie.*

"We shouldn't have drugged him," Baby whispered as she leaned closer and studied the man, who was out cold. "I bet he wouldn't have pressed charges if we had asked real nice."

"We couldn't chance it," Minnie said. "Besides, this man ain't just here for information. He's after something. I just haven't figured out what yet."

Sunshine reached out and smoothed the dark strands of hair from his forehead. "Maybe he's like everyone else and just wants a little love."

"He doesn't look like he wants love to me," Baby said. "He looks mean. And I bet he's going to be real mad when he wakes up."

Minnie chuckled and took a puff of her cigarette. "Now, I doubt that, Baby. There isn't a man alive who walks out of Miss Hattie's without a smile on his face."

Chapter Two

*Henhouse Rule #14: When unexpected things
arise... rejoice.*

THE SECOND HAND OF THE WALL CLOCK ticked past the
ten, then on to the eleven. Elizabeth Murphy waited
until its slender arm was perfectly aligned with the black
minute hand, between the one and the two of the twelve,
before she got up from her chair.

"The library is now closed," she stated in the same
no-nonsense voice she'd used since first accepting the job
as librarian over fifteen years earlier. It was irrelevant that
not a soul was in the library to hear her. Her mother had
taught her that rules and routine were what kept a person's
life on the straight and narrow.

And no one's life was more straight and narrow than
Elizabeth's.

Without the slightest hesitation, she pushed open the
gate in the circular counter and proceeded to walk down
each long aisle. As she went, she tucked in protruding
spines and checked for any misplaced titles.

Books were her babies.

She loved the woody, earthy smell of them. Loved the
smooth, crisp feel of their pages. Loved the colorful book

jackets and their straight, even spines. To a shy, awkward girl, they had been her teachers, her storytellers, her friends. To a single woman, they were her life.

She read all types of books, from nonfiction to fiction, from *New York Times* bestsellers to the reliable classics. If she had one fault, it was that she lost herself in a good story, forgoing sleep and food until she'd finished the last page. That was why she never started a book during the work week. But this was Saturday afternoon, the start of her weekend, so she took the time to pick out a number of books to take home. She had just selected a historical romance from the paperback rack when someone spoke from behind her.

"What kinda books are those, Ms. Murphy?"

The paperback slipped from Elizabeth's hand as she whirled around. Kenny Gene stood there in his tight Wranglers and pressed western shirt, his eyes squinting at the cover of the book on the floor.

"That woman sorta looks like Shirlene Dalton," he said. "Although if Shirlene paraded around with her bosom showin' like that, not one man in Bramble would get any work done."

Elizabeth held a hand to her chest. "You scared the daylights out of me, Kenny Gene. The library is closed. Didn't you hear my announcement?"

His gaze flickered up from the book. "Uh, I must've been in the men's room."

She released a long sigh at the obvious lie. "Kenny, I thought we had this discussion before," she said as she picked up the book. "If you don't want to marry Twyla right now, you need to tell her, instead of avoiding her so you don't have to set a date. Sooner or later, she's going to figure out where you've been hiding."

Kenny shook his head. "That's doubtful, Ms. Murphy. The library is the last place on God's green earth anyone would come lookin' for me—although I gotta tell you that them Scooby-doo books are downright entertainin'."

It was hard to keep a stern face. Of all the people in Bramble, Texas, Kenny was the most lovable.

"Well, I'm glad you're enjoying them. But that doesn't change the fact that you need to talk with Twyla. Just tell her what you told me—that you were thinking more a long engagement than a short one."

"That might work with someone like you, Ms. Murphy. Old maids are much more logical than ordinary women. Probably because their hopes for snaggin' a man are slim to none."

His words should've offended Elizabeth, especially since she was only thirty-seven, but she couldn't blame him. Or any of the people in Bramble. Not when she had worked so hard to achieve her old-maid anonymity.

"But Twyla don't think the same way as you do," Kenny continued. "That girl is hell bent for leather on being hitched, and after three times, I'd say she's pretty good at it."

Elizabeth bit back a smile. "I guess that depends on your point of view, Kenny."

"Well, her point of view is targeted on me, especially with Shirlene's weddin' tonight. If Twyla catches that bouquet, it's all over for me. The town will have us hitched by winter."

She couldn't argue the point. The folks of Bramble loved weddings as much as they loved football. And everyone knew how much Texans loved their football.

Kenny's eyes took on a speculative gleam. "'Course,

I wouldn't have to worry so much if some other woman caught it."

"Excuse me?"

He did an excited little hop that looked like he needed to go to the men's room after all. "You could catch the bouquet, Ms. Murphy, and then Twyla might think it was fate and be willin' to give me a little more time."

"Oh, no." Elizabeth held up a hand. "It's bad enough that I'm forced to stand there with all the young girls. I'm certainly not going to make an effort to catch it. I have no desire to get married."

"Well, of course you don't," Kenny said. "And you won't have to. No one will expect you to find a man."

She ignored the insult and shook her head. "I'd love to help you out, Kenny, but I don't think that's a very good idea."

"Just think about it, won't you?" Kenny begged. "All I'm asking for is another year of freedom."

It was hard to ignore his plea, especially when she enjoyed her own single status so much. "I'll think about it." She waved a hand toward the glass doors. "But for now, you need to let me close up so we can get ready for the wedding."

Exactly fifteen minutes later, Elizabeth stood outside the double glass doors of the library. After checking them twice to be sure they were locked, she slipped the keys in the side pocket of her tote bag and headed home.

Her house was not more than a few blocks from the library, a pretty little yellow brick single-story with a picket fence and a festoon of colorful mums growing in the flowerbeds. The front gate got stuck when she tried to open it, and she made a mental note to buy some WD-40 at the hardware store on Monday. Once inside the front door, she was greeted by a soft meow as a warm, furry body pressed against her legs.

"Hello, Atticus. Did you miss me?" she asked as she leaned down to stroke the cat's soft orange fur.

Atticus allowed her fawning for only a few seconds before he headed for the kitchen cupboard where she kept the food. At a good six pounds overweight, he had always been more interested in Meow Mix than her affection.

After feeding the cat and refilling his water dish, Elizabeth walked back into the living room to get her tote bag. The wedding was hours away. She'd have plenty of time to get in some reading before she had to get ready. Unfortunately, after deciding on a book, she made the mistake of checking her cell phone for messages. There was only one. One breathy message that completely obliterated her plans.

"Lizzie? You need to get out here. And quick."

The drive that normally took her close to an hour took only forty-five minutes, during which Elizabeth envisioned all kinds of catastrophes. Which explained why she was so surprised when she walked into the kitchen of Miss Hattie's Henhouse and found three women calmly going about their business. Minnie was sitting in her wheelchair playing solitaire at the table. Sunshine was sitting on the floor contorted in some kind of weird yoga pose. And Baby was standing at the stove, stirring something in a saucepan and staring up at the ceiling.

"What's the emergency?" Elizabeth asked as she looked around for signs of fire, flooding, or robbery.

"The Realtor came by on Tuesday," Minnie said nonchalantly.

Elizabeth released her breath and dropped her tote bag to the floor. "That's it? The reason you had me drive all the way out here was to tell me that the Realtor came by?"

She glanced over at Baby, but Baby quickly looked back up at the ceiling.

"That is an emergency." Minnie took another drag of her cigarette, her eyes squinting through the smoke. "I told you we weren't leaving." She gave Elizabeth the once-over. "Where in the hell do you get those ugly suits?"

Elizabeth wasn't the kind of person who lost her patience, but the last six months of dealing with Minnie was more than anyone should have to endure. Still, she took a deep breath and tried to remain calm.

"We can't hold on to this house, Minnie. Your social security checks put together won't even cover the gas bills for the winter." She waved a hand around. "Just look at this place. It's falling down around your ears, and it would take more money than any of us have to fix it. So, yes, I'm selling it."

The wheelchair zipped away from the table and straight toward her. But Minnie had pulled the stunt before, and Elizabeth wasn't falling for it. She stood her ground, even when the wheels of the chair came within inches of the toes of her conservative brown lace-ups.

"Let me tell you something, girlie." Minnie shook a gnarled finger at her. "You might've inherited the house, but your ancestors would be rollin' over in their graves if they knew you were plannin' on throwin' out their sister hens!"

Hens. Elizabeth cringed. She had come to hate the word. So much so, that she'd sworn off chicken, eggs, and feather pillows.

"So what do you expect me to do?" she said. "You want me to just let you live here until they turn off the utilities? Until you're forced to eat cat food—again?"

"That happened only once," Minnie said. "And only because Sunshine mistook it for a can of tuna."

Sunshine giggled. "Cathouse. Cat food."

"So are you telling me that you weren't almost starving by the time the lawyer finally located me?" Elizabeth asked.

"No." Minnie rolled back over to the table and snuffed out her cigarette. "I'll admit that we were pretty close to eating the mice that have taken over the attic. But the hens and I would've been just fine if you hadn't showed up. In fact, we just came up with a new plan."

"A plan?" Elizabeth rolled her eyes. "Is this plan similar to the one about starting your own line of lingerie?"

"That one would've worked," Minnie said, "if I hadn't let Baby come up with the slogan. 'Nighties that will entice your man to take his choo-choo on a ride in your tunnel.' What the hell does that mean?"

"Speaking of choo-choos..." Sunshine stretched a leg up over her head, something Elizabeth was quite certain she couldn't do now, let alone when she turned seventy. "Can I go upstairs now, Min? You said I could do it later? It's later. Right?"

Minnie shook her head. "In a little while, Sunshine. Right now we need to make sure Lizzie is in."

Elizabeth heaved a sigh and sat down in a chair. As much as she wanted to sell the house and completely forget her connection to Miss Hattie's, she also couldn't stand the thought of kicking the three women out of a home they loved.

"So what's this great plan, Minnie?"

Numerous cards were played and another cigarette lit before the ornery old woman finally spoke. "We're reopening the henhouse."

"Excuse me?" Elizabeth leaned closer, figuring she'd misunderstood. "Reopening as in selling sex?"

Minnie's eyes narrowed. "I don't know what that crazy mama of yours told you, but the hens never sold sex in their lives—that's what prostitutes and whores do. The henhouse was a place where men could come to be pampered and loved." She shrugged. "And if they wanted to show their appreciation with money and gifts that was their decision. Miss Hattie never spoke of money. And neither did any of the hens."

"Which might explain why you don't have any now," Elizabeth couldn't help adding.

Taking another drag of her cigarette, Minnie flipped a queen of diamonds down on the king of spades. "Did you realize that, unlike the Chicken Ranch, the henhouse was never closed down? We remained open until the last rooster flew the coop. Age is what screwed us up. Nobody wants an old hen when they can have a spring chicken." She tapped a crooked nail on the table. "'Course, the spring chickens can't just be anyone. Hen blood is either in you, or it ain't." Her eyes narrowed on Elizabeth. "And I'm havin' my doubts about you, Lizzie."

With a roll of her eyes, Elizabeth got up from the chair. "I'm selling the house, Minnie. But I give you my word that I'll help you and the hens find a good place to live."

"You're not leaving." Baby turned from the stove with a desperate look on her face. "You can't go yet." Her gaze wandered up to the ceiling.

"Let her go." Minnie reshuffled the cards, the cigarette drooping from her lip. "We should've never contacted her in the first place."

Elizabeth wished they hadn't either. Unfortunately, there was no going back. Ignoring the hens would be like leaving three blind kittens in a burning building. Someone had to watch out for the insane women. Elizabeth just wished it wasn't her.

"The Realtor will be back next week," she said as she headed to the side kitchen door. "And stop smoking, Minnie. If you don't kill yourself, your secondhand smoke is going to kill Sunshine and Baby."

"It will take more than a little smoke to kill us hens," Minnie huffed.

She probably had a point. The three would no doubt outlive most of the population of Texas.

The sun had just started to slip beneath the horizon as Elizabeth made her way around the front of the house to her car. Sunsets in west Texas were spectacular, but she didn't take the time to enjoy the vibrant splashes of color. If she hurried, she would have just enough time to change and get to the First Baptist Church before the wedding started. She'd just as soon skip the festivities and go home and read. But if she didn't attend, questions would arise. And all she needed was the townsfolk finding out about her connection to Miss Hattie's.

Unfortunately, before she even got to her car, a thought struck her. Why would Sunshine want to go upstairs when the only things upstairs were mice and empty rooms? Elizabeth might've attributed the desire to a brain that had been fried by too many drugs in the Sixties if Minnie hadn't acted like she knew exactly what Sunshine was talking about.

And if Baby hadn't acted so strange, looking up at the ceiling constantly.

An uneasy feeling settled in the pit of her stomach as Elizabeth glanced up at the second story. A part of her brain told her to ignore the feeling and get out of there. But the logical part of her brain reminded her that her name was on the deed, which meant she was liable for whatever craziness the hens had come up with. Not wanting to get in another argument with Minnie, Elizabeth decided to slip in the front door and tiptoe up the long staircase.

She had never been upstairs before, partly because the hens lived downstairs and partly because of Minnie's mice stories. It was a creepy place, filled with dark shadows and creaking floorboards. She didn't find any mice, but she did find numerous rooms—all of which were empty.

All except for the corner room.

Elizabeth pushed open the double doors, and her breath caught. While the rest of the house had minimal furniture, this room was filled to the rafters. She didn't know a lot about antiques, but the items in the room looked like they would send the appraisers on *Antiques Roadshow* into conniption fits. No wonder Sunshine had wanted to come upstairs. The room was like stepping back in time. There were plush Oriental rugs, museum-quality paintings, heavy brass lamps with stained-glass shades, and beautiful dressers and chests that gleamed in the last rays of the setting sun.

But nothing compared to the huge four-poster bed that covered one entire wall. The exquisitely carved headboard was made of dark walnut, as were the thick posts that came within inches of the high ceiling. Red-and-gold brocade draped from the canopy, partially concealing a mattress that had to be a good three feet from the floor.

Regardless of all the horror stories her mother had told her over the years, Elizabeth found herself completely and utterly enthralled by the massive piece of furniture. This wasn't just a bed. This was *the* bed. The same bed where the most famous prostitute in Texas history had slept—or not slept. A bed that had entertained outlaws and politicians alike. A bed that some museum curators would give their eyeteeth to have. And there Elizabeth stood not more than ten feet away from it.

Make that seven feet.

Four.

One.

She slid a hand down the brocade curtains and stared in at the rumpled black satin sheets. What kind of wickedness had transpired here? What kind of depravity? What kind of fun?

Before Elizabeth knew it, she had pushed back the curtain and slipped inside the shadowy cocoon. The mattress was not too soft or too hard, the sheets cool to the touch. She eased down to the pillows and breathed deeply. The smell of lilacs wasn't surprising. Being Miss Hattie's signature scent, it had been worn by all hens, past and present. But the other scent baffled her. It was an earthy scent that she couldn't quite place.

Attached to the canopy was a huge mirror. A mirror painted with a mural of a beautiful woman in a seductive red dressing gown. The painting completely obscured the dowdy old maid in the ugly gray suit, leaving only the other side of the bed visible. It wasn't hard to imagine the shape of a man's body beneath the rumpled satin sheets. Or hear his deep, steady breathing. Was he a filthy rich oil man? A lonely cowboy fresh off the trail? Or possibly a handsome hero straight from the pages of a historical romance?

As she gave her imagination full rein, a dark head separated from the black satin of the pillow and a deep voice rumbled next to her ear.

"I've been waiting for you."

Chapter Three

*Henhouse Rule #8: A man in the hand is worth two
in the bush.*

IT TOOK A HAND SETTLING OVER HER WAIST for Elizabeth
to snap out of the fantasy her mind had conjured up. By that
time, it was too late. The strong fingers tightened, and she
was pulled toward a man who looked more like a villain
than a hero. Hair as black and satiny as the sheets framed a
face of hard angles and sapphire eyes that gleamed with a
look that could only be described as dangerous and . . . hot.

Elizabeth might not pay as much attention to men as
Twyla, but she knew an attractive man when she saw one.
There was Slate Calhoun with his golden hair and hazel
eyes. Colt Lomax with his muscular body and intriguing
tattoos. And Bubba Wilkes Cates with his country boy
charm. But this man beat them all out, and she couldn't
quite put her finger on the reason why.

He wasn't handsome in the classical sense. His jaw
was a little too pronounced, his lips too firm, his forehead
too high, and his eyes too deeply set. Yet there was something in those sapphire eyes that unsettled her. A look that
reminded her of her cat, Atticus, when he had arrived at
her door soaking wet and starving.

The man dipped his head, and she realized she'd been right. He was starving. It just wasn't for food. His mouth settled over hers in a hungry glide that sent a zap of heat zinging straight through her body to the crotch of the 99-cent panties she'd gotten on sale at J.C. Penney.

This was no sloppy, inexperienced kiss like she'd gotten from Jeffrey Hunt in high school. Or the distracted, obligatory kisses she got from Marvin Migler in college. No, this man kissed like an expert who had been doing it for a lifetime—and liked doing it. His lips were hot, skilled, and consuming. So much so, that before Elizabeth even realized it, she was kissing him back and trying to remember why she shouldn't be.

A low growl came from the hard, naked chest pressed against her button-up blouse, vibrating through her mouth like a mating call. He pulled back, and she barely had time to suck in a deep breath before her skirt was being pushed up and her panties tugged down.

At this point, she needed to put a stop to things and take control of the situation. Except it was hard to take control when a warm hand skated up her thigh and one finger flicked across sensitive flesh. A sound came out of her mouth that was a mixture between a squawk and a moan. She tried to shove his hand away, but he only gave her another mind-fragmenting kiss that, this time, included the slick thrust of tongue. She resurfaced from the sensual onslaught to discover that he'd rolled completely on top of her. Hard, muscular thighs pressed into her soft ones. But it wasn't the hard thighs she noticed as much as his hard-on. A hard-on that was trying to nudge its way in between her legs. The realization that she was about to have sex with a complete stranger finally penetrated her brain, and she pulled away from his scorching lips.

"Stop this instant," she said in her most authoritative voice. But he didn't listen as well as the students from Bramble Elementary. He continued to try to ease her tightly clamped legs apart with his knee, while he kissed a trail of fire down her chin and over to the sensitive skin behind her ear.

"Don't deny me, Miss Hattie," he whispered. "I need you."

Miss Hattie?

Well, that explained a lot. This man was convinced that Miss Hattie's was open for business. And Elizabeth knew exactly who had done the convincing. Of course, she hadn't helped matters by getting so caught up in her fantasies about Miss Hattie's bed that she'd allowed him to take liberties. And not just allowed, but participated.

Still, it was time to bring the illusion to an end.

Realizing that it would take more than words to get the man out of his sexual trance, she waited for him to lift his head before she slapped him hard across the face. The blue eyes that stared back at her showed no signs he'd even registered the slap. In fact, now that she noticed, his eyes looked strange. Even as twilight settled over the room, his pupils remained tiny pinpricks of black.

Obviously, the man was stoned out of his mind. No doubt on alcohol the hens had given him. Since this wasn't the first time Elizabeth had had to deal with an inebriated man, she knew just what to do. You couldn't reason with a drunk, but you could certainly outthink them.

She ran a finger over his lips. "And I need you too, honey." She tried to do her best impersonation of Shirlene

Dalton, who everyone knew could flirt any man into submission. "But before I..." She tried to think of some naughty phrase for sex, but only one popped into her head. "Take your choo-choo on a ride through my tunnel, I need to get you some protection. You wouldn't want to risk getting a nasty STD, now would you?"

The STD part seemed to work. After only a slight hesitation, he rolled away, and Elizabeth scrambled off the bed. She made a show of opening up the nightstand drawer, which did happen to be filled with condoms. Condoms and all kinds of phallic-shaped things.

She slammed the drawer closed again. "Nope, not a condom in sight." She backed toward the door, struggling to keep her gaze away from the miles of muscle and hard, naked male. "Let me just run downstairs, and I'll be right back."

The man was drunk, but he was no fool. He lunged for her. Elizabeth started to make a run for it when the distinct clink of metal chain had her turning back around. He was stretched at an awkward angle, one arm reaching out and the other held back by the metal wrapped around his wrist.

"Oh my god." The words slipped from her mouth. "They handcuffed you?"

He looked confused for only a second before he growled and yanked his wrist, causing the sturdy headboard to shudder. Worried he was going to hurt himself, she took a few steps closer, and, for the first time, noticed the bandage on the arm that wasn't shackled. It made her feel even more sympathetic toward him and angry at the hens for taking advantage of an injured man.

"It's okay." She held up a hand. "Please don't hurt

yourself anymore. I promise I'll have you free in no time."
She was out the door and halfway down the stairs before
she realized that it probably wouldn't be smart to release
an angry drunk on a houseful of women.

Then again, maybe it was exactly what the crazy old
ladies needed to knock some sense into their heads.

The hens were right where she'd left them: Minnie
playing solitaire, Baby nervously stirring the boiling pot,
and Sunshine sitting on the floor. They all looked up when
Elizabeth entered.

"I thought you'd be gone back to your boring life in
Bramble by now," Minnie said as she rearranged a col-
umn of cards.

Elizabeth tried to keep her voice steady and her
patience intact. "Would someone care to explain why
there is a man upstairs handcuffed to the bed?"

Minnie didn't even look up from the cards. "About as
much as you'd like to explain why you're still a virgin."

Elizabeth took a deep breath and slowly released it.
"That's not what we're talking about."

"Well, it should be," Minnie said. "Your virginity is a
topic that should've been addressed a long time ago. If it
had been, you wouldn't be down here discussing the handsome cowboy upstairs, but in bed enjoying him. Although
from the look of your clothes and hair, I'd say you already
did some enjoying."

Sunshine jumped to her feet. "But you said I could
have him, Minnie!"

"'Course you can have him, Sunshine. Just as soon
as Virgin Lizzie is done with him. She needs him much
more than you do."

"No one is getting him!" Elizabeth said, much louder

than she intended. "He is a human being, not some kind of stray animal that you found in the road." She paused. "Where did you find him, anyway?"

Minnie shot her an exasperated look. "That's a stupid question if ever I've heard one. Men have always found Hattie's."

She had a point, which meant the man wasn't exactly innocent. He'd come looking to participate in illegal activities so he probably had gotten what he deserved. Still, they couldn't keep him prisoner.

Elizabeth pointed a finger at Minnie. "You're going to give me the key to his handcuffs so I can release him. And Baby, you're going to make him some strong coffee so we can sober him up before we send him on his way." She glanced over at the clock on the stove. There was no way she would make the wedding, but if she hurried she could make the reception and no one would be the wiser. She should've known that things wouldn't be that easy.

"I'm afraid we can't do that," Minnie said.

Elizabeth slammed her hands on her hips and stared the women down like she did all the children who refused to look for their lost library books. "And just why not?"

"Because," Baby said in her breathy voice, "if we let him go, he'll call the sheriff for sure."

"They aren't going to throw Minnie into jail for hand-cuffing a man to the bed."

"Not for the handcuffing," Baby said. "For the drug-ging and shooting."

There was a moment when Elizabeth felt like she might pass out. Her head got all light and airy, and she couldn't seem to catch her breath. It was Sunshine who found a brown paper bag. Sunshine who set Elizabeth down and held the bag over her mouth, telling her to take deep, even breaths. Minnie just continued to play cards while Baby looked on with wide, scared eyes.

When she finally felt less faint, Elizabeth pushed the bag away. "You drugged the man and then shot him?"

Minnie tipped her head. "Technically, I shot him and then Baby drugged him."

"But she didn't shoot him on purpose, Lizzie," Baby clarified as she wrung her hands. "It was an accident. After that, we had to drug him. We can't have him calling the police, not when the henhouse is going to reopen."

Elizabeth grabbed the paper bag from Sunshine and breathed into it for a full five minutes until the bag was soggy and limp, then she pulled it away from her mouth and reached for the cell phone in her tote bag.

"And what do you think you're doin'?" Minnie asked.

"I'm doing what that man upstairs will do when we let him go. I'm calling the sheriff. This craziness of yours has gone on long enough, Minnie. It's time we put a stop to it. You can't go around shooting and drugging men." She'd punched two buttons on her phone by the time Minnie spoke.

"You go right ahead and do that, Lizzie. I'm sure Sheriff Hicks will come hauling butt out here lickety split. 'Course, he won't be the only one. Once news gets out, reporters will flock here like a bunch of geese heading south for the winter. And it won't be a shooting and drugging that interests them." She bracketed her gnarled fingers and held them up as if reading a headline. "Extra. Extra. Read all about it. Virgin Librarian Takes Over Miss Hattie's and Handcuffs Man to Bed!"

The phone slipped from Elizabeth's fingers and hit the floor. "But I didn't handcuff him."

"No, but it won't make any difference. You're the one who owns Miss Hattie's." She smiled. "The one who has all the rights and responsibilities."

Elizabeth slumped down in her chair as the truth of Minnie's words sank in.

She couldn't call the sheriff. If word got out about the shooting, it would also get out about her connection to the henhouse. And then where would she be? She'd lose her job at the library, and, without a job, she'd be forced to leave Bramble and her quiet, comfortable life. And she wouldn't be the only one who suffered. Her mother would become the gossip of her Bunco club. Everything they'd striven to keep quiet would be out for the world to dissect.

While Elizabeth's world shattered before her eyes, Minnie flipped down a card and held up her dark-veined hands.

"Ten thousand five hundred and twenty-two wins! That should get in Guinness World Records."

Something boiled up inside of Elizabeth. Something mean and ugly and…liberating. It flooded her entire body and caused her nerves to tingle and her face to fill with blood. Just that quickly, she reached out and swiped her hand across the table, sending the cards flying.

"I don't care about some stupid solitaire record. I care that you've succeeded in ruining my life, you crazy old bat!"

Baby's, and even Sunshine's, eyes grew as big as saucers while Minnie only cackled.

"I knew there was hot hen blood in you. All it needed was a little nudge."

Chapter Four

Henhouse Rule #35: Never run from the law, just seduce it.

"HOLD IT RIGHT THERE, Ms. Murphy."

Elizabeth froze as her heart moved up to her throat. She slowly turned to find Sheriff Winslow standing not more than five feet away, the colored lights over the dance floor reflecting off the shiny, silver badge pinned to his chest.

He tipped his head, and the brim of his large, tan cowboy hat dipped. "You don't think I was gonna let you get away that easily, do ya?"

She swallowed hard and tried to speak, but it was hard when images of cold jail cells and women with tattoos and crew cuts paraded through her mind.

"You did the deed," he continued, "and now you have to pay the piper."

But she really hadn't done the deed. Three crazy old women had done the deed. Three crazy old women who had talked her into returning to Bramble as if nothing had happened. But how could a person be expected to smile and act as if everything was hunky-dory when there was a naked cowboy handcuffed to Miss Hattie's bed? It had been foolish to even think she could pull it off.

Now she would have to pay for that foolishness.

She cleared her throat. "I realize it was wrong, but I can explain."

"Wrong?" Sheriff Winslow said. "You're danged right it's wrong."

Sheriff Winslow held something out, and Elizabeth figured karma had come back to haunt her. She had allowed a man to be abducted and now she would get her turn. Except when the sheriff stepped closer, she realized that it wasn't handcuffs he held in his hand. It was a large bouquet of ugly silk flowers.

"You can't catch the darn thing and then just race off without takin' it with you," he said.

Elizabeth's shoulders sagged as her breath escaped in one long sigh of relief. "O-Of course, I don't want to forget these." She took the heavy arrangement of flowers.

Sheriff Winslow removed his hat and scratched his head. "It was shore a surprise when you went after those flowers like a dog after a rib eye. No one much thought about you wantin' to catch a man."

Elizabeth hadn't gone after anything. The only reason she'd been on the dance floor was because the townsfolk had shoved her out there, led by a beaming Kenny Gene, and the only thing she'd been thinking about catching was the first plane out of Texas. The bouquet hadn't even crossed her mind until it came straight at her like a softball fast-pitch. She had no choice but to reach out and catch it. Now, standing there staring at the sheriff's wide grin, she realized that she'd made yet another miscalculation. The first, thinking she could help out a bunch of ornery old hens.

"So what are you doin' tomorrow?" Sheriff Winslow asked.

It was a good question. One she didn't have the answer to. Most Sundays would find her in the fifth row of the First Baptist Church. But just the thought of staring up at the large wooden cross and listening to Pastor Robbins's sermon while an innocent man suffered who knew what kind of "hen-trocities" was more than Elizabeth could endure.

"I might go visit my mother in Amarillo," she said, her voice quivering only slightly. It was a lie. There was no way Elizabeth would go and visit her mother. Like most moms, Harriett Murphy had a way of ferreting out the truth. And if she ever discovered that Elizabeth had been out to Miss Hattie's, prison would be the least of Elizabeth's worries.

"Amarillo, huh?" Sheriff Winslow shook his head. "Well, that's a shame. Myra was hopin' you could come over to dinner on Monday night and meet her cousin, Jethro. He ain't much upstairs, but I figure you got enough up there for both of you."

Before Elizabeth could graciously decline the offer, Mayor Harley Sutter came hustling up with his handlebar mustache and big belly bouncing. "Now you aren't leavin' yet, are you, Ms. Murphy? I realize the bride and groom are gone, but that doesn't mean the party's over. Why, the band is just warmin'—"

"'Course she's not leavin'," Darla cut in. "My brother, Bud, was just gettin' ready to ask her for a dance."

"I don't think so, Darla." Kenny Gene joined the crowd that was forming around Elizabeth. "I just saw Bud drivin' like a bat out of hell down Grover Road." He flashed a smile and wink at Elizabeth, looking as happy as a convict on parole day.

"She don't want Bud, anyway," Cindy Lynn chimed in. "Not when she can have my Uncle Wilbur." She looked around. "Where did he go, anyway? I sent him to get her a cup of punch."

"At least Bud has a full set of his own teeth," Darla shot back. "Wilbur hasn't been able to eat steak for the last eight years."

Cindy rammed her fists on her hips. "Well, you can't expect to get Robert Pattinson when you're Meryl Streep."

Elizabeth stared at the group of people who surrounded her. It seemed that Kenny Gene was wrong. Once her fingers had closed around the thick, ribbon-bound stem of the artificial flowers, the townsfolk had stopped viewing her as an old maid who was content with her single life and had started viewing her as a prime candidate for their matchmaking. A few days ago, she would've been appalled at the idea. Now, she was more worried about spending the rest of her life making license plates.

"Meryl can have any man she wants." Rachel Dean appeared with a young cowboy on her arm. "Now a days, younger men are goin' for the older women." She smiled up at the man and winked. "Ain't they, honey?"

"Only if they're as good-lookin' as you, Ms. Rachel." The cowboy flashed a smile that had all the women sighing.

Beauregard Cates was the younger brother of the groom, Billy—or as the town liked to refer to him, Bubba. Bubba had introduced Beau to Elizabeth just that evening, but she couldn't recall a word of their conversation. Although her preoccupation didn't stop her from understanding why all the women were so awestruck by the younger Cates brother. In a black Stetson, white pleated shirt, and black tuxedo pants, he was a stunningly attractive man.

Without any warning, another attractive man flashed into her mind. A man with hair as rich and silky as satin. Eyes the color of the sky on the verge of sunset. And lips that were made to give pleasure. At the thought of the pleasure they had given her, Elizabeth blushed. But her flaming face was nothing compared to the guilt that knotted in her stomach.

"Behave yourself, you rascal." Rachel swatted Beau's arm. "I'm old enough to be your mama and then some." Her gaze swept over to Elizabeth. "But Ms. Murphy here is just old enough to make things interestin'." She unhooked her arm and gave him a shove. "Now, you two go on and dance."

Elizabeth held up a hand. "I would love to, but I'm going to see my mother tomorrow. Which means I should probably go home and pack." Or go home and have a heart attack, which was much more likely.

"Nonsense," Rachel Dean said. "I'm sure you have time for one dance."

Beau flashed another smile as he nodded his head at the dance floor. "It would sure be my pleasure, Ms. Murphy."

Elizabeth started to decline, but then realized that it would be easier to get away from one east Texas cowboy than an entire town of matchmakers. She nodded and allowed him to take her elbow and lead her away from the grinning crowd.

"So if you don't want the bouquet, why did you catch it?"

Beau's question had her glancing up at him. Most of

his face was shadowed by the brim of the cowboy hat. But what she could see was an angular jaw and lips that were tipped up in a slight smile. It wasn't as devastatingly sexy as the full one...but close.

"What makes you think I didn't want it?" she asked.

"The look on your face after you caught it for one." He nodded down at the flowers. "And the way you're holding it now—sort of like it's a rattlesnake with a sore tooth."

As distracted as she was, she couldn't help but laugh at the analogy. "Well, you're right; I wanted it about as much as you wanted to dance with me. So why don't we stop the pretense so you can go ask one of those pretty college girls to dance?"

He followed her gaze over to the group of young women who were huddled together and staring at him like he was a celebrity straight from the pages of *People* magazine. He lifted a hand in greeting and flashed them his megawatt smile as he spoke through his teeth.

"Those marriage-minded women?" Beau turned back to her and, using just two fingers, took the bouquet from her hand and flipped it down on a nearby picnic table. "I think my bachelor life will be safer with you."

With his hand riding the small of her back, he guided her onto the wooden dance floor Kenny Gene and Rye Pickett had set up on the dirt lot in front of Shirlene's childhood trailer. Grover Road was an unusual choice for a wedding reception, especially when most receptions were held at the town hall. But Elizabeth had to admit that it looked quaint and homey. Twinkle lights filled the shrubs and elm trees, and colored Christmas lights were strung from the roof of the beat-up trailer and out over the dance floor.

"I'm afraid I'm not very good at dancing," she said as he slipped a hand around her waist. "Or anything that takes coordination."

He winked at her. "Good. Because I'm not very coordinated myself."

It turned out to be an understatement. The man was clumsier than Elizabeth. At least she just stepped on his toes. He tripped on an uneven edge in the dance floor and almost took them both down. He regained his balance in time to have his toe smashed beneath her heel. A more genuine smile creased his face.

"Maybe it would help if we both weren't trying to lead."

"Sorry," she said, "but following has never been my strong suit."

Beau tipped back his head and laughed. "Mine either, which has been a bone of contention with my family lately."

"Because you don't want to get married and settle down?"

"No, because I don't want to help run the family business."

The family business was C-Corp, a large gas and oil company that had recently bought out Dalton Oil with the intention of closing it down. It was all part of a vendetta the brothers held against the town of Bramble for a murder that had happened years earlier. About a hundred years earlier. Just months after a Miss Hattie Ladue had opened the doors of her establishment.

Just the thought of Miss Hattie's had her stumbling, which threw Beau off step and almost had them colliding with Shirlene's brother, Colt Lomax. Colt was dancing with his wife Hope and his baby daughter Daffodil. For growing up the sullen bad boy of Bramble, he looked as peaceful and content as a man could get. But no more peaceful than the man who danced next to them with a wife and daughter who were carbon copies of Hope and Daffodil. Slate Calhoun grinned down at Faith and Daisy as if they were his entire world.

A thought struck Elizabeth. What if the man in Miss Hattie's room had a family? A family who was now worried sick about him? The thought of young children crying out for their father was like a cold slap of reality. What had she been thinking? It didn't matter what happened to her life, or her mother's; she couldn't continue to let Minnie hold an innocent man hostage.

Which meant that she needed to stop this farce and head straight out to Miss Hattie's so she could release the poor man. Then it would be her turn to be handcuffed.

Unless...

Unless the man didn't want people to know he had stopped by a famous whorehouse. And what family man wouldn't want to keep that a secret? The thought caused the knots in her shoulder to release and the more confident Ms. Murphy to reemerge.

Their bumbling attempt at dancing didn't seem so bad after that. In fact, she actually had started to enjoy herself when the song came to an end.

"How about one more?" Beau asked.

As much as she would've liked to try another dance, Elizabeth shook her head. "I really need to be going."

Beau actually looked disappointed. Or maybe he was just extremely mannerly. Tucking a hand around her waist, he guided her off the dance floor. "I guess I shouldn't have brought up my family's business. People must still be upset about us wanting to close down Dalton Oil."

She shook her head. "That isn't it at all. I admire a person who is willing to break from their family's profession and strike out on their own."

He reached out and snagged the bouquet from the table. "You don't want to forget this," he said with a teasing grin.

"So if you don't want to join the family business," she said as she took the bouquet, "what kind of business are you interested in?"

"I'm not sure. All I know is that life is too short to spend it worrying about making money."

She shot a glance over at him. "Thus said the man with more money than he knows what to do with."

He laughed. "True, but someone has to enjoy the fruits of my brothers' labor. It might as well be me." He continued to walk with her toward the lot next door where all the cars were parked. "So tell me, Ms. Murphy, if you could do anything in the world, what would you do?"

"I'd be a librarian in a small west Texas town," she answered. That's all she wanted. That's all she had ever wanted. She just hoped that she would be able to retain her dream.

Beau nodded. "So I get the librarian thing, but explain the entire old maid thing. I have a maiden aunt, but she's eighty-six. You don't look any older than my brother."

"I think I'm a few years older than Bubba—I mean, Billy."

"I was talking about my oldest brother."

She had heard the gossip about his oldest brother. The townsfolk were convinced he was a no-good, rotten scoundrel who still wanted to shut down Dalton Oil. Elizabeth had been willing to give him the benefit of the doubt, but now she wondered if the townsfolk weren't right. The oldest Cates brother hadn't even attended Shirlene and Billy's wedding. And only a man who held grudges would refuse to attend his own brother's wedding because he was still mad at the folks of Bramble.

"So how old is this brother of yours?" she asked.

"Thirty-eight." He took off his hat and held it out for her to precede him through the break in the hedge that separated Shirlene's property from the property next door.

Brighter lights had been strung around the lot that was filled with dinged-up American-made cars and mud-splattered pickups.

"I'm surprised that he didn't show up," Beau said as he followed her to her car. "Family means everything to him."

"Obviously, not enough." She stopped at her car and fished the keys from the pocket of her suit jacket.

"You sure don't mince words, do you, Ms. Murphy?" he said as he pulled the door open for her.

"I guess I've never believed in beating around the bush."

"Something that I find very refreshing." Beau touched her arm until she turned to him. "How about if you have dinner with me tomorrow night?"

In the bright lights, his face was even more devastatingly handsome. She studied the hard lines of his jawbone, his smiling lips, and straight non-imposing nose. But it wasn't until she reached his clear, sapphire eyes that her breath caught in her throat, and she swayed on her feet.

"Ms. Murphy?" Beau reached out and took her arm. "Are you all right?"

"I-I'm fine," she choked out before taking a deep breath of cool autumn air. "I guess all that dancing made me a little dizzy."

"Maybe I should drive you home," he said.

"No!" She shook her head and tried to calm the wild thumping of her heart. "Y-your big brother? I suppose he has hair the color of yours."

Beau laughed. "No, I'm the only one of the kids with silver hair."

"Brown like Billy's?" She squeezed the words out of her tight throat.

"No. Brant has hair like my mama's side of the family—black as a crow's."

Chapter Five

Henhouse Rule #17: The library is for reading only.

BRANT WOKE WITH A DULL ACHE in his head, an ache that eased when talented fingers pressed into the muscles that ran between his neck and shoulders. He couldn't remember the last time he'd had a massage—or a masseuse as gifted as this one. Pressure points were targeted with accuracy, and tight muscles kneaded into submission. Once he was limp and malleable, fingers slipped up into his hair and massaged his scalp with a slight scraping of nails that had his nerves tingling with delight.

He groaned and turned his face into the mattress, a mattress with the distinct scent of lilacs. While his sleep-drugged mind tried to place the scent, the masseuse's hands kneaded their way from his head down his spine. The intense pleasure had him forgetting about lilacs and closing his eyes again—until those hands reached his butt cheeks and didn't massage as much as caress, coming too close to a man's ass crack for comfort.

"What the fuck—" He jerked the pillow off his head and rolled to his back. His eyes squinted from the bright sunshine that shone in through the windows, then opened wide at the old woman who straddled him.

"All done with your massage?" she said in her soft, sing-song voice. "Ready to move on?" She stripped off her blouse.

Two thoughts registered with Brant before he slammed his eyes shut. One, bras should be worn by all women—if not for modesty, then support. And two, he hoped to God that science had come up with ways to burn memories from a man's mind.

"For the love of Pete, Sunshine," a raspy voice said, "I told you that you need to give the man time to recover from his injuries before you start ridin' the range."

"I listened, Minnie," Sunshine said. "I just wanted to give him a massage. He was the one that wanted to—"

"No!" Brant shook his head, but made sure to keep his eyes closed. "I don't want anything, except for you to get off me."

"You heard the man," Minnie said.

There was a rustle of clothing as Sunshine climbed off, although before she was gone one hand did some definite cupping. He waited a few minutes before cracking his eyes open. Thankfully, the only sight to greet him was a shriveled old woman in a wheelchair with smoke curling around her head. Images started collecting in his brain, but before the puzzle was complete, the wheelchair hummed and Minnie came closer. At least she wore a bright purple negligee that covered all the important body parts.

"See," she said. The lit cigarette bobbed from her lip. "All you had to do is ask. At Miss Hattie's we aim to please."

Miss Hattie's.

The last piece of the puzzle fell into place, and Brant

glanced down at the bandage on his arm before testing the chain of the handcuffs on his other wrist. Anger swelled up inside him. And anger had always been Brant's best subject.

"Release me," he stated in a voice very close to a growl.

Minnie didn't seem intimidated. The old gal just cackled as if she found him amusing. "All in good time, Mr. Cates."

His eyes narrowed. "Branston Cates, who happens to be friends with judges in twenty-five counties."

"No kiddin'?" She grinned. "I know a fair share of judges myself." She shook her head. "'Course, most of them are dead now or so old they probably can't remember the good times we had." She lifted his wallet from a bag that hung on the side of the wheelchair. "Branston. Now that's an interestin' name. Where would your mama get a name like that?" When Brant ignored the question, she thumbed through the wallet and stopped on the picture of Brant's parents. It had been taken when they were in their early twenties, before his mother had started dyeing her hair every color under the sun.

"Nice-lookin' couple," Minnie said. "You look like her. Same hair and eyes." She glanced back up and studied him. "Although hers aren't quite as empty."

"What are your plans?" he asked.

"Shouldn't I be askin' you that question? After all, you were the one who showed up on my doorstep, not the other way around." She quirked an eyebrow. "Didn't you read the sign out front?"

He quirked his own brow. "So you're planning on prostituting me?"

"From the looks of those panties over there, I'd say that you already have been."

Brant's gaze followed the old woman's to a pair of flowered panties that rested on the black satin of the sheets. Obviously, the erotic dream he'd had about Miss Hattie hadn't been just a dream.

"Sunshine?" The word squeezed out of his dry throat.

Minnie cackled. "Nope. Sunshine don't wear panties, and Baby and I wouldn't be caught dead in that cheap cotton." She shook her head. "I wouldn't have believed it if I hadn't seen the evidence with my own eyes, but it looks as if you had the privilege of christening the newest hen to the henhouse."

He lunged at the old woman, who had enough sense to back her wheelchair up. "When I get free," he growled, "and I will get free, this house will be nothing but kindling."

"You sure got a lot of anger inside you, boy," Minnie said. "It sorta makes me wonder what would cause such fury." Her gnarled hands flipped to the next picture. Brant felt his heart tighten as she studied the photo of the laughing woman and giggling little boy. "I knew a shrink once who believed that anger was just a by-product of hurt and pain. After livin' over eighty years on this planet, I think he might've been on to something." Closing the wallet, she tossed it to the bed before backing the wheelchair up. "I'll have Baby bring you something up to eat."

"I don't want breakfast!" he yelled. "I want release." He jerked on the handcuff until the headboard shook and his wrist throbbed, but Minnie ignored him and rolled right out the door.

When she was gone, he fell back on the bed and stared

up at the picture painted on the mirror. He tried to remember the woman who had slipped into his bed, but the only images he had were of this woman. It was this woman he had shared heated kisses with. This woman who he could still taste and smell. Except this woman was dead and had been for years.

He reached out for the panties and held them up. They weren't the lacy scraps he was used to. These were more briefs than thongs, with sturdy stitches and ordinary elastic. Just the sight of them pissed him off. It was one thing to handcuff him to a bed and another to drug him and take advantage of his basic instincts.

Brant's intention had never been to destroy Miss Hattie's.

But now, he wouldn't mind at all.

Sunlight shifted farther across the bed, and something shiny caught his attention in the mirror. He turned his head and reached out for the hairpin. For a moment, he wondered who it belonged to—the infamous Miss Hattie or the new hen who was now the main target for his anger. It didn't matter. The hairpin was just right for picking the lock of a set of handcuffs. In no time, he was free and sitting up on the bed.

Brant still felt a little groggy from whatever had been in the Wild Rooster. But despite the dull ache in his temples, he was stable enough to stand. His arm didn't hurt as much as he thought it would, but that didn't mean the old bat wasn't going to pay.

After he used the adjoining bathroom, he searched through the drawers for something to wear. He was mad, but not mad enough to run around buck naked. All he found was a bunch of old-looking lingerie, a pile of intriguing antique sex toys, about a hundred ancient condoms, and bottle after bottle of lilac perfume. He had started for the closet when Baby entered the room with a tray.

"Oh my," she cooed as her gaze drifted down.

Brant had never been the modest type, but he couldn't help reaching out and jerking the black satin sheet around his waist. It didn't seem to help. Once he was covered from the waist down, her gaze settled on his naked chest, and she breathed deeply as if she could smell him clear across the room.

"Goodness. I forgot how absolutely divine it is to have a man around the house."

Brant cleared his throat, hoping it would bring her attention back to his face. It didn't. If this was how women felt when men gawked at them, he understood why they didn't like it. He felt as cheap as a nickel slug.

"Where are my clothes?" he asked.

"Hanging out back on the line. I got up real early just so I could wash them." She lifted her gaze and blinked as if just realizing he had a face. "I also squeezed you some fresh orange juice and made you a sausage and cheese omelet. Of course, if you prefer buttermilk pancakes, I could whip you up some of those." She moved over to the nightstand and set the tray down. "I'm so glad that Minnie decided to let you go." When she turned back around, the dreamy look was replaced by a contrite one. "We really didn't mean you any harm."

Brant snorted as he strode to the closet. "And you think drugging a man isn't harmful?" The closet was half the size of the room, with rows of evening gowns, enough shoes to make any woman swoon, and box after box of hats.

"She was quite a fashion plate, our Miss Hattie." Baby came up behind him. "All her clothing was specially made just for her. Her party gowns were sent all the way from Paris." She ran a hand over the feathered trim of one gown and didn't seem to notice that half the feathers came off in her hand. "I wish I had been alive then. The parties she threw sounded like so much fun."

There was a time when Brant would've agreed with Baby, but after being shot, drugged, and violated, most of the intrigue had been replaced with anger. Jerking a silk kimono off a hanger, he slipped it on and released the sheet.

Baby giggled as he turned around. "You look just like Tony Curtis in *Some Like It Hot*. All you need is a wig and some makeup." She stared at him for a moment, her platinum blond head tipped to the side. "Or maybe not; your face is a little too rugged to pass for a woman's." When he scowled, her smile slipped. "Minnie didn't let you go, did she?"

"Nope," he said.

For an old gal in high heels, Baby moved pretty quickly. She scuttled back out of the closet and was gone from the room by the time Brant finished knotting his sash. He didn't hurry after her. Instead he took his time, stopping to check out each room he passed. There were six, not including Miss Hattie's. Each had a small adjoining bathroom and closet, and all were completely empty. No curtains, rugs, or one stick of furniture.

At the end of the hallway was a small elevator that Minnie no doubt used to get up to the second level. It looked a little too rickety for Brant so he took the stairs. Despite the need for a fresh coat of stain and sealant, the staircase was majestic. A skillfully crafted mahogany banister spiraled down the fifty-odd steps it took to get to the bottom. Brant might've taken the time to check out the main floor if a slamming door hadn't drawn his attention to the rear of the house.

Remembering the derringer, he stayed close to the wall and eased around the first doorway he came to. It turned out to be the kitchen. The room was empty, but it didn't look like it had been that way for long. Three half-full cups sat on the Fifties-style enamel and chrome table, circling an ashtray with a smoldering cigarette.

Brant wasn't interested in the contents of the table as much as the bright yellow phone that hung on the wall. He walked over and lifted the receiver. But before he could even finish dialing the nine on the rotary dial, he hung it back up. If he had learned anything by living in a small town, it was that news traveled fast. The newspaper reporters would have a field day when they learned that the president of C-Corp had been held hostage by a bunch of old women. And Brant had never much cared for publicity—good or bad.

No, he could handle things without getting the law involved. It wouldn't be hard. Brant was an expert at figuring out how to make people pay. In fact, the thought almost had him smiling when a creak pulled his attention back to the doorway. He walked out of the kitchen in time to see a woman making her way up the long staircase. To say she was an average woman was an understatement. Everything about her was average—from her height and weight to her dishwater blond hair pulled back in a haphazard bun. She wore a gray suit that reminded him of the ones his sixty-two-year-old secretary, Ms. Hathaway, wore.

He might've thought she was an unsuspecting visitor

to the house if she hadn't stopped a fourth of the way up and stared at Miss Hattie's room as if a monster lurked behind the double doors. Instead the monster stood at the bottom of the stairs.

"Looking for someone?" he said.

The woman released a terrified squeak and whirled around so quickly that she lost her balance. She would've taken a mean tumble if Brant hadn't climbed the stairs in two giant strides and caught her. Most women—especially one who knew she was in big trouble—would've played the damsel in distress card for all it was worth, clinging to his chest and acting as if he was the bravest of heroes. Surprisingly, this woman didn't waste her time . . . or his. Once he set her back on her ugly brown shoes, she straightened her suit jacket and got right to the point.

"So I see you escaped." Her gaze flickered over his body, and her face flamed a bright red before her eyes moved back up to his.

Considering that his borrowed robe had come untied, he understood her embarrassment. He was starting to pull the silk edges together when he noticed her mouth. It was an unusual mouth. With the top lip slightly bigger than the bottom, it made her look as if she was pouting upside down. But it wasn't the shape that held his attention as much as the memories that flashed through his mind. He remembered these lips, remembered the feel, taste, and texture. Remembered the hard pull and passion.

She no more than blinked before he had her against the wall. He thought she would scream. Instead she just studied him as if expecting his anger.

"You were the one who came to my room last night," he growled.

Her face got even brighter, but she didn't look away. "Yes. And I'd like to explain, Mr. Cates, if you'll just let me." A tense smile tipped her lips. He had a hard time looking away as she continued.

"I realize you probably won't believe this, but it was all just a comedy of errors. Minnie didn't mean to shoot you, and Baby only drugged you so you wouldn't call the sheriff."

"And I suppose you handcuffed me to the bed and seduced me just to be hospitable," he said more than a little snidely.

Her eyes widened, and then suddenly she was laughing. Not a soft chuckle, but a full-out laugh that brought tears to her eyes. It only served to piss Brant off more, and his hands tightened on her waist.

"You think that's funny, do you?"

She stopped laughing, but her eyes behind the glasses still twinkled with humor. "If you knew me, Mr. Cates, you'd think it was funny, too. I've never seduced a man in my life."

"So what were you doing in my bed last night?"

Her mouth opened, but nothing came out. She closed it and swallowed hard. Before she could try again, a gunshot rang out. Brant exchanged looks with her for only a second before he released her and headed down the stairs.

Minnie's derringer was still smoking when Brant shoved open the front screen door. He didn't waste any time pulling the gun out of her hand.

"You crazy old woman. I should call the sheriff."

"I don't think we need the sheriff." Beauregard poked his head around the trellis of honeysuckle that surrounded the porch. "But after that scare, I might need a change of underwear."

Chapter Six

*Henhouse Rule #10: Some men take a little more
time to come around.*

"Ms. MURPHY?" Beauregard Cates pulled off his hat, and
his confused sapphire eyes, so much like his brother's,
settled on her.

Elizabeth probably should be upset that Beauregard
had found her at Miss Hattie's, but after discovering that
the man she'd left handcuffed to the bed was also the
president of one of the biggest companies in Texas, Elizabeth had resigned herself to the fact that the jig was up.
And her life, as she knew it, was over.

"Hello, Beau," she said, trying to keep the quiver of
fear from her voice. "It's so nice to see you again."

Beau still looked confused but was mannerly enough
to play along. "The pleasure's all mine, ma'am. I sure
enjoyed our evening together last night."

"Last night?" Branston Cates's gaze snapped over to
her. "You were with my brother last night?"

Minnie cackled. "The girl has more potential than I
thought she did. Fresh out of bed with one, and on to the
next. And brothers, no less. Although you need to be careful with relatives, Lizzie. The Dickens boys got in a brawl

over me and caused ten thousand dollars' worth of damage that they never did pay back."

Elizabeth's face flamed when it finally dawned on her what Minnie was talking about. "No! Beau was just teaching me how to dance."

Baby sighed. "That's how it happened to me. One second, I was doing the jitterbug with Jimmy Foster, and the next, my feet were brushing the roof of his daddy's Cadillac."

Before Elizabeth could defend her honor, Brant's fingers bit into her upper arm.

"If you drugged my little brother," he whispered in her ear, "so help me God, I'll—"

"Okay, so what's going on?" Beau cut in. "I get why you're here, Brant—the same reason I am—you were curious about the place where our great-grandfather got shot. But why did you miss Billy's wedding? And why are you wearing that ridiculous robe?"

Brant glared at Minnie. "Because she didn't happen to miss me with the derringer."

"She shot you?" Beau's blue eyes widened right before laughter erupted from his mouth. In fact, he got to laughing so hard, he had to sit down on the front step. "Wait until I tell the family about big, bad bro getting taken down by a bunch of little old women," he gasped. "Billy and Beck are going to love it."

Minnie's eyes narrowed. "Who you callin' old, Mr. Smartie Pants?"

"Beg pardon, ma'am." Beau wiped at the corners of his eyes. "But you've got to admit it's pretty danged funny."

A smile creased Minnie's face as Sunshine sat down on the step next to Beau.

"What about this one, Minnie?" She ran a hand along Beau's cheek, which took the last of the laughter from his eyes and replaced it with a look of discomfort. "Since Lizzie got the last one, can I have this one?"

Before Minnie could answer, Beau politely extracted himself from Sunshine and got to his feet. "So how do you fit in all this craziness, Ms. Murphy?"

All eyes turned to her, and she found her mouth suddenly dry. She had just worked up enough moisture to speak when a car pulled up in front.

Not just any car, but a sheriff's car.

Minnie's eagle eyes landed on Brant. "So you called the law on us, did ya?"

"He didn't call them. I did," Elizabeth stated as she straightened her suit jacket and tried not to act like her knees were knocking at the thought of spending time behind bars. "What we did was wrong. And as owner of this establishment, I need to take responsibility for that. No matter what the consequences are."

Beau's mouth dropped open. "The old maid of Bramble owns a whorehouse?"

"Watch your mouth, sonny boy," Minnie warned. "Miss Hattie's has never been a whorehouse." She shot a mean glare at Elizabeth. "It's a gentlemen's club that I refuse to let be brought down by a snooty woman who doesn't know shit from Shinola." She zipped the wheelchair over to the edge of the porch and pasted on a big smile. "Well, howdy, Sheriff Hicks. You come to get your butt whipped at poker again?"

The man wending his way through the weeds looked nothing like Bramble's sheriff. This man was young, tall, and lean, and when he removed the tan cowboy hat, a sharp gaze took in the occupants on the porch in one sweep.

"No, ma'am. I learned my lesson the first time." He rolled the brim of his hat around in his hands. "Havin' a party, Miz Minnie?"

"It sure looks that way, don't it?" She tipped her head and blew a puff of smoke up in the air. "'Course we're gonna need a lot more booze if that's the case."

Sheriff Hicks didn't even crack a smile. "So what's this I hear about a shooting?"

"It wasn't really Minnie's fault." Baby clicked her way forward with a desperate look in her magnified eyes. "It was all just a—"

"Minor accident," Brant's deep voice cut off Baby. Elizabeth watched as he discreetly slipped the small gun into the pocket of the kimono before he reached out a hand to the sheriff. "Branston." He nodded at Beau. "And this here is my brother, Beauregard. I was on my way to my brother's wedding in Bramble when I got lost and ended up here."

Sheriff Hicks's eyes narrowed for a heart-stopping second before returning to Minnie. "So you were waving guns around again. I thought I warned you last time about that."

"I know, Sheriff," Minnie looked duly chastised. "But you can't expect three helpless old women not to have some form of protection."

The sheriff snorted. "I don't think there's a person on God's green earth that would call you women helpless." His gaze wandered over to Elizabeth. "So I take it that you're the one who called."

Elizabeth took a step toward him and held out a hand.

Unfortunately, her legs were still a bit wobbly, and she ended up tripping and almost taking a nosedive off the porch. Only Brant's quick reflexes kept her from it. His arm encircled her, and she was pulled up against his hard chest. A chest that was barely covered by the oriental-print kimono. How could a man be so blatantly masculine in a thigh-high kimono? And why was she so aware of it? Every nerve ending in her body tingled as if she'd just stuck her finger in a light socket. It took everything she had in her not to melt at his feet.

What made matters worse was that Brant Cates seemed to know it. His hands tightened for a fraction of a second before he released her and she was able to catch her breath. But even then, her mind was so scrambled that she had trouble remembering what she had been about to do.

Minnie reminded her—or more like took charge.

She waved the cigarette at Elizabeth. "This here is my niece, Elizabeth, who came out for a visit. She's a little slow on the uptake—somethin' she gets from her mama's side, not mine. She called you without gettin' the facts straight."

Slow on the uptake? There was a moment when Elizabeth really wanted to blurt out the truth and set Minnie on her ear. But relief that Mr. Cates wasn't going to press charges had her holding her tongue.

Still, the sheriff stared at her for a good heart-stopping minute before he nodded. "Well, I hope you enjoy your stay, Elizabeth."

"Thank you," she said, although she had no intention of staying there for longer than it took to sell the house. If she had learned anything in the last twenty-four hours, it was that her mother was right. Miss Hattie's was nothing but trouble.

The sheriff slipped his hat back on and pointed a finger at Minnie. "And you had better call me the next time some stranger shows up, instead of waving around guns."

"Will do, Sheriff," Minnie said with an innocent look that wasn't fooling anyone.

The Sheriff's car had barely pulled out of the driveway before she was holding out a hand to Brant. "I'll take my gun back now."

"I don't think so," Brant said. "Just because I didn't turn you over to the sheriff, doesn't mean I'll forgive and forget."

Beau snorted. "That's an understatement. He's still holding a grudge about the baseball mitt I borrowed and left at the park—and that happened more than twenty years ago."

"Now, I can't see any reason for you to hold a grudge," Minnie said as her twinkling eyes landed on Elizabeth. "Seems to me you've been paid in full for any damages— virgins are high commodities here at Miss Hattie's and don't you forget it."

Beau choked so hard that Sunshine raced over to pat his back while Elizabeth stared at Minnie in stunned shock. Did the old woman have dementia or had she just lost her ever-loving mind? Elizabeth hadn't had sex with Branston Cates. But before Elizabeth could deny it, Brant latched onto her arm and pulled her back inside the house. He paused for a moment to look around the entryway, then chose the first door on the right.

It was the library, the only room in the entire house that Elizabeth wanted to own. Or at least she wanted to own the contents of the room. She would've loved to take home the first-edition classics that lined the shelves. Unfortunately, she might own the house, but the hens owned everything in it. And they refused to part with anything that had belonged exclusively to Miss Hattie or her ancestors.

The door slammed shut, and Elizabeth turned away from the book-filled shelves to look at the man who leaned against the door with arms crossed and dark scowl in place.

"You've got exactly five minutes to explain what a virgin was doing in my room last night before I call that sheriff back out and have you arrested for sexual assault."

"Sexual assault?" She placed a hand on her chest where her heart was thumping out of control. "I did not sexually assault you."

"Are you saying you weren't the woman in my arms last night?"

Her face flamed with heat. "No. I'm not saying that at all. I'm just saying that I didn't force you to do anything you didn't want to."

"I was drugged, for Christ's sake!" he snapped as he came away from the door.

Elizabeth was not used to being yelled at, and she didn't care for it one bit. She wasn't blameless, but she certainly wasn't the villain he was making her out to be.

"I wasn't responsible for you being drugged, Mr. Cates," she said. "You have the hens to thank for that. In fact, I didn't even know you were drugged until we almost..."

"Screwed?"

The word drained the embarrassment right out of her and replaced it with anger.

"Watch your mouth, mister." She pointed a finger at him. "And no, we were not even close to that. I merely stumbled into your bed by accident."

"So Minnie didn't send you?" He answered the question for himself. "Of course she didn't send you. She's not the owner of the henhouse. You are. Which makes me wonder if you weren't doing exactly what Minnie said you were—trying to seduce me into not pressing charges."

It was hard to think when the kimono had come undone again. The glimpse of hard thigh was bad enough, but the teensy weensy peek of dangly flesh had her blushing so much she now could empathize with her mother's hot flashes.

She turned away and walked over to the bookshelves. "I told you before, Mr. Cates, that I'm not the seducing type. The only reason I was there was because I was curious as to why Sunshine was so anxious to get upstairs."

He moved up behind her, so close his breath ruffled the hair on the back of her neck. "So we didn't have sex?"

"Absolutely not."

There was a pause before he continued. "Then explain how your panties got in my bed, Ms. Murphy?"

She froze, her hand resting on the binding of *War and Peace*. Since there was no way she could talk with this man about what had taken place in Miss Hattie's bed without dying of embarrassment, she stretched the truth a little.

"I don't know what panties you're talking about."

Only a fraction of a second slipped by before she was spun around. The kiss he laid on her was as hot and steamy as her nightly baths. It had the same effect: her muscles turned to jelly and she was ready for bed.

Miss Hattie's bed. With this hot angry man who was an extremely good kisser.

Without even being aware of it, her lips opened, and her tongue greeted his in a slide of heat that had her releasing a deep moan. She hooked her arms around his shoulders and started to thread her fingers through the curls at the back of his neck when he pulled away.

For a second, Brant stared at her with confusion, as if he didn't quite understand what had just happened, then just as quickly the confused look evaporated and hard anger slipped back into place.

"You're a liar," he stated. "I remember your kisses." He leaned down and his hand slipped under her skirt and over her panties. "I remember your panties." Two fingers dipped beneath the elastic, and Elizabeth closed her eyes and tried not to groan. "And I remember your heat."

His hand slipped away, but it took a full minute for Elizabeth to realize that he'd moved. She opened her eyes to find him standing by the door. His lips still held the wet glimmer of shared heat, but his eyes remained as cold as an arctic sea.

"I'm not through with you, Ms. Murphy. Not by a long shot."

Chapter Seven

Henhouse Rule #4: Pleasure is best shared.

"HOLY SHIT."

Brant looked back at Beauregard, who had stopped in the doorway of Miss Hattie's room to stare at the massive bed that covered one entire wall. Even after spending a night handcuffed to it, Brant had to agree with his little brother. The bed was impressive and an antique that he would love to add to his collection. The wood was a rich walnut, the carving on the headboard and footboard definitely early eighteenth century. Since most colonists at the time had made practical furniture, Brant would almost bet that this ornate bed had been brought over from Europe—more than likely, from England.

"The infamous Miss Hattie's bed," Beau breathed. Tossing his cowboy hat onto a chair in the corner, he strode over and bounced down on the high mattress. "It's about as comfortable as a bed can get. No wonder Miss Hattie did so well. Most men would've paid good money just to sleep here for the night."

"I doubt seriously that the mattress is over a hundred years old," Brant said as he placed the suitcase he'd gotten from his truck on the end of the bed. The old women were a sneaky lot. They'd hidden his truck out behind the barn in a forest of weeds.

"Hey, don't screw with my fantasies." Beau flopped back, and his breath whooshed from his lungs. "Damn, is that her? Is that Miss Hattie?" He scooted over on the mattress. "It's like I'm lying in bed with her right next to me."

Why the thought of his brother in the bed with a woman who had been dead for over fifty years should bother Brant, he didn't know. All he knew was that he wanted Beau off the black satin sheets as quickly as possible.

"What, were you raised in a barn?" He reached out and knocked his brother's boots off the end of the bed. "Mama would yank a knot in your tail if she saw you disrespecting someone else's property like that."

Beau rolled to a sitting position and cocked a brow. "No more than she plans on yanking a knot in yours and Brianne's for not showing up to Billy's wedding. I've got to tell you, Brant, Billy was pretty hurt."

The thought of hurting his brother had Brant mad all over again at the crazy group of women. Especially Ms. Elizabeth Murphy. Or maybe he wasn't as angry with the woman as much as he was with his reaction to her. What in the hell was the matter with him, anyway? He could understand what had happened when he was drugged. But what had caused his reaction to her only moments ago in the library? One second, he'd been angry about her lying, and the next thing he knew he'd wanted to press her back against the shelves and dip into her like a tortilla chip into hot salsa.

And Elizabeth was hot. Which meant that Minnie was

wrong. No uptight virgin would heat up as quickly as that woman did. Every time he touched her, she was wet and ready. It was like she walked around in a constant state of arousal. Just the thought had his dick coming to life. Not wanting to embarrass himself in front of his little brother, he tried to get his mind back to their conversation.

"So I take it Billy didn't come to his senses and call off the wedding," he said as he unzipped the suitcase.

Beau shook his head. "He loves Shirlene, Brant. And when you meet her, you're going to love her, too. She's Billy, but in a woman's body."

"Last time I checked," Brant said as he took out a pair of jeans, "Billy wasn't a gold digger."

In a flash, Beau jumped up from the bed with his fists clenched. "Shirlene's not a gold digger. She's a sweet gal that we had no business kicking out of her house."

It wasn't surprising that Beau stood up for Shirlene. Ever since he'd been a kid, he'd had a thing for helpless girls—or what he viewed as helpless girls. From what Brant knew about Shirlene Dalton, she was about as helpless as a barracuda. But for some reason, she made Billy happier than he'd been in years, and his family's happiness was all that mattered to Brant.

"So Brianne didn't show up at the wedding either?" He pulled a shirt out of his suitcase, annoyed by the wrinkles that creased the sleeves and waist.

"No," Beau said and flopped back down on the bed. "Brianne might be getting a 4.0 in college, but she's dumber than a box of rocks if she thinks Mama will forgive and forget. Mama's almost as good as you are at settling scores." He glanced back at Brant. "Please tell me you're not planning on kicking that group of harmless old women out on the streets just because our granddaddy was supposedly killed here. I would've thought that you learned your lesson after trying to ruin the town of Bramble."

An hour ago, Brant would've delighted in tossing the old broads out on their behinds. But his temper had cooled since then. At least, toward the old hens. The new one was a different matter.

"The only lesson I learned was 'check your facts more thoroughly,'" he said. He pulled on a pair of boxer briefs. "And the only proof we have that our grandfather was shot here at Miss Hattie's is the word of Moses Tate, a man you said yourself is as ancient as the hills and spends most of his time sleeping on the bench in front of the Bramble pharmacy. Moses probably has trouble remembering his name, let alone a story he heard from his grandfather years ago."

"You wouldn't be saying that if you'd met the man," Beau said as he leaned over the opened nightstand drawer. "He's more alert than half the people in town." He lifted a long, phallic-shaped object from the drawer and squinted at it. "But even if Moses Tate got his facts wrong, and our grandfather really was killed in Bramble, it's not going to change anything. You can't get revenge by closing down Dalton Oil, Brant, not when Bramble is Billy's new home."

Beau had a point. With Billy and his new family living there, closing Dalton Oil was out of the question. It was a hard pill to swallow. In the last year, revenge on Bramble had consumed Brant's thoughts. Now all he had were the nightmares and bizarre dreams of Miss Hattie.

"So if you feel that way, why did you come all the way out here?" Brant asked.

Beau tossed the antique dildo back in the drawer and grinned brightly. "Because I'd never been to a whorehouse before and I wanted to see one before I die."

Brant might've laughed if Beau hadn't just finished up chemotherapy. There was nothing funny about his little brother dying.

"What did the doc say at your last visit?" he asked as he walked over to one of the chairs in front of the fireplace and sat down to tug on his boots.

Beau rolled his eyes. "You sound as bad as Mom. She calls me every day to ask how much sleep I've gotten and what I had for breakfast, lunch, and dinner. Of course, she worries about everyone in the family. She thinks Harvard has ruined Beckett. Brianne is too spoiled and headstrong to ever catch a man. And you're a recluse who will end up as nutty as Aunt Milly."

"Aunt Milly isn't off her rocker." Brant tugged on a boot. "She's just a lonely old woman who lives in the past." When Beau didn't say anything, Brant looked up at his brother, who was watching him with what could only be called sympathy. "Are you saying I'm a lonely old man who lives in the past?"

"No," Beau said. "I'm saying you're a man who's still grieving for his wife and son and is looking for anything or anyone to blame. The legend of the Cates Curse just happened to be a convenient explanation. But I think both of us know that the tornado that killed Mandy and B.J. wasn't caused by something that happened a hundred years ago."

There was a part of him that knew Beau was right. Up until Mandy and B.J. had died, the Cates Curse had only been a ghost story he and his brothers had delighted in retelling when they were camping in the backyard with their flashlights and sleeping bags. But if he didn't have the curse to blame for the huge emptiness that his family's death had created inside him, then what could he blame? There was nothing he could do about fate. And if he blamed God and renounced all faith, then he couldn't believe in heaven. And without heaven, his wife and son would just be decaying in the hard, cold ground.

Brant couldn't live with that.

"Why don't you take some time off," Beau said. "You haven't had a vacation in years. We could go hiking through Europe or motorcycle riding through Taiwan—or climb Mount Ever—"

There was a tap on the door, and Baby walked in with a silver tray that held two cut-crystal glasses and a bottle of brandy.

"Minnie thought you two would like a little refreshment."

Beau didn't hesitate to hop up from the bed. "That would sure be nice, ma'am. I'm pretty parched myself."

"Don't touch that," Brant said. "Miss Hattie's likes to slip people mickeys."

Baby giggled as she brought the tray over to the table next to Brant's chair. "Minnie thought you would feel that way, so she had me get an unopened bottle." She peeled off the seal and removed the cap, then splashed a little in a glass. "It's the best bottle of cognac we had. But nothing's too good for our guests."

Even with the seal, Brant refused to take the glass, but Beau had no such reservations. He accepted the drink with a smile that had Baby's eyes almost bugging through her glasses before he took a seat in the chair next to Brant's.

Baby quickly slipped a footstool under his feet, then hurried across the room and returned with a humidor.

She flipped it open right in front of Beau, who examined the contents.

"Cuban?"

"Of course." Baby smiled. "Miss Hattie's wouldn't have anything else."

After a careful inspection, Beau selected a cigar and ran it under his nose. "Nice."

Since Beau had probably never had a Cuban cigar in his life, Brant had to grin. Baby held the humidor out to Brant. As much as he wanted to, he couldn't resist the smell of rich tobacco. When he chose one, Baby looked like she was about to burst with happiness.

"Would you boys like a foot massage?" she asked as she lit his cigar.

"I would—" Beau started, but Brant cut him off.

"No, thank you, Baby."

"What about a back scratching?" she asked.

"That would be great—"

Brant threw his brother a warning look. "Thanks, but we're good."

Baby's face fell. "All right then, I guess I'll just leave you two to enjoy your cigars."

Once she had clicked her way out of the room, Beau relaxed back in the chair and blew out a puff of smoke. "This is the life. The gals might be old, but they sure understand what men like." He took a sip of the brandy and closed his eyes in ecstasy.

"You might feel differently when you wake up handcuffed to a bed," Brant said as he sat back and savored his own cigar.

Beau cracked open one eye. "I noticed those. Don't tell me the old hens took advantage of you."

"Not the old hens, but the young one."

Beau's eyes popped open. "Ms. Murphy? Are you kidding me? I thought Minnie was joking."

"Not in the least." It was hard to keep the anger from his voice. "What do you know about her?"

Beau laughed. "A lot less than you seem to know." Brant sent him a hard stare, but his little brother only grinned wider. "Not much. She's the librarian in Bramble who helped Billy with research. The first time I've ever talked with her was last night at the wedding after she caught the bouquet Shirlene tossed."

The thought of the woman going to a wedding and celebrating while he was chained to a bed had Brant almost snapping the cigar in half.

"She sure doesn't seem like the type to force herself on a man." Beau continued. "But I guess it makes sense with her being the owner of Miss Hattie's and all." He shook his head. "What a great disguise. She's the last person I would think of as a madam."

The word "madam" bothered Brant more than he cared to admit. Or maybe what bothered him the most was the image of other men getting what he'd sampled but couldn't remember.

"Of course, it's not like she's a real madam," Beau continued. "Miss Hattie's isn't a working whorehouse." He puffed out a stream of smoke and glanced over at Brant. "Right?"

Before spending the night handcuffed to a bed, Brant might've agreed. Now he wasn't so sure.

"Good morning."

The airy voice had them both turning to the door where Sunshine stood holding a plate of chocolate chip cookies. Homemade chocolate chip cookies that Brant could smell clear across the room.

Beau put his drink down on the table and rubbed his hands together. "This place just keeps getting better and better." He collected a handful of cookies from the plate before Sunshine offered them to Brant. The image of her without her shirt flashed through Brant's mind, and he shook his head.

"No, thank you," he said. "But I do have a question. Just how did Ms. Murphy get ownership of Miss Hattie's?"

Without the slightest hesitation, Sunshine answered. "Minnie had the lawyer give it to her."

It wasn't hard to figure out how a lawyer had played into it. "So she inherited the house?"

Sunshine nodded.

"But inherited it from whom?" Beau directed the question at Brant. "Kenny Gene told me that her mother was a retired schoolteacher in Amarillo."

"Oh, but she didn't inherit it from her mama," Sunshine said. "She inherited it from the hen."

Beau and Brant exchanged glances before looking back at Sunshine.

"The hen?" they both said simultaneously.

"The head hen." Sunshine beamed. "Elizabeth is the great-great-granddaughter of Miss Hattie Ladue."

Chapter Eight

*Henhouse Rule #26: Seduction is a weapon. Wield
it carefully.*

"I JUST CAN'T BELIEVE that you would do something like
that, Elizabeth."

Elizabeth adjusted the cell phone to her ear and continued to alphabetize the books in Miss Hattie's library.

"It's not the end of the world, Mother. It's only a bouquet," she said as she moved John Steinbeck to the "S"
shelf behind Shakespeare and Shelley. "How did you find
out about it, anyway?"

"I have my sources," her mother huffed, and Elizabeth
figured she was doing her morning calisthenics, which
included exactly twenty-two minutes of jogging in place,
followed by three sets of jumping jacks. "And believe me,
it's not the bouquet as much as the act of catching it. The
entire town of Bramble now thinks that you want to get
married." The word "married" came out sounding like
the worst form of torture a person could endure.

And according to Harriett Murphy, it was. Only
vapid ignoramuses wanted to participate in an institution
thought up by men to ensure they always had a sex partner
and slave on hand. Unfortunately, men were controlled

by their baser instincts—hunting and procreating—and those weren't stifled by a wedding band and vows. In fact, in most cases, marriage only exacerbated those instincts.

Thus the popularity of places like Miss Hattie's Henhouse.

Elizabeth didn't blame her mother for her beliefs. Growing up in a house of ill repute would taint just about anyone's views of men and marriage. Elizabeth was just getting sick of hearing about it. Although this time, as her mother went on and on about the animal instincts of men, a perfect example popped into Elizabeth's mind.

Branston Cates.

If any man was a hunter and procreator, it was Branston. Testosterone seeped from the man's pores like honey from a hive, and it was hard not to want to lick it off like a starving bear cub. Which explained her behavior where the man was concerned. Having never been around such a virile man, she'd lost her head.

And her panties.

But she wasn't about to let either happen again. Branston Cates might not be through with her, but she was more than through with him. Fortunately, the hens had ensured that Branston wouldn't be staying long. What man in his right mind would want to stay in a rundown old house with a bunch of crazy old women?

"Are you listening to me, Elizabeth?" her mother asked.

"Yes, Mother," she said. "Men are the scum of the earth. Now I better go so I can burn Shirlene's bouquet before it works its voodoo."

"I'm not amused, Elizabeth," her mother huffed. "I'll call you tomorrow."

After she hung up, Elizabeth continued to organize the books. Not that she was afraid of leaving the library and running into Brant. She just happened to like organizing books. The front door slammed, and she raced over to the window in time to see Brant and his brother heading down the front steps.

There was no denying the Cates brothers were a handsome lot. She had met the youngest brother, Beckett, at the wedding, and he was just as good-looking as Billy, Beau, and Brant. They were all tall and lean with broad shoulders that filled out a western shirt to perfection. Although there was something about the way Brant's starched shirt fit that made Elizabeth's stomach feel like she'd swallowed a herd of butterflies. She watched as he disappeared around the corner of the porch. Suddenly, the butterflies were gone, leaving behind a hollow emptiness.

She turned from the window and went back to the books, but not even discovering a first edition F. Scott Fitzgerald made her feel any better. Thinking she was only tired and needed some sleep, she left the library and headed for the kitchen to say her good-byes.

Except the hens weren't in the kitchen. Or their bedrooms. Or in any of the rooms on the main level. She had just started up the staircase when the elevator caught her eye—and not the elevator so much as the lit arrow above it—an arrow that pointed down.

Elizabeth wasn't surprised that there was another level in the house she knew nothing about. After discovering Miss Hattie's room, it was obvious that she needed to have Minnie give her a full tour before the Realtor arrived in the morning.

The ride down to the bottom floor in the rickety elevator

could only be described as hair-raising. Relieved to be alive, Elizabeth pushed back the metal spring door and stepped out. She had expected to find a room as empty as the ones on the main floor or as filled with antiques as Miss Hattie's. What she didn't expect was a Seventies jungle-themed nightmare.

Purple shag carpeting was the canvas for fake-fur and animal-print furniture, brightly colored pots with artificial plants, and Art Deco end tables that held slow-blobbing lava lamps. A huge Andy Warhol painting hung over the leather and chrome bar, a bar that stood just to the right of a small dance floor. Strobe lights flashed and reflected off a disco ball, causing dots of light to bounce around the room as if dancing to the beat of the Bee Gees' song that blasted through the overhead speakers.

Between the noise and the lighting, Elizabeth felt more than a little disoriented, and it took her a moment to locate Minnie. The old woman was sitting in an orange fur chair that clashed with her purple negligee. Or not sitting as much as sleeping. The cigarette that hung from her mouth had a three-inch line of ash.

Weaving her way between a ceiling-high, plastic ficus tree and the zebra-print couch, Elizabeth reached out for the cigarette. But before she could take it, Minnie's eyes flashed open.

"What the hell!" Minnie sat up. Surprisingly, the cigarette remained on her lip. Along with the ash.

Exasperated, Elizabeth grabbed an ashtray off the end table next to Minnie's chair and held it out to her. "If you're not careful, you're going to wake up in flames one day," she yelled above the music.

Minnie snorted. "I've never doubted that for a second."

Once the cigarette was out, Elizabeth set the ashtray back on the table and sat down on the couch. What she thought was print turned out to be actual zebra, the hair stiff and very horselike. Since she was an animal lover, this discovery was more than a little disconcerting. "How come you didn't tell me this room was here?" she asked. Minnie cocked her head, and Elizabeth repeated the question louder.

"Because you weren't a hen until last night," the old woman yelled back. "This part of the house is hens only. Our break room, so to speak."

Elizabeth looked around. The basement was about as far from an office break room as she was from a hen.

"Who decorated it?" she yelled. "This certainly isn't late eighteen hundreds."

The song cut off abruptly, as did the strobe lights. But the refracting lights of the disco ball remained, dancing over Minnie's wrinkled face.

"Your grandma," she said. "She had an interior designer come all the way from Dallas to do it." She shook her head. "That man was as queer as a three-dollar bill. But I'll tell you what. He was the best damned dance partner I ever had." Her eyes grew distant as if picturing herself dancing with the gay designer from Dallas.

It was the first time Elizabeth had ever thought of Minnie as handicapped. The woman was such a tyrant that it was hard to think of her as being human. The image of a younger, dancing Minnie had Elizabeth feeling sympathy for the woman. Unlike her own mother, who when she wasn't nagging Elizabeth was quite content reading or watching birds through her binoculars, Minnie had a zest for life. Being confined to a wheelchair had to be the worst form of torture.

"I'm sorry, Minnie," Elizabeth said.

Minnie's eyes refocused, and she reached for the cigarette that was no longer there. "No need to feel sorry for me, Lizzie. I've lived more than any human has a right to. And I ain't done yet."

Elizabeth released her breath. "Minnie, we're not going to keep—"

Another song came through the speakers. Instead of loud and disco, this one was soft and jazzy. Elizabeth started to tell her that she'd called the Realtor and asked her to come back out in the morning, but Minnie shushed her.

"Shhh. You need to watch and learn." She pointed across the room.

To the left of the dance floor sat a bright blue baby grand piano, and on top of the piano sat Baby. Elizabeth didn't know how she'd gotten into the room without her noticing. Or how she had gotten up on the piano for that matter. But there she sat, her legs crossed in the slit of the long white dress, one bright red high heel teasingly keeping time to the beat of the music. From that distance, she looked exactly like Marilyn, her platinum-blond hair gleaming in the disco lights.

She lifted the microphone to her ruby-painted lips and in a breathy voice started to sing.

"There's a somebody I'm longing to see. I hope that he…turns out to be…someone to watch over me."

The words brought a heaviness to Elizabeth's heart as Baby put all her emotions into the beautiful, and surprisingly talented, rendition of the song. But it turned out that Baby wasn't the only one who had slipped into the room unnoticed. Suddenly Sunshine danced out of the shadows, two feathered fans covering her from neck to knee. She danced as she walked, her legs moved gracefully to the beat of the music while her arms manipulated the fans like a swan stretching his wings. Elizabeth caught glimpses of bare skin, but never enough to know if Sunshine was completely naked beneath the trembling feathers.

"It's a lost art," Minnie said, her voice low and filled with awed reverence. "It's fallen prey to a bunch of pornography and vulgarity. Everyone's in such a hurry to get to the act of sex that they completely forgo the best part," she paused as Sunshine manipulated the fans, "seduction."

Elizabeth was too caught up in the dance to say a word. Minnie was right. The dance was like a form of art. A moving art that left the viewer as speechless as the sight of a priceless Monet. Every sweep of the feathers was like the stroke of an artist's brush, painting a picture that was breathtakingly beautiful.

And yes, totally seductive.

It didn't matter that it was being performed by a woman twice Elizabeth's age. The painter was only a faceless genius completely hidden by the beauty of the canvas.

Elizabeth had never been much of a crier, but she couldn't help the emotion that welled up in her throat. There was something about the dance that spoke to her and her alone. Something that touched her like nothing else ever had. When it ended in a swirl of feathers, Elizabeth was left wanting more yet, on the other hand, relieved that the emotional torture was over.

"It was Hattie's dance," Minnie whispered. "The

music has changed over the years, but never the movements." Her gaze took in Elizabeth's flustered state. "You
can't sell the henhouse. It's part of your heritage. Part of
who you are."

There was a moment when Elizabeth started to believe
Minnie's words, but then the dance floor lights shut off
and someone switched on the bright overhead lights.
When Elizabeth's eyes finally adjusted, she found herself
sitting on a zebra-skin couch in the most famous whorehouse in Texas.

Seduction might be a lost art form, but what happened
after the seduction was still cheap when it was being
paid for.

She turned to Minnie. "As much as you sugarcoat it,
Minnie, you're still exchanging sex for money."

Minnie's eyes filled with disappointment. "You don't
get it, Lizzie. You see Miss Hattie's as a sex store, and I'm
not going to argue that sex took place here. But sex isn't
what Miss Hattie's is about. And until you figure it out,
you'll never find happiness."

"I'm selling the house," Elizabeth stated.

"Over my dead body," Minnie countered just as Baby
came tiptoeing across the shag carpeting in her high heels,
followed by Sunshine, who was wearing a tan leotard.

"So what did you think, Lizzie?" Baby asked.

It was hard to answer when she was struggling with
the strong desire to wrap her fingers around Minnie's
throat and take her up on her offer. "The song was beautiful and the dance breathtaking."

Baby beamed while Sunshine shot her a sullen look.
It seemed she still hadn't forgiven Elizabeth for getting to
Brant first.

"I can't wait to perform it for Brant," Sunshine said.

Surprisingly, the thought of Sunshine performing the dance for Brant didn't exactly set well with Elizabeth. Which was silly. Especially when Brant was long gone.

"I'm afraid that the Cates boys have already left, Sunshine," she said.

Instead of looking disappointed, Sunshine looked smug. "No, they haven't. Beau is taking a nap in Miss Hattie's room, and Brant is out in the lilac garden looking for his great-grandfather's bones."

Elizabeth thought she had been mad at Minnie, but it was nothing compared to how she felt about Mr. Cates wandering around the henhouse. She had made a mistake not releasing him last night, but that did not give the man the right to snoop around her property without her permission.

She jumped to her feet and headed for the elevator.

"Where are you going, Lizzie?" Baby asked.

Elizabeth slammed the elevator gate closed. "To deal with a bully."

Once the elevator was on its way up to the main floor, Baby turned to Minnie.

"Maybe we should go after her. She looked a little murderous."

Minnie nodded thoughtfully. "You're right, Baby, she does look a little angry. And come to think of it, she didn't start showin' a little piss and vinegar until Branston showed up."

Baby sat down on the couch. "You don't think he forced himself on her when she found him in the bedroom, do you?"

Sunshine tugged at her leotard that had ridden up on her butt. "It didn't look like he was forcing her when they were kissing in the library."

Minnie's eyebrows lifted. "They were kissin' in the library?"

A guilty look crossed Sunshine's face. "I wasn't spying, Min. I was just going to ask Branston if he needed anything."

It only took a minute for Minnie to start cackling. "I was only teasing Elizabeth about losing her virginity, but it looks like I wasn't too far off the mark. And if Branston is the one that can heat up her hen blood, then Branston is the key to us gettin' to keep Miss Hattie's."

Baby looked puzzled. "But how are we going to keep him here?"

"By giving him what he wants," Minnie said.

"Sex," Sunshine piped up.

A sly smile slipped over Minnie's face. "His great-granddaddy's murderer."

Chapter Nine

*Henhouse Rule #33: Never send a man on his way
without giving him the full tour.*

BRANT HAD EVERY INTENTION OF heading back to Dogwood,
but first he wanted to take a look around. It would be stupid
to have made the trip clear out here and then not check out
the property. Beau tagged along, although it didn't take him
long to get bored and head back to the house for a nap.

From what Brant could figure out by the barbed wire
fences, Miss Hattie's property included a couple of acres.
The barn and house took up a big chunk, and the rest was
covered in weeds, mesquite, and overgrown lilac bushes.
The lilacs didn't surprise him. Not after spending an
entire night with the scent. What did surprise him was the
amount of bushes. They grew twice as high as the weeds
and were twice as difficult to get through.

Brant had just about given up on finding anything in
the lilac-weed jungle when he came across a headstone.
The weeds had been cleared from around the base of the
mauve-colored stone, but an overgrown lilac bush covered most of the front. He reached out and brushed back
the branches until he could see the chicken statue perched
on top and the name engraved beneath.

Miss Harriett Lillian Ladue

Brant didn't know why he knelt at the marker, or why, after a few moments of silence, he started snapping off the lilac branches that covered the headstone. Maybe it was his way of paying tribute to the grand madam. Or maybe he just couldn't stand the thought of a person's last resting place being completely undetectable. When some of the branches proved too thick, Brant got up and headed to the barn to see if he could find some pruners. He took an armload of branches with him, dumping them in one of the trash bins that sat against the side of the barn. He had just put the lid back on when a snooty voice spoke from behind him.

"Are you planning on taking up gardening?"

He turned to find Elizabeth standing only a few feet away, her hair smoothed back in a tight bun and her clothes much less rumpled than they had been earlier that morning. With her glasses reflecting the overhead sun, he couldn't see her eyes, but her cheeks were a rosy red. Which seemed to be their constant condition. Except this time, he didn't think it was from embarrassment as much as anger.

Brant brushed his hands off on his jeans. "As a matter of fact, my doctor has recommended that very thing. He claims it alleviates stress."

"Well, you need to relieve your stress elsewhere," she stated in a voice that reminded him of his second-grade teacher, Miss Shultz. And Miss Shultz had been one uppity pain in the ass. "You've worn out your welcome here."

He shrugged. "I would've been more than happy to leave

yesterday. It was you who kept me from doing so. Therefore, I'll leave when I'm ready." He narrowed his eyes. "I owe you, Ms. Murphy, and I don't take my grudges lightly."

Annoyingly enough, she didn't look that worried. "I don't doubt that for a moment, being that you're the same grudge holder who was willing to put an entire town out of work just because someone shot your relative a hundred years ago."

"So you *do* know who I am. That makes things a lot easier."

"How so?" she asked.

"Now you'll know exactly what to expect."

Her lips pressed into a firm line that took the plumpness right out of them. "If you felt that way, then why didn't you just tattle to the sheriff?"

"Because I prefer to handle my own retribution."

"Sort of like God?"

He tipped his head. "Sort of."

"Well, sorry if I don't wait around for judgment day, but I need to get back to Bramble and you need to leave." She straightened her suit jacket. "I wish I could say it was nice to meet you, Mr. Cates. But unlike your brothers, I find you to be a disagreeable man." She turned and started to walk off, but he reached out and grabbed her arm. She felt more fragile than she looked. Something he'd noticed earlier on the stairs and again in the library.

Of course, he'd noticed other things in the library as well. Like how soft her lips were and how sweetly they opened up to his. Even pressed in a firm line, they were tempting, which made his next question come out a little meaner than he had intended.

"How did you become the owner of Miss Hattie's?"

She jerked her arm away. "Do you always go around bullying people, Mr. Cates?"

"In business, it's called getting your questions answered." He crossed his arms. "Bullying is when you force someone to do something they don't really want to."

"You do seem to persevere, don't you? I've already apologized for that, while you haven't once apologized for your brash behavior. It sort of makes a person wonder what kind of women you've been hanging out with."

"The kind who don't lie about how they lost their panties."

Her face brightened, and there was a moment that Brant thought she might actually punch him, but he should've known that Ms. Murphy had more self-control than that.

"Which means," he continued, "that you're probably not going to tell the truth about how you came to own Miss Hattie's. Since I can't understand why a librarian would want a whorehouse, the only feasible answer to the question would be that you inherited it like Sunshine said." He laughed. "Although the woman is a little confused about whom you inherited it from. My guess would be that you're somehow related to a businessman who bought into the house years ago."

She slowly clapped her hands. "Bravo, Mr. Cates. No wonder you're one of the wealthiest men in Texas—you know how to put two and two together. Now that you've finished your detective work, you can let me go and be on your way."

That would've been the smart thing to do. But there was something about Elizabeth's demeanor that bothered him. She had acquiesced almost too easily. So instead of releasing her, he reached up and pulled off her glasses. The eyes that stared back at him were big and brown and filled with tiny golden flecks that reflected the sunlight. Eyes identical to the ones in the mural over the bed.

"Shit," he breathed.

She released an exasperated huff. "So eloquently put. I must admit that I thought the same thing when I discovered the connection. But we can't help who our relatives are, now can we? Something I'm sure your brothers, Beau and Billy, understand completely. So if you're done interrogating me, I would appreciate it if you'd give me back my glasses and be on your way. As you've pointed out, I own Miss Hattie's and I want you to leave."

Brant might've complied if he hadn't been so stunned by the fact that the same whiskey-colored eyes that had occupied his dreams for the last month were identical to the eyes staring back at him now. It was a relief when she pried the glasses from his numb fingers and covered those eyes. Except covering them with thick glass didn't seem to stop his imagination.

Now that he knew what lay beneath, all kinds of sexual images flashed through his mind. Images that he was no longer certain were real or just part of his screwed-up psyche. Either way, he couldn't seem to keep his head from dipping toward her lips. And as mad as she seemed to be, Elizabeth didn't do one thing to stop him.

"Hey, you two!"

His brother's voice caused them to pull back. Brant gave her upside-down mouth one last look before turning to Beau, who tramped through the weeds toward them with a knowing grin on his face.

"I hope I'm not interrupting anything."

"Not at all," Elizabeth said. "Mr. Cates was just saying good-bye."

Beau looked at Brant. "No kidding. Well, I'm glad I caught him before he left. It seems that Miss Minnie just remembered something that might help us find out if our granddaddy was here. I guess Miss Hattie kept a record of all her visitors. There's just one problem. Miss Minnie doesn't exactly know where it is. Although she thinks it might be up in the attic."

Brant didn't even hesitate before heading toward the back door.

"Now wait one second," Elizabeth said as she hurried after him. "I didn't give you permission to go searching through my attic."

Brant glanced back at her. "What are you going to do? Call the sheriff?"

The stairs that led to the attic were steep, narrow, and dark. The dim flashlight Minnie had given Brant gave off about as much light as a firefly as he, Elizabeth, and Beau moved up the worn steps.

"Isn't there a light switch?" Elizabeth asked as she swatted at a cobweb.

"An exterminator would be more appreciated," Beau said. "I think I just got bit by a spider."

"This should be right up your alley," Brant said. "You used to drag me to every haunted house in Dogwood on Halloween."

"Except those creepy critters were the dime-store variety. And I don't think what just ran across my boot was made of rubber."

Elizabeth latched on to Brant's shirt and almost pulled him back down the stairs as she turned to Beau. "Was it a mouse?"

"If it wasn't, then it was the biggest spider in Texas."

Elizabeth scuttled up on Brant's step. "Well, kill it."

"I would love to, ma'am, but I'm a little skittish myself," Beau said. It was easy to detect the teasing note in his brother's voice. "Now Brant, on the other hand, has never been scared of anything. He could slay a dragon if he took the notion, which means a little ol' mouse wouldn't stand a chance."

Brant ignored his brother's foolishness and tried to climb the last step, but Elizabeth had a stranglehold on his shirt. He wasn't exactly happy with the woman, but he couldn't ignore her fear, either. He slipped his hand in hers and gave it a comforting squeeze. "Mice are more terrified of you than you are of them."

"Unless it's Willard," Beau said.

"Shut up, Beau." Brant pulled Elizabeth up the last step. He shined the flashlight at the wall and, spotting a switch, reached out and flipped it on. One single bare bulb came on, but its light was enough to reveal the mountains of clutter that were piled almost to the rafters.

"Holy shit," Beau said, before muttering an apology. "Sorry, ma'am, but this is one big pile of crap."

It was. Except Brant didn't view it as crap. He viewed it as a gold mine of precious history. There were old televisions and radios. Leather trunks and suitcases. A stockpile of paintings and a grandfather clock that made his hands sweat. Or maybe that was the heat emanating from Elizabeth's.

"Does the saying, 'finding a needle in a haystack'

mean anything to you?" Beau asked with a smirk in his voice. A cackle came up the stairwell, and Brant released Elizabeth's hand and called down to the old woman who sat at the bottom.

"Can you remember what you stored it in?"

"I think it was a trunk," Minnie called back up.

Brant looked back at the clutter. There had to be at least a hundred big trunks stacked amid the furniture and cardboard boxes, but he had never been one to be intimidated by work. He didn't waste any time pulling out the first trunk and opening it up.

"Don't tell me you're going to look through every one," Beau said.

"Now why would I do that when I have a helpful little brother?" He searched through the trunk of old clothing.

"Oh no." Beau stepped back. "I'm not spending my time in some musty, old, rat-infested attic looking for a book unless it's filled with some of Miss Hattie's x-rated stories."

"Beau's right," Elizabeth said as she walked over and slammed the lid of the trunk down, almost catching Brant's fingers in the process. "Once I sell the house, there will be plenty of time to pull all the things out of the attic and look through them. If I should find anything about your grandfather, I'll be more than happy to contact you."

Brant ignored her and grabbed another trunk. "Well, that's real nice of you, Ms. Murphy, but since I don't trust you as far as I can throw that grandfather clock over there, I think I'll just look myself."

Another cackle drifted up the stairs, followed by Minnie's raspy voice. "All of that stuff belongs to us hens, and if Branston wants to go through them, that's fine with us. Isn't that right, Sunshine?" Sunshine chirped her agreement, which made Elizabeth's brow pucker all the more.

"And if Beau doesn't want to hang out up there," Minnie continued to yell up, "I've got a few things he could help me with down here."

Beau didn't waste any time accepting the offer. "Good luck, big bro," he said as he clattered down the stairs.

When he was gone, Brant took off his cowboy hat and hung it on an old hat rack before rolling up his shirt-sleeves. "You don't have to stay, Ms. Murphy. I'm quite capable of handling the job alone."

"I don't doubt that for a second, Mr. Cates. But I also don't trust you as far as I can throw you."

He laughed as he took a seat on the trunk he'd just opened. "So you're planning on selling the house?"

"There isn't any other choice." She glanced around the attic floor before taking a seat in the rocking chair across from him, but a scratching noise had her quickly hooking her feet up on the bottom rung.

"And if there was?"

Her gaze flickered up to his, direct as ever. "You're right, I still wouldn't keep it. Miss Hattie's was my great-grandmother's dream, not mine."

"From what I've read, it was quite a dream," he said as he pulled the next trunk closer. "It's hard to believe this is the same house they wrote about. Although Miss Hattie's room certainly does the legend justice." He unhooked the latches, but waited to lift the lid. "I'll give you a good price for the bed if you're interested in selling."

Her gaze snapped up from the floor, and she studied him for only a second before speaking. "It's not mine to sell. It belongs to the hens, and considering how they hate to part with Miss Hattie's things, it's doubtful that they'll sell it."

Refusing to let his disappointment show, he pulled up the lid of the trunk. This one wasn't filled with clothes, but stacks of yellowed newspapers. He went to pull the first one out when Elizabeth stopped him.

"Be careful with those. If they're as old as they look, the paper could tear easily." She scooted the rocking chair closer.

"I know how to handle old things," he said. He hadn't meant it in a derogatory way, but when her gaze swept over to him, he couldn't help shooting her an overtly innocent look. "Present company excluded, of course."

"These are Bramble *Gazette*s," she said after only a glance. "I loaned your brother Billy copies of these." She carefully leafed through the stack in the trunk. "I'm afraid you won't find anything in here about your grandfather," she pulled out a newspaper that looked smaller and older than the others, "except for this false story that they printed about him being shot in the middle of town."

Brant took the page of the newspaper she offered him and quickly read through the short article:

Shooting On Main Street

William Cates from Lubbock was shot dead by Sheriff Wynn Murdock on Wednesday, August 5, after a dispute with Mayor Fillmore over the dedication plaque Cates had made for the new town hall. According to the mayor, who was the only witness to the shooting, Cates became violent when the mayor refused to pay him for the plaque, forcing the sheriff to use his Colt 45.

"It's the sheriff's job to protect the citizens of Bramble," Mayor Fillmore said. "And Cates had no business getting all riled up about money when the plaque had the wrong date."

Sheriff Murdock refused to comment.

"And what makes you think this is false?" Brant said after finishing the article. "It sounds accurate to me."

She looked up. "It did to me as well until I heard Moses' side of the story and took another look at the newspaper. Don't you find it strange that the mayor was the only witness to the shooting when it took place on Main Street? It's also strange that this wasn't a headlining story. The entire front page was dedicated to Elma Winter's canned green tomatoes taking first at the State Fair."

"So you're saying that the mayor, sheriff, and newspaper were all part of a cover-up?"

"I know it sounds strange," she said. "But it does make sense when you think about it. Not only did the men of the town not want to tell your grandmother that her husband was killed in a bordello, but I don't think they wanted attention brought to Miss Hattie's."

He placed the newspaper back in the trunk. "I still won't believe Moses' story until I have proof."

"Like a book with your grandfather's name in it?"

"Exactly."

Elizabeth stared at him for only a few seconds before she nodded. "Fine, Mr. Cates. I'll help you look for it."

Her sudden about-face had him squinting at her until

the light went on. "So you're afraid I might still close down Dalton Oil."

She shook her head. "With as much as Billy loves Shirlene, I doubt that will happen."

"Then why?"

Elizabeth stared down at the newspapers for a moment before she answered. "Maybe I just want to force you to admit that you're wrong."

Brant got to his feet and pulled down another trunk. "Then you might want to get a heavier jacket, Ms. Murphy, because that will be a cold day in west Texas and hell."

Chapter Ten

Henhouse Rule #47: Hens always dress for dinner.

"THE CATES BROTHERS ARE NOT STAYING FOR DINNER," Elizabeth stated. "Nor are they staying the night. I'm willing to let them look for information about their grandfather, but that's where my generosity ends."

It was a nice speech, but not one hen paid her any attention. Sunshine was busy carrying in the fresh sheets she'd just taken off the line. Baby was standing over a stove filled with all kinds of bubbling pots. And Minnie was sitting at the kitchen table, playing solitaire and humming "Someone to Watch Over Me."

"Are you listening to me?" Elizabeth said. "The Cates brothers are not staying. Beau might be a nice person, but Brant is not. He's the same man who tried to close down Dalton Oil and still would, if not for his brother."

She glanced up at the ceiling, having second thoughts about leaving such a dishonorable man alone in the attic with all the antiques. Of course, losing a few antiques was better than losing something else. Like her virginity. Within one short hour of being in the attic with Brant, she knew the exact angle of his jaw and the length of his eyelashes. Knew the breadth of his shoulders and trim lines of his waist. When she caught herself staring at the bulge beneath the zipper of his fly, she decided that she trusted Brant in the attic by himself much more than she trusted herself with him.

"Branston can't be all that bad," Minnie said as she flipped down another card. "After all, he didn't call the sheriff on us."

"And why was that? What law-abiding citizen that you know wouldn't call the sheriff after what we did to him?" Elizabeth leaned over Minnie's shoulder and went to move the four of spades to the five of diamonds, but Minnie slapped at her hand before she could accomplish it.

"Maybe he likes us," Baby said.

Minnie snorted. "I don't think it has anything to do with us. Obviously, Lizzie here has more talent than I thought she did."

Try as she might, Elizabeth couldn't control her blush, which she thought would have Minnie cackling like a fool. Instead, the woman glanced up and studied her through a swirl of cigarette smoke.

"Isn't that the same ugly suit you had on last night?"

Elizabeth tugged on her jacket. "I didn't exactly have time to shower and change when my entire life was about to go down the drain."

"Well, you better clean up. Men don't like a woman that looks like she's been rode hard and put away wet." Minnie grinned. "Unless they're the ones who have been doin' the ridin'."

"I don't care if Mr. Cates likes me or not." Elizabeth lifted the lid of the pot on the stove. Baby didn't smack her, but she did take the lid and push her out of the way with one curvy hip.

"Then take a shower for us hens," Minnie said. "Your stink is makin' my eyes water. And of course Brant and Beau are staying for supper," she continued, "Hens have never sent a man away hungry, and we never will."

She went back to her card game. "But if you don't want to stay, Lizzie, that's up to you. The hens and I can entertain the boys just fine without your help."

"Not likely—"

The kitchen door opened and Beau came in with an armload of cedar wood. As he pushed the door closed with his elbow, he took a deep breath. "What is that smell?" Elizabeth stepped back before she realized he was talking about Baby's cooking.

"Chicken and dumplings." Baby beamed.

Beau flashed a smile at Elizabeth that would make any woman a little breathless. "Please tell me I'm invited for dinner."

As much as she didn't want the Cates brothers to stay, she couldn't bring herself to be rude. "We would love to have you..." she cleared her throat, "and your brother stay for dinner." She narrowed her eyes at Minnie. "I'll just go freshen up."

"You'll have to use Hattie's bathroom," Minnie said with a gleeful note in her voice. "Ours is cluttered with a shower bench and a bunch of old woman stuff."

Miss Hattie's bathroom was as luxurious as her bedroom, but there was little doubt that it had been remodeled—during a time when pink toilets and sinks were popular. The only thing that looked like it had come from the eighteen hundreds was the huge bear-claw bathtub. A bathtub that Elizabeth didn't hesitate to fill.

The water that came out of the faucet looked a little

rusty at first, but after a few minutes it turned clear and steamy hot. Elizabeth usually took a shower before work—a three-minute shower to be exact—but, at night, she enjoyed the muscle-relaxing heat of a full bath. But her tub didn't come close to being as big as Miss Hattie's. She could stretch her legs completely out and still not touch the other side. She had just rested her head against the rim of the tub when she heard a soft click. She sat up, sloshing water over the edge as Sunshine walked in, holding a key she had undoubtedly unlocked the door with.

Her gaze fell on Elizabeth, sitting in the tub with her hands clamped over her breasts, and she released a snort. "I don't know what he sees in you. A toothpick has more curves." Then she gathered up Elizabeth's dirty clothes and disappeared out the door before Elizabeth could do more than sputter.

Unless she wanted to go down to dinner in a towel, Elizabeth had no choice but to finish her bath and head to Miss Hattie's closet.

She'd expected to find hanger after hanger of revealing, inappropriate clothing. And there was plenty of that. But surprisingly, there was also conservative clothing. Walking dresses with high-buttoned collars, shirtwaist blouses and full skirts, and cashmere suits with furred collars and knee-length hems.

As she searched through the racks, she couldn't help but wonder which outfits had been worn by whom. Had Miss Hattie worn the southern belle-styled dress with the numerous petticoats? Had her great-grandmother, Lillian Ladue, worn the teal chiffon? Had her grandmother, Millicent Ladue, worn the bell bottoms and fringed vest?

Her grandmother.

Elizabeth was just as intrigued by Millicent as she was by Miss Hattie. Why would her grandmother will the henhouse to a granddaughter she'd never even met? She understood why she hadn't willed it to her mother; Harriett Murphy wanted nothing to do with the henhouse. But why had her grandmother thought that Elizabeth would?

A flash of scarlet satin had Elizabeth separating the hangers and pulling out the long, satin dressing gown. The very same gown Miss Hattie wore in the mirrored picture. Elizabeth didn't know why she took it off the hanger or why she slipped her arms through the belled sleeves. Maybe she just wanted to see if it would fit. Or maybe, like the bed, she just wanted to see what it felt like to step into Miss Hattie's shoes for a moment.

She walked over to the beveled mirror at the back of the closet. The gown didn't fit. The bodice was too loose. The hem too short. Still, there was something about her in it that Elizabeth couldn't seem to look away from. Even with the damp waves of hair that spread around her shoulders, she didn't look like herself. She looked different. Pretty. Sexy. With her gaze riveted on her own reflection, she didn't notice Brant standing behind her until she heard his sharp intake of breath.

Elizabeth's face turned as bright red as the dress, and she pressed a hand over the low neckline before turning around. Except Brant's gaze wasn't riveted to her insufficient cleavage. His eyes were staring straight into hers as if she was a stranger. Or maybe not a stranger as much as some kind of a ghost.

"I'm sorry," he said in barely a whisper. "Minnie told me I could clean up for dinner in Miss Hattie's bathroom."

It took her a moment to find her voice. Even then, it

sounded quivery and breathless. "Of course. I'll just be a second more."

Brant nodded, but didn't seem to be in any hurry to leave. And the funny part about it was that Elizabeth wasn't in any hurry for him to leave either. She wanted him standing there looking at her in the gown. In fact, she wanted him to reach out and touch it.

To touch her.

Then just that quickly the moment was shattered, and without a word, Brant walked out of the closet and closed the door behind him. Once he was gone, Elizabeth didn't waste any time taking the gown off. She tried on numerous other outfits before she settled on black cigarette pants and a sweater set. The only bra she found in the lingerie drawer was a heavy-duty contraption that made her breasts jut out like two missiles getting ready to launch. But, with the cardigan buttoned, she didn't think she looked all that bad. At least, that's what she thought until she walked into the kitchen.

"Well, it's an improvement," Minnie said as her gaze ran over Elizabeth. "But not much of one."

Dinner parties weren't something Elizabeth was used to. Growing up, she and her mother had always eaten at the kitchen table. After moving to Bramble, she usually took her food into the living room where she would sit on the couch and nibble while she read. So she felt completely out of her element sitting in the cavernous dining room at the linen-covered table Beau and Brant had moved in from the kitchen. It didn't help that Brant sat across from her, studying her like a map written in a foreign language. His deep-set gaze made her so nervous she became a klutz. She dropped her fork twice, dripped gravy on her sweater, and knocked over her water glass. Finally, she gave up trying to eat altogether and just sipped her wine and listened to Beau, who turned out to be as good at telling stories as he was at smiling.

"...I swear I've never seen such a sight in my life as Billy standing on stage in those girlie tights, spouting out a bunch of crazy Shakespearean lines." Beau heaped his plate with another helping of chicken and dumplings. "The town of Dogwood didn't know whether to laugh or start looking for another quarterback."

"Well, I think it was sweet," Baby cooed. "Especially since he did it all for the love of Juliet."

Brant snorted. "Some Juliet. She dumped him after just a week for a freshman running back at UT. Not that he didn't deserve it for making such a fool of himself."

"Something, I assume, you've never done," Elizabeth said. Into her second glass of chardonnay, she was feeling a lot more relaxed.

Before Brant could answer, Beau laughed. "Brant make a fool of himself? You don't know my big bro, Elizabeth. He doesn't like to do anything that draws unwanted attention. He broke up with a woman once just because she spoke too loudly." Beau refilled Elizabeth's glass with wine before filling his own. "But enough about my family. Let's talk about Miss Hattie's. How long have you been here, Minnie?"

Minnie took her time chewing before she washed it down with the same brand of beer that Brant was drinking. "Longer than you've been around, squirt."

Beau grinned. "That long, huh? Were you here when Miss Hattie was alive? Did you ever meet her?"

Elizabeth assumed Minnie would be as vague as she always was when answering questions. Instead she surprised her.

"Once," she said. "She was old, of course. Most of her beauty hidden behind wrinkled skin and fading eyes. Yet, there was still an aura about her that I can't explain. I remember she gave me a stick of gum from her pocket and a pat on the head. That was when the henhouse was at its height of popularity. World War II was over and there were plenty of boys who needed some tender lovin' care to help them forget the calamities they experienced. I wasn't livin' here then, but my mama gave me a tour of the house. With its gleamin' chandeliers and richly upholstered furniture, it was the most beautiful place I'd ever seen." Her eyes stared off as if remembering. "But my favorite spot was always the lilac garden. The stone benches and fragrant flowers were right out of a fairytale."

Elizabeth didn't know how having a prostitute for a mother was out of a fairytale, but she kept her thoughts to herself.

Beau glanced around. "It's a shame all that history was lost."

"It's here, Beau," Minnie said. "All a person needs to do is look," she glanced over at Elizabeth, "with more than just their eyes."

The only person who couldn't see was Minnie. She refused to accept the fact that the henhouse would never be what it had once been. Which was why Elizabeth had called the real estate agent earlier that morning and asked her to come out tomorrow. The sooner she got it on the market, the sooner Minnie would give up her fantasies and Elizabeth could get back to her life.

"Who would like some coffee and dessert?" Baby asked. "I hope everyone likes homemade apple pie and vanilla ice cream."

"I appreciate the offer," Brant said as he blotted his mouth. "But I think we need to be going."

Minnie shot him an annoyed look. "You can't leave. Baby would be devastated if you didn't try her apple pie. In fact, why don't you and Elizabeth head on out to the front porch while Sunshine and Baby get dessert ready? Beau, you can help me get the after-dinner brandy."

Since the last thing Elizabeth wanted was to be alone with Brant, she pushed back her chair with every intention of declining dessert and the front porch. Unfortunately, Brant had other plans.

"As a matter of fact, there are a few things I'd like to discuss with Ms. Murphy," he said as he got up.

Minnie cackled. "In my day, the front porch was used for a lot more than just discussin'."

Chapter Eleven

*Henhouse Rule #44: Don't give away the cart
unless you've sold the horse.*

"I REALLY CAN'T TAKE ANY MORE VERBAL BATTLES
today," Elizabeth said as she walked out the screen door
Brant held open. "So if that's your intention, I'd rather go
back in and help the hens."

"Actually, I would like to call a truce." Brant allowed
the door to slam closed behind him.

"What happened to retribution?" The cool night air
had Elizabeth feeling a little light-headed so she moved
over to the porch swing and sat down. Or maybe it wasn't
the night air as much as the wine she'd had for dinner.

Brant leaned a shoulder on one of the posts and crossed
his arms. "As much as you think otherwise, I'm not the
type of man who punishes someone for another's crime.
Despite the panty story, I've decided that you weren't
lying when you said you stumbled into Miss Hattie's bed
accidentally."

"Well, thank you so much, Mr. Cates. Now I can die
happy."

An "almost" smile tugged at the corners of his mouth.
"After last night, Mr. Cates seems a little formal, don't

you think? Why don't you call me Brant. And do you like Elizabeth, or do you prefer Lizzie?"

It was a bad idea. Elizabeth was having a hard enough time remembering she didn't like the man without adding the familiarity of first names. But he did have a valid point. "Mister" should be reserved for men who hadn't placed their tongues in your mouth.

"Elizabeth," she said. "I hate Lizzie. Although don't tell Minnie or she'll use it twice as much."

The slight smile returned. "She is an ornery old thing, isn't she?"

"That's putting it mildly," Elizabeth said as she leaned back in the swing. "I guess it's understandable given her childhood."

Brant sat down next to her. The scent of starched shirt and man made her even more light-headed, and she edged as close to the arm of the swing as she could get without being obvious. "Her story about coming here as a child was pretty eye-opening." Using just a boot heel, he set the swing in motion. "I never thought about the women who worked here having children."

Elizabeth nodded. "When the lawyer called and informed me that I had inherited the henhouse, I did some research. One book that I found online had entries from numerous journals and diaries. I was surprised to discover that a lot of working women got pregnant and decided not to get rid of the children. Instead, they farmed them out to relatives who raised them as their own."

He glanced over at her. "Is that what happened to you?"

Elizabeth had never enjoyed talking about herself and, like Minnie, had become quite adept at vague answers. But for some reason—the wine or the man who stared back at her—she answered truthfully. "No. My mother was raised right here at Miss Hattie's, but left before I was born."

"So she chose not to take up her mother's profession?"

Elizabeth laughed at just the thought of her tight-laced mother working at Miss Hattie's. "My mother decided to go in the opposite direction."

"Ahh." He looked away. "A man hater. That explains a lot."

Elizabeth scowled. "What do you mean? I do not hate men."

He glanced back at her. "Then why haven't you married?"

"Just because I enjoy my single life, doesn't mean I don't like men." She pointed a finger at him. "You're single, and no one thinks you hate women."

"I don't dress in a way that wards women off, either."

The insult had her spine stiffening. "I dress professionally, Mr. Cates."

"You dress frumpy," he hesitated for a brief second before adding, "Elizabeth." His gaze wandered down to her pointy breasts. "But I must say that I like that outfit. Of course, I liked the red dress better."

She blushed and looked away, crossing her arms over her chest. "No doubt, every man in Texas loved that gown."

"And is there something wrong with dressing to please a man?"

Was there? Her mother had always thought so. Harriett Murphy had believed in dressing to please oneself. But now that Elizabeth thought about it, maybe Brant was right. Maybe there was nothing wrong with dressing to please a man. Not every man, but just one. One man who looked at you in a mirror like you were a vision he couldn't take his eyes off of.

"So why *did* you try on the dress?" he asked.

She shrugged. "I'm finding out that one's history is hard to ignore."

"Amen to that," he said as he turned away.

As he continued to push the swing with his boot heel, she studied his profile. He had obviously shaved before dinner. His jaw was smooth, as was the skin above his lips. Lips that smiled much too rarely.

"Is that why you're so wrapped up in finding out where your grandfather died?" she asked. "After meeting you, I can't believe you're the type of man to buy into a fanciful legend about a curse."

His gaze stayed pinned on the stars that glittered on the horizon. "When a man needs answers, you'd be surprised at what he's willing to believe in."

It was an unusual choice of words. He didn't want answers. He needed them. And "need" was a much more vulnerable word than "want."

"So I'm assuming you didn't find any proof in the attic that your grandfather was here," she said.

Brant leaned back in the swing. "Actually, I did."

"What?" She stared at him. "You found the register? Why didn't you say anything?"

"Because a faded and barely legible signature isn't exactly proof."

She leaned closer and pointed a finger at him. "It's his, and you know it. You just don't want to admit to being wrong."

"I'll admit that the handwriting looks like his, but I wouldn't start gloating just yet," he said. "None of the pages were dated, which means he could've shown up here before he went to Bramble."

Elizabeth couldn't argue the point. Nor could she argue the fact that the mystery of William Cates was starting to intrigue her. This was much better than an Agatha Christie novel, and she had the opportunity to be right in the middle of it.

She turned to him. "Have you done a lot of research about your grandfather online?"

"A little," he said. "But my internet skills leave a lot to be desired."

"I could help," she blurted out.

Elizabeth didn't know who was more surprised by the offer. Brant stopped pushing the swing and cocked an eyebrow while her face burned like a late August brush fire. He recovered much more quickly than she did.

"I'd appreciate it." He went back to pushing the swing.

After that, they didn't talk. The swing creaked back and forth as they stared out at the barren country that stretched as far as the eye could see. Soon she found herself relaxing back against the swing. But it only took a subtle tightening for her to realize that the hardness she rested against wasn't the wood of the swing but Brant's arm. She started to sit back up when Brant shifted toward her, and she found herself looking up into a pair of deepset eyes.

If someone had told Elizabeth a few days ago that a mere kiss could scramble your brains like a whisk through eggs, she would've thought they had read too many romance novels. But that's exactly what Brant's kiss did to her—scrambled her brains so much that all logical thought fled and all that was left were the feelings the man evoked with his hot mouth and skilled tongue.

He kissed like he seemed to do every other task, with

complete concentration and focus. Elizabeth, on the other hand, couldn't focus at all. Her mind was a whirl of sensations that bounced from one point to the other. The heat of his mouth on her lips. The hard press of his knee between her legs. The feather touch of his fingers on her breast.

Brant lifted his head and looked down. "What the hell is this bra made of—cast iron?" His hand slipped under both sweaters and to the hooks at the back. With a couple of flicks of his fingers, the bra billowed up.

"I think we need to—" Elizabeth started, but then Brant's warm hand settled over her bare breast, and she forgot what she was going to say. It was like he held her heart in his hand and increased the beat with each caress of his fingers. When her head tipped back and a moan escaped her lips, he pulled her onto his lap and kissed his way along her neck.

"So this entire virgin thing," he spoke against her throat. "Minnie was kidding, right?"

"Mmm," she hummed as he nibbled his way to her ear. Elizabeth didn't understand what he was talking about, nor did she care. She was like a kid in a candy store, and she wanted to taste everything offered to her before the store closed. She turned her head and hesitantly touched her lips to the side of his neck.

His breath rushed out. "I just want to make sure you're not some religious nut saving herself for her husband."

"What husband?" She ran her tongue over his earlobe, and he released a hiss from between his teeth.

"Exactly what I was thinking," he groaned before bringing his lips back to hers.

Their kisses grew more heated and Brant's hands more marauding. If his caresses weren't causing her nipples to pucker with desire, they were fanning the flame that burned beneath the crotch of her cigarette pants. She could feel the hardness of him beneath her bottom, and she wiggled her hips, wanting to get closer to that hardness. His breath hitched, and he pulled away from the kiss.

"The way I see it, we have two choices," he said. "We can go up to Miss Hattie's room or we can go to my truck. But make the decision quickly, sweetheart, because I don't think I can wait much longer. And I'd hate to freak out a bunch of little old women."

Elizabeth wasn't sure if it was the mention of Miss Hattie that dropped a bucket of ice water on her desire or the mention of the hens. Either way, the heat slipped out of her body like a cup of coffee placed in the deep freeze.

"Let me go," she said as she pushed against his shoulders.

His eyes narrowed. "What?"

"Let me go. I want to stop."

For a second, she wondered if she might have to give him the same slap she'd given him when he'd been drugged. Fortunately, it didn't come to that. He slipped her off his lap and rolled to his feet. He moved to the edge of the porch in a stiff walk that looked almost painful.

"I'm sorry," she said, "but I don't think this is a good idea." She tried to smooth her hair back into the braid she'd put it in, but it was a lost cause. "I mean, I don't even know you. And we don't even..."

"Like each other," he finished for her.

"I was going to say have a lot in common."

He kept his back to her. "You don't have to have a lot in common, Elizabeth, to have sex. Nor do you have to like each other." He ran a hand through his hair. "But you're right. Having sex with you *would* be a mistake."

Since she had been the one to put a stop to things, she should be happy he was agreeing. Instead, the words just made her feel annoyed. She leaned up and tried to refasten the bra, but the ancient hooks refused to cooperate. Her struggles caused the chains of the swing to rattle, drawing Brant's attention. He walked back over and sat down.

"Turn around." His warm fingers brushed her skin as he hooked the bra, sending gooseflesh racing down her spine. He tugged down the sweater and cardigan, then stood and pulled her to her feet. "Come on. Let's go rescue my little brother from the hens."

Except when Brant and Elizabeth got to the dining room, Beau wasn't there and neither were the hens. Nor were they in the kitchen, library, or upstairs in Miss Hattie's room.

Which left only one room.

When Brant pushed back the gate of the elevator, Elizabeth wasn't sure what she would find. But it wasn't Beau on the dance floor dancing to the Bee Gees and waving around two huge feather fans.

Fortunately, he was still fully clothed.

"Come on in and join the party," he yelled, his words slurred enough to make Elizabeth worried that the hens had drugged him.

Brant seemed to be of the same mind. He rounded the couch where all the hens sat and pinned Minnie with a dark look. "Tell me you didn't give him a Wild Rooster."

"'Course not," Minnie huffed. "He's young enough to be my grandson. He just can't hold his liquor worth a damn, is all. I swear he only had two glasses of brandy."

"And three glasses of wine at dinner," Brant said as he sent an exasperated look at his brother who was "Staying

Alive" with a bump and grind that had Elizabeth blushing as bright as Minnie's fur chair.

"Come on, 'Lizbeth." Beau placed one fan up on his head and the other on his wiggling butt. "Come dance wiff me."

"I think it's time to call it a night, Beau," Brant said as he walked onto the dance floor and tried to hook an arm around his brother. "We'll get back to Dogwood well after midnight as it is."

But Beau wasn't having any of it. He ducked under his brother's arm, then brushed the feather fan over Brant's head until his dark hair stood straight up with static electricity. Brant jerked the fan away, but not before the hens were crowing with laughter. Even Elizabeth had trouble biting back a smile.

"Stop being such a party p-pooper, Big Bro," Beau said. "And let's celebrate." He waved the other fan around while he did a little jig. "After all those lectures you gave me on becoming responsible, you should be overjoyed to hear that your kid brother has just become a business owner."

Brant stopped trying to grab his brother and went perfectly still. "What do you mean, Beau? You're already a business owner. You own a percentage of C-Corp."

"That's always been yours and Billy's company. This one is going to be mine." Beau held the fan over the lower half of his face and wiggled his eyebrows at Brant before twirling on a boot heel and almost falling on his butt. When Brant reached out and steadied him, Beau dropped the fan and flashed him a drunken smile.

"Take a good look at the soon-to-be owner of Miss Hattie's Henhouse."

Chapter Twelve

*Henhouse Rule #21: The best deals are always made
in the bedroom.*

BRANT PULLED BACK THE LACE CURTAINS and stared out
the water-spotted window. In the middle of the weeds and
overgrown lilac bushes, he could just make out the top
of Miss Hattie's headstone. Even from that distance, it
looked as if the hen statue was thumbing her beak at him.

A groan came from behind him, and he turned away
from the window to the huge bed his brother slept in.
Except for the cowboy boots Brant had taken off last
night, Beau was still fully clothed, his head hidden
beneath one of the black satin pillows.

"Rise and shine, little brother," Brant said.

Another groan followed, and Beau's muffled words
came through the pillow. "What time is it?"

"Almost seven-thirty." He walked over and hit Beau's
stocking foot. "So get your ass up. I want to get on the
road."

Beau waved a hand. "You go on. I'll catch up with you
back in Dogwood."

Moving over to his suitcase, Brant stripped off the
towel that he'd tied around his waist after bathing in Miss

Hattie's bathtub and pulled on a pair of boxer briefs. "I'm afraid not. I'm not leaving you here after what happened last night."

Beau pulled off the pillow and sat up. He blinked at the room for a few seconds before his face turned a chalky white. Holding a hand over his mouth, he scrambled off the bed and headed for the bathroom.

It was nothing to be concerned about. Brant had suffered a few hangovers himself in his younger days. But as much as he tried to act like it wasn't a big deal that his brother was tossing his cookies, Brant couldn't quite pull it off. The sound of Beau throwing up brought back too many memories of the weeks his little brother had suffered through chemotherapy. Within minutes, Brant was sitting on the edge of the bathtub with a wet washcloth in his hand and a tight band of pain squeezing his chest.

"Holy shit," Beau took the washcloth and pressed it to his face as he flopped back against the vanity. "Remind me to never try to keep up with Minnie again. The woman can hold her liquor better than Gramma Wilkes." When Brant didn't say anything, Beau lowered the washcloth. "You can stop looking at me as if I'm going to drop dead at any second. I'm okay. I just drank too much is all."

"Nice to know," Brant said before he thumped his brother upside the head.

"Oww!" Beau held a hand to his head and glared at him. "What the hell was that for?"

"For drinking more than you should've." He thumped him again. "And that's for getting a bunch of old women's hopes up." While Beau continued to glare at him, Brant got up and moved to the sink. "Those women actually believe you're going to buy Miss Hattie's and reopen it, and nothing I could say would change their minds." He pulled out the shaving cream from his travel kit. "So as soon as you get cleaned up, I expect you to go down there and apologize to those women and set things right."

With another groan, Beau got up from the floor and sat down on the vanity stool next to the sink. His face was still as white as the marble tile behind him. With his silver hair, he looked ghostly.

"Except there's nothing to apologize for."

Brant's hand stopped in the process of lathering his face. "You're going to apologize, Beau, or I'm going to whup your ass into the middle of next Sunday."

"As if," Beau said with a slight grin. "But what I'm saying is I don't need to apologize because I still plan on buying The Henhouse."

Brant whirled around, sending shaving cream flying. "Have you lost your mind?"

Beau shrugged. "I'm sure that more than a few people will think so. All I know is that, while I was sitting there talking with the hens, things became crystal clear to me. Everything just made perfect sense." Brant started to argue, but Beau held up a hand. "Don't try to act like you don't know what I'm talking about. You said the same thing happens to you when you decide to buy land or a new company. Besides, you were the one who said I didn't have to join C-Corp if I didn't want to—that you would be behind me one hundred percent if I found something else I was interested in."

"I wasn't talking about a whorehouse."

Beau grinned. "Well, you should've been more specific."

"Beau," Brant growled.

Beau laughed. "Fine, so I'm not going to run a whore-house. But all the attention the hens showered on me got me to thinking. What man doesn't like to be pampered?" He stood up and started to pace with excitement. "I'm talking about the kind of pampering Mom used to do, but without the chore of taking out the garbage. What man do you know who isn't sick of the itty bitty food they serve at restaurants or the frozen entrées he gets at home? What man wouldn't love to come to someplace for home-cooked, rib-sticking meals that would be served any-where they wanted them—bed, poker table, or in front of a fifty-eight-inch flat screen? And after dinner, they could sit back and have a smooth brandy brought to them, along with a Cuban cigar. I'm talking about a place where men can be themselves without getting their ass chewed out for putting their feet on the sofa or their dirty socks on the floor. It would be like a spa retreat for men, except with-out the froufrou stuff." He paused. "Although I think we should offer massages and a steam room."

Brant turned back to the mirror and finished applying shaving cream. "So you would expect men to pay good money to come to Miss Hattie's just to be pampered with food and drink?"

"You're right." Beau pointed a finger at his reflection. "We need to come up with some other forms of enter-tainment." He started to pace again. "What if we set up a shooting range and offer hunting guides for quail and dove? And we could put a bar in The Jungle Room with a lot of televisions for all the major sporting events."

Brant stopped shaving and looked at his brother. "You're really excited about this, aren't you?"

Beau stopped pacing. "I think it could work, Brant.

And if it doesn't work for a men's retreat, I can always turn it into a bed and breakfast. Men and women alike are intrigued by what went on at Miss Hattie's."

Since Brant had spent the last month dreaming about the brothel, he couldn't argue the point. Of course, he didn't need to. There were a lot of other points to argue.

"I don't like the thought of C-Corp being connected to a house of ill repute," he said.

"I don't plan on involving C-Corp. Thanks to my big brother's business sense, I've got enough investments to get things started. People will just look at me as the renegade brother who doesn't have any sense."

"You're still a Cates, and those investments you're talking about should remain where they are."

The smile fell from Beau's face. "For what, big brother? For a rainy day? If I've learned anything in the last year, it's that life is short. I'm not waiting for a rainy day, Brant. I'm going to enjoy every penny and every second I have left."

There was a part of Brant that held tight to the belief that the cancer would stay in remission and Beau would live to be an old man. But the other part, the part that held the clear picture of the faces of his wife and son at the morgue, knew that tragedy could strike at any time. And if he tried to talk his brother out of this now, it might be just one more thing he regretted later.

"How much more money do you think you'll need?" he asked.

Beau flashed a bright grin. "I'm not sure. I was hoping my business advisor would be able to figure that out. Especially since he knows all about history and antiques."

It was a mistake. Brant could feel it in his bones. Still

he nodded as he tipped his chin up and shaved his neck, wondering if he'd just cut off his nose to spite his face.

Minnie didn't waste any time bulldozing Beau's offer through. The real estate agent was sitting at the table when Brant and Beau came downstairs. Baby was cooking at the stove, while Sunshine was sitting on the floor in some pretzel shape that looked like it hurt. Elizabeth stood in one corner with her arms crossed. She had gone home the night before and was wearing an ugly pantsuit and a look that said she was fit to be tied. Of course, the woman always looked fit to be tied. Brant's gaze settled on her upside-down lips.

Well, maybe not always.

"I've tried to get it through Minnie's head that Beau isn't going to buy the house," Elizabeth said. "But she refuses to listen. So I'm hoping you can explain things to Ms. Connors?"

Brant pulled his eyes away from Elizabeth's lips and over to Ms. Connors, who had just gotten up from her chair. She was an attractive woman with long, dark hair and a body that filled out her yellow business suit quite nicely.

She held out a hand. "Elena Connors."

He took her hand in a brief shake. "Brant Cates. And this is my brother, Beau."

Beau flashed a smile as he took her hand. "Pleasure, ma'am."

A dazed look entered her eyes, but she shook it off and returned her gaze to Brant. Which told him exactly what Ms. Connors was most interested in.

"I read the article they did about you in *Fortune*

magazine," she breathed. "It's amazing how you and your brother, Billy, achieved so much after starting out with just a small farm equipment company. I mean, how did you know that the land you bought would have such a big pocket of natural gas beneath it?"

Elizabeth cleared her throat. "I'm sure Mr. Cates doesn't want to waste your time with that story. Especially when we've already wasted your time enough." She looked at Beau. "Tell her that you aren't really interested in buying the house."

"Well, actually, Elizabeth—" Beau started, but Brant cut him off.

"We are going to buy the house." Brant wasn't sure why he'd attached the "we." Maybe he just liked ruffling Elizabeth's feathers. Or maybe he wanted to get back at her for filling his mind so full of hot kisses and sweet, wet centers that he wasn't even tempted by Ms. Connors.

Elizabeth's eyes widened behind her glasses. "We? But why would you want to buy a rundown old house? What are you planning on doing with it?"

Brant lifted his eyebrows, and Elizabeth's face flamed bright red. But it was Ms. Connors who spoke.

"Why, Mr. Cates, you don't mean to tell me that you're starting up a brothel?"

"Now that would be illegal, wouldn't it, Ms. Connors?" he said.

"Please call me Elena."

He dipped his head. "Brant."

She shot him a seductive look, one filled with an open invitation. "So what *are* you going to do with it, Brant?"

"I think it's best to keep everyone guessing." He accepted the cup of coffee Baby handed him and took a sip. Damn, it was better than Starbucks. Too bad he only got to take one more sip before Elizabeth snagged his arm.

"Do you think I could talk with you for a moment in private, Mr. Cates?" she said through her teeth.

He set his cup of coffee on the counter. "Please call me Brant."

"Brant," she gritted out before pulling him from the kitchen. He really wished she had chosen a different room to take him to. The library got him thinking about things he had no business thinking about. She must've had the same thoughts because she stopped suddenly and whirled around, looking a little like a caged animal.

He had to hand it to her. She recovered quickly.

"Just what do you think you're doing?" she asked.

Brant walked over to the bookcase and examined the titles. "I'm buying your house."

"Why?"

"That's not any of your concern as long as I give you your asking price." He pulled down a copy of *East of Eden* and turned it to the title page. His jaw dropped when he saw the inscription from the author to a Miss Lily Ladue. He reverently closed the book and carefully placed it back on the shelf. "What is your asking price, anyway?"

The number she gave him was fair, even considering the condition of the house. His gaze swept the room. Now that Beau had put the idea of restoring the house in his head, Brant couldn't help imagining how the library would look restored. The shelves sanded and stained a deep mahogany. The chair reupholstered in rich leather. Tiffany lamps scattered around and a soft-cushioned couch in front of the fireplace.

How that fit into his brother's vision he didn't know.

Nor did he care. This would be his room when he came to visit, a place where he could read and not be bothered by work.

The thought surprised him. Work had been his salvation since the tornado. But suddenly, he realized he hadn't checked his cell phone and e-mails once while he'd been here. And the more surprising part was he hadn't even missed it. Maybe his mother was right. Maybe he needed some time off from work.

"I'll double the price," he stated.

"Excuse me?"

He turned to Elizabeth. "I'm willing to double your asking price."

Her mouth dropped open for a brief second before it snapped back closed. Her eyes narrowed. "With what stipulation?"

His laughter seemed to take them both by surprise. Brant stopped suddenly, and Elizabeth stared at him as if he were some strange reptile that had crawled in the door uninvited. He didn't waste any time covering his uncharacteristic reaction.

"With the stipulation that I keep everything in the house, including Miss Hattie's bed."

"And the hens?" Minnie rolled into the room with cigarette dangling. Brant took one look at the smoke that curled around her head and strode across the room to take the cigarette from her mouth.

"I'm not buying the hens," Brant said, tossing the cigarette in the brass spittoon that sat by the door.

"Well, that's too bad." Minnie lifted her chin. "Because Beau already said we could stay."

Beau strutted into the room with a cup of coffee in one

hand and a delicious-looking cinnamon roll in the other. For being hungover, it sure looked as if he hadn't lost his appetite. He took a big bite of the bun and rolled his eyes in ecstasy.

"Only if that includes Baby. These are the best cinnamon rolls I've ever eaten." He held it out for Brant to take a bite, but Brant only glared at him. "Oh, come on, big bro. The old gals will just add color when we reopen. The guests will eat Minnie's stories up with a spoon."

It wasn't like Brant had much of a choice. Beau wanted the house, and it was obvious that the ladies weren't leaving it. Besides, how much trouble could three little old women be?

"Fine," he said. "They can stay, but on one condition." He pointed a finger at Minnie. "No more smoking. I won't have all these classic books damaged any more than they already are."

Minnie opened her mouth to argue, but Beau winked at her and whispered for all to hear. "I'm planning a cigar room."

Minnie cackled with glee as she rolled out of the room, followed by Beau.

When they were gone, Brant turned to Elizabeth. "So is it a deal?"

He expected a fight. Instead, while he'd been bickering with Minnie, it seemed that Elizabeth had resigned herself to the idea. Her gaze swept over to the doorway before it returned to Brant. A smile brightened her face. It was the first time one of her smiles had been directed at him, and it did something funny to his equilibrium.

"Deal," she said as she held out a hand.

He made the mistake of taking it. While most women's

hands were cool to the touch, Elizabeth's hand surrounded him like an electric blanket on a wintry night. He was surprised at how chilled he felt when she pulled away.

"I'd like to ask for one thing," she said. When he lifted his eyebrows, she continued. "I'd like you to forget my relationship with Miss Hattie Ladue."

Brant nodded, but as he stared into those amber eyes, he realized that forgetting might be a promise he couldn't keep.

Chapter Thirteen

Henhouse Rule #2: Never forget where you came from.

"WELL, MORNIN', Ms. MURPHY," Rachel Dean called as Elizabeth stepped inside Josephine's Diner. Before Elizabeth could lift a hand in greeting, half the men in the restaurant jumped up and headed for the door.

It was a phenomenon that had taken place often in the last week. Single men would take one look at Elizabeth and head for the hills. It all had to do with Shirlene's bouquet. It seemed that there wasn't a man in Bramble who wanted to get hitched up to an old maid. Which suited the old maid just fine. However, it didn't suit the more stubborn matchmakers in town.

"The men in this town are really startin' to annoy me." Twyla's eyes narrowed at the front windows. Kenny Gene strutted down the street looking as happy as a puppy off his leash. "If he thinks he's gettin' away from me, he's got another think comin'," she mumbled under her breath before looking back at Elizabeth. "Don't you worry, Ms. Murphy. My second cousin, Barney, who lives in Big Springs, is comin' out for a visit next week, and he's been shoppin' for a wife ever since his last one ran off with that carnival guy who guesses your weight. The carnie was under by twenty pounds, and that was all it took to win Edna's heart."

"Ms. Murphy ain't interested in some old rodeo clown," Rachel said as she followed Elizabeth to her usual booth. "Not when she's got her eye set on Beauregard Cates." She winked as she set down a cup of tea in front of Elizabeth.

"But there is no way in hell—" Cindy Lynn piped up, but Rachel cut her off with a stern look.

"Be quiet, Cindy, and eat your eggs before they get cold."

Elizabeth was touched that Rachel was willing to defend her, but she couldn't let the craziness continue. "Actually, Rachel, Cindy's right. Beau isn't interested in me. Which works out nicely because I'm not interested in him."

Rachel looked mind-boggled. "You ain't? Why, that man is hotter than jalapeño pepper sauce on a chile relleno."

"No hotter than Shirlene's husband Bubba," Twyla sighed. "And did you see the youngest brother, Beckett? Lordy," she fanned her face with a menu, "them Cates produce better genes than Wrangler. Sorta makes you wonder what the oldest one looks like."

At just the mention of Brant, Elizabeth felt her face heat up. Along with a spot much lower.

"A snake." Rachel Dean's eyes narrowed. "Because no one but a lowdown, dirty snake would want to buy Dalton Oil just so they could close it down and ruin Bramble."

"But wasn't Bubba in on that, too?" Darla was sitting on a stool at the counter, knitting the longest scarf Elizabeth had ever seen. "I thought that's why the sheriff threw him in jail."

"Exactly," Rachel said. "Bubba paid his due for his crime. Not only did he spend time in jail, but he almost lost Shirlene." She shook her head. "Purt near broke my heart when he was apologizin' for what he did. The oldest one, on the other hand, doesn't seem a bit sorry. He didn't even have the guts to show up for his brother's weddin'."

"Rachel's right," Twyla jumped in. "Kenny Gene told me that if the man steps one foot in Bramble he'll find himself tarred and feathered and run out of town on a rail."

Most people would assume that Twyla was exaggerating. That in this day and age, no one would actually tar and feather another human being. But after living in the town for fifteen years, Elizabeth knew better. If Brant stepped foot in town, she didn't doubt for a second that he'd find himself wearing more feathers than Sunshine during her fan dance.

Elizabeth smiled. She didn't want anyone hurt, but Brant could use a good dose of humility. And the town was right; he did owe them an apology. But knowing what she did about the man, she figured it would be a cold day in hell before they would get one.

The bell over the door jingled as the twins, Hope Lomax and Faith Calhoun, entered with their babies, Daffodil and Daisy, hooked on their hips. Hope was busy talking to the mayor who followed closely behind them. It was common knowledge that when Mayor Sutter retired, Hope would take over his spot. She was always coming up with one project or another to better the town and had set up a website to attract more businesses to Bramble.

The women clustered around Hope and Faith, vying for turns to hold the babies who looked as identical as their mothers. In the midst of the coos and ahhs, Faith glanced up and saw Elizabeth. She quickly handed off Daisy to Rachel and hurried over.

Since Faith had moved to Bramble, she and Elizabeth had become friends. Not only did they share a passion for books, but Elizabeth was helping Faith with online classes she was taking to get her teaching certificate.

"I was hoping I'd run into you," she said as she slipped into the seat across from Elizabeth. "I wanted to ask you about the grant for the new computer section in the library. Have you heard anything?"

Elizabeth shook her head. "I haven't heard a thing, but they said it could take up to six weeks. I certainly appreciate you helping me put it together."

"After all the help you've given me with my homework, it was nothing." Faith looked down and fiddled with the salt and pepper shakers. "I was also going to ask you if you'd like to come to dinner tomorrow night." She paused. "I thought I'd invite Slate's assistant football coach, Travis."

Elizabeth laughed. "Not you, too?"

Faith looked up and grinned. "So you didn't mean to catch the bouquet? And here I thought I'd been a horrible friend because I didn't know you wanted to get married."

Hope slipped into the seat next to her sister. "I tried to tell her that nobody in their right mind would want to be on the receiving end of Bramble's matchmaking, but she wouldn't listen."

The similarities between the two women always left Elizabeth a little speechless. It was like looking at mirror images. Of course, it didn't hurt that they wore almost identical clothing—something Faith had told her was more accidental than planned.

"But it's too late now," Hope continued. "Once the town gets something in their head, it's hard to get it out. And believe me, I know."

Faith laughed, and Elizabeth couldn't help but smile at just the thought of the "Daddy Search" that had taken place when the townsfolk had thought that Hope had been impregnated by some Hollywood loser. Fortunately, things had all worked out, and Daffodil had gotten the perfect daddy.

"So I hear that Colt's custom motorcycle shop will be opened by the first of the year," Elizabeth said.

"That's what we're hoping." Hope took one of the triangles of wheat toast Rachel had just delivered to the table. "Colt has been working his butt off to get things completed. So much so, that I'm starting to feel like a single parent." She munched on the toast. "I think he's still a little worried that C-Corp will close down Dalton Oil. Especially since the president is a real butthole."

"Now, Hope," Faith spoke in her usual soft voice, "let's not jump to conclusions. I think there's probably a very good reason for his bad behavior. I told you what Billy told Slate about his brother's wife and son."

Elizabeth choked on the sip of tea she'd just taken, and it took a couple rib-jarring back smacks from Hope before she could catch her breath.

"Brant is married?" she wheezed out.

"Brant?" Hope exchanged a look with Faith.

Elizabeth couldn't hide her blush or her flustered reaction. "Uhh, I mean, Mr. Cates." She clutched her shaking hands together as images flashed through her mind of all the kisses she'd shared with Brant. "So he has a wife and son? I thought he was single."

"He is single," Faith said, causing Elizabeth's body to melt back against the booth. "Slate said Billy wouldn't go into details, but I guess he lost both his wife and son in some sort of accident."

"Well, that still isn't an excuse for wanting to shut down Dalton Oil and put a bunch of good people out of work," Hope said.

Faith shook her head. "No, I guess it doesn't excuse him, but it might explain why he's so obsessed with the curse and his grandfather's death. And Slate did say he was going to find jobs for all the employees of Dalton with C-Corp."

Hope rolled her eyes. "I'll believe that when pigs fly." She got to her feet. "Speaking of which...we need to go pick up Sherman at Shirlene's house. I figure the kids have tuckered him out by now."

Sherman was Hope's pet, a cute pig that had won the entire town over with his sweet disposition and almost human-like behavior.

"I'll stop by the library later," Faith said as she got to her feet.

Once they were gone, Elizabeth didn't waste any time paying her bill and heading to the library. Her conversation with the twins had made her a good five minutes late, and she had to hustle to get back on schedule. While she took the books out of the night drop-off box, she couldn't help thinking about what Faith had told her about Brant's wife and son.

It was a tragedy. And Faith was right. It didn't excuse

Brant's actions, but it sure explained them. Elizabeth
hadn't even known her father. He had left before she was
born and never contacted her once in all the years after.
And yet, when she had gotten the news of his death, she'd
been devastated. It didn't matter that she hadn't ever met
him, or he hadn't loved her enough to want to be part of
her life. He was her father. She could only imagine how
much more painful it would be if you lost someone you
knew and loved.

And not just one person, but your entire family.

For the rest of the morning, Elizabeth was kept busy
with children's story time and a class field trip from Bramble Elementary. When she finally had a break, she found
herself back at her desk, typing Brant's name into the
Google search. The sites that came up were staggering.
There were so many articles about Brant on the internet
that Elizabeth only had time to skim through each one.

Still, it was enough. Besides learning more than she
would ever want to know about C-Corp, she learned
about his personal life. Brant had been born in Dogwood,
a small town in east Texas. He was the second son to a
family of five boys and one girl. Buckley, Branston, Billy,
Beauregard, Beckett, and Brianne. But Elizabeth soon
discovered a newspaper article about the oldest son, Buckley, dying after his car had been hit by a train. And there
was another article about Brant making a huge donation
to The Cancer Society in the name of his brother, Beauregard, who was undergoing treatment for cancer.

Finally, she stumbled upon a story about Amanda and
Branston Cates Junior, who were killed when a tornado
swept through east Texas. Elizabeth had found very few pictures of Brant, and none of him posing for the camera. He

wasn't posing in this newspaper photo, either. He was standing in the midst of the remains of a demolished house, nothing more than a tall silhouette against the blue of the sky.

Elizabeth's hand slipped off the computer mouse. And suddenly, she wondered if maybe Brant wasn't so crazy after all. Maybe there *was* a Cates Curse that followed him around. How else could you explain the string of tragedies?

She returned to her work, but her mind never strayed far from Brant and his Curse. During her afternoon break, she returned to her computer to look up information on William Cates. There was very little to be found. The only thing she discovered was that he'd been born in Cedar Rapids, Iowa, in 1870, which meant that he had only been twenty-two when he died. She had just pulled up an article from an old Lubbock newspaper about a Cates metalsmith business when Moses Tate shuffled past the desk.

Moses was over ninety and hard of hearing so he didn't even acknowledge Elizabeth when she called out a greeting. He just continued over to the newspaper section, where he would read a little and sleep a lot more. Normally, Elizabeth would go right back to what she was doing. But today she realized that Moses' arrival was perfect timing. He was the one man in town who might be able to help her.

"Good afternoon, Mr. Tate," she yelled as she stepped out from behind her desk.

Moses dropped the newspaper he'd just pulled off the wooden rack and held a hand to his chest before turning and squinting at her. "No need to yell, Ms. Murphy. I ain't deaf. Besides, I thought you was supposed to be quiet in libraries."

Elizabeth bit back a smile. "That's true. I'll try to keep it down."

Moses nodded before grabbing another paper and heading over to one of the reading couches.

Elizabeth followed him, picking up the newspaper he'd dropped and placing it back on the rack. "So I was wondering if you could tell me a story, Mr. Tate."

The newspaper rattled as he opened it up. "And which one would that be? At ninety-one, I got my fair share of 'em."

"The one about William Cates," she said as she took a seat on the couch across from him.

His bushy white brows lifted. "I heard you was interested in one of them Cates boys, but I didn't put much store in it. Guess I was wrong."

Giving up on correcting the assumption, she repeated Rachel's description of Beau. "Yes, well, he's as hot as jalapeño sauce on a chile relleno."

Moses shook his head. "Don't eat spicy things myself. They give me gas." He squinted at the newspaper. "So I figure you've heard the town's version of the story. And they got the first part right. William did get all riled up about the mayor not paying him for the plaque he'd made. And I can't say as I blame Will. It wasn't his fault that the town hall wasn't completed by the date on the plaque." He shook his head and turned to the next page. "The towns-folk have always been as slow as molasses."

"So that's when Sheriff Murdock supposedly shot him?" Elizabeth prompted.

"Yep, that's the story the newspaper came up with. But my grandpappy saw Will that very night at Miss Hattie's and got the story straight from the horse's mouth. It seems the mayor had calmed William down by offering him a night at Miss Hattie's Henhouse."

"Where he was shot," Elizabeth finished for him. "And did your grandfather ever tell you who shot him?"

"Nope. He was upstairs at the time."

Not wanting to discuss what his grandfather had been doing upstairs, Elizabeth forged on. "But he said it was in a poker game. Did he mention who was playing poker that night?"

He licked his finger and turned to the next page. "Nope."

Elizabeth fell back on the couch. "So all we know is that William Cates was shot to death in a poker game on the night of August fifth." She was so into her thoughts that she didn't realize that the afterschool program had come into the library until a couple kids raced past on their way to the story pit.

Knowing that she would need to corral the children before they got out of hand, Elizabeth got up from the couch. "Thank you, Mr. Tate. I'll let you get back to your reading."

She started to head to her desk to get the book she'd picked out for this afternoon when Moses stopped her.

"It wasn't on August fifth."

Elizabeth turned back around. "Excuse me?"

"William Cates wasn't killed on August fifth. That was the day he showed up in Bramble, but that wasn't the day he was shot."

"But I thought you said that the mayor treated him to a night at Miss Hattie's?" Elizabeth said.

"He did." Moses grinned, revealing his pink toothless gums. "But no man alive can only stay one night at The Henhouse."

Chapter Fourteen

Henhouse Rule #16: A man's past is best left there.

A STORM HAD MOVED INTO DOGWOOD. It split the dark skies with jagged spears of light and left a crackle of electricity in the thick humid air.

Brant stood on his bedroom balcony, staring out at the night.

Storms were the worst. He could ignore the pain in sunlight, but there was no ignoring it when each gust of wind and rumble of thunder caused questions to pelt his mind like the cold, unrelenting rain that fell from the sky.

Did they wake up in time to be scared? Did Branston Junior cry from his crib in the other room? Did Mandy make it to him in time? Did they suffer any pain? Did they call out his name?

The questions rolled around and around in his head until Brant tipped his face up to the skies and dared the powers that be to finish the job. To strike him dead where he stood and put him out of his misery. But as always, he was left standing on the flagstone balcony drenched in rain... and pain.

He didn't know how long he stood out there before he

finally turned and walked back inside. After a hot shower, he climbed in bed with his laptop. Work seemed to be the only thing that helped shut out the storm. It was well past one o'clock when the lightning finally stopped and the rain slowed to a drizzle. Exhausted, he saved his files and shut off the computer. But when he went to set his laptop on the nightstand, his gaze got caught by the books resting next to the lamp.

The one on top was his great-grandmother's diary. A book he'd read from cover to cover, at least four times. Ever since Billy had discovered it at their Aunt Milly's. Brant hadn't learned anything about his great-grandfather's death in the diary. Most of the entries consisted of his great-grandmother complaining about Texas and how much she wanted to return to Iowa. The only time she'd mentioned his grandfather was at the end of the diary, when she ranted on and on about William's body not being returned to her for a proper burial.

Ignoring the diary, Brant slid out the book beneath it. It was a history book, one of the many he had read before heading to Miss Hattie's. But this one he had kept for the picture on the cover. It wasn't as sensual as the one painted on the mirror above the bed. This woman was dressed in a high-collared dress with big puffed sleeves. But it had never been Hattie Ladue's clothes that had intrigued Brant.

His gaze wandered over her face—the pointed chin, the full mouth, the slim nose—until he reached the eyes. Even in the dull grays and browns of the sepia-toned photograph, there was a sparkle of life in the depths that held Brant transfixed.

As he stared at the picture, another pair of eyes

drifted into his mind, eyes that were similar yet drastically different. Elizabeth's eyes didn't carry a sparkle. They were direct and at times disconcerting, but never filled with the joy of a life well lived. Maybe that was what intrigued him so much about Miss Hattie. In her eyes, she seemed to have held the secret of what made life worth living—something Brant had lost the night of the tornado.

Placing the book back on the nightstand, he reached out and turned off the light. To keep the nightmares at bay, he visualized the picture of Miss Hattie in the red satin gown. But somewhere between sanity and fantasy, Elizabeth's hot kisses slipped in, and his dreams were filled with both women.

Brant awoke to sunlight streaming in through the balcony doors and the ringing of his cell phone. He sat up and made a grab for his phone on the nightstand.

"Mornin', Big Bro," Beau's voice came through the receiver.

"What time is it?" Brant asked as he swung his legs over the edge of the bed.

"Around seven, I think," Beau said.

"And exactly what are you doing up so early in the morning? I've never seen you get up before—" A thought struck Brant, and he jumped to his feet. "Is something wrong? Did you get the results back from your last doctor's visit?"

Beau laughed. "Nothing's wrong. I just thought you'd like to know that we found some of Miss Hattie's journals."

Brant released his breath and sank down on the bed. "Journals? I thought I looked through every trunk in the attic."

"They weren't in the attic." Beau's voice grew softer, like he'd pulled the phone away from his mouth. "Thanks, Sunshine, but I don't need a massage right now. But I sure could use a cup of coffee." Brant heard Sunshine's muffled voice before Beau returned to their conversation. "I guess Minnie found them in some old trunk out in the barn."

"How did Minnie get out there in her wheelchair?"

"Beats me," Beau said. "The hens are always slipping around. For a bunch of old women, they're pretty damned quick."

"So have you read them?" Brant asked.

"I thought I'd leave that up to you."

Brant didn't know why he felt so relieved by the information. This weird connection he had with a dead person had to cease. Still, he couldn't stand the thought of Beau looking through Miss Hattie's private journals.

"Overnight them to me," he said.

"Sorry, bro, but no can do. Minnie insists that they stay at Miss Hattie's. She says if you want to read them, you'll have to read them here. Of course, I tried to tell her you were much too busy a man to be able to do that."

Beau was right. Brant was busy. Even with this being Saturday, he had numerous phone calls to make and a couple of contracts he needed to go over. But it was doubtful he'd get anything done when his mind was consumed with all the secrets he might discover in the books. As if reading his thoughts, Beau jumped back in.

"Of course, if you can't come, I can start reading them to see if there's anything about our grandfather. Although I figure they're probably just filled with a bunch of dirty sex stories."

"I'll be there by noon," Brant said. Before he hung up the phone, he heard his brother's laughter.

"If I had known you were so damned filthy rich," Minnie yelled above the sound of the helicopter lifting off from the circular driveway, "I would've had Elizabeth ask for more money."

Brant took the cigarette from Minnie's mouth and flipped it down to the porch where he stubbed it out with the toe of his boot. "So where are they?"

Minnie shot him a mean look before reaching in the side pocket of her wheelchair. "I've got one right here." She pulled out a battered, bound book. Brant reached for it, but Minnie pulled it back. "Of course, it wouldn't be right to let you read it before Elizabeth gets to—her being Miss Hattie's relative and all. She works today, but tonight I'll give her a call and have her come out first thing tomorrow." She placed the book back in the side pocket. "And in the meantime, you can help your brother weed the lilac garden."

Brant's gaze moved over to Beau, who was reclining back on the porch swing, eating what appeared to be oatmeal cookies with raisins.

"Don't look at me," he said around a mouthful of cookie. "I wanted to hire professional gardeners."

"And I told you, Beauregard," Minnie said with a shake of a gnarled finger, "that I'm not having some untrustworthy, ham-handed workers destroyin' Miss Hattie's lilacs. Those plants are delicate and need a gentle hand."

Beau held up a hand filled with cookies. "And you think these hands are gentle?"

"He's got a point," Brant said. "Beau is a bit of a klutz

with everything but women. He broke more of our mother's china and lamps than all the brothers put together. Besides, I didn't fly all the way out here to weed a garden. I'm here to read Miss Hattie's journals." He held out a hand. "I'm sure Elizabeth won't mind."

Minnie shook her head. "You're not gettin' them until Lizzie gets here. There's hen protocol to consider."

"I'd give it up, Brant," Beau said as he rolled to his feet. "If I've learned anything in the last week, it's that there's no getting around the hens when they set their mind on something. Point me in the direction of a hoe, Miss Minnie." Beau laughed at his pun. "I'm your humble servant."

The smile that settled on Minnie's face left little doubt in Brant's mind that his brother had wiggled his way into the woman's heart. And for that reason, and the fact that he couldn't wrestle an old woman for a diary, Brant accepted his fate and followed Beau around to the barn.

Doc Connelly turned out to be right. Gardening was soothing. There was something about uncovering a tiny rosebush beneath a sea of weeds, or sculpting a lilac bush into a smooth rounded shape, that eased the tight knot in his stomach and the tension in his shoulders. Long after Beau had quit and stretched out in the hammock beneath one of the cottonwoods, Brant kept working. By the time the sun had started to ease behind the horizon, Miss Hattie's garden had started to appear.

"Damn," Beau breathed after waking up from his nap. "Who would've guessed that something this beautiful was under all those weeds? Although I don't know how it will fit into my man-cave concept, and I don't think the hens will let me cut it down." His eyes lit up. "Maybe we could do the shooting range right inside the garden—you know, have moving targets pop out from all the bushes."

Brant shook his head as he leaned down to pick up the old set of hedge clippers. "And maybe we could leave it as a garden. And instead of a cigar room, patrons could sit out here and smoke."

Beau looked thoroughly disappointed with the idea. "Yeah, maybe. But in winter, it's going to be damned cold. Of course, we could get some of those space heaters, I guess."

Brant didn't really care how Beau worked it out. He just didn't want the garden destroyed for some stupid shooting range.

"Supper's ready," Baby called from the back door. "I hope you like pot roast and mashed potatoes."

Beau didn't even wait for the back door to close before he started toward the house. "Come on, I'll help you clean up the tools after dinner."

But Brant had never been one to leave a job unfinished, so he waved his little brother on and gathered up the tools to take back to the barn.

The barn was as cluttered as the attic, except in here the antiques were larger. An enormous amount of furniture filled one side of stalls, while an old tractor, a flatbed wagon, and a couple classic cars filled the other. One of the first Harley motorcycles ever made sat amidst a pile of old bicycles. A moonshine still was right next to a popcorn machine. What Brant *didn't* see were trunks, and he couldn't help but wonder where Minnie had found the journals.

He had just put the tools back in the tack room when he heard the distinct sound of a car backfiring. He didn't know why he hurried out of the barn and around to the front of the house, or why he felt so disappointed to find a beat-up Grand Prix with four bald tires rather than Elizabeth's Ford Escort.

The door of the car creaked open, and a young girl stepped out; a young girl who looked like she was going to prom. And not just any prom, but Brant's in the early nineties. Her brown hair was piled high on her head, and she wore a black velvet dress that was too small for her body. She was talking to someone, although whoever it was had to be lying down in the back of the car because Brant couldn't see them.

"Head up and shoulders straight, Starlet. Smile, but don't giggle nervously. And remember, you're only as good as you—" She looked up and released a startled yelp when she saw Brant.

"Oh." She held a hand to her ample chest. "You scared me. I didn't see you standing there—" She paused and her eyes narrowed. "Are you a john?"

Brant bit back a smile. "No, I'm a Brant. And you are?"

"Starlet." She held out a hand as if she expected Brant to kiss it. Instead, he gave it a quick shake as she continued. "Starlet Brubaker, but my Auntie and Uncle Bernard just call me Star on account of the fact that I've won every talent show there is in Mallory County." She flapped a hand. "I can sing any show tune you name. You want to hear me sing a song from *Funny Girl*? People say I sound just like Babs." She took a deep breath and started to belt out the song. The noise that came from Starlet's mouth sounded nothing like Barbra Streisand. In fact, it sounded a little like a calf during branding.

"What the hell is going on?" Beau came out the front

door with a biscuit in one hand and a glass of milk in the other. "It sounds like you're killing a—" He stopped when he saw Starlet. Brant didn't know who looked more surprised: Beau, that a young girl could make that kind of a noise, or Starlet, who looked as if she'd just run into her favorite teen idol.

She stopped singing in mid-note, and her brown eyes glazed over. Since most women reacted that way to Beau, Brant wasn't surprised. The only one who didn't seem to be caught up in his brother's good looks was Elizabeth.

Which made Brant more than a little suspicious of the woman.

"Pardon me," Beau said. "I didn't know we had company." He popped the rest of the biscuit in his mouth before wiping off his hand on his jeans and holding it out. "Beauregard Cates."

Starlet's eyes only got bigger as she stared at his offered hand and tried to stammer out a reply. "Umm, I-I…"

"This is Starlet Brubaker, Beau," Brant said, unwilling to waste any more time. "Starlet was just about to tell us why she's here." When she continued to stare at Beau, Brant stepped in front of her.

Once she could no longer see Beau, her trance ended. Although she still looked a little loopy. "Huh?"

"What are you doing at Miss Hattie's?" Brant repeated.

"Oh. Well, I'm here because I was invited." She lifted a hideous pink purse off her shoulder and dug through it until she pulled out a lavender envelope with writing sprawled across the front. She handed it to him.

"I got it a couple weeks ago, but I had to put in notice

at the Putt-Putt and come up with a good lie to tell my aunt and uncle. They would skin me alive if they knew I was here."

Brant pulled out the card. The scent of lilacs filled the air. And even before he started to read the dark script, he knew it wasn't going to be good.

As the descendant of the famed Starlet O'Malley, you are cordially invited to Miss Hattie's Henhouse, where you will have the honor of being inducted as a hen as soon as you complete the proper training and pass the final exams. Please read the list of henhouse rules attached and…

The rest of the invitation went unread as Brant crumpled the cardstock in his fist.

"I'm going to wring that hen's neck."

The hen Brant was referring to sat at the window of the library watching as he strode up the porch steps and banged through the front door.

"He's really mad, Minnie," Baby said. "Maybe we shouldn't have brought him back by forging Miss Hattie's journals."

"We didn't forge anything." Minnie wheeled her chair around. "The journals are real. They just aren't Miss Hattie's. Besides, how else were we going to get Brant here? Brant is the key to getting Elizabeth to discover her henness. Without him, we'll lose her. And it won't matter if we locate all the other hens. Miss Hattie's won't be Miss Hattie's without the head hen."

"But Elizabeth doesn't even act like she likes him—or us," Baby said.

"Oh, she likes him, all right," Minnie said. "And as for liking us, we'll grow on her. We always do."

"But how are we going to get them together? No matter what you said to Brant, Elizabeth won't care anything about reading Miss Hattie's journals."

A door slammed somewhere in the house as Brant called Minnie's name.

Minnie thought for a moment before she smiled. "Maybe we don't need to bring Elizabeth out here. Maybe all we need to do is send Brant to her."

Chapter Fifteen

Henhouse Rule #31: A laid hen is a happy hen.

ELIZABETH WOKE WITH A START. She lay there for a few seconds with her heart thumping while her mind tried to figure out what had awakened her. The answer wasn't long in coming. A floorboard creaked. Most women might've started screaming at this point, but Elizabeth had never been a screamer. Especially when this wasn't the first time this had happened.

On more than a few occasions, her next door neighbor, Elmer Tate, got so drunk that he forgot where his house was. Which was why, in a town where no one locked their doors, Elizabeth had taken to locking hers. Unfortunately, tonight her mind had been so consumed with what she had learned about Brant and William Cates, she had forgotten.

Elizabeth rolled over with the intent of stopping Elmer before he stumbled any closer to the bed. But before she could say a word, he stepped on Atticus, who must've gotten up for a midnight snack. The cat released a yowl that threw Elmer off balance and had him tumbling to the bed.

Leaving Elizabeth pinned under a drunk.

"You have to stop doing this, Elmer," she said as she tried to shove him off.

"Elmer?"

The deep voice stopped her struggles, and her gaze lifted. It was too dark to see much more than an outline, but she would recognize the thick wavy hair anywhere.

"Who's Elmer?" Brant asked.

"The neighbor. What are you doing here?"

He rolled off her, and she leaned up and switched on the lamp. The bright light had her squinting for a few seconds. Once her eyes adjusted, she couldn't help but wonder if it would've been better to leave the lamp off. With it on, Brant seemed bigger, closer, and so handsome it took her a moment to find her voice.

"So why are you sneaking into my house, Mr. Cates," she glanced over at the red digital numbers on the clock, "at twelve twenty-two at night? Is this tit for tat—I stumbled into your bed so now you're stumbling into mine?"

"It only seems fair." His intense blue-eyed gaze ran over her from the top of her bed-head to the chenille bedspread that spilled over her lap. Slowly, it moved up again until it settled on the front of her pink nightshirt. "For some reason, I thought you would wear one of those flannel nightgowns like my granny's."

She swallowed hard and crossed her arms over her chest. "I get hot at night."

"Which explains the neighbor," he said. Before her mouth could finish dropping open, Atticus jumped up on the bed. Brant eyed him balefully. "Jesus, what the hell is that? A basketball with legs?"

She ignored the question. "So are you going to get to the point of why you're here, or not?"

He pulled his gaze away from the chubby orange cat that had flopped down next to Elizabeth. "Did you think you'd pulled a fast one on me when you saddled me with three crazy old women?"

She started to deny it, but then realized she couldn't. She *had* saddled him with a bunch of crazy old women. She'd just hoped that he wouldn't realize it until after they closed on the house.

"I didn't force you to agree to let them stay," she said. "I believe that was Beau's doing."

"You're right." He reached out and scratched Atticus's head. Always one for a good scratching, Atticus started purring to beat the band. "But you could've warned me about their plans to reopen Miss Hattie's."

Just the sight of his strong fingers gently stroking the cat's fur had heat flooding her face—along with other body parts. Needing some space between them, she inched closer to the opposite side of the bed.

"I thought it was harmless enough," she said. "Especially now that you and Beau are buying it."

"Well, you might want to tell that to the women they sent invitations to—or girls might be a better description."

"What girls?" she asked.

"The girls they plan on teaching to be hens."

"What!" She yelled so loudly that she startled Atticus, and he jumped down from the bed.

Brant studied her. "So you don't know about the invitations?"

"Of course I don't! How could you even think that?"

"I don't exactly know what to think of you, Elizabeth," he said. "One minute you're telling me you're a virgin, and the next I discover you're entertaining the neighbors." Before she could defend her honor, he held up a hand. "But I didn't really believe you were the brain behind this hare-brained idea. Minnie was trying a little too hard to convince me of that." His head tipped, and his gaze narrowed. "Where are your glasses?"

Surprised by the sudden change of topic, it took her a moment to answer. "On the nightstand. People don't usually sleep with their glasses on."

His eyes pierced straight through her for several heart-stopping seconds before he glanced over at the nightstand. Her glasses rested next to the book she'd been reading, and he leaned over and read the title. "*Whorehouses of the West*. So did you find anything about my grandfather?"

"No," she said. "But Moses Tate had some interesting information. According to Moses' grandfather, William Cates stayed more than just a night at Miss Hattie's."

Brant's gaze lifted from the book. "He has evidence?"

"Nothing solid, but he swears his grandfather told him that William was killed the night of November tenth."

Brant leaned back on the pillows, the same pillows Elizabeth had been sleeping on not more than five minutes earlier. And if she thought he'd taken up too much space when he was sitting on the bed, it was nothing compared to having him stretched out on it.

"But that's more than three months later," he said, completely unaware of her discomfort. "The article in the Bramble *Gazette* said August fifth."

She inched so far off the bed her entire leg was hanging over the edge. "Exactly," she said. "But what was funny was that when I looked back at the newspaper, it came out November 30, 1892. Now I realize that news was slower back then, but four months slower?"

"So you think William was at Miss Hattie's for three months before the mayor and sheriff concocted the story about his shooting. But that's crazy."

"You don't know Bramble. We're a pretty crazy town," she said as she watched him toe off a cowboy boot. The boot hit the floor with a thud that had Elizabeth jumping. "Just what do you think you're doing?"

Brant cocked an eyebrow. "Worried I'm going to piss off your boyfriend Elmer?"

"Elmer is not my boyfriend. He's married, for goodness sakes."

The other eyebrow joined the first. "Are you sure you're not behind the invitations?" He toed off the other boot, and it thumped to the floor.

It was difficult to pull her gaze away from the big stocking feet that now hung over the end of her bed. "Did Minnie actually invite young women out to the house to become prostitutes?"

"It appears so," he said as he tucked his hands behind his head. "Although she refuses to use that word."

"Except we both know that it's the same difference. Has she lost her mind?"

"I think that would be a yes," he said.

"Well, you'll just have to contact the women and let them know the situation."

He turned to her. "Me? I'm not the owner of Miss Hattie's. And you can be damned sure that I won't be until this is cleared up."

Elizabeth was afraid of that. "Fine. I'll contact the women. How many invitations did she send out?"

"According to Baby, only ten. And five have already declined, which leaves five, minus the one that's already there."

Elizabeth stared at him. "There's a girl at Miss Hattie's?"

"Starlet Brubaker to be exact." He rolled to his side and propped his head up on his hand. "According to Minnie, she's a direct descendant of Starlet O'Malley."

Elizabeth knew the name. "The hen who moved to New York and starred on Broadway?"

"That would be the one, which is why Starlet is at Miss Hattie's. She's convinced that her road to stardom starts as a hen."

"Good grief." She flopped back on the bed. "Please tell me she's over eighteen."

"Barely." He reached out and caught a curl of her hair that had fallen over the edge of his pillow. "I thought it would be shorter and more brown." He stretched out the strand and studied it in the light of the lamp. "Not long with hints of gold."

At another time, the sight of his fingers caressing her hair might've turned her into a witless wonder. But the thought of going to jail for soliciting kept her on topic. "So this Starlet is still at the house? Why didn't you explain things and send her on her way?"

"Because I've always been a sucker for tears." He wound the piece of hair around his finger. "And not only does Starlet have a voice that would send African elephants charging, she also cries so loudly it had me saying anything to get her to stop. Which means the job of kicking her out is all on you."

"Fine," Elizabeth said. "I'll deal with it first thing in

the morning." She looked over at him. "And now that we have that settled, you can go."

But Brant seemed in no hurry to release her hair, or leave. In fact, he continued to wind the lock around his finger until the tension had her moving closer.

"So tell me about Elmer." His breath fell hot against her lips.

"There's nothing to tell. He's just a neighbor who forgets where he lives when he gets drunk," she said as she tried to unwind her hair. It only took him closing his fist to crush her hopes of freedom.

"Maybe he doesn't forget," he said. "Maybe he knows exactly what he's doing."

Her gaze lifted to his. In his eyes, she saw desire. The same desire that swirled around inside of her. Brant had come here because of invitations. Now it looked as if he was issuing one of his own. Except he didn't wait for her reply before his head tipped and his lips brushed over hers.

The man had a way with kisses. He had all these subtle techniques of soft sips and gentle little nips that left Elizabeth completely and utterly mindless. All she could think about was the heat of his mouth and the tingles that filled her body with each sweep of his tongue. It didn't take much for him to coax her into participating, and once she offered up her mouth to his skillful assault, all sanity was lost.

Releasing her hair, he pressed her back against the pillows. His hand skated over the cotton of her nightshirt as he reshaped her breast to fit his palm. He brushed his thumb over her nipple and heat zinged from the hardening point to the spot between her legs. The intense sensation left her breathless and stunned, forcing her to pull back from the kiss or pass out from lack of oxygen.

While she gasped for air, Brant blazed a trail of kisses down her neck and over her breasts, his mouth creating little damp spots on her shirt. Elizabeth had just caught her breath when his mouth settled over her nipple and took it away again. The combination of hot tongue and wet cotton stroking over her nipple brought the ache between her legs to a fevered pitch. She couldn't breathe, but she no longer cared. All she cared about was Brant continuing what he was doing. A primitive groan came from her throat, and Brant answered the guttural sound by jerking up her shirt and touching his hot, rough tongue to her tight, bare nipple.

The hard pull of his lips had her hands gripping his hair and her hips bumping up against his thigh as she searched for a way to alleviate her aching need. The bedspread and sheets had bunched up between them, cushioning the hardness she craved. As if reading her thoughts, Brant jerked the blankets free and sent them sailing to the floor before his hand curved over her bare bottom.

He pulled his head back and glanced down. The sexual haze lifted, and she tried to tug the shirt over her most vulnerable spot. But Brant wasn't having it. He curled his strong fingers over hers and lifted the shirt back up amid her stammered excuses.

"I-I don't just run around without my panties. I read this article that said it was a good idea at night to let… certain body parts," she swallowed hard, "sort of…you know…breathe."

He stared at the light brown patch of hair for an inordinately long amount of time before his gaze lifted to hers.

The heat in his eyes had her face flushing, and her pulse throbbing.

"I couldn't agree more," he said as he slipped his hand between her legs, causing a current of desire to zing straight through her. "We wouldn't want *this*," he slid a finger inside her slick heat, and she wondered if she might pass out after all, "not to be able to breathe."

Before she could do more than groan, he removed his hand and lowered his head to kiss her there. And not a brief sweet kiss, but a long, deep one with plenty of tongue. She knew about oral sex. She just didn't *know* about oral sex. Now that she did, she didn't think she could ever go without it again. It was like an addictive drug that sizzled through her veins and up to her brain where it completely reconfigured all her synapses.

Gone was the Elizabeth Murphy who had spent most of her life ignoring her sexual needs. In her place was a woman who wanted to explore every one of them.

And Brant didn't seem to have a problem helping her.

With each stroke of his tongue, he brought out more and more of her passion, turning her into a wanton woman who held on to his head and urged him on with her groans. The tight knot of desire grew and grew until Elizabeth felt like a stretched rubber band just waiting to be released. The intensity of her orgasm took her by surprise. Suddenly, she was sailing through the heavens in a meteor shower of sensations that had her thighs clamping around Brant's head and words flying from her mouth.

"Oh, yes! Yes! Yes!"

She landed back on earth with a satisfying plop. She enjoyed the feeling of contentment for only a moment before the sound of tearing foil made her open her eyes.

Brant knelt above her, completely naked. She was so wrapped up in the sight of all those lean muscles that she didn't notice what he was doing until his hands dropped away from his condom-covered penis.

Correction. His mammoth condom-covered penis.

Her eyes widened as her heart started beating erratically again. But this time, not with passion. With fear. She jerked down her shirt and crab-walked closer to the headboard. She tried to look away, but she couldn't seem to get her eyes to cooperate. Or her unruly mouth.

"You're huge."

Brant tossed the condom wrapper to the nightstand, a smile teasing the corners of his mouth. "Thank you."

"I didn't mean it as a compliment. What I meant was—" Her eyes widened as he eased down next to her. "What are you going to do with that?"

He arched one brow. "Do?"

"I mean, I know what you want to do with it, but I just don't think it's possible. That," she pointed a finger down, but refused to look, "is not going to fit."

His laughter took her completely by surprise. She had rarely seen the man smile, let alone laugh until tears dripped from the corners of his eyes. She should've been angry that he was making fun of her. But the sight didn't fill her with anger as much as a warm, cozy feeling that settled in her stomach and had her smiling back.

He stopped laughing, but his lips still tipped up at the corners. And it was really hard to think when he smiled at her. His smile wasn't as flashy as Beau's, but it was twice as sexy. He had white, even teeth and a dimple. Just the sight of that little dent in his cheek caused her heart—and a spot much lower—to flutter.

"Believe me, sweetheart," he said. "I'm not laughing at you. It's just that I've never been with someone who is quite so straight to the point." His smile faded. "So I guess my assumption was wrong. You really are a virgin." When she nodded, he released his breath and rolled to his back, covering his eyes with the back of his forearm. "Would you care to explain how a woman your age is still a virgin? Or let me guess: you're saving yourself for marriage."

She probably could've lied and saved herself an embarrassing explanation, but she had never been good at lying. Especially to a man who had just given her the best orgasm of her life—the only male-induced orgasm of her life.

"No. I don't want to get married."

He lifted his arm and looked over at her. "Every woman wants to get married."

"I don't," she said. "I'm quite happy being single."

He rolled over onto his side to face her. "So are you telling me that the reason you're still a virgin is that you just haven't found the right fit?" He reached out and smoothed back her hair, trailing a line of fire from her forehead to her ear.

"I haven't looked that hard." Her gaze swept down to the condom-covered thing that rested against her thigh. "Have you found women that fit?"

He chuckled. "A few." He leaned over and brushed his lips across hers until her brain was so scrambled she couldn't think. "Did you know you have the prettiest lips?" He deepened the kiss. Between the compliment and his hot kisses, Elizabeth started to wonder if size really didn't matter.

"Fine," she whispered against his mouth. "I'm willing to try. But if it doesn't work, you'll have to promise to stop."

Brant pulled back and studied her for a few minutes before he shook his head. "Sorry, but I don't do virgins. You might not be saving yourself for marriage, but you should be saving yourself for someone you care about."

Brant was right. The first time should be with someone she cared about. And she certainly didn't care about this man. But if that was true, then why did she suddenly feel so disappointed?

"Well," she tugged at the hem of her t-shirt and tried to scoot away from him, "thank you for the...orgasm. And I would appreciate it if you'd lock the door when you leave."

His dimple reappeared. "Who said anything about leaving?" His hand slid up her leg, pushing her t-shirt to her waist.

"But I thought you didn't want—"

"Oh, I want," he said in a gravelly whisper. "But just because I can't have what I want doesn't mean we still can't have a little innocent fun." His hand slipped between her legs, and his thumb brushed over her.

Elizabeth closed her eyes as hot tingles spread upward.

She didn't know how innocent it was...but it sure was fun.

Chapter Sixteen

Henhouse Rule #11: No man stays past his welcome.

THERE WAS A MAN IN ELIZABETH'S BED.

A man with huge feet that dangled off the end and an armspan that took up the entire width of her double mattress. Elizabeth was pinned beneath one of those arms. Pinned like a butterfly to a display board, she was unable to do more than stare at the ceiling and try to figure out how she had ended up in this position.

She wasn't some impulsive woman who was easily swept off her feet. In fact, Elizabeth wasn't impulsive at all. She prided herself on her rational thinking. Before she made any decision, she always did her homework, weighed the pros and cons, and considered every angle.

So what had made a rational woman act so irrational?

The answer came quickly enough. Shifting in his sleep, Brant's fingers brushed the lower swell of her breast, and every nerve ending in Elizabeth's body tingled to attention.

It seemed that while the mind could be rational, the physical body had no such ability. It functioned only on its senses.

And the man who lay next to her knew how to cover all five. He looked delectable even with morning stubble. Smelled as good as freshly baked bread. Tasted better than Josephine's rhubarb pie. Touched her in a way that made her mindless. And whispered naughty sweet nothings that could have the strongest woman melting at his feet. Elizabeth couldn't help but wonder if this was how Miss Hattie had started her life of sin. With one very sexy cowboy who knew his way around a woman's body.

Except Elizabeth wasn't an uneducated, seventeen-year-old farm girl with no money or means to support herself. She was an intelligent woman who refused to let her physical body rule her logical brain. An intelligent woman who had a good job and a comfortable life. A comfortable life she wanted to get back to.

For a brief moment, she thought about shaking Brant awake and asking him to leave. But then she realized that if her nerves tingled from just an accidental brush, there was no telling what would happen from an intentional one. The man was an expert at seduction, something he had demonstrated over and over again the night before.

Innocent fun.

There was nothing innocent about what they had done. She still had her maidenhead, but her innocence had been lost the first thirty minutes of being in Brant's arms. The man knew every trick under the sun for finding satisfaction without actually having intercourse. And she couldn't blame what happened totally on him. She had been a willing student, participating in his lessons with the enthusiasm and dedication she had applied to all her schoolwork.

Now that the lessons were over, she had nothing to show for them but sore muscles, humiliation, and a bed hog.

Glaring at the bed hog, Elizabeth carefully eased out from under his arm. Once her feet were firmly on the floor, she breathed much easier. She tiptoed around the bed and tripped over Atticus. The cat opened his eyes and sent her a look that was both hostile and accusing.

"Don't judge me," she whispered, "you liked his petting as much as I did." She hurried to the bathroom, planning to be all showered and collected before Brant woke up.

Unfortunately, plans don't always work out.

Elizabeth had just started soaping up when the shower curtain was jerked back. The soap slipped from her fingers, and she released a squeak of surprise as Brant stepped into the bathtub.

"Mornin'," he said as he pulled the curtain closed.

Stunned, all she could do was stand there with her mouth open.

"Geez, woman," he growled as he bent to adjust the faucet. "Is it hot enough for you?" He bent down and picked up the bar of soap, sniffed it, then proceeded to run it over his chest and armpits.

Elizabeth followed his sudsy hands until they got to his penis and testicles, and then she didn't know where to look. Naked male skin seemed to fill every nook and cranny of the small shower.

Brant was oblivious to her embarrassment. He just continued to wash and rinse off as if he showered with a woman every day. And he probably had. Not only had he been married, but there was little doubt that he was one of those men who attracted women like the clusters of bubbles that clung to his shoulders.

"I think I must've breathed in about half-a-cat's worth

of hair last night," he said before he rinsed out his mouth. "What is it with single women and cats, anyway?" He took the razor from the shower caddy. "Why don't you get yourselves a nice dog to protect you?"

After searching through the products on the shelf, Brant reached for the soap again and lathered his face. "Of course, my dog, Max, wasn't exactly what you would call a guard dog. He was too busy chasing squirrels. I swear that animal would chase anything that moved— trash, leaves, the neighbor kids on their bikes."

He tipped his head back to shave his throat. "I had this laser on my key ring and that dog would go crazy trying to catch the beam of light I flashed around on the floor. And the crazier he got, the louder B.J. giggled—" His hand stilled in mid-stroke, but it only took him a second to recover. "Anyway, dogs are a lot less hairy than cats." He handed the razor back to her and rinsed off, and, just that quickly, the curtain was jerked back and Elizabeth was alone.

Before she could even get her mouth closed, he peeked his head back in. "I realize that women like to take long showers, but I'd sure appreciate it if you hurry things up a little. I'm so hungry I could eat the ass out of a bear."

It took the door clicking closed for Elizabeth to snap out of her trance. She blinked and tried to figure out what had just happened. When it finally dawned on her, anger replaced shock. Just who did he think he was telling her to hurry? She jerked back the shower curtain, almost ripping it from the hooks. And how had he gotten in when she was positive that she'd locked the door behind her? Even if she hadn't locked it, a mannerly man would've knocked before barging in. Not only on the bathroom door, but on the front door.

Of course, a woman who cared about mannerly behavior should've pointed that out, instead of allowing him into her shower—and into her bed—without saying one word to stop him.

By the time Elizabeth was dried off and dressed, her hands were shaking so badly from anger she couldn't even get her wet hair up in its usual bun. It only got worse when she walked into the living room and discovered the Sunday paper spread out on the couch and her computer booted up.

A cupboard door slammed in the kitchen, and Elizabeth's eyes narrowed.

She found Brant squatted down next to Atticus, who had gotten over his annoyance at being evicted from the bed and was rubbing against Brant's legs. More than likely because the man held a bag of cat food.

"Hold on there, boy," Brant said as he poured the food into the bowl. "No need to be a glutton." Once the bowl was brimming with more food than an overweight cat should have, Brant gave Atticus a good scratch and rose to his feet. He walked back over to the pantry to put the bag of food away, the muscles of his bare back rippling as he set it on the upper shelf.

Elizabeth must've made some sound, possibly from the steam releasing from her ears, because Brant turned. His gaze slid over her suit, and a slight smile tipped up the corners of his mouth.

"Please tell me you have coffee. All I could find was about a hundred boxes of herbal tea." He reached out and lifted his blue shirt off the back of a chair. "And do you have an iron? This sure needs it."

It was the final straw.

Marching across the kitchen, Elizabeth ripped the

shirt from his hand and tossed it to the floor. "No! I will not iron your clothes. Or make you breakfast. Or go buy you coffee." She whirled and headed out into the living room where she lifted up a section of newspaper and shook it at him until it rattled. "And did you ever consider the fact that some people prefer to read the newspaper when it's all neatly stacked?" She tossed it to the couch and moved over to the computer. "Or that a computer is as private as mail and snooping around on someone else's should be a federal offense?"

He tipped his head and squinted at her. "Are you into something that you don't want people to know about?"

She scowled at him. "That's not the point. It's none of your business what I'm into. You have no right to be on my computer." She pointed a finger at the kitchen. "Or count my herbal tea boxes. Or feed my cat." She poked herself so hard in the chest it hurt. "My cat. Mine!"

Elizabeth was about to move on to his shower etiquette when the doorbell rang. All anger fizzled right out of her as her gaze went to the door and then back to Brant, who was leaning against the doorway to the kitchen with his arms crossed and a semi-smile pinned on his face. If she hadn't been so terrified by the possibility of her mother standing at the door, she might've slugged him.

Instead, she started racing around like a chicken with its head cut off. Not a hen. Never a hen.

"Quick!" She grabbed up the newspaper and shoved it into his hands. "You need to hide." She pushed him back toward the bedroom. "But not in the bathroom. Mother always checks to see if I'm cleaning my toilets properly." She shoved him inside the bedroom and closed the door in his face just as the doorbell rang again.

With her heart thumping, she smoothed back her hair and headed for the door. It wasn't her mother who stood on the other side. But her visitor was almost as bad.

"Well, good mornin', Ms. Murphy." Wilma Tate nodded her head, causing the plastic cherries on her purple felt hat to bounce. "We were startin' to think you weren't at home."

Elizabeth glanced over at Elmer, who stood off to the side, looking tired and hungover. No doubt from a Saturday spent at Bootlegger's Bar.

"Good morning," she said as brightly as possible. "Are you two on your way to church?"

"Of course. What else would a person do on Sunday?"

An image of Brant sprawled across her bed flashed in Elizabeth's mind, but she quickly pushed it out again.

"So we were just curious about that truck," Wilma said as her gaze shifted to Beau's SUV that was parked out in front. "Do you know whose it is?"

Elizabeth stared at the vehicle and showed the appropriate surprise. Until that very second, she hadn't given a thought to how Brant had arrived at her house. Now she would have to do some quick thinking if she wanted to avoid becoming the main item of gossip in town. But before she could come up with a good lie, Wilma continued to ramble.

"If I listened to other folks, I might think you had yourself a boyfriend, Ms. Murphy." She laughed so hard her cherries jiggled. "But like I told Rachel Dean, that's just pure foolishness. What would an old maid do with a boyfriend? At our age," she winked, "all women need to keep them warm at night is a heatin' pad and a tube of Ben-Gay." She looked back at the truck. "No doubt it belongs to someone visitin' across the street. That teenage daughter of Delia's is as wild as a March hare."

Elizabeth didn't know why Wilma's words bothered her. They weren't anything she hadn't heard before. And maybe it was the fact that she wasn't the only one who had heard them. Even though she had told Brant to hide, something told her he wasn't the hiding kind. This was confirmed when a hand slipped around the door, and Brant appeared in all his shirtless glory.

"Why, Elizabeth, honey," he said, his voice dripping with a smooth, east Texas drawl. "You didn't tell me we had company."

Wilma's mouth dropped open so wide that Elizabeth thought her false teeth might fall out and hit the cement porch. It certainly wasn't funny that Brant was standing half-naked in front of one of the biggest gossips in Bramble. Which didn't explain why Elizabeth giggled.

Brant looked down at her, and his own smile turned into something more real.

"And just who are you?" Wilma asked.

Brant shot her a look that could only be described as annoyed. "Bra—"

"Brad Murphy," Elizabeth jumped in. "He's my cousin who is visiting from Amarillo."

Wilma's eyes narrowed. "I didn't know you had family besides your mama."

"Distant cousin." Elizabeth didn't know why she lied. After this morning, Brant wasn't exactly on her good side. Still, bad manners didn't justify a tar and feathering.

Elmer stepped up and held out a hand. "I'm Elmer Tate. It's a real pleasure to meet you, Brad."

One of Brant's eyebrows popped up. "The Elmer who forgets where he lives?"

For a man who spent most of his time in a bottle,

Elmer was no dummy. He quickly took Wilma's arm and pulled her toward the porch steps. "Come on, dear. We don't want to be late for church."

Before the Tates could even make it to the front gate, Brant called out. "I'd make sure I have the right house next time, Elmer. I'm real protective of..." he glanced down at Elizabeth, "my cousin."

Elmer nodded and struggled to open the gate for his wife. Elizabeth watched them hurry down the sidewalk and had little doubt of what the gossip would be at church that day.

"You should've stayed in the bedroom," she said as she turned and walked back inside.

"The woman annoyed me." He followed her and closed the door. "Why do you let her talk to you like that when you won't even let me mess up your newspaper without throwing a tantrum?"

Her mouth flapped a few times before she could speak. "I did not throw a tantrum."

"I don't know what you'd call it." He tipped his head and studied her. "Somethin' wrong, Beth?"

The nickname caused her stomach to hurt. Not a bad hurt, just a needy one. Although she didn't have a clue what Brant could have that she possibly needed. To hide her discomfort, she walked over and picked up his shirt from the floor. "Nothing's wrong."

He had her in his arms before she could finish placing the shirt on the back of the kitchen chair. She had forgotten how warm his skin was and how good he smelled. Even masked by her feminine soap, he reeked of virile male.

"Tell the truth, Beth," he said. "Are you regretting the fun we had last night?"

Was he right? Was that why she was so angry? Did she regret allowing him such sexual liberties? She thought back to the night before, from the first kiss to the last tingle of orgasmic sensation.

"No," she said, "I don't regret what happened last night. It's just..." She tried to put her thoughts into some kind of logical order. "It's just that, when I woke up with you lying in my bed, I guess I got scared. I've never had a man stay the night before, and I was worried that my life had suddenly changed forever." She looked up at him. "And I like my life, Brant."

One eyebrow quirked. "Are you telling me that you've had your fun and now you're through with me?"

"Yes."

He laughed. It was such a nice laugh that it was a shame that he didn't use it more often. And a shame that it ended too soon.

"Fair enough," he said as he brushed the strand of hair from her forehead. "And for the record, I didn't expect you to make me breakfast or iron my shirt. I can do those things for myself."

"And the messed newspaper and entering my bathroom without knocking?"

"I have no excuse for those. I guess I'm just a guy." He studied her, and for a moment, she thought he was going to kiss her. Instead he dropped his arms and stepped back. "Would it be too presumptuous of me to take you to breakfast? I'll let you pay."

She laughed. "In that case, I'll iron your shirt."

He ended up ironing his own shirt while she went back to the bathroom to fix her hair. She had just stabbed in the last hairpin when he called to her. She walked into the bedroom to find him standing in front of her dresser.

"Where did you get this?" he asked as he held up the silver chest she kept her few pieces of jewelry in.

"My mother gave it to me when I turned sixteen. It was the only thing she took with her from Miss Hattie's." She moved over to stand next to him. "Why?"

"Because my mother has one just like it." Brant turned over the chest and pointed to the engraving on the bottom. "Not only was it made by my great-grandfather, but it was made in October of 1892. Over two months after he supposedly died."

Chapter Seventeen

*Henhouse Rule #36: Every hen has a talent...some
are just more entertaining than others.*

THE YOUNG WOMAN THAT GREETED Elizabeth as she
stepped off the henhouse elevator could only be described
as cherubic. Dark curly hair surrounded a round, chubby
face with a button nose and big brown eyes. At least, they
were as big as saucers now.

"You're related to Miss Hattie?" Starlet said in disbelief. "But you look just like my old Sunday school teacher.
She liked to wear them old maid suits too."

Elizabeth could've easily ignored the comment if she
hadn't started having her own doubts about her ward-
robe. Suits that had once seemed professional and modest now seemed hot, uncomfortable, and...frumpy. Just
that morning at breakfast, she caught herself envying a
woman for her comfortable-looking jeans, western shirt,
and cowboy boots. Or maybe she envied the fact that the
woman had caught Brant's eye. The thought of envying
women Brant merely glanced at had her straightening her
frumpy suit jacket with a jerk.

"I'm Elizabeth Murphy," she said as she held out a
hand, "and you must be Starlet Brubaker."

The girl grabbed her hand and gave it an exuberant shake. "Yes, ma'am, I sure am. It's a pleasure to meet you. I've been working all morning on my audition. Minnie already told me that I'd have to get past the head hen before I could stay."

"About that, Starlet…" Elizabeth's words were left hanging as Starlet charged across The Jungle Room, her bright fuchsia prom dress slapping around her legs. She slipped behind the baby grand piano, and the sound system clicked on. There was a squeal before Starlet's voice came through the speakers.

"Testing. Testing."

The background track for "Someone to Watch Over Me" started, and Starlet moved around the piano. She tried to sit up on it like Baby had, but ended up tearing a bigger slit in her dress. While she examined the tear, she missed her cue and had to run back over and restart the song. This time she skipped sitting on the piano and leaned against it seductively instead. Her elbow slipped on the slick wood, and she almost took a nosedive to the floor. She caught herself and was able to start the song in the nick of time.

After only two notes, Elizabeth realized that Starlet didn't need a microphone. Her voice resounded off the low ceiling like a foghorn at high tide, and it took a strong will for Elizabeth not to cover her ears. Starlet, on the other hand, didn't have a clue how she sounded. Her face was scrunched up in concentration as she belted out the words.

Her performance was a complete antithesis of Baby's. While Baby had the husky jazz style down cold, Starlet just sounded like what she was—an awkward young woman with no musicality whatsoever.

Still, Elizabeth smiled brightly and applauded when she was finished.

After returning the microphone to the stand and turning off the sound system, Starlet walked back with an apprehensive look on her face.

"What did you think? It's a little out of my range, but Baby says I'm improving every time I sing it." She clutched her hands to breasts that spilled over the top of her too-tight dress. "So can I stay? I promise to work harder than any hen in the history of the henhouse. Minnie already says I have plenty of potential."

Elizabeth stared at the young girl and understood why Brant hadn't been able to kick her out. She looked a lot like a pitiful puppy at the pound with her big, pleading eyes.

"It's not about potential, Starlet," she said. "It's about the fact that Minnie had no business inviting you here. The henhouse doesn't even belong to her, and it won't belong to me after next week."

"I know that," she said as she flopped down on the couch and hugged a fur pillow to her chest. "The Cates brothers are going to buy it." Her eyes glazed over. "Have you ever seen eyes as blue?" she breathed. "They're the color of the pretty gem ring my mother got from one of her boyfriends."

An image of Brant's blue eyes looking back at her over the rim of his coffee cup popped into Elizabeth's head, forcing words to pop out of her mouth.

"Sapphire," she said in a voice almost as awed as Starlet's. "Brant's eyes are sapphire."

"Brant?" Starlet said. "I wasn't talking about Mr. Cates. I was talking about Beau." She smiled slyly. "So you have the hots for Mr. Cates?"

"No!" The answer came out a little too quickly, and Elizabeth tried to recover. "Mr. Cates and I are only business acquaintances." Who'd had a little innocent fun. Wonderful, body-sizzling fun. She cleared her throat, but it was harder to clear the images of body-sizzling fun.

"Which brings us back to the subject at hand," she said as she sat down next to Starlet. "Miss Hattie's is not going to reopen—at least, not as it was. Brant and Beau are planning to open a men's resort."

Starlet looked confused for only a second before a knowing look entered her eyes. "Of course, a *men's resort*." She leaned in closer to Elizabeth and whispered. "You think we're bugged? Minnie said we had to be careful about who we told because we didn't want the feds on us." She sat back up, her eyes big and innocent as she spoke in an overly dramatic voice. "Well, of course it's going to be a men's resort. Just like I'm here to visit the place where my dear old great-grandmother used to work—as a maid."

Suddenly, Elizabeth understood why Starlet's grandmother had ended up on Broadway—overacting must run in the family. She also understood why Brant didn't want to deal with her. The girl was determined to stay here, which meant Elizabeth needed to be more blunt.

"I realize how exciting it must've been for you to receive an invitation in the mail from the infamous hens. But you can't stay here, Starlet. I'll help you pack your bags, and Mr. Cates has offered to buy new tires for your car so you can get home safely."

The girl's entire face drooped. "But I can't go back to my hometown. I told them I was headed to Broadway. I can't go home until I'm as big as Starlet O'Malley. And

I just know if I get some polishing from the hens, I can do it."

Elizabeth didn't know what hen "polishing" entailed, but she had an idea. And she couldn't believe that Minnie would be so devious as to try to corrupt a girl this young and naïve. Once she was finished explaining things to Starlet, she had a few things to say to Minnie.

"This doesn't mean that you should give up your dream," Elizabeth said. "Mr. Cates told me all about the talent shows you've won. It certainly sounds like you're on the right road to fame and fortune. But I think for now, you should head back home. I'm sure your family and all your friends will be happy to see you."

The look in Starlet's eyes went from sad to downright terrified. She didn't yell or scream or throw a tantrum. She just got to her feet, looking as if Elizabeth had just destroyed her entire world.

"No, they won't," she said. "They won't because everything I told Mr. Cates was a lie. I didn't win any talent shows. I was just the fat girl in school that nobody liked. The black sheep in a family of pretty, talented people." She swallowed hard. "I was just hoping that the hens could find something in me that no one else could."

She turned and ran across the room, disappearing behind the large philodendron.

Elizabeth stared at the artificial plant and felt like she'd been kicked in the stomach. Starlet's painful confession brought back memories of her own childhood. She hadn't been overweight, but she had still been an outcast. The kid in grade school that no one picked for kickball. The nerdy bookworm no one invited to prom. The old maid in town who people thought couldn't get a date without help.

She didn't know what to say to Starlet to make her feel better, but she had to try. Except when she got up and crossed the room, she didn't find a young girl huddled in the corner in misery. She found a doorway. And inside the doorway she found a stairway leading up. Beau was standing on the first flight of stairs, his gaze following a flash of bright fuchsia. When he noticed Elizabeth, he started down the stairs.

"I guess that Starlet didn't take the news so well."

"That's putting it mildly." Elizabeth continued to look up. "So where do these lead?"

"To the upstairs rooms. Each one has its own secret door in the closet. I guess there are all kinds of hidden passages in the house. I've stumbled upon a few, but I think the hens are keeping some to themselves."

"So did you see what room Starlet was going to?" Elizabeth started to walk past Beau and head up the stairs, but he stopped her.

"It's been my experience with weepy women that it's best to give them a little time to themselves."

If anyone knew how to deal with weepy women, Elizabeth figured it would be Beau. No doubt the man had broken hearts from Texarkana to Amarillo. So she followed him back into The Jungle Room and watched as he walked over to the bar and pulled out a bottle of beer from the mini-refrigerator.

"I'm surprised Minnie lets you hang out here," she said. "She told me it was hens only."

He pulled off his John Deere cap and flashed his megawatt smile. "Minnie made an exception, seeing as how I'm going to be the new owner and all." He walked over to the couch and flopped down. "But I've got to tell ya, it could sure use a big-screen TV. The Cowboys played today, and I had to sit in my truck and listen to it on the radio. It just wasn't the same, especially when Starlet kept sneaking around staring at me like I was a freak show at the carnival."

Elizabeth took a seat next to him. "She's much better off with you than with the hens. Hopefully, they haven't corrupted her too much."

"She's nineteen," Beau said. "I'm sure she's learned more from reality television shows than she could possibly learn from three old ladies."

"So you think I should let her stay?"

He swallowed a sip of beer and shrugged. "I don't see why not. Once she figures out that the henhouse isn't going to be as much fun as she thought it would be, I'm sure she'll head back home soon enough."

For being so young, Beau was certainly logical. And since Elizabeth wasn't looking forward to any more tears, she figured it wouldn't hurt to test Beau's theory. At least for a few days.

"Will you keep an eye on her?" she asked.

"Nope." Beau shook his head. "One of the reasons I found the staircase was because Starlet showed up in my room last night. She might be naïve, but she's not shy. Besides, Minnie's not going to let anything happen to her. She's already warned me about keeping my distance." He took a deep swallow of beer. "As if I have time to worry about women when I have a business to get started."

Elizabeth shot him a skeptical look. "And it looks like you're working real hard on that."

He grinned. "Noticed that, did you? I'm afraid I'm not the worker bee my brother is. I prefer to enjoy life to the fullest."

"I'm sure cancer will do that to a person." The words were out before Elizabeth could stop them, and she quickly apologized. "I'm sorry, Beau. That's none of my business. Sometimes I speak before I think."

Beau studied her in a way that was so much like his brother she couldn't help but blush. "That's what I like about you, Elizabeth. You don't mince words." He rested his head back on the couch. "Ever since I've been diagnosed, people have tiptoed around the subject. My family still won't use the word around me. It's like if they say it, it might make the cancer come back."

"Maybe they are just worried about scaring you," she said.

Beau snorted. "If that's the case, it's a waste of their time. I'm already scared shitless." He opened his eyes and stared at the Andy Warhol painting. "I have these nightmares that the grim reaper is standing over my bed looking down at his watch, just counting the seconds until he can suck the life right out of me."

"So it's not in remission?" she asked.

There was a pause where she thought Beau was going to lie, but then he glanced over at her. "I don't know. And I've decided that I don't want to know. If it's back, the chances of me living to see my next birthday are slim to none, so why shouldn't I just enjoy whatever life I have left without going through the hell of treatment?"

She leaned up. "Because that's stupid."

Beau's eyes widened before he started laughing so hard that he sloshed the beer out of the bottle. But Elizabeth saw nothing funny about it.

"You can't just stop going in for check-ups. Even if the cancer is back, I've heard of people having cancer more than once and surviving. Of course, they were fighters while you're obviously a...weenie."

"A weenie?" He sobered and sat up. "You try going through weeks of chemo and radiation, and we'll see who's a weenie."

"I realize it had to be hard, Beau," she said. "But you can't just give up. It's not just about you. It's about Brant and Billy, and everyone who loves you."

He released his breath and flopped back. "Maybe I don't want to carry the burden of my family like Brant does. Maybe I'm a selfish prick who just wants to think about himself."

"So think about yourself and go get a check-up. There's a good chance that the grim reaper might be staring at his watch for another sixty years."

"Are you always so sure of yourself?" Beau asked.

It was laughable. Ever since waking up that morning with a man in her bed, Elizabeth had been completely unsure of herself. Not only had she started to doubt her clothing selection, but also her values and beliefs.

"It's much easier to figure out what other people should do than it is to figure out what you should do," she answered truthfully.

"And what are you having trouble figuring out?" he asked.

Try as she might, Elizabeth couldn't keep her face from heating up. And Beau didn't waste any time drawing the correct conclusions.

He flashed a smile. "So you and Brant do have a thing going. I was starting to have my doubts. Especially since you don't exactly act like you like each other."

"I like your brother just fine," she said. "But we don't

have a thing going. We're merely..." Her voice dropped off when she realized she didn't know how to finish the sentence.

"Friends?" Beau finished for her. When she didn't reply, his gaze wandered over her from the top of her head to the tips of her shoes. This time, his smile was less flashy and more sincere. "Come to think of it, a friend might be exactly what my brother needs most."

Chapter Eighteen

Henhouse Rule #38: The man never picks the hen.
The hen picks the man.

ELIZABETH LOOKED DIFFERENT. Gone was the tightly buttoned Ms. Murphy in somber gray suits, and in her place was a relaxed woman in a red sweater and a pair of faded Levi's that showcased her long legs and hugged her curvy hips. But it wasn't her clothing that held Brant's attention. Her entire demeanor had changed. She sat in the shade of the monstrous cottonwood tree, her bare feet tucked up on the hammock and her finger twisting a strand of hair as she read one of Miss Hattie's journals. It was a seductive pose. At least, it looked damned seductive to Brant.

"You holdin' up that hoe or is the hoe holdin' you up?"

Minnie's voice startled Brant out of his voyeurism, and the hoe he'd been leaning on shifted beneath his weight. A slower man would've fallen flat on his face, but Brant was quick enough to regain his balance. Just not before his cowboy hat went tumbling to the ground.

Minnie cackled. "I guess that answers that."

He picked up the hat and slapped it against his thigh. "You need to quit sneaking up on people."

"A chargin' elephant could've snuck up on you," she

said, and her gaze wandered over to Elizabeth. "Makes a person wonder just what held your attention."

He tugged his hat back on. "Daydreaming, is all. And I thought I asked you to quit smoking." He reached for the cigarette that hung from her mouth, but she swatted his hand away.

"It ain't even lit."

"So why do you need it?"

"The same reason you need to keep that chirpin' cell phone latched to your belt." Her eyes narrowed. "Although it looks like you've misplaced it."

Brant hadn't misplaced his phone. It was on the dresser in Miss Hattie's room, no doubt chirping as one e-mail after the other filled his inbox. Normally, he'd be chomping at the bit to get back to it and his laptop, but for some reason, answering e-mails and reading contracts no longer seemed that pressing. His gaze swept back over to Elizabeth before he picked up the hoe and went back to chopping the waist-high weeds.

"You're doin' a fine job," Minnie said. "It won't be long before the garden will look as pretty as it once did. Of course, the house still needs some work."

"I've already contacted the contractors," he said as he wrestled with a more stubborn weed. "They'll be out this week as soon as we close on the house." He stopped and shot her a warning look. "But I'm not signing anything until you give me your word that you won't be sending out any more invitations."

Minnie held up a wrinkled hand. "Hen's honor." She shook her head. "It didn't do much good anyhow. Ten invitations and all we got was three girls."

He turned to her. "Three?"

She shrugged. "There were the two before you got here. But I sent them on their way quick enough. Much too full of themselves. One even had the audacity to ask if we had a stripper pole she could audition on." She shook her head. "What is the world comin' to?"

Brant couldn't help but grin. Something that was happening much too frequently. "Did you get a good look at the chest I left in the kitchen?" he asked. "Do you remember it?"

"Of course I remember it," she said. "It was once—" she stopped and took a deep puff of her unlit cigarette, "Miss Hattie's."

Brant leaned on the hoe. "So it was Miss Hattie's?"

"One of her most prized possessions. According to the stories, she even slept with it on occasion." She squinted at him. "But I didn't realize your granddaddy had made it. How did you figure it out?"

"My father gave one to my mother when they got married that's almost identical," he said. "I recognized it immediately when I saw it in Elizabeth's bedroom—" He cut off quickly, but not quickly enough. Minnie latched on to his words like an alligator on raw chicken.

"Well, I guess that proves two things," she said almost gleefully. "Your grandfather was here. And Elizabeth is no longer a virgin."

Elizabeth was still a virgin, but barely. For a man who prided himself on control, he'd lost most of it the night before. When he ignored the comment and went back to chopping weeds, Minnie cackled.

"I'd say it's about damned time." She wheeled closer to him. "Unless you're a slam-bam-thank-you-ma'am kind of man."

In the last year, Brant probably could've been described as a slam-bam-thank-you-ma'am kind of man. On the rare occasions that he'd needed sex, he'd spent little time with the woman after the act was over.

Which was why he should've been relieved to discover that Elizabeth wasn't a clingy type of woman. And he was relieved. He didn't need, or want, a serious relationship. His life was complicated enough. Still, there was a part of him that felt a little annoyed by Elizabeth's lack of interest after their night together. Maybe he wasn't annoyed as much as confused.

Shouldn't a virgin be a little enamored of the man who had given her multiple orgasms? The first time he'd had oral sex, he'd followed Melissa Coolidge around like an orphaned baby duckling until her mother had reported him to the sheriff as a stalker.

Elizabeth, on the other hand, wasn't the stalker type. He didn't wake up to find her staring dreamily at his face. She hadn't ogled him in the shower. Hadn't rushed to fix him coffee or breakfast. She hadn't melted against him when he'd kissed her. In fact, she'd treated him the same way she'd always treated him: indifferent with a slight measure of contempt.

He glanced over at her. There she sat, sipping the iced tea Baby had brought out to her and reading one of Miss Hattie's journals as if the man she'd just enjoyed a night of sexual delights with wasn't standing less than twenty feet away. It was enough to really piss Brant off. Hoping to figure out what made Elizabeth different from every other woman he'd been in bed with, he turned to Minnie.

"So tell me about her. I know she was an only child, but why didn't her mother inherit the henhouse?"

Moments ticked past, and he started to wonder if there was some hen code that stopped Minnie from answering. But finally she relaxed back in her chair and spoke.

"Harriett never loved the henhouse the way a hen should," Minnie said. "And I can't say as I blame her. She didn't have it easy. Instead of havin' her go live with relatives like most hens did, her mama made the mistake of lettin' her grow up here. It was a bad decision. One her mother lived to regret." She pulled the cigarette from her mouth and stared at the unlit tip. "But no matter how much you want to, you can't go back and fix things. You just have to live with your mistakes."

"You sound like you know a lot about the subject," he said. "Do you have any children, Minnie?"

Minnie flipped the cigarette out into the weeds. "Not a one that I deserve."

Her gaze wandered over to Elizabeth. "Growin' up with Harriett and all her hang-ups about men has made Elizabeth more than a little distrustful." She looked back at him. "Which is where you come in. You need to prove to her that all men aren't assholes."

"And what makes you think I'm not?" he asked.

Minnie snorted as she backed up the wheelchair. "I've been around men all my life. And believe me, I know an asshole when I see one."

After Minnie went back inside, Brant continued to chop weeds and think about what she'd said about Elizabeth's childhood. A mother that hated men explained a lot. Elizabeth's virginity. Her frumpy clothes. Her old maid lifestyle. And he agreed with Minnie that Elizabeth needed a man in her life. Brant just wasn't that man.

Which didn't explain why Brant remained outside with

Elizabeth, even when he started to suffer from heatstroke. Or maybe heatstroke was only the excuse he used for what happened next. With one eye pinned on Elizabeth, he stripped off his shirt, something he rarely did, and proceeded to perform feats of strength. He moved large rocks for no good reason, grunting as if he were leg-pressing a good five hundred pounds. He welded the hedge clippers like Edward Scissorhands. And hoed like a lumberjack bent on clearing half the Sierras.

It was heatstroke. It had to be. There was no other way to explain a thirty-eight-year-old man flexing and posing for a woman like some goddamned body builder in a competition.

And the worst part about it was she didn't pay him the slightest bit of attention. Not when he almost threw out his back lifting a cement stepping-stone, and not when he doused himself with the hose and shook off like a naked blonde in some sex video. She just sat there completely oblivious to his humiliation.

Unfortunately, his little brother wasn't so oblivious.

"What are you doin', Big Bro?"

Brant dropped the hose and turned to find Beau standing at the back door, an overly bright smile on his face.

"Just cooling off," Brant said as he grabbed up his shirt. "I was hot."

Beau glanced over at Elizabeth, and his smile got even brighter. "I bet you are."

"Hi, Beau!" Elizabeth lifted her hand in greeting.

Brant scowled. Here he had worked his ass off for the last half hour trying to get her attention and all his little brother had to do was walk out the door?

As if reading his thoughts, Beau shrugged before

turning back to Elizabeth. "Well, don't you look all cool and comfortable," he said as he waltzed right over and flopped down on the hammock with her. And if Beau's familiarity with Elizabeth didn't piss Brant off, her reaction certainly did. She closed the diary and had the audacity to give Beau her full attention.

Brant should've gone inside. He didn't need this kind of aggravation. Unfortunately, his feet didn't seem to listen to his common sense.

"What are you two talking about?" he asked as he strolled over. It annoyed the hell out of him that he sounded exactly like a kid who had been left out of the playground basketball game.

"I was just telling Elizabeth how pretty she looks in jeans." Beau threw Elizabeth a wink, and she blushed brightly. "Hey, would you watch it, Brant?" He tried to shove Brant back with his boot. "You're dripping all over."

Brant didn't apologize, nor did he move. It was only after Elizabeth's jeans had numerous damp dark spots that she looked up at him. She obviously didn't need her glasses for reading because they were hooked in the front of her sweater, leaving her pretty hazel eyes exposed. Along with the direct and annoyingly indifferent look in them. "You might want to put on some sunscreen." She pointed to his chest. "It looks like you're getting a burn."

"She's right," Beau said. "You do look a little pink, brother."

Ignoring the comments, Brant nodded at the notebook. "So did you discover anything interesting?"

She opened the book back up. "Not really. Although given that none of the entries have dates, it's a little confusing."

Beau leaned way too close to Elizabeth, and it took everything Brant had not to wrestle his brother to the ground. Something of what he felt must've shown on his face because Beau sent him an innocent look before leaning even closer. "Have you found my grandfather's name?"

She flipped through the pages. "No, but I found Buddy Holly. Which doesn't make any sense considering the fact that my great-grandmother would've been long gone by the time he was popular."

"Maybe it's a different Buddy Holly," Beau said, before taking a deep breath. "What perfume do you use, Elizabeth? You smell good enough to eat."

"Watch it, Beau," Brant growled.

"Watch what, big brother? I was just making a comment."

"One that was out of line."

"Now why would that be? Unless..."

"You're probably right about Buddy Holly," Elizabeth said, completely unaware that a fight was about to break out. "There are a lot of men's names in here."

That got Beau's attention. "Does Miss Hattie go into detail about what happened with those men?" he asked.

Elizabeth shook her head. "No. The only thing she goes into detail about is the weddings. It seems that a lot of the hens got married. Which I guess makes sense given the fact that the men outnumbered the women twenty to one."

Right now two to one was too many for Brant.

"So Miss Hattie's was a little like Match.com?" Beau said.

Elizabeth laughed. "I wouldn't go that far."

It was hard to think when Elizabeth laughed. When

she laughed, the stern lines of her face softened, and she looked all womanly and approachable. All Brant wanted to do was pull her into his arms and kiss those upside-down lips.

"Well, we shouldn't play up that angle too much," Beau said. "The men who come here will want to get away from marriage talk. Which brings up the reason I came outside in the first place. I was talking with the hens, and we think we should have ourselves a celebratory dinner tonight. Baby has some t-bones, and Minnie said she could dig up some champagne. Of course, we'll have to talk Elizabeth here into staying."

"I really couldn't, Beau," Elizabeth said. "I need to get home and feed Atticus."

It would probably be best if Elizabeth went back to Bramble. There was something about her that turned Brant into an adolescent idiot. The next thing he knew he'd be locating a skateboard and trying to "catch some air." But instead of leaving well enough alone, he jumped on Beau's bandwagon.

"It wouldn't be much of a celebration without the owner of Miss Hattie's," he said. "Besides, I think I gave your cat enough food this morning to last him a while." He didn't know why he'd brought up the fact that he'd been at Elizabeth's house that morning. Maybe he wanted Beau to know. And maybe he wanted Elizabeth to remember. Either way, it was about as ill-bred as he could get.

"Then it's settled." Beau got to his feet. "I'll just run in and tell the hens to set another place."

Brant probably should've followed after his brother. Instead, he took Beau's place on the hammock. Except his boots slipped out from under him, and he fell down into the hammock so hard he almost bounced Elizabeth off the other end. He reached out to keep her from falling off and, once his hands closed around her arms, he couldn't help pulling her close.

She did smell good. Like the soap in her shower and lilacs. Or maybe the scent of lilacs came from the garden. He had wanted to talk more about the journal. But when she looked up at him, he forgot all about the past and only cared about the present.

As usual she wore no makeup, her skin smooth and slightly blushed. Her lips were pressed together in a stern line, but that didn't stop his head from dipping closer for a taste.

Unfortunately, Elizabeth wasn't as cooperative as she had been the night before.

She placed a hand on his bare chest and pushed him back. "What are you doing, Brant?"

He leaned in and nuzzled her neck. "Is it that hard to figure out?"

She pulled away. "I realize I'm naïve about relationships, but I thought we both decided that last night was more of an accident. You were in my bed, and we just sort of…" She let the thought trail off. "And if that's the case, then why are you trying to kiss me now?"

It was a good question. One he had been trying to avoid all day. But staring into her direct, honest eyes, he realized he couldn't avoid it any longer.

"Because, Beth," he reached out and smoothed the wayward strand of hair from her eyes, "I've discovered that one night wasn't enough."

Chapter Nineteen

*Henhouse Rule #25: If you don't have something
nice to say, keep your beak shut.*

"MY UNCLE LETS ME HAVE A GLASS OF WINE at Thanksgiving," Starlet grumbled when Baby handed her a glass of Sprite.

"This ain't Thanksgiving, Short Stuff," Minnie said. "There'll be plenty of time to drink when you're older." She glanced over at Beau who stood at the bar in The Jungle Room pouring champagne. "And plenty of time for men."

Starlet looked confused. "But isn't that what...?"

Minnie shook her head in disgust. "Greenhorns." She held up her champagne glass. "To Miss Hattie's. May it be a sparkling oasis of love in the dry desert of life."

Elizabeth held up her glass and clinked it with the others, trying to ignore the man who sat next to her on the zebra-skinned couch. It was impossible. Especially when he sat so close that she could smell the scent of his spicy soap and feel the crisp starch of his shirt every time he leaned up to talk with Beau. And maybe it wasn't his proximity that bothered her as much as his words, which bounced around in her head like the pinball in the machine at Bootlegger's Bar.

I've discovered that one night wasn't enough.

It was an underhanded thing to say. Especially when up until that point, Elizabeth had been doing so well. Regardless of how fluttery her stomach felt and how much her pulse rate increased whenever he was around, she had been able to keep her emotions hidden. She'd gotten through breakfast without a hitch and had almost made it through the day at Miss Hattie's. Which was quite a feat since every time she looked up there was some other temptation to resist.

Brant's butt in a pair of soft worn jeans. The muscles of his back flexing beneath the cotton of his shirt. The breathtaking flesh he revealed when he stripped off his shirt.

But how in the heck did a woman ignore those words?

And how in the heck did a man say those words and then just move on as if nothing had happened?

All through dinner, he'd chatted with Beau and Minnie about plans for remodeling, tried to convince Starlet that college was a good backup plan for a singer, and asked Sunshine about what it was like growing up in the sixties. Elizabeth had just sat there staring at Brant like Starlet was staring at Beau—sort of like he was the second coming.

After the third bottle of champagne had been emptied, Baby suggested karaoke, and everyone took turns getting up and singing their favorite song—most quite badly. The only ones who didn't remind Elizabeth of nails scraping down a chalkboard were Baby and Brant.

Baby had pulled Brant up for a jazz duet of "Summertime," and Brant's singing voice turned out to be as deep and rich as his speech. But he didn't showboat. After only one chorus, he handed the microphone off to Minnie, who finished the song in an off-key voice that was almost as bad as Starlet's. But Elizabeth enjoyed listening to bad singers much more than she enjoyed Beau pulling her up on stage.

All her life, Elizabeth had hated being the center of attention. She couldn't sing, was too clumsy to dance, and too shy to act. So she just stood there and blushed as Beau got on one knee and sang a country love ballad with a thick, exaggerated twang.

Fortunately, Brant stopped him in mid-song.

"I think we've all had enough singing for one night, little brother," he said as he took Elizabeth's hand from Beau. "Why don't you put on something slow, Baby, and I'll see if I still remember how to waltz."

Brant remembered quite well. Unlike Beau, he moved in a graceful glide that put Elizabeth's dancing to shame.

"I like the jeans," he said.

She stared at the tiny smattering of dark hair that showed above the collar of his shirt and cleared her throat. "Thank you. I borrowed them from Miss Hattie's closet. Although I would assume that they belonged to another hen."

His hands slipped down to her waist, and he hooked his thumbs under the worn belt loops, leaving his finger-tips to brush the top swell of her hips. "Possibly, but Levi's have been around for a while so you never know. Hattie seemed like the type of woman who enjoyed slipping into something snug and comfortable."

Elizabeth stumbled, and he pulled her closer.

"The key," he breathed against the top of her head, "is to trust your partner completely. Do you trust me, Elizabeth?"

She looked up from her feet and into a pair of mischievous blue eyes. "Are we talking about dancing?"

One side of his mouth quirked up. "You don't mince words, do you?"

"You didn't this afternoon."

He released his breath. "I apologize for being so blunt. It's just that I don't exactly know how to handle you."

The words snapped her out of her euphoric state, and she stumbled to a stop. "Excuse me?"

"Maybe 'handle' isn't exactly the word," he said. "What I'm trying to say is that naïve virgins aren't my specialty."

Elizabeth went from only slightly mad to furious so quickly she felt light-headed. "Are you saying that you handle worldly sluts better?"

His eyebrows popped up. "No. That's not what I'm saying at all." He tried to guide her back into the dance, but she flat-out refused.

"Then what are you saying, Brant?" she said. "Because call me a naïve virgin, but I'm just not getting it."

"Would you keep it down," he whispered as he looked back at the bar, where Beau was entertaining the hens with some story. "I'd rather not have everyone in on our relationship."

"What relationship? Didn't we just decide this morning that we don't have a relationship? And then not more than four hours later, you were telling me that one night wasn't enough."

"You should talk." He glared down at her. "You didn't mind cuddling up next to me all night like your damn cat, but in the morning, the cuddly kitten had turned into a prudish prig."

Her eyes widened. "A prudish prig? And I was not

cuddled up next to you," she said. "Your big-assed body takes up the entire bed." The cuss word surprised them both, but Brant was the one who recovered more quickly.

"Then I guess I'll take my big-assed body and leave you alone." He turned and yelled at Beau. "I'm going to bed. Are you coming?"

Beau shook his head. "You snore worse than our old Labrador Honey. I'll crash down here on the couch."

Brant nodded and, without looking at Elizabeth, headed back toward the elevator. She might've mentioned the hidden stairway if she hadn't been so mad. Stomping over to the bar, she joined the party and even downed two more glasses of champagne. She soon discovered that she was a sullen drunk, for instead of enjoying Beau's humorous stories, she just sat at the bar and mulled over her argument with Brant.

Virgins weren't his specialty.

He'd said it as if she was some rare breed of animal that he had bagged but didn't know what to do with. Well, Brant Cates hadn't bagged anything. And if "one night wasn't enough" that was just too bad. One night was all he was going to get.

The evening finally came to a close. Because she drank too much, Elizabeth felt it was prudent to stay the night. At well after one o'clock, she slipped beneath the sheets of Baby's double bed.

"Wasn't this a fun evening?" Baby said as she slid in next to Elizabeth. When Elizabeth didn't say anything, she rolled over and faced her. "I guess not so much for you. Did you and Brant have a fight?"

"I wouldn't call it a fight. A fight is what friends or lovers have. Brant and I are neither."

"So you didn't have sex with him?" Baby sounded confused. "Minnie said that you did."

Elizabeth probably could've denied it on technicalities. Unfortunately, it would still be a lie. She and Brant hadn't had intercourse, but they'd had sex. Steamy, orgasmic sex that she couldn't seem to get out of her mind.

"It was a bad idea," she said. "I mean, what kind of person agrees that what you had was just a one-night thing, and the next second he's telling you that he wants more?"

"A man."

Elizabeth glanced over, but all she could see was the outline of the hairnet that covered Baby's platinum-blond hair. "What?"

"Sex really screws with a man's mind," Baby said. "His body tells him he can't live without a woman, but his mind tells him he can't live with one. It's really a Catch-22 for the poor dears."

"So why do we even mess with them?"

Baby giggled. "Because it's fun. And because once they get past the battle between their minds and bodies, they can be really sweet and loving. And you have to admit that Brant is sweet. What man would take on a bunch of old women? He reminds me of this cute boy I once knew. Johnny Daniels was the strong silent type that made all the girls go crazy. I had a major crush on him in college."

Elizabeth's head came up off the pillow. "You went to college?"

"Cornell. Magna cum laude."

Elizabeth was glad it was dark because she couldn't hide her surprise. "But why did you come here? I mean... couldn't you find a better job?"

"It wasn't about the money," Baby said. "It was about finding a safe haven." She hesitated for a moment before she continued. "After I graduated from college I moved to New York City and became a buyer for Macy's Department Store. I was so cocksure of myself. I had my own apartment and piles of clothes. But since I didn't have family or many friends, I was lonely.

"And then I met Michael. He was handsome and funny and a dapper lawyer who was as full of himself as I was. It was love at first sight, and we married and moved to Austin where he'd gotten a new job. Everything might've been okay if I hadn't had trouble getting pregnant." She rolled on her back and placed a hand over her eyes. "Look at me, after all these years, I'm still trying to blame myself for the abuse."

"He hit you?" Elizabeth asked.

"'Beat' would be a more accurate word. Michael didn't stop until I was bleeding and half unconscious. Beneath his wool suit and crew cut was the worst kind of monster."

"So why didn't you leave him?"

"I finally did, but not before he had practically beat me to death. I don't even remember how I made it to the car. I drove for a good fifty miles until I was pulled over by the sheriff." She glanced over at Elizabeth. "Joe was a friend of your grandmother's. He took one look at me and brought me here."

"And you stayed?" Elizabeth asked. "But didn't you hate men?"

"With a passion," Baby said. "I couldn't even be in the same room with them at first. But then Minnie talked me into singing. Music was my salvation. Still, it took years before I decided to try sex again." She laughed. "Jasper was his name—the sweetest little farmer you'd ever want to meet. He even proposed to me, but by that time, I wasn't willing to leave Miss Hattie's."

Elizabeth looked up at the ceiling and tried to place Baby's story inside the image she carried around with her of the henhouse, but it just wouldn't fit. Where were the sordid details her mother had hinted at? The naked women running around? The sex-crazed men?

"And Sunshine?" Elizabeth asked. "How did she end up working here?"

"Sunshine has never worked here," Baby said. "Your grandmother went to Dallas on a shopping trip and found her living on the streets—too drugged out to even know her name. She brought her back to Miss Hattie's, and she's been here ever since. Your grandmother gave her a new story. A new life."

There were no words to express all the feelings that crowded up inside. So Elizabeth just lay there and looked up at the ceiling. After a few moments, Baby spoke.

"I realize it's hard to understand. And I'm certainly not going to justify anything that has taken place here at Miss Hattie's. Men *have* come here for sex. But Hattie's is so much more than that. It saved my life and helped me become the type of woman who isn't afraid to go after what she wants." She paused for only a breath before she continued. "So what do you want, Elizabeth?"

Elizabeth turned to her. "What do you mean?"

She reached out and patted her hand. "You told me that Brant hasn't had enough. Now the question is, have you?"

Chapter Twenty

*Henhouse Rule #42: Sometimes a roll in the hay is
all a hen needs to unruffle her feathers.*

BRANT COULDN'T SLEEP.

His shoulders and back stung like hell from his sunburn, and his ego stung like hell from a blunt-talking librarian who didn't understand the first thing about men.

Or maybe she knew too much.

What was he doing? Since when did he pant after women like a dog in heat? He hadn't even chased after Amanda. Their relationship had just evolved from their friendship. But friendship wasn't what came to mind when he thought about Elizabeth. Steamy sex did. And maybe that was the problem. Maybe he was still getting Elizabeth confused with all his fantasies about Miss Hattie.

He rolled over onto his stinging back and stared up at the painting. He didn't know if it was a trick of the moonlight that filtered in through the curtains or his own sleep-deprived mind, but Miss Hattie's eyes no longer looked seductive as much as accusing. Almost as if she didn't care for the way he'd treated her granddaughter.

"Fine," he said. "I admit it. I was a little bit of an asshole tonight."

"True, but I wasn't exactly nice."

Brant blinked at the painting before his gaze moved over to the doorway where Elizabeth stood. He sat up, and his heart started to pound so loudly he had trouble hearing her next words.

"So you couldn't sleep either?" She came closer, her steps hesitant.

"What are you doing here?" he asked. It was a really stupid question, and he wished like hell he could take it back. He didn't care why she was there. He was just glad she was.

She cleared her throat, something he suddenly realized she did a lot. "I brought you the first journal. I'm not quite finished with it, but I thought you'd like to take a look." She stopped about a foot from the bed. Close enough for him to smell the scent of lilacs. Close enough for him to see the outfit she wore.

"What do you have on?" His gaze swept up her long, bare legs to the satin shorts that flared at her hips, then up the matching top that clung to the jut of her nipples.

"Baby loaned them to me," she said. "I think she calls them baby dolls." She smoothed a hand down the satin in a way that took all the moisture from Brant's mouth. "Which makes sense given that her name is Baby. Here," she held out the notebook, "I'll just let you get back to whatever you were doing."

He reached out to take the book, but instead took her wrist.

"I-I shouldn't have bothered you," she stammered as he pulled her closer. "I-I just thought that I'd—oh!" The diary thumped to the floor, and she tumbled onto his lap.

"Beth." He didn't know why he said her name. It just came out. Like an exhalation. Like a whispered prayer.

His lips covered hers as the desire that had goaded him all day grew thick and intense. Still, he refused to give in to the pressing need. Instead, he reined it in, cradling her jaw between his hands and sipping at her mouth as she had sipped the expensive champagne just that evening.

Brant didn't know how much experience she'd had with kissing, but if it was limited she was a fast learner. After only a few sips, she ran her hands through his hair and sucked him into the heat of her mouth. Her tongue was hesitant at first, but grew bolder with each stroke of his. He eased her top up, his hand gliding over her breast. The sweet flesh seemed to swell in his hand, and he squeezed gently before strumming her nipple with his thumb.

Her moan had barely died in his mouth when she reached up and covered his hand with hers to stop him.

He pulled back from the kiss. "Did I hurt you?"

She shook her head. "No. It felt wonderful." She cleared her throat, and he knew she was blushing. "It's just that I was hoping that this time I would get to touch you."

The words were as hot as they were sweet, and Brant didn't waste any time taking her up on the offer. Easing her off his lap, he stretched out on the bed.

He expected hesitant caresses. What he got was a thorough inspection that left him struggling to retain control.

"What's this bump?" she asked as she pressed against a rib.

"Football injury," he croaked.

"Star quarterback?" She caressed the spot.

"No, bench-warming tight end."

"Hmm, tight end?" Her hand settled over his pectoral muscle, causing it to twitch. "I can see where that would fit." She dipped her head and covered his nipple in wet heat.

Brant tried to regulate his breathing, but it was a lost cause. Virgin or no, Elizabeth had a talent for seduction. Every stroke of her tongue, every suck of her mouth, had his breath chugging in and out worse than the time Beckett had talked him into running a marathon.

She didn't stop with one nipple, but moved on to the next. When she'd finished turning it into a tight nub of need, she nibbled her way down his ribs, trailing a line of fire to the satin sheet that spilled over his hips. Without hesitation, she pulled back the sheet. Since the waistband of his briefs had irritated the sunburn on his lower back, he'd gone to bed naked. He actually found himself blushing as she studied his bobbing length.

"Oh. It's not as big as I thought."

He lifted his head. "Excuse me?"

She giggled. Something he couldn't remember ever hearing her do. "I mean, it's mammoth," she corrected.

"That's better—" The words ended on a groan as she encased him in her fist. He expected her to be unsure, but Elizabeth never reacted the way he expected. And he suddenly realized that was what he liked most about her.

She caressed him from tip to base before her mouth settled over him, all hot and mind-blowingly wet. She was awkward, but it was her awkwardness that turned him on the most. Elizabeth might not be experienced, but she was thorough. She left no area unexplored and tried out different techniques until she found the one that had him moaning the loudest.

Then suddenly, when he was just about to go over the edge, she lifted her head and gazed up at him. "I think we should give it a shot."

Brant blinked. "What?"

She sat up. "I think it might fit. And if it doesn't, at least we tried." When Brant started to say something, she held up her hand. "I know. You think I should save my virginity for someone special. But what if no one special shows up, Brant? What if I die without ever knowing what it feels like to have a man deep inside me?"

The "deep inside me" part added another inch to Brant's erection, and he groaned and closed his eyes. What was he doing? He had no business being back in bed with Elizabeth. His insane behavior today had more than proved that. If he wanted to keep his sanity, the best thing he could do would be to climb out of bed and never look back.

Unfortunately, he couldn't bring himself to do that. Not when he opened his eyes to find Elizabeth completely naked and bathed in moonlight. And not when she took him in hand and kissed the very tip of his penis. And not when just the thought of another man being "deep inside" her made him completely and utterly insane.

"Come here," he said as he guided her mouth away from him and pulled her back up his body, enjoying the cool slide of her soft skin. "Are you sure this is what you want?" He kissed her gently on the mouth. "There's no going back."

"Positive," she said before deepening the kiss.

A wave of heated excitement coursed through him, but he took things slow, enjoying the feel of her lips against his and the softness of her breast in his palm. He continued kissing and fondling her until she hugged his thigh between her legs and bumped her hips against him. Then he rolled her over and kissed his way down her body to the patch of golden brown hair. He planned on taking his time, trying to alleviate any fear she might have with passion. But it turned out that Elizabeth was less fearful about losing her virginity than he was. After only a few flicks of his tongue, her thighs tightened around his head, and she tugged on his hair.

"Please, Brant," she whispered, "I want you in me."

With a knot of apprehension tightening his stomach, he sat up and reached for his wallet on the nightstand. "If I hurt you, you need to tell me." He pulled out the condom. "Whenever you want to stop, we'll stop." He might've continued to ramble if Elizabeth hadn't taken matters into her own hands. Once he was suited up, she wasted no time in pulling him down to her warm, waiting body.

He eased in inch by inch until sweat broke out on his brow and his arms started to quiver. She was so damned tight that it was hard not to drive deep inside her. He stopped halfway in to catch his breath and regain some willpower.

"It's not as bad as I thought," she said. "In fact, it just feels like a tingly stretching. Although I think it would feel better if you moved."

It would feel better all right. Brant just wasn't sure he could stand it feeling much better. He pushed in a little deeper, then slowly pulled back out. He figured he could've kept up his measured movements if Elizabeth hadn't started participating. With a tilt of her hips, she pushed up and took him deep. The tight, hot sheath and friction had him driving into her with a force that banged the headboard against the wall. He would've apologized if she hadn't wrapped her legs around his waist and pulled him closer.

"Don't stop," she panted.

That was all it took for his lust to take over. His hips pumped against her, and she met each thrust with one of her own. He tried to hold off and wait for her, but it was no use. Within seconds, he was spiraling down into an amazing orgasm. He drove into her one last time, riding the intense sensations out. It was a long ride. Just before the last tingle died away, Elizabeth climaxed, tightening around him and sending one last shower of sparks raining over him.

He rolled off her and flopped over onto his back. Sleep deprivation from the last two nights had finally caught up with him, and he could barely keep his eyes open. He had just tucked an arm around her waist and pulled her close when she giggled.

"Well, what do you know?" she whispered against his chest, "we fit."

Brant woke to warm sunlight. He squinted and waited for his eyes to adjust. It didn't take him long to figure out where he was, and even less time to look around for Elizabeth. He thought she'd be long gone before the sun came up, scurrying back to the security of Baby's room. Instead he found her leaned back on the headboard, reading Miss Hattie's journal.

He lifted his head and she glanced up from the book and smiled. It was almost as bright as the sun that streamed in through the window.

"I take it that you're in a better mood than you were in yesterday?" he said with a smile of his own.

She blushed. "As long as you don't expect me to iron your shirt, we're good."

"I would never even consider it." He laughed and plumped the pillows up so he could sit next to her. "So did you discover anything?"

"A lot, actually," she said. "I didn't realize the hens

were so charitable. Did you realize they supported local orphanages and helped with the war efforts?"

"War? What war would that be?"

"I don't know." She flipped through a few pages. "It doesn't really say."

He relaxed back on the pillows, his gaze falling to the edge of the sheet that inched down her bare chest. To keep from devouring the soft swells like a ravenous dog, he tried to distract himself. "Read me something."

She went back to the page she was on, and started reading in a voice that was soothing and articulate. A librarian voice if ever he heard one. It was sexy as hell.

" 'The hens went to town today. The women ignore us, and the men avoid us like the plague. It's funny when you think about how friendly they'd been the night before.' " Elizabeth turned the page. " 'J.D. stopped by tonight. I like J.D. He has big feet that smell like stagnant water after a good rain, but he's sweet and kind. They say his wife—' " She paused and started to close the book, but he stopped her and leaned closer.

"Why did you stop? I want to hear it."

She looked at him and then went back to reading. " 'They say his wife died a year back. Some kind of a fever that took hold after she gave birth to their baby boy.' " She swallowed hard. " 'He cries sometimes after we're finished, and I hold him until he stops.' "

Just that quickly, the joy of the morning ended. Pushing back the sheets, Brant swung his legs over the edge of the bed. But before he could do more than sit up, Elizabeth had wrapped her arms around him from behind.

She pressed her cheek between his shoulder blades. "I'm sorry."

The words were simple, but heartfelt. Against his back, he could feel the damp moisture of her tears. It was his undoing. The pain he'd tried so hard to keep inside broke free, and tears dripped from the corners of his eyes. He didn't know how long they sat there like that, her clinging tightly and him silently crying.

It was Elizabeth who finally pulled away.

"Why didn't you say anything?" she said. "Your back is really burned." She gently stroked a hand down his spine before she scrambled off the bed and headed for the bathroom.

By the time she got back, Brant had pulled himself together enough to enjoy the sight of her walking toward him completely naked. She had a phenomenal body, breasts full and heavy with the palest pink nipples he'd ever seen. Her waist nipped in, and her hips curved out then tapered down to shapely legs. And Brant had always been a leg man.

He reached out to pull her into his arms, but she side-stepped him

"Later," she said with a teasing smile. "Right now, you need to lie down so I can get this on your back."

"This" turned out to be a face-cleansing cream that instantly cooled the burn and had him groaning into the mattress. Or maybe the groans came from the feel of her cool hands gliding over his muscles, or her sweet center against his buttocks as she straddled him.

"Tell me about your wife and son."

The request snuck up on him, and he leaned up to end the massage. With a strength that surprised him, Elizabeth pushed him back down. Still, she wasn't that strong or heavy that he couldn't have easily gained his release.

But maybe he didn't want to be released. Maybe it was time to talk about it.

"She grew up on a farm only a half mile from my house…"

Once he started, the words slipped out effortlessly. Elizabeth didn't ask questions. She just continued to stroke his back and shoulders…and listen. He talked about the good times. The fun he and Mandy had had as kids, the crazy things they'd done as teenagers, and the first years of their marriage. He couldn't bring himself to talk about Brant Junior so he ended the story at his son's birth.

A long silence passed before Elizabeth finally spoke.

"It wasn't your fault, Brant. Even if you had been there, you wouldn't have been able to save them."

"No, but I would've died with them," he said. "And maybe if I had never married Amanda, she wouldn't be dead now."

Elizabeth stopped stroking his back and allowed her fingers to rest at the curve of his spine. "The curse?"

He rolled to his side, forcing her to move off him. "Do you think I'm crazy?"

She sat next to him, her legs folded to the side. "No. I think you're trying to make sense of the senseless things that have happened to your family. And sometimes people do stupid things to make themselves feel better." She fiddled with the edge of the sheet. "Even though my father left before I was born and never once called or came to see me, after he died I drove all the way to Idaho to see where he was buried."

Brant reached out and caressed her knee. "I'm sorry."

Her gaze lifted from his fingers to his face. "Why are you interested in me? You were right. I am an inexperienced virgin."

"Were." He pulled her down next to him. "Now you're a temptress that has me making a complete fool out of myself just to get your attention."

"Well, you have it, Mr. Cates," she said. "Now what?"

"Now I intend to enjoy it." Leaning up on an elbow, he kissed her. Her mouth opened instantly and desire pumped through his veins with each slide of her lips. He started to press her back down to the pillows when she stopped him.

"I meant where do we go from here?"

It was a discussion he would've preferred to have later. Much later. But he also knew that it would be better to get things out on the table before they went any further.

He pulled back, although he kept a hand on her waist. "I can't make any promises, Beth. Marriage and love aren't things I even consider anymore. But I enjoy being with you. I like your intelligence and wit." His finger drew a figure eight on her hip. "And I like this—a lot."

It wasn't exactly his best speech, but he'd given worse. Of course, he hadn't cared if the other women told him to take a hike. He cared if Elizabeth did, but he still wasn't willing to lie in order to keep her in his bed.

Fortunately, Elizabeth was a logical thinker.

Maybe a little bit too logical.

Her eyes scrunched up in thought. "So we'll sort of be like friends with benefits."

"I wouldn't exactly say that."

She tipped her head. "So what would you call it?"

Brant stumbled around in his mind for an answer, but he couldn't find one. She laughed at his stunned silence before she leaned over and gave him a kiss that curled his toes into the satin sheets.

"Friends with benefits it is."

Chapter Twenty-one

Henhouse Rule #29: Never waste time on good-byes—they'll be back.

"WHAT HAPPEN TO THE WABBIT, Miss Mow-fee?"

The words pulled Elizabeth out of her daydream, and she realized she was sitting in the middle of the reading pit with an open book in her hands and a group of children circled around her feet.

Brody Cates leaned up on his knees with a naked Barbie clutched tightly in his hand and continued to talk in a voice too deep to belong to a three-year-old. "Did he get away from Mistow McGregow?" His eyes narrowed. "That McGregow is a mean one. Almost as mean as my Uncle Bwant."

It was ironic that the child had brought up the same person who had caused Elizabeth to zone out in the middle of story time. Although her daydreams weren't about the mean "Bwant" Cates who never smiled and who had tried to close down Dalton Oil. Her daydreams had been about a hot, sexy cowboy who had told her funny stories about his childhood while sitting with her in Miss Hattie's huge bathtub. A sweet lover who had fed her Baby's pumpkin pancakes, helped her get dressed, and then walked her out to her car where he'd given her a kiss that left her faint and giddy.

Four days later, she was still faint and giddy.

"Isn't Uncle Bwant mean, Mama?" Brody yelled back at Shirlene Cates, who was sitting at the edge of the reading pit with the other mothers. Of course, Shirlene looked nothing like the rest of the mothers in her designer jeans, diamonds, and sky-high-heeled boots.

Shirlene flashed a brilliant smile at her son. "Now where would you hear somethin' like that, honey?"

Brody looked confused. "Fwom you."

Shirlene's smile drooped only slightly before she glanced around at the other mothers. "Don't kids say the darnedest things?" She shifted a sleeping Baby Adeline to her other shoulder. "Now turn around, Brody. Your constant chatterin' is gettin' Ms. Murphy all flustered."

Flustered was an understatement. Elizabeth was more than just flustered. She couldn't eat. She couldn't sleep. And she couldn't even read a children's book without images of the man flashing through her mind like a PowerPoint slideshow.

"I don't think it's Brody who has her all flustered," Sue Ellen said as she tried to get her cell phone away from her toddler. "I think she's worried about catching a husband."

"No need to worry about that, Ms. Murphy." Missy bounced the newest addition to the Jones clan. "Not with the entire town on the hunt. I have a great-uncle who would be perfect for you."

"Thank you," Elizabeth said, "but I'm not really interested in getting married."

The women exchanged knowing looks before Darla spoke.

"Of course you're not. That's why you knocked Twyla out of the way to catch Shirlene's bouquet."

"Now, y'all stop teasin' Ms. Murphy," Shirlene said. "She can catch a man without any help from us." She looked over at Elizabeth and winked. "Got anyone in mind, honey?"

Elizabeth had someone in mind all right. But there was no way she would catch him. And maybe that's what had her all flustered. The man she had her eye on was way out of her league. Brant was handsome and rich and could get any woman he wanted. Elizabeth had just been convenient. She had called their relationship *friends with benefits*. But she shouldn't delude herself. Brant wouldn't be contacting her for conversation...or sex.

She just needed to realize it and move on.

It was easier said than done. Her mind had a will of its own. She got through the Peter Rabbit story, but couldn't seem to focus on anything else. She was standing behind the counter, checking out Brody's books when Shirlene reached out and took a book from her hands.

"You've scanned that six times now, Ms. Murphy. I'd say it's checked out."

Elizabeth looked down at the monitor screen. "I don't know what's wrong with me. Maybe I have the flu."

"It looks more like man-itis to me," Shirlene said as she placed the book in the bottom part of the stroller where Adeline slept. "Brody," she called to her son, who was kneeling on the floor in the children's section, "don't be sticking Naked Barbie in the heating vents. Remember how upset you were when you got purple marker on her leg?" She looked back at Elizabeth and smiled. "So I guess you did mean to catch my bouquet after all."

"No!" Elizabeth said much louder than she intended.

"Now don't go gettin' your panties in a bunch. All of us have been there." Her perfectly plucked eyebrows lifted. "Some more than others. You'll either get over it or succumb." Her green eyes moved over to the doorway where a tall, lean cowboy had just entered. "As for me, I succumbed."

For a moment, Elizabeth's heart stopped. It started again when the man pulled off his black Stetson and ran a hand through his chestnut hair. Still, the similarities between Billy Cates and his brother had her face flaming. Especially when his gaze settled on Shirlene and turned to smoldering heat. He strutted right over and pulled her into his arms.

"Hey, Shirley Girl, want to run away to a Caribbean island?"

Shirlene smiled. "We just got back from a Caribbean island."

He gave her a quick kiss. "Then I guess I'll have to settle for lunch at Josephine's."

After Shirlene and Billy left, Elizabeth had an even harder time keeping her mind on her work. She would no sooner start a task than she would catch herself daydreaming about Brant, and she had to wonder if maybe Shirlene was right. Maybe there was such a thing as man-itis. Of course, she refused to succumb to it. She would treat it like a cold and let it run its course.

With that thought in mind, she made herself a strong cup of hot tea and sat down at her desk to e-mail some reminders to delinquent patrons. She had just sent off a reminder to Kenny Gene for *Scooby-doo and the Zombie's Treasure* when her cell phone started to buzz. She dove for the phone like a drowning victim for a life vest, splashing tea onto her wool skirt and her keyboard.

"Hello," she said, sounding more breathless than she had ever sounded in her life. Unfortunately, it wasn't Brant's deep, sexy voice that came through the receiver.

"Are you sick, Elizabeth?" her mother asked. "Is that why you haven't returned my phone calls?"

Elizabeth cringed and mentally kicked herself for not checking caller I.D. before she answered the phone. All she needed was another lecture from her mother. Unfortunately, it looked as if that was exactly what she was going to get.

"I thought I taught you common courtesy, but I guess I was wrong. It seems you've turned into one of those women who completely ignore their mothers, who spent hours in labor to give them life."

Elizabeth rolled her eyes. "I'm sorry, Mother. I've just been a little busy lately."

"With what?" her mother asked. "Or maybe I should say with whom?"

Elizabeth choked on the sip of tea she'd just taken.

"Sit up straight, Elizabeth, and clear your air passages," her mother directed. "Do you have any water around?"

She grabbed her water bottle and took a few sips until she could breathe again.

"What are you talking about, Mother?"

"I'm talking about the man you've been shacking up with." This time Elizabeth choked on nothing but air as her mother continued. "Don't act so surprised. You can't keep things from a mother. We have our sources."

"Minnie." Elizabeth assumed she'd just thought the word until her mother gasped.

"Minnie? How do you know Minnie?"

"Uhh…" Elizabeth scrambled through her brain for an answer, but all her brain cells had been spent dealing with man-itis, and there wasn't one left to deal with her mother. So she told the truth.

"I've talked with the hens," she said, purposely leaving out the part about inheriting the henhouse. It was a good decision seeing as how contacting the hens was enough to send her mother over the deep end.

"How could you, Elizabeth!" she ranted. "Didn't you learn anything? Those women are nothing but a bunch of immoral prostitutes. And I have little doubt that they are responsible for 'the cousin' Wilma Tate said she saw at your house. Did he hurt you? Do we need to call the police?"

"He didn't hurt me, Mother," she said. "And we certainly don't need to call the police."

But her mother was no longer listening. The mention of Minnie had sent her into a downward spiral of craziness. Or maybe her mother had always been a little crazy. Something Elizabeth was just now realizing.

"Well, we might not need to call the police on him, but we certainly need to call the police on Minnie. That woman needs to be behind bars."

A few weeks ago, Elizabeth would've agreed with her mother. But somewhere along the line, Minnie had wiggled her way into Elizabeth's heart. She was still a cantankerous pain in the behind, but she was an endearing one. And Elizabeth wasn't about to let her mother harass the old woman.

"You aren't going to call the sheriff, Mother. Minnie didn't do anything wrong."

"Nothing wrong?" her mother yelled. "What about corrupting my innocent daughter by sending a no-good, lying man to her house—"

"That's enough, Mother," Elizabeth said. She didn't know where the words came from. She had never talked back to her mother. But once the words were out, others burst forth like withheld water from a dam.

"I'm not an innocent child. I'm a thirty-seven-year-old woman who has lived on her own for the last fifteen years. A woman who can think for herself and make her own decisions. And if that includes having men over to my house, then that's my choice, not anyone else's."

She took a deep breath before continuing. "I know that growing up at Miss Hattie's couldn't have been easy, and I don't blame you for being a little jaded about the hens. But I think you're wrong about them being nothing but immoral prostitutes. They're people just like you and me. People who survived in the only way they knew how. I can't blame them for that, just like I can't blame you for your hatred toward men."

When the words finished spilling out of her mouth, Elizabeth fell back in her computer chair in stunned silence. It was the most she'd ever spoken to her mother in her life. And the only time she'd ever stood up for herself. It felt wonderful and liberating. But it also felt sad. Because, for the first time, she realized what an unhappy woman her mother was.

"Well," her mother huffed, "it looks like Minnie has won again. She's brainwashed you, just like she tried to do to me." When Elizabeth didn't say anything, she continued. "So I guess that's that. It looks like you've made your choice."

"I haven't made a choice," Elizabeth said. "You're still my mother."

There was a long pause before her mother spoke. "Not if you continue your relationship with the hens."

The phone clicked dead.

Most daughters would be surprised, but most daughters hadn't grown up with a mother as unbending as Elizabeth's. After she set the phone down on her desk, she sat there thinking. Not just about the phone conversation, but about her life up until that point. Her mother was right. Elizabeth had been brainwashed. Just not by Minnie. Harriett Murphy had brainwashed her daughter into believing that Miss Hattie's was a skeleton that needed to be hidden and that women were better off without men.

Except being at the henhouse had made Elizabeth realize that she should be proud of her heritage, and being with Brant had proved that some men were well worth the effort. She might not ever hear from Brant again, but that didn't mean that she couldn't date other men. And her brief experience with Brant had given her enough self-confidence that when Peter Sanders showed up to install new software on her computer, she stopped what she was doing and started up a conversation.

It proved to be a mistake. Not only was Peter boring, spewing out an overabundance of technical words that Elizabeth didn't understand, but he had the annoying habit of cleaning his ear with anything that happened to be handy. His index finger. A key on his overcrowded key ring. The eraser end of the pencil on Elizabeth's desk.

She had just removed her favorite pen from his reach when her cell phone rang. Grateful for the excuse, she grabbed her phone and walked out from behind the counter. She expected to hear her mother continuing her rant. Instead, a deep voice had her stomach fluttering and her heart tightening.

"Elizabeth? This is Brant."

"Oh," she said as if she was talking to a 411 operator instead of the man who had her heart thumping like a kettle drum. "How are you?"

When he answered, there was a smile in his voice. "Fine. How are you?"

"I'm well. Thank you."

For some reason, he laughed. "I'm glad to hear it. So what are you doing?"

She took a deep breath and released it. *Just answer the questions, Elizabeth. Nothing hard about that.* "I was sitting here talking with Peter."

There was a long pause, and when he came back on, he didn't sound so happy anymore. "Who the hell is Peter?"

"The county computer tech," she said. "He comes every other Friday."

"Alone?"

"Of course. Why would he bring someone?" She fiddled with the neck of her sweater as she waited for him to speak again.

"Look," he sounded annoyed, "I was calling to see what you were doing, but if you're busy—"

"I'm not busy," she said a little too quickly.

"Does that mean you might be interested in seeing me this weekend?" The smile was back in his voice.

The fluttery feeling came back even more intensely, but she held it together and walked farther away from the desk so Peter wouldn't eavesdrop. "You can come by on Saturday night. But I'd appreciate it if you'd park your truck down the street. And you'll need to leave before the Tates get up."

"That sounds nice," he said, "but I was thinking more of taking you to dinner."

"Why would you do that?" she asked.

"Why the hell wouldn't I?" He sounded angry again.

"Because we decided we were just friends with benefits," she explained. "Which means you don't have to wine and dine me. I'm what you guys refer to as a sure thing."

"Damn it, Elizabeth!" Brant swore. "I'm taking you to dinner."

"Fine," she said, no longer feeling all aflutter. "But we can't go to Josephine's. Not unless you'll enjoy being tarred and feathered for dessert."

"I was thinking more of flying you to Houston for the weekend."

"Flying? Like on a plane?"

"Are you afraid of flying?"

She wasn't afraid of flying. She was more than a little afraid of losing her mind. She had never felt so loopy in her life. Still, there was no way she would decline another night spent with Brant Cates.

"What time do I need to be ready, and what is the attire?"

"Four…and I liked those baby dolls quite a bit."

"I can't wear pajamas out to—"

He laughed. "I'm teasing, Elizabeth. I'll pick you up at your house on Saturday, and whatever you choose to wear is fine."

The phone clicked, and Elizabeth stood there staring at it until a smile tipped up the corners of her mouth.

It looked as if the old maid of Bramble had a date.

Chapter Twenty-two

Henhouse Rule #49: If you're gonna sling chicken shit, prepare to get hit.

THE MISSION-STYLE MANSION was twice as big as Brant's own house back in Dogwood and surrounded by three times as much land. The house had been built by Lyle Dalton, a man Brant had met on more than a few occasions and liked. What he didn't care for was the way Lyle had run Dalton Oil into the ground. Of course, Lyle's bad business decisions had fed right into Brant and Billy's plan to destroy Bramble. A plan that had dissolved when Billy fell in love with Lyle's widow.

Brant parked the beat-up truck he'd borrowed from the owner of the airstrip in front of the large mansion and climbed out. The flight from Dogwood had taken less time than he'd thought. And since Elizabeth didn't get off work for another two hours, he had plenty of time to visit with his brother.

Seconds after Brant rang the doorbell, the door was pulled open by a boy no bigger than a gnat. From behind him came the sounds of a large family. The low mumble of a television. The hard thump of rap music. A baby's squeals of delight. Husky feminine laughter. And the scream of an angry sibling.

"I swear, Jesse Rutledge Cates!" A dark-headed teen-age girl raced past the door. "If you don't stop taking things from my room and selling them..."

Brant stared down at the little boy who didn't seem to be concerned at all by the racket going on around him. He just stood looking at Brant and stroking the wild blond hair of his naked doll.

"Hi," Brant said, trying not to think about the fact that B.J. had been close to the same age as this little boy when he'd died. "My name is Brant Cates. Is your..." He tried to remember if Billy's adopted kids called him Daddy or by his name. Before he could decide, the door slammed in his face.

Brant blinked, then reached out and pressed the door-bell again. With all the racket, it took a full five minutes for it to be pulled back open. This time by a sullen-looking kid with mussed red hair and calculating brown eyes.

"You here for the iPhone, Mister?"

"No. I'm here to speak to my brother, Billy Cates."

The boy's eyes narrowed, but before he could slam the door, Brant caught it with the toe of his boot. Sending the kid a warning look, he pushed it open and stepped into the foyer.

"Jesse, honey," a woman called out. "Who's at the door?"

"That Bad Bwant!" The little demon who had first answered the door popped up from behind a couch and started shooting Brant with a squirt gun. And not a little squirt gun, but one almost as big as the kid. Brant was thoroughly doused before Billy came around the corner.

"What the—?" When he saw Brant dripping on the tile, Billy's eyes widened and he burst out laughing. He laughed so hard that Brant wondered if he was going to drop the little girl he held in his arms.

"Just what is so doggoned funny, Billy Cates?" A stunningly beautiful woman strutted out from behind Billy, along with the teenage girl. They both took one look at Brant and joined the laughter.

"I'm glad you find this amusing," Brant said, just as another stream of water hit him in the ear.

The woman stopped laughing long enough to take the squirt gun from the little boy. "I think that should about do it, Brody."

"But he's Bad Bwant, Mama," the little boy yelled in a voice too deep to belong to a kid. Billy hooted even louder as Brant shot Brody an annoyed look.

"That would be Uncle Bad Brant to you, Squirt."

Shirlene handed the gun to the teenage girl, and her smile faded. "Well, it's sure nice to know you got yourself a little sense of humor, honey. I was startin' to have my doubts."

Brant pulled off his hat and glanced over at his brother, who had finally pulled himself together.

"I think she's still a little miffed about you not showing up to the wedding," Billy said.

"The wedding I could live with." Shirlene's eyes narrowed. "Shutting down Dalton Oil is another matter."

Hooking an arm around his wife, Billy pulled her close. "I thought we've been over this, Sugar Buns. If you forgave me for trying to shut it down, I figure you can forgive my brother."

"Only because you changed your mind." Shirlene looked back at Brant. "He hasn't."

Brant had never enjoyed eating crow. But the few times it had been served, he'd eaten it without complaint.

"You're right," he said. "I didn't think Dalton Oil was worth the time or effort. But my brother here proved me wrong. After looking at the quarterly reports, I'd say that Dalton Oil is doing much better than I expected." He brushed the water off the brim of his hat. "And about the wedding, I'd like to apologize for not being there. I'd planned on it, but I ran into a bit of unexpected trouble on the way."

"Unexpected trouble?" Shirlene studied him, her green eyes delving and intense. After a few seconds, however, the smile returned. It was just as contagious as Billy's and Beau's. "Well, I guess I can understand that. I've had my share of unexpected trouble in the past year."

Brant held out his hand. "So is it too late to welcome you to the family?"

Shirlene's eyebrows shot up. "Not like that, honey." In two steps, she had Brant in a bear hug. Although she pulled back in a hurry. "Lord, you're soaking wet." She hooked an arm through his. "Come on, honey, let's get you dried off."

Fifteen minutes later, Brant was dressed in his brother's western shirt and sitting on an opulent white couch with a margarita in his hand. His image of a money-grubbing, snooty gold digger had been replaced by the charismatic woman who sat on the couch across from him. A woman who didn't seem to mind if Brody got chocolate from the brownie he was eating on her designer jeans or if Baby Adeline drooled on her expensive blouse. She was as patient as a saint with the kids, getting up numerous times to walk over to the breakfast bar and help Jesse and Mia with their homework.

But it wasn't Shirlene's way with the children that won

Brant over as much as her way with Billy. People had always thought Billy was an easygoing redneck, but Brant knew that beneath his good ol' boy smile was an intensity that bordered on anal. Billy had been almost as wrapped up in the Cates Curse as Brant was. He was the one who had discovered that William Cates's body had never been returned to Lubbock. The one who had plotted Bramble's demise with Brant. That intensity was gone now, replaced with a contentment that seemed to be centered around the redheaded woman who snuggled beneath his arm and looked up at him with adoring eyes.

"...and you better not be gettin' any ideas about hangin' out at Miss Hattie's," Shirlene said. "I'm an extremely possessive woman." She reached out and smoothed down Billy's shirt collar.

The sight brought a pang to Brant's stomach. Mandy had always straightened his shirt collars. Something he'd tried to forget.

Billy grinned. "I'll keep that in mind, Shirley Girl." He looked over at Brant. "I still can't believe you let Beau buy into a house of ill repute."

Jesse's head popped up from his homework. "House of Ill Repute? Is that like The House of Screams that they have in Houston? Man, that's so cool. I can't wait to tell my friends that my uncle owns a haunted house. Can they all get in for free, Uncle Brant?"

Billy choked on laughter, leaving Brant to field the question.

"It's not a haunted house, Jesse. But I think you'll have fun with all the secret passages and old rooms. Once we finish renovating, I'll invite you and a group of your friends out for a night."

As Jesse let out a whoop, Billy turned to Brant. "We? Don't tell me you've bought into Beau's crazy scheme."

Brant set his margarita down. He had never been much of a mixed drink kind of guy and found he missed the smooth brandy of Miss Hattie's. "Actually, I don't think it's so crazy. And while I don't know if I'm sold on the idea of a men's retreat, I do think that Miss Hattie's is a piece of Texas history that shouldn't be lost."

"And what about our grandfather?" Billy asked. "With all your plans of renovating Miss Hattie's have you had time to investigate how he died?"

"I haven't discovered how he died," Brant said. "But I now know for certain that he was at Miss Hattie's. He gave her a silver chest almost identical to the one Daddy inherited from our grandmother. Except this one was dated a good two months after he supposedly died."

Billy sat up even straighter. "You're kidding? So he was killed at Miss Hattie's later?"

"Or maybe not at all," Brant said. "The only proof we have is from a ninety-year-old man who heard it from his grandfather. I located Miss Hattie's journals, but so far they haven't mentioned William Cates. Which means we may never know what happened."

Billy studied him. "And can you live with that, Brant?"

It was funny, but the curse that had consumed him after the death of Mandy and B.J. was no longer such a driving force. It had been pushed out by other things. The renovation of Miss Hattie's. A bunch of crazy old hens. And a librarian with baby soft skin and pretty gold eyes.

Brant glanced down at his watch. He had a good hour before he had to be at Elizabeth's house, but suddenly he didn't want to wait any longer.

He rolled to his feet. "I need to be going."

"Oh no, you don't." Shirlene got up from the couch. "Cristina is making her green chile-infused turkey, and I've already told her to set another spot at the table."

"I'm afraid I'll have to taste that another time," Brant said. "I have a date tonight."

Billy shot him a surprised look. "A date as in with a woman?"

"Is there another kind?" Brant headed for the door, keeping an eye out for Brody, who had disappeared mysteriously. The little boy showed up again when the family congregated around Brant to say good-bye. But this time he only had a cap gun. Still, it was a little disconcerting for Brant to step out the door and know that it was pointed straight at his back.

"Next time, be sure to bring your girlfriend," Shirlene called out as Brant climbed into the pickup.

His girlfriend.

The words rolled around and around in his head as he started the engine and drove down the tree-lined entryway. And soon, the words were joined by the image of Elizabeth sitting at a dinner table with him, Billy, and Shirlene. It was a nice image. So nice that he allowed it to develop into a daydream. And Brant had never been much of a daydreamer. Which probably explained why it got so out of control. One moment, he was enjoying dinner with his brother and sister-in-law, and the next, he was sitting on the white couch with Elizabeth tucked against his side like Shirlene had been tucked against Billy's. Children were playing around their feet, but not Brody and Adeline. These were different children. Children with a mixture of dark and light hair, and gold and blue eyes.

It was a crazy dream. But no matter how crazy it was, it remained with him all the way into Bramble, warming him from the inside out. Making him feel alive and part of a world he'd given up on. He was so wrapped up in the daydream that it took him a moment to realize his phone was buzzing. He pulled it from his shirt pocket and answered.

"M-Mr. Cates?" a quivery female voice came through the receiver. "This is Starlet Brubaker."

He adjusted the phone. "Is everything okay, Starlet? Did something happen to one of the hens?"

"Oh, no. They're all fine." She paused. "It's just that I overheard something that I thought you needed to know."

"Please don't tell me they contacted another girl."

"Actually," Starlet said, her voice clogged with what sounded like tears. "It was your brother I overheard talking."

Knowing how much Starlet was enamored with Beau, Brant thought he knew what had her so upset. "I wouldn't worry about it, Starlet," he said. "Beau talks to a lot of girls. It was probably just one of his childhood friends from Dogwood."

"But it wasn't a friend. It was a doctor."

Just that quickly, Brant's good mood dissipated, and his hands started shaking so badly that he was forced to pull over to the curb.

"What did the doctor say?" he asked. "Is the cancer back?"

"Cancer?" Starlet released an earsplitting sob.

This time, Brant had no patience for the girl's theatrics. "Be quiet!" he ordered. The wailing stopped immediately, and he took a deep breath before he continued.

"Now tell me exactly what happened and what you over-heard."

Starlet sniffed. "I was in Miss Hattie's closet, and I overheard Beau talking on his cell phone. He sounded really upset about some x-ray. Is that why he went to Houston on Monday, Mr. Cates? He went for x-rays?"

Brant had known that Beau had gone to Houston on Monday. But Brant thought he'd gone to hang out with a college buddy. His brother hadn't mentioned anything about tests.

"Where is Beau now, Starlet?" he asked. "Did he head back to Houston?"

"I don't know." Her voice cracked as a sob broke free. "The entire time he was packing, he just kept repeating the same thing... 'I want to live.'"

Chapter Twenty-three

*Henhouse Rule #40: All women have a little "hen"
in them.*

WHOEVER HAD INVENTED EYELASH CURLERS had
never taken into consideration inept women with no
coordination. Elizabeth stared down at the clump of
eyelashes still attached to the brand-new shiny instrument
hooked on her thumb and forefinger. Her gaze moved back
up to the bathroom mirror to verify the fact that the lashes
on the curler belonged to her. They did. The woman who
looked back at her was a good ten lashes short of a row.

The missing lashes weren't the only reason Elizabeth
felt like throwing up.

The new blue eye shadow she'd gotten at Sutter's Pharmacy was too dark, the black eyeliner too thick, and the
rose blush too bright. Instead of the beautiful, sophisti-
cated woman she'd hoped for, Elizabeth looked like a pre-
schooler who had gotten into her mother's makeup.

Dropping the eyelash curler into the sink, she was
reaching for a washcloth with every intention of wiping
off the hideous makeup when the phone rang. She carefully made her way back into the bedroom, trying not to
twist an ankle in her new high-heeled shoes.

She picked up her phone from the dresser and pressed the talk button. "Hello."

"Hi."

Brant's deep voice sent her into hyper mode, and she started removing the curlers that were still in her hair. It was easier said than done. One curler after another got tangled and refused to come out.

"I'm almost ready," she said as she left the curlers dangling and hurried over to the closet to get the black dress she'd bought at Duds 'N Such. "Are you outside?" She finished zipping the dress and stared at herself in the mirror. The dress had looked sexier on the hanger. On her, it looked like a black potato sack with arm holes.

There was a long pause. "Actually, I called to tell you that I can't take you to Houston."

Her shoulders relaxed. "Thank God. To be perfectly honest, I don't think I'm date material. Why don't I fix us something here to eat, and then we can—"

"I can't come over, Elizabeth."

She dropped her hands away from the curlers, not knowing if she felt depressed that he couldn't come over or that he hadn't called her *Beth*. "Oh. Well, that's okay. Did you want me to meet you out at Miss Hattie's?"

There was another long pause, this one much more terrifying than the last.

"Listen, Elizabeth, you were right to keep our relationship on a friendship basis. You don't want to get involved with me. Not when everyone around me seems to..." He released his breath, and she could almost picture him running his hand through his hair. "Look, I need to go, but I want to tell you something first. You're a beautiful

woman, Elizabeth Murphy, and any man would be lucky
to be with you."

The phone clicked dead, and Elizabeth was left to
stare at the image in the mirror of the garishly painted
woman in an ugly black dress and dangling curlers. *Beautiful?* She turned away from the mirror. She wasn't beautiful. If she was beautiful, Brant wouldn't be breaking their
date.

And not just their date, but whatever relationship
they'd had.

No longer in a hurry, Elizabeth took her time unzipping the dress and hanging it back in the closet. It wasn't
even four o'clock, but she still dug through her drawers
until she found her old pair of flannel pajamas. Once she
had them on, she made one more attempt at getting the
curlers out. When she failed, she left them dangling and
walked to the kitchen. She'd been so nervous about her
date that she hadn't eaten lunch, which might explain the
sinking feeling in the pit of her stomach.

She went through every cupboard and refrigerator
shelf, but nothing looked good. She finally settled on a
container of week-old yogurt. Curled up on the couch,
with Atticus cuddled close, she spooned in one bite after
the other and tried to think logically.

Logically speaking, she had never stood a chance with
Brant Cates.

Brant deserved to be with gorgeous women who knew
how to use eyelash curlers and hot rollers. Women who
made anything they put on look sexy. Women who were
comfortable hopping on a private jet and flying to a big
city for dinner. Not some frumpy librarian who had spent
the last fifteen years in a town with only one main street.

A town that suddenly felt like a vast black hole that was sucking her in.

Or maybe it wasn't the town that was a black hole, but her life.

All Elizabeth could see were endless days spent exactly the same way. Shower at six fifteen. Josephine's for tea and toast at eight twenty. Open library at nine. Eight hours later return home.

Home.

She looked around the sterile living room. It didn't feel like home. There were no knickknacks or colorful throw pillows or bright Andy Warhol paintings. It was a depressing thought to realize that The Jungle Room was homier than her house. Despondent, she did something she rarely did. She reached for the television remote. But before she could click it on, the doorbell rang. She was up off the couch in a flash, sending Atticus flying and curlers swinging. She had the door open before she even considered how she must look. She started to make excuses, but they died on her lips when she saw the four women standing on the porch—make that three standing and one sitting in a wheelchair.

"Good God," Minnie said. "What the hell did you do to yourself, Lizzie?" Without waiting for an invitation, she pressed the button on the arm of her chair and almost mowed Elizabeth over.

Elizabeth jumped out of the way just in time. "What are you doing here?"

"We came to cheer you up," Baby said. She pulled a container of ice cream out of a grocery sack and handed it to Elizabeth.

"Because Brant dumped you." Sunshine beamed.

While Elizabeth was trying to figure out how the hens knew she'd been dumped, Minnie rolled farther into the living room and glanced around.

"It's worse than I thought. This house has 'old maid' written all over it."

Even though Elizabeth had been thinking the same thing, she bristled. "I haven't had time to put a lot of effort into decorating. And just how did you know Brant broke our date?"

Minnie examined the books in Elizabeth's bookcase. "Brant talked to me after Starlet told him about Beau flyin' the coop, and he thought you might need some company."

"Beau left?" Elizabeth's eyes narrowed. "What did you do, Minnie?"

"Minnie didn't do anything," Starlet jumped in. For the first time, Elizabeth took a good look at the young woman. She looked worse than Elizabeth. Her cheeks were wet with tears, and her makeup was smudged beneath puffy, bloodshot eyes.

"Beau left because he's…" She released an earsplitting wail, "d-dying!" She flopped down on the couch and placed a hand over her eyes.

For a moment, Elizabeth felt like doing the same thing. "Beau's dying?"

"Now, we don't know that for sure, Starlet." Baby came hurrying back in from the kitchen with a handful of spoons.

Starlet peeked over her arm. "Then why was Brant so upset when he found out Beau had been talking to a doctor right before he left?"

Elizabeth's heart tightened as Starlet's words sank in.

No wonder Brant had broken the date. He had other things to worry about. Like Beau dying. She hated to even think the thought, but there was no getting around it. If Beau had talked with a doctor and then disappeared, something was very wrong. And Elizabeth felt responsible. She was the one who had pushed Beau to go for a check-up. The one who convinced him to make an appointment at the earliest opportunity. And now it looked as if the worst scenario possible had happened. And if she felt this upset by the news, there was no telling how upset Brant would be.

The feeling of icy cold had her glancing down at the small container of ice cream that she was squeezing in her hand. She quickly gave it to Baby before heading toward the bedroom.

"I have to find Brant. He's upset and will need someone to talk to."

Once in her room, she didn't waste any time changing into the jeans and sweater she'd taken from Miss Hattie's. She was standing at the dresser mirror, still struggling with one stubborn curler, when Minnie rolled into the doorway.

"You can't go runnin' off half cocked, Lizzie."

Elizabeth ignored her and pulled a pair of scissors from the top drawer. But before she could snip the curler free, Minnie reached up and grabbed her hand.

"Sit down, Elizabeth," she said. Since it was the first time Minnie had used her given name, Elizabeth found herself listening. Still, she only perched on the edge of the bed as Minnie tried to work the curler free. She was gentler than Elizabeth had expected. Although her next words hurt more than if she had ripped the chunk of hair out by the roots.

"Brant doesn't want to be with you right now. If he did, he would be here. Normally, I'd call him a chicken-livered bastard for breaking his date with you, but sometimes there are good excuses for bad behavior. And I'd say that the fear of losing your brother is a pretty damned good one. Especially for a man who loves his family as much as Brant does." She paused. "But that doesn't mean he won't need you later on."

Tears welled up in Elizabeth's eyes, and not from the gentle tugs on her scalp. "He won't need me later," she said. "In fact, I'll be surprised if I ever see him again."

She waited for Minnie to deny her words. Instead she only confirmed them.

"You might be right." She gently worked to free the curler. "Men can bring a lot of joy to a woman's life. They can also bring a lot of sorrow—and sometimes, unrelenting pain. Which is exactly what happened to your mama."

"My father?" Elizabeth asked.

"No, your father was just an asshole. I'm talking about that bastard Dwayne Connor."

Uncaring of the pressure on her scalp, Elizabeth turned and looked at Minnie. "Dwayne Connor? Who is that?"

Minnie handed Elizabeth the curler and then rolled her chair back a few inches. "Dwayne Connor was your mother's first crush. A no-good, two-bit criminal who preyed on the innocence of a seventeen-year-old girl." She nodded at Elizabeth. "Your mama was a lot like you. She spent most of her time in the library at Miss Hattie's, reading books and dreaming. Then one day, she starts wearing makeup and dresses, and I figure she's found herself a beau." Tears filled Minnie's eyes. "We just didn't realize it was a man six years her senior until after he'd taken her out on a date and raped her."

Elizabeth tried to take a deep breath, but she couldn't seem to fill her lungs. "So that's why she left the henhouse?"

Minnie nodded. "I think she blamed it and the hens as much as she blamed Dwayne."

"Did she press charges?"

"No," Minnie said. "But that didn't mean he didn't get exactly what he had coming to him. We hens watch out for each other."

Elizabeth's eyes widened. "You shot him?"

"No, but I would've liked to. Right where it counts. Instead I just had every law enforcement officer in west Texas keepin' an eye on him. It didn't take long for Dwayne to do something stupid. He robbed a bank in Big Springs and took a pot shot at the sheriff. Turned out the sheriff was a better shot." She searched through the side pocket on her wheelchair and scowled. "Darn fool man, taking my cigarettes."

"So that's why she hates men," Elizabeth whispered under her breath. "And I guess my father leaving her didn't help matters."

"No, I'm sure it didn't." Minnie moved closer and took her hands. "But excuses are like assholes; everyone's got one. And what happened to your mama doesn't excuse what she did to you, Elizabeth. She had no right to put her fears and mistrust on you. People aren't perfect, and some are more imperfect than others. But we can't give up on the entire race because of the actions of one. Brant might not ever call you. And you might meet another man, and he could hurt you as well. That doesn't mean you just give up on living. I can tell you, life is much too short to waste it on fear."

*   *   *

The women stayed the night with Elizabeth, refusing to leave her even when she tried to convince them that she would be all right. She had to admit that there was something comforting about having the house filled to the brim with hens, although Minnie snored so loudly that Elizabeth got very little sleep. At around five o'clock, she gave up and tiptoed through the living room past a sleeping Starlet, who snored even louder than Minnie.

The early morning air was colder than she expected. She started to head back inside for a jacket when she noticed Sunshine sitting cross-legged on the front step of the porch.

"It's too cold to be out here, Sunshine," she said. "Why don't you come on back inside where it's warm?"

Sunshine didn't turn around. "I'm not dumb, you know. I know if I'm cold or not. And I'm not cold."

Elizabeth eased the door closed behind her. "I know you're not dumb. You know things that I'll never know."

Sunshine looked back at her. "Like what?"

"Well," Elizabeth sat down in the wicker rocker, "you knew how to bandage Brant's wound. And you're good at massages. And I could never bend like that, or dance with feather fans."

"The fan dance is easy. Anyone can learn to do it if they have a teacher like your grandmother."

Elizabeth leaned back in the chair. "I've heard that she was quite an amazing woman."

"She wouldn't have lost a good-looking man once she had him, that's for sure." Sunshine turned back around and stretched her arms over her head.

Elizabeth smiled. "No, she wouldn't have. Was she as beautiful as Miss Hattie?"

Sunshine glanced over her shoulder and studied her with clear, innocent eyes. "No. You look more like Miss Hattie."

If she hadn't worried about Sunshine's feelings, she would've laughed. Instead, she wrapped her arms around herself and rocked back and forth in the chair. After a while, the sun peeked over the horizon, spreading a layer of orange marmalade on the roofs of the houses across the street. She had spent most of the night listening to Minnie's snores and thinking about everything that she had learned in the last few hours—Beau's cancer and what had happened to her mother. Now her mind took a break and just enjoyed the view.

"We won't be able to stay, will we?" Sunshine finally spoke.

Elizabeth lifted her head from the back of the rocker. "What?"

"Now that Beau is gone, we'll have to leave the henhouse."

Elizabeth had so many things cluttering her brain that she hadn't given much thought to what Beau's leaving meant to the henhouse. Now that he was sick, it was doubtful that he would want to finish the renovations and reopen it. And Brant had never been interested in the house for anything besides answers about his grandfather's death.

Which meant that Sunshine was right. The hens would have to move.

Elizabeth was surprised at how upset the thought made her, especially when no more than a few weeks ago she was the one who had wanted the hens out. But that was before she had come to know the three women. Before

Starlet had arrived. Before she had heard all the stories about her ancestors. Before she realized that Minnie was right; the henhouse wasn't just a whorehouse.

It was her heritage.

The sun finally crested over the roofs, spilling onto the porch and warming the chill from her cheeks.

"No one is leaving the henhouse, Sunshine," Elizabeth said. "Us hens have to stick together."

Chapter Twenty-four

Henhouse Rule #22: Always take a bull by his horn.

CANCER OR NO, Brant was going to kill Beau.

It had taken Brant a good five weeks to locate his brother. Five weeks of hell where he hadn't been able to concentrate on anything but the image of Beau wasting away in some seedy hotel room. Except that the cocky cowboy who stood on the railing of the rodeo chute didn't look like he was wasting away. He looked as virile and healthy as the huge Brahma bull that slammed against the railing beneath his boots.

While Brant watched in disbelief, Beau secured his cowboy hat and settled down on the bull's back.

"Tonight we're lucky enough to have a new rider," the announcer's voice echoed around the high ceiling of the indoor arena. "Hope you folks will give a warm welcome to Beau Cates, who will be riding Pissed Off."

Pissed Off?

Oh, Brant was pissed off, all right. He was so spitting mad he could hardly see straight. He shoved his way through the group crowded against the railing next to the chutes, not even realizing they were young women until one spoke.

"I'd like to be his first ride," a blonde in a bright pink shirt gushed.

"Who wouldn't?" another said. "Did you see his hair? High ho, Silver." She waved her cowboy hat over her head.

The gaggle of girls giggled and pushed closer to the railing. Realizing he wasn't going to make it through the rodeo groupies in time, Brant gave up and yelled over their heads.

"Beauregard!"

Beau stopped adjusting the bull rope around his hand and looked up. He registered surprise before a smile eased over his face.

"Come to watch the show, Big Bro?"

The crowd of girls shifted as they turned to look at Brant. He took the opportunity given him to move closer to the rail. "Quit messing around and get your ass off that animal. Now!"

Beau's smile got even bigger. "No can do. But I wouldn't worry too much. I only plan on staying on for a few seconds. Eight to be exact."

"Beauregard," Brant said, but the warning had barely hissed through his gritted teeth before Beau nodded and the gate flew open.

The eight seconds Beau had mentioned seemed more like eight hours. Time slowed to a heart-stopping drip that had Brant gripping the cold railing in his hands as he watched his brother try to stay on the kicking, twisting beast.

Beau surprised him. Instead of being bucked off as soon as the bull was released from the pen, he continued to hold on. And not just hold on, but actually resemble a pro bull rider. With each high-kick of the bull, Beau's back arched, his legs gripped the bull's sides, and one hand waved above his head. The buzzer went off, but Brant couldn't release his breath until Beau was safely on the ground.

It happened in a blink. One second, Beau was riding, and the next, he was sailing through the air. He landed with a bone-crushing thump right beneath where Brant stood. Brant's heart skipped a beat until Beau jumped to his feet, flashing a smile and a wave at the cheering crowd.

Unfortunately, the bull wasn't as happy. It whirled around and came directly at Beau with horns lowered. Without thinking, Brant grabbed onto the railing and catapulted down into the clumped dirt of the arena. His landing attracted the bull's attention, and the animal swung in his direction. He braced for the hit, but before he went flying over the bull's horns, a rodeo clown flapped a red silk hankie in front of the crazed animal's eyes. The bull turned toward the new distraction. The other clowns helped out, and soon the bull was directed back toward the holding pens, the gate slamming closed behind him.

Beau picked up his hat and dusted it off on his thigh. "Now that is what I call fun."

It took all three rodeo clowns to pull Brant off his brother.

"Damn, Brant," Beau said as he pressed the bag of ice that the bartender had given him to his nose. "I think you broke it."

Brant took another drink from the long-necked bottle. "You're lucky I didn't break every bone in your body."

"Too late." Beau rolled his shoulder. "I think Pissed Off might've beaten you to it. That was one ornery bull." He lowered the ice pack and looked at Brant through the eye that wasn't swollen shut. "I would've gotten out of the way, Brant. That was one of the first lessons I learned from you—steer clear of trouble."

"Then what the hell were you doing on the back of that bull?"

"Living."

"Well, if you keep that shit up," Brant said, "you won't be living for long."

Beau paused, the beer bottle inches from his mouth. "I might not be anyway."

The words took the last of the anger out of Brant, and the hopeless despair that he'd been living with for the last month returned. He should be used to the feeling. It had been his constant companion for years—after Buckley had died, then years later when Mandy and B.J. were killed. But somehow, this time it seemed worse. The news that Beau's cancer had returned had completely broadsided Brant, leaving him frustrated and angry. And so scared that his hand shook as he drained the last of the beer.

It was his own fault. He had let down his guard. Had started to believe that his luck had changed. That happiness was within his reach. But it had all been an illusion. There would be no happy ending for him.

Or, it seemed, for his little brother.

That's what tore Brant up the most. He might be able to jump in front of a pissed off bull and save Beau, but there was no way to jump in front of a disease. All he could do was sit back and watch as his brother got trampled.

The bartender brought over two more beers and set them down. "Those two young ladies at the end of the bar would like to buy you fellas a couple drinks."

Brant glanced down the bar at the two women in the short jean skirts and boots. They waggled their fingers at him. He acknowledged them with a tip of his head before declining the beers.

"Tell them thanks, but we can't stay." As the bartender left with the two beers, Brant slipped off the stool. "We need to be going. I called Doctor Thornton while the rodeo doc was checking you out and told him to meet us at the hospital."

Beau smiled at the women before turning back to Brant. "Maybe you weren't interested, but I was. And when are you going to figure out that I'm not the baby brother who used to follow you around everywhere you went? I'm a big boy now, Brant. And I'm not going to any hospital."

For a second, Brant thought about grabbing Beau by the back of the shirt and physically dragging him out. But then common sense prevailed, and he set his hat back down on the bar and took a seat.

"I realize the news about the cancer coming back shocked you, Beau. And I understand that anyone would need some time alone to adjust to that. I even understand why you wanted to ride that damned bull. But with the cancer back, we don't have time to waste. We need to get you into treatment now."

Beau dropped the ice bag and looked at him. "Doc Thornton told you I had cancer?"

Brant shook his head. "He refused to tell me anything, even after I threatened him with bodily harm and C-Corp taking back the money for the new wing."

The laughter that came out of Beau's mouth worried Brant. Obviously, his brother was closer to the edge than he had first thought. Of course, he had to be pretty damned upset in order to climb on the back of a Brahma bull.

Brant motioned for the bartender and ordered two double shots of whiskey. When they arrived, he downed one before handing the other to his brother.

Beau stopped laughing long enough to toss the drink back, but was still chuckling when he set his glass on the bar. "I'm sorry, but the thought of you threatening a little bald-headed doctor is pretty funny, and so is Doc refusing to give in to my big bad brother. I never really cared for the man, but now I think he's growing on me. So who told you I had cancer?"

"Starlet overheard your phone conversation and called me. Of course, she didn't quite understand what she had overheard until I mentioned cancer. Then she started sobbing so loudly she almost broke my eardrum."

Beau's smile faded. "She was crying?"

"Wailing would be a better description," Brant said. "She's a dramatic little thing."

"And a bad eavesdropper," Beau said as he finished off his beer.

"What do you mean?"

"Doc Thornton said that the test results weren't conclusive. He saw what looked like a suspicious spot on one of my lungs, but he wanted to run more tests to be sure."

To say Brant was relieved would be putting it mildly. It felt as if the weight of the world had lifted off his shoulders, and he hugged his brother close, uncaring of the narrow-eyed looks he received from the rough cowboys that filled the Austin bar.

"That's great news, Beau." He pulled back and reached for his hat. "Which is even more reason to get back to the hospital."

Beau stopped him. "I'm not going to a hospital, Brant."

"I don't understand. There's a chance that it could be anything. A shadow. A mistake of the radiologist. Or something that's completely benign."

"Or it could be cancer," Beau stated.

"But you won't know until they run more tests."

Beau released his breath. "I know this is hard for you to understand. You haven't spent a year of your life being poked and prodded, undergoing all kinds of tests and treatment. I went through all of it, Brant. The radiation. The chemo. The sickness. The hair loss."

He paused as if remembering the horrors. "Don't get me wrong. I appreciated you, Billy, and Beckett—and even crazy Brianne—shaving your heads so I wouldn't feel like a freak. But shaving your head isn't the same as having no hair on your entire body, including your testicles.

"But I survived it. I did everything any doctor asked me to do with a smile on my face. I did it because I didn't want to die, but also, because I didn't want to hurt you, Brant. Because I didn't want you to go through the pain you went through when you lost Mandy and B.J."

He placed a hand on Brant's shoulder. "I'm not telling you this to make you feel guilty. I'm telling you this so you'll understand why I can't go through it again—why I won't go through it again. If the cancer has metastasized to my lungs, we both know that my days are numbered. So it makes no difference if I go back for more tests or not. And if I only have a few days left, I want them filled with something other than pain. I want to experience life to the fullest. Try things I've always wanted to do, but might never get a chance to."

"Like riding a Brahma bull." Brant spoke around the

wall of pain in his chest. Beau flashed his grin. A grin Brant wasn't sure he could live without.

"Yeah," Beau said. "That and a whole lot of other things that would make you crazy if I told you. Did you tell Mama and Daddy about the cancer?" When Brant shook his head, Beau squeezed his shoulder. "I'm counting on you to continue to keep it a secret. Not only from our parents, but from the rest of the family. It will only make them worry."

"And if it is cancer?" Brant couldn't keep the quiver from his voice. "If there's a chance I could've saved you and didn't, how will I live with myself then?"

"Damn it, Brant. Stop trying to save the world. You couldn't stop Buckley from being a teenager and attempting to outrun a train. You couldn't stop a tornado from leveling your house. And you can't stop cancer from killing me. Call it fate or divine will, shit happens, Big Bro, and there's not one thing you can do to stop it."

"So that's it?" Brant glanced over at him. "I'm just supposed to let my little brother walk off into the sunset and never worry about him again. Because that's not going to happen, Beau."

Beau leaned closer. "I'm not walking off into the sunset. As long as I'm breathing, I'll still be family. I'll still call my big brother for advice. And I'll still stop by Miss Hattie's when I'm in the neighborhood. How's the renovation coming, anyhow?"

Brant held the shot glass up to the bartender. "I stopped renovations when I heard about you."

Beau scowled at him. "Sometimes you can be such an asshole, Brant."

"Because I've been more worried about you than a dilapidated old house?"

"No, because you're more worried about me than your own happiness. Miss Hattie's is good for you. You smiled there more than you've smiled since Mandy and B.J. died. You can't tell me that you don't love the history of the house, or hanging out in that weed-infested garden, or talking with those crazy old hens."

It was true. He had loved those things, but Beau's illness had eclipsed everything. Well, maybe not everything. It hadn't eclipsed Elizabeth. Even when he was insane with worry about his little brother, Elizabeth had slipped in. He went to sleep at night with the scent of lilacs and amber eyes clinging to the edges of his mind. Woke up with the strong desire to find her sleeping next to him. And in between, he dreamed of her. Finding his only redemption in the warmth of her arms and the heat of her body.

"So if you stopped renovations, I wonder how they pulled it off," Beau said as he accepted one of the shots the bartender had brought over. "Even with the money I left them, it couldn't have been easy for three old gals."

Brant downed his shot and savored the wave of alcohol bliss. "What couldn't be easy?"

"Reopening Miss Hattie's," Beau said as he turned on the stool and leaned back against the bar. "Is it my imagination or are we being mad-dogged?"

"You must've misunderstood, Beau. There's no way the hens could reopen Miss Hattie's," Brant said as he swiveled around on his stool to see what his brother was talking about. Beau was right. The entire bar did seem to be mad-dogging them.

"Then how do you explain the invitations that were sent out? It appears that the list we made up of prospective clients was used wisely. Miles Cooper called me the other day and couldn't wait to talk about the grand opening of Miss Hattie's. He's viewing his invitation like an invitation to the Playboy mansion."

Brant's gaze moved away from the mean-looking crowd. "When?"

"This Saturday," Beau said before the biggest cowboy Brant had ever seen walked up to them and tipped back his Stetson.

"We don't take kindly to your kind," the man said around a mouthful of chew.

"And what kind would that be?" Beau asked.

Another man stepped up. "The type that goes around ignorin' beautiful women and huggin' on men. This here is a hetter-o-sexual bar. So we figure it's time for you two sensitive girlie guys to find another place to drink."

Brant was still trying to absorb the fact the hens had sent out invitations for Miss Hattie's reopening so it took him a moment to react to the ludicrous assumption. A moment that had Beau slipping his arm around Brant's neck and tugging him closer.

"Well, I'm as sorry as I can be to hear that," Beau said in an exaggerated effeminate voice. "Because me and my partner aren't finished with our drinks." He turned to Brant. "Are we, honey?"

Brant lifted an eyebrow. "So am I to assume that a bar fight is something else you'd like to experience?"

Beau didn't even finish flashing his smile before a fist plowed into his jaw.

Chapter Twenty-five

Henhouse Rule #41: If a hen has time to lean, she's got time to clean.

ELIZABETH WAS EXHAUSTED. But it was a good tired, the kind that came after accomplishing a huge task. After close to six weeks of constant work, the restorations on Miss Hattie's were almost complete. There were still a few workers around, touching up baseboards, setting up the computer in the library, and hanging the chandelier in the foyer. But for the most part, Miss Hattie's was ready for the grand opening. The exterior boasted a brand-new red metal roof and freshly painted wood siding, multi-paned windows, and pretty green shutters. The sagging porch had been replaced, the weeds cleared from the front, and Elizabeth had planted brightly colored mums in the flowerbed like the ones at her house.

Surprisingly, the inside hadn't taken as much work. The banister and hardwood floors had had to be sanded, stained, and sealed, but the rest of the work had been cosmetic—a fresh coat of paint, new linoleum in the kitchen, and the elevator oiled and refitted with new hardware and two shiny metal doors.

The biggest chore had been pulling all the things out

of the barn and attic, cleaning off the cobwebs and mouse feces, and sending them to be refinished or reupholstered. It was a daunting task. Elizabeth didn't know how much furniture the hens had sold before she got there, but it appeared that they had twice as much stored. Fortunately, they'd retained the older antiques. Antiques from Hattie's time. Huge armoires, four-poster beds, loveseats, lavishly carved sideboards, and a dining room table and chairs that could've easily been at King Arthur's court. There were Tiffany stained-glass lamps similar to the ones in Miss Hattie's room, Persian rugs and velvet drapes, and lead-crystal wineglasses and fine English china.

Along with more books than there were in Bramble's library.

The antiques were so plentiful that Minnie could've easily sold some of them and made enough to buy out the Cateses. Of course, when Elizabeth had suggested doing just that, the older hen had refused to even consider it. Not only did she refuse to part with anything that had belonged to the head hens, but she had some crazy belief that the Cates brothers would be back.

"They need Miss Hattie's as much as us hens," she'd said. "They'll be back. You mark my words."

Elizabeth hadn't argued. Not only because she'd yet to win an argument with Minnie, but because she had a secret hope Minnie was right. She wanted Brant to come back. She wanted to see his face one more time. To hear his voice. And yes, to feel his arms. And when she wasn't working on the house, she was reading the journals, searching for any tidbit of information about Brant's grandfather in hopes that she could use it as an excuse to call Brant.

She didn't find anything. The diaries didn't mention a William Cates once. It mentioned every other man. Including a man named Harry, who popped up about three years in and was mentioned in almost every entry thereafter.

Harry smiled at me for the first time today, and my world became about seven shades brighter. When Harry cuddles next to me, I feel like I could just float away on happiness. I wish I could keep Harry with me forever, but the hens don't agree.

It went on and on until Elizabeth actually grew sick of Harry. Even today, as she stretched out on Miss Hattie's bed reading one of the notebooks, she couldn't help but skip over the entries that had Harry's name in them. What she didn't skip over was an entry about The Jungle Room.

The new designer came out today to redo The Jungle Room. He sleeps on the wrong side of the bed, but, boy, can that man dance. We stayed up most of the night cutting a rug—

Elizabeth's hand slipped off the edge of the book. It fell closed as her mind struggled to fit the pieces together. It didn't take long. Especially when she knew how devious Minnie could be. She should've been mad that Minnie had tricked her. Instead, she was mildly amused by the woman's audacity.

Taking the diary with her, Elizabeth walked into Miss Hattie's closet and pushed back the long, formal dresses to reveal the door that led down to The Jungle Room. Unfortunately, when she reached the bottom of the stairs, she didn't find Minnie. Instead there was only Starlet, sitting on the couch strumming a guitar.

Elizabeth hadn't realized Starlet owned a guitar, or that she could play so well. Her fingers ran over the strings without thought as she started to sing. Elizabeth braced herself for the booming off-key voice. Instead, the sound that came out of Starlet's mouth was soft and sweet, with just enough country twang to bring forth images of small towns and home.

The song was about a kiss, a good-bye kiss that started a love affair and, at the same time, ended it. Starlet's softer voice wasn't perfect. It didn't hit all the right notes with all the right pitches, but it was that imperfection that made it so captivating. The quiver of youth and raw emotion struck a chord inside of Elizabeth that had tears trickling down her cheeks.

A sob escaped, causing Starlet to glance up and stop singing mid-chorus. Setting the guitar down, she hurried over to Elizabeth and pulled her into her arms.

"It's okay," Starlet said as she awkwardly thumped her on the back. "I guess it finally sank in. Miss Minnie said it would. She said that sometimes women don't figure out that they love a man until he's gone."

Elizabeth wanted to deny Starlet's words, but realized she couldn't. Minnie was right. It took Brant leaving to figure out that she loved him, that she had loved him from the moment he tumbled into her bed.

Once the realization hit her, there was no holding back the tears.

"I don't know how it happened," she sobbed. "I had it all planned out. We were just going to be friends."

"That's the worst kind." Starlet's voice quivered. "It's those friends that will get you every time."

"But I'm not even his type," Elizabeth continued. "I'm a frumpy old librarian who doesn't know how to dress or curl my eyelashes."

"M-Me neither," Starlet started sobbing. "And I look like a big fat cow in a prom dress, which is probably why Beau only gave me a quick kiss good-bye. Who wants to kiss a big fat cow in a prom dress?"

The thought of Beau leaving had both of them crying even harder. They stood there clinging to one another and sobbing out their heartache.

"You're not fat, Starlet," Elizabeth said. "You're what men would call curvaceous."

"And you're not frumpy," Starlet said. "You're what men would call skinny."

It wasn't exactly a compliment, but Elizabeth decided it wasn't the time to point that out.

"Would you look at us?" she sniffed and pulled back. "If the hens could see us, they'd be getting out the ice cream all over again."

Starlet's watery eyes lit up. "Maybe that's not a bad idea."

Elizabeth laughed. "Maybe not." She looked over at the guitar on the floor. "I didn't know you could play."

Starlet walked over and picked it up. "I'm not very good. You should hear my cousin play. Now she's got talent."

Elizabeth hadn't had much time to talk with Starlet since the night she had showed up on her porch with the hens. She had been too busy with the restorations. But she had heard Minnie and the hens discussing the young woman, trying to come up with ideas that would build her self-esteem. Maybe Elizabeth had stumbled onto it.

"I think you've got talent," she said. "That was one of the most touching songs I've ever heard. What's the name of it?"

Starlet shrugged. "I was thinking about calling it 'The Good-bye Kiss.' Does that sound too stupid?"

Elizabeth stared at her in disbelief. "You wrote that?"

She blushed and nodded. "I wrote it for Beau after he…" Her voice trailed off. "It doesn't matter. He'll never get to hear it."

"You don't know that for a fact, Starlet," Elizabeth said. "He could come back. But even if he doesn't, other people should get to hear that song. In fact, Baby plans on singing at the grand opening. I don't know why you couldn't sing as well."

Starlet shook her head. "I wouldn't be comfortable singing something I wrote. I'm much better at performing show tunes."

The thought of Starlet bellowing out a show tune at the grand opening had Elizabeth clearing her throat. "Yes, well, sometimes a person needs to step out of their comfort zone and try something different. Stretch their wings, so to speak."

"Is that why you decided to help reopen the henhouse? You wanted to stretch your wings?"

Elizabeth hadn't really thought about it like that, but now that she did, she realized that Starlet was right. Reopening the henhouse had been a step out of her comfort zone. And so was loving Brant. She was surprised to discover that she regretted neither one.

"Yes." She leaned closer and whispered, "But don't tell Minnie that I've loved every second of it."

"Oh, she already knows," Starlet said. "She figures it will only be a matter of time before you quit your job in Bramble and move back in with us."

It seemed very unlikely. Elizabeth had enjoyed being

part of bringing Miss Hattie's back to life, but it was hard to imagine herself living here. She glanced down at the journal that was still in her hand.

"Where is Minnie?"

"She's in the kitchen with Baby, making Sunshine some chicken noodle soup for her cold," Starlet said. "Minnie's worried sick that Sunshine won't be able to perform the night of the grand opening."

As Elizabeth turned to the elevator, she wondered if that wasn't for the best. It was one thing to have Baby and Starlet sing and another to have a woman perform a strip-tease.

Elizabeth didn't find Minnie in the kitchen. She found her in the lilac garden, puffing away on a cigarette. When she saw Elizabeth, she quickly tossed it into the weeds.

"You know you could burn down the entire house with your negligence," Elizabeth said as she walked out to her.

"Nothing has burned up yet," she said. "And I've been doin' it now for going on fifty-seven years."

"I'm sure that was when the weeds weren't almost past your head." Elizabeth pushed back the tall weed and made sure the cigarette was out. "I don't know why you refused to let the lawn company finish the garden."

"Because this garden is Branston's project. And he needs to finish it."

Elizabeth sat down in the lawn chair next to her. "He's not coming back, Minnie. And it's time we both face it."

"He'll be back."

"Because of this?" Elizabeth lifted the diary. "This isn't Miss Hattie's, is it."

Minnie studied the book for only a second before

she cackled. "It took you long enough to figure that out, Lizzie. What gave it away? Buddy Holly or did I mention my infatuation with Clint Eastwood?"

"The designer from Dallas," Elizabeth said.

"Darn fool." Minnie shook her head. "Good dancers have always made me forget myself."

Elizabeth handed the book back to her. "So you lied to keep Brant and Beau here so they would save Miss Hattie's."

"The house had nothin' to do with it. Beau wantin' to buy the house was as big a shock to me as it was to you. The diary was all about getting you in touch with your hen-ness."

Elizabeth relaxed back in the chair. She should be mad at Minnie for her manipulation and for wasting her time looking for something that wasn't there. But surprisingly, she wasn't. Elizabeth had enjoyed reading the diaries of an outspoken woman who refused to hide from anything. Not the people who criticized her for her profession. Or the bill collectors who barked at her door like wolves. Or a prudish librarian who was convinced her mother had been right.

Minnie's diaries had helped Elizabeth understand the woman behind the layer of makeup and sharp comments. Helped her to realize that Minnie wasn't a crazy old prostitute who needed to be locked away in a retirement home. She was a woman to be admired. A woman who believed in women's rights. In donating to charities. And volunteering with veterans. A good woman who loved to dance to Buddy Holly. Enjoyed a strong drink and a good smoke. And who cared about the men who came to visit her—especially a man named Harry.

"I'm sorry, Minnie," Elizabeth said. When Minnie glanced over at her, she continued. "I'm sorry I tried to get you to move. I'm sorry I didn't take the time to listen to you and understand that Miss Hattie's was so much more than just a..." She left the sentence incomplete.

A smile bloomed on Minnie's face. It was the first time Elizabeth had seen her smile like that. It wasn't a sly grin or a smirk. This smile completely consumed her withered face and lit her eyes with happiness and tears.

"Is," she stated in her no-nonsense voice. "Miss Hattie's *is* more than just a whorehouse. And it always will be."

Chapter Twenty-six

Henhouse Rule #19: Never surprise a man when his pants are down.

MISS HATTIE'S HENHOUSE had come back to life. From the newly bricked circular drive to the peak of the weathervane that spun in the stiff west Texas breeze, the house was the exact replica of what it had looked like in the eighteen hundreds. Except no dull sepia picture could convey the majestic allure of the mansion Brant Cates stood in front of.

He felt like he had stepped out of a time machine. Or possibly onto a movie set. Everything, including the full harvest moon that hung low in the sky, seemed surreal and almost... magical. It was as if the house had a life of its own. As if it beckoned all weary men to come inside and find peace. The stone fountain in front trickled and splashed its soothing symphony. Each window glowed with a welcoming warmth. And even the wind carried the calming scent of lilacs.

But Brant wasn't calm. He was angry. Angry that he had been so hungover and battered from his bar fight with Beau that he hadn't been able to get there in time to thwart whatever craziness the hens had thought up.

Hopefully, they weren't planning on doing what he

thought they were planning on doing—reopening Miss Hattie's with all the services offered in the eighteen hundreds. Although it seemed possible, given that the only people climbing out of the trucks and SUVs parked in front were men. Of course, that had been Beau's plan as well. But Brant couldn't see the hens being happy with just serving food and drinks. Whatever was going to take place tonight wasn't going to be good. And what made it even worse was that Brant's name was still on the deed.

As he made his way up the porch steps, he couldn't help but notice the new solid oak pillars, the glazed cement floor, and the freshly painted railing. And maybe that was another reason Brant was angry.

The hens had restored Miss Hattie's without him.

Beau had been right. Working on Miss Hattie's had been good for Brant. It had taken his mind off the tragedies of the past and had given him something to look forward to in the future. He'd started to believe that if there was a chance an old dilapidated house could be brought back to life, there was a chance that he could, too.

"It ain't quite right."

Startled out of his thoughts, Brant turned to find an ancient old man sitting in one of the new wicker rockers that sat on the porch.

"The roof's a little brighter," the old man continued. "And the color of the sidin' is off a couple shades." He switched the lump of tobacco in his mouth to the other side, revealing a set of toothless gums in the porch light. "But when the roof and paint weathers a bit it should be close enough."

Brant took off his cowboy hat. "You were here when it was still open?"

The man pulled out a bent plastic cup from his shirt pocket and spit a stream of tobacco into it. "More than a few times." He wiped off his mouth with the back of his hand and squinted up at Brant. "You get one of them fancy invites?"

That was something else that pissed off Brant. He was partial owner, and he didn't even get an invitation?

"Surprised the hell out of me when I opened that dadgum mailbox and found mine." The old guy shook his head. "I didn't exactly leave Miss Hattie's on the best of terms."

Brant probably should've gone inside and put a stop to whatever the hens were up to. Instead, he couldn't help but sit down next to the man. As he eased back in the chair, he released a groan.

"Looks like you got in a tangle yourself," the old man said.

"That's an understatement." Brant stared out at the road and the sign that had been repainted. The words TRESPASSERS WILL BE PROSTITUTED were now the same green as the shutters. "So tell me about Miss Hattie's," he said. "What was it like?"

The man shook his head. "I can't tell you about the early days. I wasn't here during Miss Hattie's reign, but by the time I was old enough to get in, it was still like nothing you could ever imagine." He grinned his toothless grin at the memory. "It was like a beautiful oasis smack dab in the middle of a dry, unforgivin' land. There was music and laughter and the finest food, drink, and smokes a man could ask for without havin' to spend a fortune. In fact, money was never an issue at Hattie's. If you had some, you gave it. If you didn't, you gave extra when you did.

'Course, the rich fellers didn't seem to mind carryin' the load for us poor folks. When you walked through the door of Miss Hattie's, all men were created equal."

He paused to spit. "Dirt poor farmers mingled with wealthy oil men. And I figure there were more than a few criminals mixed in to boot. 'Course if Miss Millicent found out you were the unsavory sort, you got tossed out on your ear. That woman didn't put up with any tomfoolery."

"And were you one of the ones to get kicked out?" Brant asked.

There was a long silence, and Brant wondered if the old guy had gone to sleep, but then his voice came out soft and heartfelt.

"I guess you could call it tomfoolery. I fell in love with her and asked her to marry me."

"And she tossed you out for that?"

He looked back at Brant. "She tossed me out for expecting her to leave Miss Hattie's." He shook his head. "And she was right. It was a foolish notion."

"But how could she expect you to marry her and still allow her to be a—"

"Watch it, son," the older man said. "Or I'll add a black eye to the one you already got. Miss Millicent is the finest woman you'd ever want to meet."

Brant had to admire the old guy for sticking up for his woman after all these years. It was too bad that Miss Millicent was long gone. He got to his feet. "What do you say we go inside and see if the brandy and cigars are still as good?"

The old guy nodded. "Might as well."

Even if Brant had only been involved in the planning stages, he couldn't help feeling a twinge of pride when he stepped through the front door. The inside of Miss Hattie's was more amazing than the outside. A soft Persian rug cushioned his feet, a huge crystal chandelier glittered overhead, and the grand staircase gleamed in rich, high-polished mahogany. The doors of all the rooms were thrown open, and men of all ages lounged in overstuffed chairs and couches with glasses in one hand and cigars in the other.

The hum of a wheelchair drew Brant's attention, and he turned to see Minnie rolling out from around the staircase. Gone was the hideous magenta wig, and in its place was a head of soft silver hair and artfully done makeup. Instead of the gaudy negligee, she wore a pretty red gown that reminded Brant of Miss Hattie's.

The swift kick of pain that punched him in the gut took him by surprise. It shouldn't have. Since stepping from his truck, Elizabeth had never been far from his mind. Luckily, Minnie didn't notice his reaction. It appeared she only had eyes for the little old man standing next to Brant, holding his water-stained felt hat over his heart.

"Hello, Millicent. You're lookin' as pretty as ever."

Millicent? Brant looked back at Minnie, who was actually blushing. Without the thick makeup and wig there was something very familiar about her features.

"Hello, Moses," Minnie said with a smile. "Long time, no see."

Brant's gaze shifted back to the man. Moses? As in Moses Tate? But before he could confirm the man's identity, Baby came hurrying into the room. If she had looked like Marilyn before, it was nothing compared to how much she looked like the actress now. In the white dress and red lipstick, she was a carbon copy. All she needed was a puff of air blowing up her skirt to finish the picture.

She leaned down to Minnie. "She threw up three times while I was getting her ready, but I think she's going to go through with it." She glanced up and saw Brant, then gasped and covered her mouth.

"Who threw up?" he asked.

Baby started to stammer, but Minnie cut her off. "Starlet. She's performing tonight and has a little stage fright, is all." She noticed Brant's face for the first time. "What the hell happened to you?"

Brant ignored the question. "I'm warning you, Minnie. If you are intending something else for Starlet, I'm going to have you carted off to an old folks' home."

"Over my dead body," Moses said as his eyes narrowed on Brant.

"Enough," Minnie held up her hand. "I don't want any fighting tonight." She looked around and a peaceful smile slipped over her face. "Not when my dream has finally come true. I just want to sit back and enjoy it. And as far as Starlet is concerned, I would never do anything to harm that child. She's going to make us hens proud. If you stick around for a while, you'll see just what I'm talking about."

She whipped the chair around and spoke in a voice loud enough to be heard clear to Dogwood. "If you fine gentlemen will follow me into the ballroom, we have something very special in store for you."

If Starlet was performing, special didn't quite cover it. The poor girl was about to be completely humiliated, and Brant wasn't about to let that happen. Unfortunately, the men didn't waste much time following after Minnie. They emerged from every room like ants on the way to a picnic and proceeded to block Brant from getting to her.

It was an eclectic group of men. Brant recognized a

banker, an older senator, a natural gas mogul, Sheriff Hicks, and one of the contractors he'd hired to restore Miss Hattie's. When the contractor saw Brant, he tried to hide behind one of his carpenters, but Brant reached out and stopped him.

"Hello, Hank," Brant said. "You care to explain how Miss Hattie's got finished? Especially since I instructed you to stop the renovations."

Hank swallowed hard. "Well, sir, uhh...those hens can be pretty persuasive. And the boys and me didn't see any harm in doing a little extra work for them on the side."

"A little?" Brant glanced around.

Hank coughed. "Well, maybe more than a little. I couldn't seem to keep the boys away once Miss Minnie told them that they were all invited to the grand opening and would be the first to get to spend the night once the place was in full operation."

"Is it in full operation, Hank?" Brant asked.

"No, sir," he said. "We still need to do some work in the upstairs bedrooms, but Miss Lizzie thought it was important to get people talking."

Brant's heart thumped in overtime. "Miss Lizzie as in Miss Elizabeth Murphy?" He must've looked a little angry because Hank took a step back.

"Yes, sir. Miss Liz—Elizabeth has been the one in charge of all the renovations. And I'll tell you one thing, that woman runs a tight ship. I'd hire her myself if she wasn't going to run Miss Hattie's."

Brant's shock was such that the foyer was completely empty by the time he snapped out of it. *Elizabeth was going to run Miss Hattie's?* Hank had to be mistaken. There was no way that Elizabeth wanted to be associated with the house. Once he and Beau had signed the letter of intent, she couldn't get away fast enough.

Still, Hank didn't seem like the type of man who got his information wrong.

The soft strum of a guitar had Brant moving toward the ballroom. The room was so crowded that he couldn't see who played the instrument. But he could hear. He braced himself for Starlet's off-key voice. Instead, a sweet youthful sound swelled over the heads of the gathered men. There was something about the voice that made Brant feel lonely and, at the same time, completely loved.

It must've had the same effect on the other men in the room because they collectively moved closer. Brant skirted the edge of the ballroom until he could see who it was that was singing. The young woman perched on the edge of the bar stool with the guitar strapped around her shoulder looked like Starlet, yet completely different.

Gone was the awkward girl in a too-tight prom dress. In her place was a shy young woman in a simple blue dress that fit to perfection. She sang with her eyes closed and her chin tipped toward the ceiling. Sang like a woman who had known love and lost it. The song ended on a soft, sweet note, and her hand rested against the strings of the guitar.

There was a slight hesitation before the men applauded, but no one louder than Brant. He couldn't explain it, but he almost felt like a proud father. When Starlet's gaze fell on him, he couldn't help but give her a broad smile and a thumbs-up. She answered with a smile of her own before mouthing one word.

Beau?

Brant knew how she felt. He still worried about Beau,

but he had also come to terms with the fact that there wasn't a thing he could do about it. Beau was a grown man with his own mind. A man who wouldn't want Starlet to waste her youth worrying about him. He touched his forefinger and thumb together in an okay sign, and Starlet's shoulders sagged in relief as Minnie rolled in front of her.

"If you gentlemen will move back a few steps, we have one more surprise for you. This next performance was started way back when Miss Hattie's first opened. Since then it has been handed down from one hen to the next, and it just wouldn't be a grand opening without the feather dance being performed." She backed out of the way. "I hope you enjoy it."

A hush fell over the room as a man that Brant didn't recognize stepped over to the piano and began to play. Baby appeared out of a side door, having changed from the white dress to a deep midnight blue. As she slowly walked to the piano, she lifted the microphone and started to sing.

"There's a somebody I'm longing to see. I hope that he…turns out to be…someone who'll watch over me."

A fluttering drew Brant's attention back to the doorway. Two huge feathered fans filled the opening, quivering like leaves in a strong breeze. They moved forward, propelled by two shapely legs and a pair of glittery gold spiked heels that clicked against the parquet floor. Brant had to admit that for an old gal, Sunshine had a great set of gams. Although he worried a little bit when a few steps from the middle of the floor, she twisted her ankle. She covered her falter by turning around and lowering one fan to reveal a creamy white shoulder and a fall of blond-streaked hair.

Brant blinked.

Sunshine had dyed her hair? It didn't seem likely knowing her earthy nature. Still, Minnie and Starlet had changed for the grand opening so it made sense. She moved hesitantly at first, the feathers of the fans trembling with each step she took. Then slowly she grew more confident and started to manipulate the fans around her body.

Brant might've stopped the dance if he could've actually seen something. But the way Sunshine was twirling the fans, you couldn't see more than her legs and an occasional glimpse of skin. It was enough to rile the crowd. The men inched closer, and a few whistles split the air. Brant really couldn't blame them. In the dim lighting, Sunshine's body looked years younger. And after she stopped moving so awkwardly, Brant had to admit that the quivery feathers and swaying blond hair were pretty seductive.

It was too bad that this would be Sunshine's last feather dance.

He wasn't about to let Miss Hattie's become a peep show.

If Hank was right, and Elizabeth was in charge, what had she been thinking to allow this kind of craziness to take place? Of course, she probably had no idea what was happening. She was probably back at her little house on Maple Street, snuggled on her bed next to her fat cat.

Why the thought would make him hard, Brant didn't know. One second he was half-watching Sunshine strut around, whipping huge feather fans around her body, and the next, he was as hard as a stone. Talk about awkward. He started to move toward the door when the song ended in a flurry of feathers. The men applauded much louder than they had with Starlet as Sunshine moved back to the doorway. But before she slipped inside, she lowered the fan enough to smile brightly at the crowd.

A smile that quickly replaced Brant's desire with cold, hard anger.

Chapter Twenty-seven

Henhouse Rule #27: An angry cock is better than a passive one.

ELIZABETH WAS SO THRILLED to have finished the dance without falling on her butt that it took a moment to notice the man walking toward her. And not walking so much as stalking like a predator after his prey. She couldn't see his face beneath the brim of the cowboy hat, but she didn't need to. His body, in jeans and a starched western shirt, was familiar enough.

She didn't know why she turned in a flurry of feathers and hurried up the stairs. She had never been scared of Brant. Maybe it had nothing to do with being scared and everything to do with being caught in a tight beige leotard that crawled up her butt. Or the fact that he had just witnessed one of the most embarrassing moments of her life.

What had she been thinking letting Minnie talk her into doing the dance? Or believing her when she said that she hadn't invited anyone that Elizabeth would know? No, she had just invited the only man Elizabeth had ever loved! And that was the main reason she was running away. She was terrified that she would be unable to keep that love from showing.

Fortunately, it was easier climbing up the stairs in the painful high heels than it had been climbing down them. What wasn't easy was trying to maneuver the huge fans through the narrow passageways. The tread of cowboy boots on wooden stairs had her dropping the fans and hurrying down the narrow corridor at the top. There were a number of rooms she could've come out in, but she chose the one that had more things to hide behind.

Except the paneled door that led to Miss Hattie's closet got stuck, and no amount of shoving would get it opened. Before she could turn and head in another direction, a hand settled around her waist, and she was pulled up against a hard body she remembered all too well.

"It looks like the shy librarian has come out of her shell," Brant breathed close to her ear.

Since his words were rather snide, she shouldn't have felt desire. Yet, there it was, heating the crotch of her leotard and taking all the air out of her lungs. If Brant had turned her around and kissed her, she would've let him and even fully participated. But instead, he turned into a bit of a Neanderthal.

Scooping her up in his arms as if she weighed no more than one of the feather fans, he kicked open the door and maneuvered her through the small doorway. Once inside, he carried her through the dark closet into the bedroom where he tossed her down on the bed.

"Just what the hell did you think you were doing?" he said as he took off his hat and sent it sailing over to the chair in the corner.

Now that he wasn't touching her, she could think a little more clearly. And the first thing that popped into her head was that she didn't particularly care for his arrogant attitude.

"I believe it's called the feather dance. Not to be confused with the one done by the Southwestern American Indians."

He stepped closer to the bed. "I'm not kidding around."

"Ha!" Elizabeth snorted. "As if I would ever think that Branston Cates was kidding around. No, I realize you're mad, Brant. But since it seems to be your natural state, I'm not overly concerned."

It was too dark in the room to clearly see his features, but she thought she detected a flash of white teeth. It had to have been her imagination because his next words had no smile in them whatsoever.

"Well, you should be concerned," he said. "I'm still the owner of this establishment, and I never intended for it to be a strip club."

"I did not strip!"

"No, you just made a bunch of men horny as hell by dancing around half naked."

Anger fizzled right out of her, and a bright smile lit her face. "I did?"

He stared at her for a few seconds before he sighed in frustration and sat down on the edge of the bed. "What happened to the virgin who prefers the light off? A virgin who would never be caught dead doing the . . . feather dance?"

It was a good question. One she really didn't have the answer for. She didn't know what had happened or why she had agreed to put on a skin-toned leotard and dance for a room filled with men. She could blame it on Sunshine's flu, Baby and Starlet's pleading, or Minnie's reverse psychology—telling her she couldn't pull it off. But she realized none of those reasons would have forced her into doing something she didn't want to do.

"Maybe I'm tired of the status quo," she said. "Maybe I just wanted to try something different—something completely out of character."

He snorted. "Well, that was it. Hell, you can't even walk in those crazy shoes."

Suddenly Elizabeth had the strong desire to kick him hard in the back with her crazy shoes. Instead, she scooted toward the opposite side of the bed.

"If you'll excuse me, I need to change and go down and help the hens."

But before her feet could even hit the floor, Brant had pulled her back and trapped her beneath him. "Since when do you want to help the hens reopen Miss Hattie's? I thought you didn't want anyone knowing your connection to a whorehouse."

"It's not a whorehouse," she stated indignantly, although it was hard to be indignant when her entire mind was wrapped up in the hard body pressed against hers. She could feel the texture of his blue jeans against her thighs, the cold metal of his belt buckle just to the left of her hipbone, and the flex of his biceps on either side of her shoulders.

"I don't believe this," he said. "Minnie has finally succeeded in pulling you into her crazy hen psyche. Next you'll be smoking cigarettes and talking about all the men you've slept with."

"And what difference does that make to you?"

In the shadow of the bed curtains, she couldn't distinguish his features, but she could feel his eyes boring into her.

"You're right. It shouldn't make a difference." He rolled over onto his back and rested his forearm over his eyes.

If Elizabeth had wanted to leave, now was her opportunity. But the truth was that even an arrogant, controlling Brant was better than no Brant at all.

"You don't have to worry about the Cates name being associated with bad press," she said. "That will be the last time the feather dance will be performed. Minnie just wanted something special for the grand opening, and Sunshine got sick."

"Is she all right?" He lowered his arm and glanced over, and she gasped. In the shaft of moonlight that spilled across the bed, his face was a mosaic of tiny cuts and bruises.

"Oh my God, what happened to you?" Even as annoyed with him as she was, she couldn't help reaching out and tentatively touching the purplish knot on his jaw.

For a brief second, he leaned into her hand before he pulled away. "It was just a stupid misunderstanding I had in a bar. One that Beau enjoyed making worse."

"How is he?"

Brant looked away and released his breath. "He refuses to go back to the hospital to have more tests done. He claims that even if they find something, he won't go through any more surgery and treatment."

"I'm sorry."

"No more than I am," he said. "But the funny thing about it is that I don't blame him. I'd probably do the same thing if I was in his shoes."

"No, you wouldn't."

He turned back to her. "And what makes you think so?"

"Because you care too much about what it would do to your family." She rolled to her side. "Anyone that knows anything about you, Brant, knows that your family comes first. And always will."

Time slowly ticked by as they stared at one another. Finally, he lifted his hand and smoothed back the piece of hair that had fallen over her eye. "I'm sorry. The last thing I wanted to do was hurt you."

She started to deny his words, but then realized she couldn't. At that moment, she felt hurt. Hurt that she couldn't love him the way she wanted to love him. And hurt that he didn't love her at all.

"You never promised me anything, Brant," she whispered. "Everything I did, I did because I wanted to."

"And now?" he asked. "What do you want now, Beth?"

"You," she said, even though she knew it was an impossibility. "I want you."

With a groan, he pulled her into his arms, holding her as if he never wanted to let her go.

"God," he whispered against the side of her head. "How did this happen?" Not waiting for a reply, he pulled back just enough to kiss her. It wasn't a brief sip, but a deep, hungry kiss that held a desperate plea Elizabeth had no trouble answering.

Somewhere in between the hot slide of lips and tongues, they stripped free of clothing and came back together in a tangle of heated skin. His hands seemed to be everywhere at once. Caressing her trembling flesh. Gliding over her straining muscles. Dipping into her wet heat. It had been over a month since he had touched her, a month with only fantasies to keep her warm, so it didn't take long for her to find release.

Her orgasm struck like a flash of lightning—hard, bright, and electrifying. When the pieces fell back into place, she was lying on top of Brant.

"I need to be inside you, Beth," he whispered as he rained

kisses along her neck. He lifted her limp body and sucked her nipple deep into his mouth before he bit down gently. The sensation had desire zinging through her again and her legs tightening around his hips. She could feel him probing to get inside, and she helped him by grasping his throbbing penis in her hand and, inch by inch, guiding him in. When he was two-thirds of the way in, she sat down fully, wiggling to adjust the fit.

"Jesus," Brant groaned and dug his head back into the pillow.

His excitement excited her, and she wiggled a little more. When she got the same reaction, she realized that she liked the feeling of being on top and in control. She liked it even better when Brant encircled her waist and taught her the exact way to move. His hands set a slow pace. And while it felt good, it wasn't enough friction, and soon she took over and pumped against him hard and fast.

"Slow it down, babe," he said between his gritted teeth. "I'm too damn close."

Except Elizabeth didn't want to slow down. She'd spent her entire life doing things slow and concise, and tonight she wanted to push the limits. To test the edge. To spin out of control.

Or maybe she just wanted Brant to spin out of control. For her.

So instead of listening to him, she moved faster, causing his hands to tighten on her waist and his breath to rush out in short, quick pants. She enjoyed the feel of him deep inside her, but no more than she enjoyed watching his excitement build. When he reached orgasm, she expected his eyes to close. Instead, his gaze locked with hers. In the molten-blue depths, she saw ecstasy, but also something else. Something that made her love him even more than she already did. She saw Brant before the tragedies. Before the pain. Before he'd built the wall so high that no one else could enter. She saw the sensitive heart beneath. His vulnerability brought tears to her eyes and a tidal wave of emotion that forced words from her mouth she'd never had any intention of saying.

"I love you."

He stared at her for only a second before his eyes closed, and he rode out the last ripples of his orgasm. When his muscles had relaxed and his body sagged back into the mattress, he opened his eyes again. But the vulnerable Brant was long gone, replaced with the hard, determined man who rolled her over and proceeded to wipe all thoughts from her mind with long, deep kisses and sweet, hot caresses.

A man who wasn't satisfied until he'd given her two more amazing orgasms and left her too exhausted to do more than sleep.

Chapter Twenty-eight

Henhouse Rule #39: Never smoke in bed.

WHEN ELIZABETH WOKE, it was still dark. She reached out for Brant, but felt nothing but the cold slickness of satin sheets. Sitting up, she glanced around the room. Brant stood by the window, his back to her.

"You don't love me, Elizabeth," he stated without turning around.

How he knew she was awake, she didn't know. Or maybe he just spoke to himself. Either way, she swung her legs over the edge of the bed and turned on the lamp.

"I might be a novice at these things," she said. "But I don't think that's your decision to make."

He turned, his naked body glorious in full light. "Whatever happened to friends with benefits?"

She got to her feet, uncaring that she was completely naked. "I guess I fell in love with my friend."

Brant's gaze ran over her body in a hot slide before he turned back around. "You only think that because I'm the first man you've ever had sex with. But it will pass." He paused as if struggling with the words. "Someday you'll meet the right man and get married. Until then, I plan on signing the henhouse back over to you."

"So you're leaving," she whispered.

There was a long silence before he finally spoke. "It's for the best. You've done a great job with renovations, and I have little doubt that you can finish getting the henhouse up and running. Still, I'll set up an accountant for you in Bramble, just in case you need it."

She laughed. It was a brittle, hard sound that came straight from her breaking heart. "I guess I'm a hen in all respects now."

Brant turned away from the window. "Excuse me?"

Her smile faded. "Sex for money? Isn't that what you're offering me?"

"No, my offer has nothing to do with...sex."

Trying to ignore the pain that accompanied his choice of words, Elizabeth walked to the nightstand and picked up the journal she'd been reading. "Oh, so I get it. Signing the house over to me has more to do with guilt." She tried to casually thumb through the pages, but her hands shook so badly that she was forced to snap the book closed. "Well, I'm afraid I'm not going to make it that easy for you, Brant. I don't want your guilt money. All I want from you is something you can't give."

"Damn it, Elizabeth!" Walking over, Brant took her by the arms and spun her around. "You don't want to love me. Don't you see what loving me gets people? It gets them swept away in some tornado. Or hit with some life-threatening disease." He gave her a shake. "And I'll be damned if I'll go through that again. I won't have you being pulled into the curse that seems to follow me."

She jerked free and glared at him. "That is such bullshit, Brant."

He blinked. "Excuse me?"

"You heard me. You're an intelligent adult who should understand the difference between fact and fiction." She spoke like she did with her preschool kids, her words slow and precise. "A curse is fiction. A legend. Some story passed down by creative, but uneducated people, to explain the calamities that happen to them. You are no more cursed than I am."

His face darkened. "You haven't had people you love die all around you."

"No," she said. "I haven't. Probably because I grew up with only a mother. You, on the other hand, have been blessed with a huge family. And yes, some of them have died. But that doesn't mean you're cursed. Nor does it give you the excuse to act like an asshole." She leaned up and got in his face. "If you don't love me, Brant, then be man enough to say so. Don't hide behind some fictitious curse."

His jaw worked, and there was a moment when she thought he was really going to lose his temper. She wished he had. At least then, she would've known he had some feelings. Instead, he picked up his clothes and headed for the door.

Once it clicked closed behind him, Elizabeth's legs gave out, and she wilted down to the bed. She felt like she'd been repeatedly kicked in the stomach. Pain throbbed deep down inside her, and she couldn't seem to catch her breath. She didn't know how long she sat there before the slamming of a car door drew her attention to the window.

She hurried over in time to see Brant walking away from his truck, wearing nothing but his jeans. Just the sight of his muscular chest in the moonlight had heat surging through her body, melting her brain cells so quickly that she almost didn't notice the suitcase he was carrying. The implication of the suitcase pulled her out of her desire-drugged state and back to reality.

If Brant Cates thought he was going to spend the night at Miss Hattie's, he had another think coming. Elizabeth might not be an expert on the dos and don'ts of dating, but she knew enough to know that once you dumped a girl, you had no business spending the night in her home.

Suddenly she realized that Minnie had been right all along. For better or for worse, Miss Hattie's *was* Elizabeth's home.

Heading for the closet, she grabbed the first robe that she found. She didn't realize it was the red satin dressing gown until she went to tie the sash. Since the last thing she wanted was for Brant to think she was trying to seduce him, she started to take it off when a loud crash had her glancing over at the door that led down to The Jungle Room.

Elizabeth's eyes narrowed. Quickly, she retied the sash before pulling open the door. How dare Brant think that he could sleep in the hens' private sanctuary? His audacity had her feet flying down the steps. But she came to a halt when she rounded the artificial philodendron plant.

There *was* someone in The Jungle Room. But it wasn't Brant. Not unless he was a quick-change artist. The man who moved around the dimly lit room was dressed completely in black, from the top of his stocking cap to the toes of his boots. And he was smaller than Brant, smaller and a lot less agile.

He stumbled over a tiger-skinned ottoman and bumped into the bar, knocking over the hula dancer lamp and causing numerous bottles of brandy to wobble precariously.

Elizabeth watched as the man grabbed one of the bottles and opened it. But instead of drinking it, he did the strangest thing. He walked over to Minnie's fuzzy orange chair and poured the entire contents all over it. Then before Elizabeth could blink, he pulled out a lighter and flicked it to life. The face that wavered behind the flame had Elizabeth gasping.

"Mother?"

Harriett Murphy looked over, and her eyes widened. "Elizabeth? What are you doing here?"

Elizabeth stepped into the room and flipped on the light switch. "I think that should be my question." She waved a hand at the chair. "Why in the world would you do that to Minnie's chair?"

Her mother released her thumb from the lighter. "I think you're intelligent enough to figure that out."

It only took a second for the pieces to fall into place. Still, Elizabeth couldn't quite bring herself to believe it. "You were going to burn down Miss Hattie's?"

Her mother moved over to the bar, but this time she poured herself a brandy and downed it in one swallow. Elizabeth had never seen her mother drink. Of course, she'd never seen her dressed in solid black either. Her mother preferred the less dramatic colors of gray and beige. And Elizabeth had to admit that the black turtleneck looked good with her mother's champagne-colored hair and amber eyes.

"This," her mother waved the empty glass around, "should never have happened. The henhouse shouldn't reopen. In fact, it should've closed long before it did."

"So you were going to close it permanently by committing arson?"

"If I have to," she stated without the least bit of remorse. "What other options do I have? I probably could've ignored things if the hens hadn't tried to suck you into their craziness." Her gaze drifted over the red satin robe. "Just look at you standing there in Miss Hattie's dressing gown as if you belong here. Didn't I teach you anything?"

"Yes." Elizabeth walked over to the bar. "You taught me a lot of things, Mother. You taught me how to read, and how to tie my shoelaces so they wouldn't come undone. And you taught me how important it is to be prompt and logical. And burning down Miss Hattie's isn't logical. It's crazy."

When her mother didn't say anything, Elizabeth continued. "I know you're worried about me, but no one has sucked me into doing anything I didn't want to do. Not Sunshine. Or Baby. Or Minnie." She paused as a realization hit her. "Or even Brant."

Her mother shook her head. "I suppose that this Brant is the man you've been shacking up with?"

"Yes," Elizabeth said without hesitation.

"And am I to assume by the dreamy look on your face that wedding bells are in the future?"

There was a time when Elizabeth would've laughed at the mere idea of marriage, but she wasn't laughing now. After realizing her love for Brant, she had started to dream about a wedding similar to all the ones she'd attended. With one small exception. At this wedding, she was the one walking down the aisle toward the man she loved.

Except the man she loved didn't love her in return.

"No," she said. "There won't be a wedding."

Her mother snorted. "I tried to warn you. Women would be a lot less hurt and disappointed without men."

"Is that why you never dated, Mother?" Elizabeth asked. "You were afraid of being hurt and disappointed?"

Her mother looked away. "I didn't date because I didn't want some man controlling my life." She looked at Elizabeth. "Your life. It was safer for both of us if I remained single."

"But life shouldn't be safe, Mother. It should be thrilling and fun." She thought of her shattered wedding dreams. "And sometimes sad and disappointing." She covered her mother's hand that rested on the bar. "Minnie told me about what happened to you, and I'm sorry. But Miss Hattie's isn't to blame for the actions of a monster."

Tears welled up in her mother's eyes. It was the first time Elizabeth had ever seen her cry, and rather than feel upset by the tears, she only felt relief. Relief that her mother was human after all.

"But Dwayne was right," her mother said as she wiped at her eyes. " 'If you look and act like a whore, then you are one.' I did wear a tight, short skirt that night. And I did brush up against him every chance I got. And I did live in a whorehouse."

"But that didn't give him the right to rape you," Elizabeth said. "He was the one who was wrong, Mother. Not you."

Her mother sat down on the bar stool and rested her head on her arms. "You're right; it wasn't my fault. But it *was* my mother's. It wouldn't have happened if she'd just put me up for adoption like all the other hens did with their children. Instead, she made me the sexual joke of every kid in town."

"It was a mistake."

Between her mother's sobs and her own thumping heart, Elizabeth hadn't heard the elevator. So she was surprised to turn and find Minnie sitting there in her wheelchair. But no more surprised than she was by the tears that trickled down Minnie's wrinkled face.

"I'm sorry, Harry," she said. "Sorry I was too selfish to let you go."

"Harry?" Elizabeth stared at Minnie, then slowly lifted a finger to point at her mother. "This is Harry? But I thought Harry was the love of your life."

Minnie's gaze never wavered from Elizabeth's mother. "She is."

"But then that would make you my . . ."

"Grandmother," Minnie said as she rolled around the couch.

Elizabeth was stunned. "But why didn't you tell me?"

"Because I had promised your mother that I wouldn't."

Her mother looked up and wiped at her eyes. "But that didn't stop you from contacting her."

"The henhouse is her heritage, Harriett. She had the right to accept it or decline it." Minnie smiled at Elizabeth. "I'm glad she's accepted it."

"Because you hens have brainwashed her," her mother snapped. The tears were gone, and Elizabeth didn't think they'd be back. "Well, I won't put up with it. I'm taking her out of here even if I have to tie her up and drag her."

Minnie shook her head. "Give it up, Harry. Elizabeth is happy here. And you'd be too if you'd pull that corn cob out of your ass. You act just like your father—the Senator had a stubborn streak a mile wide."

Elizabeth flopped down on the bar stool next to her

mother. "You mean my grandfather was a Texas senator?" She glanced over at her mother. "You told me you didn't know who your father was."

"Because I didn't want you getting any false hope that his family would acknowledge you. The one time I wrote the man, he answered with nothing more than a ten-thousand-dollar check."

"Which you promptly cashed," Minnie said.

"Of course I cashed it, Mama! I was raising a daughter and trying to put myself through school."

"Fine." Minnie held up her hands. "I'll be the first to admit that your father was an asshole. But your choice in men wasn't any better."

"At least I was smart enough to quit after two!" Elizabeth's mother yelled back. "You just kept on going. How many men have you been with, Mama? Thirty? Forty?" She hopped up and glared at Minnie. "A hundred!"

"Twenty-six," Minnie said. "And that's only if you count oral sex."

Harriett rolled her eyes before looking over at Elizabeth. "See? See what I had to live with?"

"Stop being so dramatic, Harry." Minnie fumbled around in the side pocket of her bag until she found her pack of cigarettes. She pulled one out and stuck it in between her lips. "You're worse than Starlet."

"Are you talking about that innocent young girl who sang tonight or the one you taught to feather dance?"

Elizabeth turned away, hoping her mother hadn't seen the blush that heated her cheeks.

Minnie's eyebrows lifted. "So you were snooping around, Harry?"

"It didn't take much snooping to realize that you

intend to reopen Miss Hattie's exactly as it was." She leaned down and pointed in Minnie's face. "And get this through your head, Mama. I'm not going to allow it. I don't care what I have to do." She whirled and headed for the elevators.

"Mother, wait," Elizabeth called out.

"Let her go, Lizzie," Minnie said. "She's as hard-headed as they come. It's enough to make a person go back to their bad habits." She struck a match on the arm of her chair. It took the flickering glow of the tiny flame for the severity of the situation to hit Elizabeth.

"Minnie, no!" Elizabeth's fingers closed around Minnie's thin, wrinkled wrist. Unfortunately, before Elizabeth could blow out the match, it dropped from Minnie's fingers.

In slow motion, Elizabeth watched as it tumbled through the air and landed on the fuzzy chair. Within seconds, the flaming orange really was flaming. But the burning chair didn't bother Elizabeth as much as the burning edge of Minnie's negligee. The flames ate their way up to Minnie's knees before Elizabeth could rip the material away from her body.

"Mama!" Elizabeth's mother returned with a throw blanket and tossed it over Minnie's legs, smothering the last of the flames.

But that wasn't the worst of it. When they turned, the entire room seemed to be ablaze. The bar. The zebra couch. The Andy Warhol painting.

"Oh my God," her mother breathed. "What have I done?"

Chapter Twenty-nine

*Henhouse Rule #30: If a man wants to rescue you,
let him.*

AFTER GETTING HIS SUITCASE FROM THE TRUCK, Brant headed to the library. He tossed his bag in a corner and then stripped down to his boxer briefs. But instead of lying down on the leather couch in front of the fireplace, he proceeded to pace between the door and the desk. Where had his Elizabeth gone? What happened to the sweet librarian who thought so logically? The woman who hadn't expected anything from him except what he was willing to give? What happened to the friend with benefits?

Okay, so maybe he hadn't been that good of a friend. A friend wouldn't have canceled a date so abruptly, or not called for over a month. And a friend wouldn't have gotten pissed off at her for dancing provocatively for a room filled with horny men.

But she hadn't exactly kept her end of the friends-with-benefits bargain either.

Friends did not use the l-word. Especially the way that Elizabeth had used it. She had waited until his defenses were down. Waited until he was so mindless with desire that he couldn't shield his heart from the look in her eyes or the words coming from her lips.

Of course, he didn't believe that she loved him. He was just the first man she'd ever been in bed with, the first man to give her an orgasm. And sex was a powerful motivator. There was actually a moment when the l-word had almost slipped out of Brant's own mouth. Except it hadn't been during sex when it had happened. It had been earlier, when they had been lying on the bed together and talking about Beau. There had been a moment when she had looked at him with those empathetic amber eyes when he'd wanted to give up the battle he waged and just let go.

It had to be desire that motivated the feeling. What else could it be? He'd closed himself off from love a long time ago. Even now, just the thought of Elizabeth standing there completely naked had his penis standing at attention. He ignored it. His desire for Elizabeth had already caused enough damage. If he'd learned anything tonight, it was that sex without strings was an impossibility.

Realizing that sleep was out of the question, Brant padded over to the bookcase. The collection still amazed him. He had just pulled down a copy of *The Adventures of Huckleberry Finn* when his gaze got snagged by the silver chests sitting side by side on the shelf just above him.

Brant had gotten the other chest from his mother and sent it to Miss Hattie's so he could compare the two. After the news about Beau, he'd forgotten all about them. Now he took the time to study the two together. It was obvious they'd been made by the same man. The sizes and shapes were identical, as were the beautiful etchings that covered the tops and sides.

He took Elizabeth's chest down and looked at the inscription on the bottom, wondering how it had come to be in Miss Hattie's possession. The loud pop of the embers that still burned in the fireplace startled him from his thoughts, and the chest slipped from his fingers and hit the wooden floor with a tinny clank.

When he squatted down to pick up the chest, he noticed the wide crack that had opened up along the seam at the bottom. Through it, he could see the folded edge of a paper. He quickly carried it over to the desk and pulled out the high-backed leather chair. Once he was seated, he turned on the lamp and closely examined the gap. It looked as if there was another compartment attached to the bottom. After some searching, he found the two small releases hidden in the intricate design and pressed them simultaneously. The entire bottom swung open and a bundle of letters fell onto the top of the mahogany desk.

Brant stared at the bundle for only a moment before reaching out to untie the red ribbon that held them together. He took the first letter from the top and carefully opened it. The penmanship was perfect and precise. And very similar to the faded signature in Miss Hattie's register.

Harriett,
The trip to Lubbock was uneventful. I ran into a little hail that got the horse skittish, but I managed to find shelter before the worst of it hit. I know I said I wouldn't write, but I just wanted to let you know I got home safely.

William

It wasn't much of a letter, but Brant wasn't as interested in it as he was in the date at the top—September 4, 1872. So William had stayed close to a month at Miss Hattie's.

Brant lifted the second letter. It didn't reveal much more. His grandfather talked about the weather and a silver inlaid saddle he was making for a wealthy rancher. The rest of the letters continued along the same lines. But what intrigued Brant was that each one was dated not more than a few days apart. And this was after his grandfather had said he wasn't going to write.

Had his grandfather had feelings for Miss Hattie? If he had, he'd been as bad at expressing them as Brant was. In the next twenty letters, there were no mushy words, no plagiarized poetry, not even a "Love, William." His grandfather continued to talk about the weather and his job ad nauseam, and Brant couldn't figure out why Miss Hattie had kept them.

Then he stumbled upon the second to the last letter William had written:

Harriett,
It snowed today for the first time, and I had to pull out my heavy coat. I didn't want to. I can't stand the thought of the cold, bleak winter ahead. It's foolish I know. One cannot stop the change of the seasons. Nor turn back the hands of time. Yet, I can't help but long for the warmth of August and the sweet scent of lilacs. So much so, that I don't think I can continue without them.

William

Brant sat back against the cool leather of the chair before reaching for the final letter. It was dated November 1, 1872 and held only one line:

I'm leaving Elsa and will arrive soon.

Brant allowed the letter to slip from his hand and join the rest on the top of the desk.

William *had* loved Miss Hattie. And if the carefully kept letters were any indication, Miss Hattie had loved William. So what had happened after? Had William returned to Miss Hattie and died over a card game like Moses Tate believed?

Slowly, Brant collected the letters and carefully slipped them back into the compartment. He pressed on the soft metal until the gap closed. He thought about showing the letters to the family, but then decided against it. They didn't explain how William had died—or if he had even died at Miss Hattie's. All they explained was why Miss Hattie had the box in her possession. And what good would it do to let his family know that their grandfather had fallen in love with a madam and had planned to leave his wife for her?

Brant stood and replaced the chest on the shelf. His gaze wandered over to the other chest. Was it possible that it also had a secret compartment? This time, it didn't take him any time at all to locate the releases. But instead of a bundle of letters, he only found one neatly torn-out diary page. And since he'd spent numerous hours searching through the diary Billy had found in Aunt Milly's attic, it didn't take him more than a second to recognize the handwriting.

"That's Lizzie's."

The softly spoken words had Brant looking up toward

the doorway. Sunshine stood there, looking pale and ghostly in her long, white nightgown.

"That's Lizzie's box," she said as she walked into the room. "You shouldn't be touching it."

Brant placed the page back in the compartment and snapped it closed. "How are you feeling, Sunshine? Elizabeth told me that you've been sick."

"She did my dance."

"I know. And it looked like you did a good job of teaching her."

Sunshine smiled, but it was a weak attempt. Now that he really studied her, she didn't look well at all.

"Here," he placed the chest back up on the shelf, figuring he'd have plenty of time to read his grandmother's diary page later, "let's get you to bed."

Her eyes wandered down his body, and Brant realized that he was in his underwear. "I can't have you," she said with a look of complete disappointment. "Hen Rule #28 clearly states that no hen can cavort with a man that another hen loves." She cocked her head to one side. "Unless you don't love her."

Ignoring the comment, he grabbed the throw blanket from the couch and wrapped it around his waist. "I promise I'll only tuck you in."

"That's what Harriett did," Sunshine said as she allowed him to guide her back to the room she was sharing with Starlet. "She tucked me in and told me to do something." She stopped in the doorway. "But I can't remember what it was."

"Harriett as in Miss Hattie?" Brant asked, wondering if Sunshine was more delusional than he thought.

Sunshine laughed. "Of course not, silly. Miss Hattie is

dead. Harriett is Elizabeth's mother. Minnie named her after Miss Hattie." She covered her mouth with her hand as her eyes widened.

"Minnie is Elizabeth's grandmother?" Brant asked, even though he didn't need her confirmation. Last night he had thought Minnie looked familiar, and now he knew why. Although he didn't know why they had kept the secret from him. Unless...

"Does Elizabeth know?" he said.

Sunshine finally removed her hand and shook her head. "And please don't tell. Minnie will be real mad." The alarm clock next to Sunshine's bed went off, causing Starlet to sit straight up in bed with a startled yelp. Sunshine's eyes lit up. "That's it. At exactly three o'clock, Harriett told me to wake up Minnie and tell her that the Jungle Room was on fire."

"What?" Brant yelled above the ringing, and then repeated himself when Starlet finally shut off the alarm. "What did you say?"

"The Jungle Room is on fire," she repeated.

It was such an unlikely scenario that Brant thought Sunshine had dreamed the entire episode, until he smelled smoke. Hurrying down the hallway, he headed for the elevator. The curl of smoke seeping through the crack in the new doors had his chest tightening and his heart thumping against his ribs. The heat that greeted his fingers when he touched the metal was even more alarming.

He turned around to find Sunshine and Starlet standing right behind him. He spoke to Starlet in a stern voice. "You need to go wake up Baby and get outside. I'll get Minnie."

Except when Brant got to Minnie's room, he didn't

find the old woman. He found a sleepy-eyed old man in saggy red long johns.

"What's all the commotion?" Moses asked as he rubbed his eyes. "And where did that ornery woman run off to now?"

Brant didn't waste any time jerking back the covers. "You need to get outside. There's a fire in The Jungle Room."

Moses moved faster than Brant had ever seen him move. "And Minnie?"

"I don't know, but I'll find her," Brant said as he helped Moses to the door.

It turned out that Minnie wasn't in any of the downstairs rooms. And since there was no way she could've used the elevator, that left only one other option.

The Jungle Room.

Brant took the stairs two at a time. He started calling Elizabeth's name before he even reached Miss Hattie's room, then flung open the door with such force that it slammed into the wall. The smoke was thicker here, and Brant slipped the blanket from his waist and covered his nose as he raced over to the bed.

It was empty.

Wetting a towel in the bathroom, he tied it around his nose and mouth before heading through the closet. He threw open the panel door to even more smoke. But it wasn't the smoke that tore his heart in two, but the coughing that came from within.

He froze. It was like every nightmare he'd experienced in his life. Buckley, Mandy, and B.J. were all calling for him, but he couldn't seem to move. All he could do was stand in the doorway with his eyes burning, his lungs tight, and his mind frantically chanting.

No. No. No. Not again.

"Please don't give up, Mother."

It was Elizabeth's plea that finally snapped Brant out of his terror, and placing a hand over the wet towel, he charged into the smoke. It was so thick that he had to feel his way along the banister and down the flight of stairs. On the first landing, he ran into a familiar body. His arms went around Elizabeth's waist, and all he wanted to do was jerk her up in his arms and head back up to safety. He should've known it wouldn't be that easy.

"No," she coughed. "Take Minnie."

It was then that Brant realized that Elizabeth was holding Minnie by the arms and trying to pull her up the stairs. He quickly took Minnie from her with every intention of pushing Elizabeth in front of him. Instead, she pulled away.

"M-My mother," she coughed before she headed back down the stairs.

The fear he felt as he saw her disappear into the smoke was even worse than before. But this time, instead of freezing, his body went into hyperdrive. He charged up the stairs. The closet now had as much smoke as the stairwell so Brant hurried into the bedroom and left Minnie sitting by an open window.

He found Elizabeth only a few steps from the top, her arm hooked around her mother's body. Both women were coughing so much they couldn't talk. He scooped up her mother and herded Elizabeth in front of him. Once in the closet, he kicked the paneled door closed behind them and carried Elizabeth's mother over to the window where Minnie was still struggling to catch her breath. After he set Elizabeth's mother down, he probably should've started thinking about how he was going to get all the women out of the house. Instead, he jerked the towel from his face and pulled Elizabeth into his arms.

Words bubbled up inside him and would've spilled out if a loud thump hadn't pulled everyone's attention to the window. He couldn't help but smile when a bald, age-spotted head came into view. Moses peered over the top of the ladder, his mouth spread in a wide, toothless grin.

"Did you think I'd let you keep all the hens to yourself?"

Chapter Thirty

Henhouse Rule #15: Never let them see you cry.

"HOW IS SHE?"

Elizabeth turned from the hospital bed where Minnie slept to find her mother standing in the doorway. She was still dressed in black, but now her face was smudged with smoke and soot. All except for the tear tracks that ran down each cheek.

"I didn't mean for anyone to get hurt." Harriett stepped farther into the room, allowing the door to sweep closed behind her. "I told Sunshine and set her alarm, but even then I planned on making sure everyone got out safely before the fire spread. I just didn't think it would spread so quickly." She looked down at the bed and more tears raced down her cheeks. "And now..."

As much as her mother was probably due a good dose of guilt, Elizabeth couldn't prolong her agony. "Minnie's just sleeping," she said. "The doctor gave her something to help her relax." She got up from the chair. "Which is exactly what you need to do. Why wouldn't you let them get you a room, Mother?"

"Because I'm fine." Her mother ignored the chair and

went to stand by Minnie. "Besides, after all that smoke, I just wanted to stay outside and breathe in some fresh air."

"So that's where you've been?"

Her mother nodded. "I was out in the courtyard reading this." She held up Minnie's journal that had been on the nightstand. "I figured if it was the one thing you refused to leave behind then it must be worth reading."

Elizabeth didn't know what had possessed her to grab the diary before it was her turn to climb down the ladder. But looking into her mother's tear-filled eyes, she figured it had been a good choice.

"I never knew," her mother whispered as she moved closer to the bed. "I always thought the reason she kept me with her was to get another hen for the henhouse." She took Minnie's hand that wasn't connected to the I.V. "Now I realize it was because she couldn't live without me." Tears raced down her cheeks as she bent over the bed. "Why didn't you tell me, Mama? Why did I have to find out after I almost killed you?"

Minnie's eyes opened. "Quit your caterwaulin', Harry. I ain't dead yet, and I don't plan to be for a while." She took the oxygen tubes from her nose and pushed the tubing up on her head. "Leastways, not until we've rebuilt the henhouse."

"Good Lord." Elizabeth's mother rolled her eyes and she stepped back from the bed. "Is that all you can think about, Mama?"

"No." Minnie sat up. "I could use a couple eggs, some bacon, and a cup of coffee. Followed by a cigarette. Elizabeth, go see if you can find a cigarette machine."

Elizabeth grinned. "I don't think they'll have one in a hospital, Minnie."

"You don't need a cigarette, Mama," her mother said. "That's exactly what got us in this situation."

Minnie pointed a finger. "What got us in this situation, Harriett, was you being an overprotective mama. Now apologize to Elizabeth for almost ruinin' her life so we can move on to talkin' about what it's going to take to get Miss Hattie's up and runnin' again."

"Me apologize?" Elizabeth's mother looked like she was about to explode, which happened to be a nice change. "You should be apologizing to me for ruining my life by keeping me at the henhouse."

Minnie's eyebrows lifted. "I think you've made me pay for that, Harry, ten times over."

Elizabeth's mother's lips pressed into a firm line, and she flopped down in the other chair like a sullen child who had just been put in her place. But Minnie wasn't about to let her off that easy.

"Harry, acknowledge the mistakes you've made with Elizabeth, or I'll rethink what I told Sheriff Hicks."

What Minnie had told the sheriff was exactly what happened. She'd just left out the part about Elizabeth's mother dousing half the room in brandy. Something that Elizabeth figured Minnie would use in the future to manipulate her daughter at every given opportunity. Except when Harriett turned to Elizabeth, she didn't look like she was being manipulated. She looked sincere.

"I'm sorry for interfering in your life, Elizabeth. You're a grown woman, and if you want to stay at Miss Hattie's, then that's your choice." She cleared her throat. "And I'd also like to apologize for perhaps forcing my views of men on you."

Minnie snorted. "Perhaps?"

"Fine," her mother snapped, "I did! But from the look of things, she didn't take my lessons to heart."

"Well, we need to thank God for that." Minnie winked at Elizabeth. "And a tall, dark Texan." She looked around. "Where is that tall, dark Texan, anyway?"

Elizabeth glanced over at the door that Brant had exited not more than five minutes earlier. Brant had barely left her side since arriving at the hospital. Another woman might take that as a sign of affection, but Elizabeth knew better. Brant was just doing what he thought was right.

"He got a call and left the room to take it," she said.

"Well, go get him," Minnie directed. "Not only do I want to ask him about the insurance, but I want to thank him for saving my life. If it had been up to you two, we would've all died in that damn stairwell."

"Oh, that's real nice, Mama," Harriett said. "We almost die trying to save you and that's the thanks we get."

"Good Lord, Harry, would you stop being so dramatic—"

Elizabeth slipped out the door before Minnie could finish. A smile tickled the corners of her mouth as she walked down the hallway. Most people might be upset that their family members couldn't seem to get along, but Elizabeth was just happy to have a family. A family who loved one another regardless of the way they verbally sparred.

She found Brant in the waiting room. One of the firemen who had responded to Baby's call had loaned him a t-shirt, and he wore the navy shirt with a pair of pale green scrubs and booties. Most men might look scruffy in the mixed clothing. Brant just looked hot and endearingly rumpled. The complete opposite of what she must look like in the hospital gown she wore over Miss Hattie's tattered satin dressing gown.

Brant was still talking on the phone, with his back to her and his head cocked down. When she touched his arm, he turned and his gaze ran over her from head to toe. Funny, but he didn't look like he thought she looked horrific. In fact, his eyes sparkled with something that looked a lot like relief. But he glanced away so quickly she couldn't be sure.

"Listen, Beau," he said. "I'll keep you updated." He pressed a button and lowered the phone. "How's Minnie?"

"As ornery as ever," Elizabeth said. "She's already talking about rebuilding."

Brant grinned. "Well, rebuilding may not be the right word. The fireman I talked with said that the sprinkler-system on the main level kicked in once the fire came up the elevator shaft. It sounds like we'll just need to deal with the damage done to The Jungle Room and some smoke and water damage."

" 'We'll?' "

Brant's gaze shifted away. "I was thinking that maybe I would stick around for a couple weeks." His Adam's apple slid up and down as he swallowed hard. "I mean, if you want me to."

There was nothing that she wanted more. Unfortunately, a couple weeks would only be enough to completely destroy a heart that was already broken.

"I realize that I'm already indebted to you for buying the house and for rescuing my family from the fire," she said in a voice that betrayed none of the emotions that threatened to overflow. "But I was wondering if I could ask one more favor."

He turned back to her and stepped closer. "Anything."

She lifted her gaze to his and tried to etch every feature into her memory. The dark, wavy hair. The high forehead. The deep-set eyes. The strong nose. And the firm mouth that gave up smiles so infrequently that, when it did, it could brighten an entire world. Her entire world.

"I want you to leave," she said in a voice husky with smoke and emotion. "I want you to leave and never come back." A tear dripped down her cheek. "Never."

Brant didn't know how he made it to his truck that was parked out in front of the regional medical center. He felt like someone had dropped a three-hundred-pound barbell on his chest. His heart hurt, and he was having trouble breathing. Not to mention his blurred vision. He wanted to blame it on smoke inhalation, but if that was the case, then why had it only started after Elizabeth told him to leave?

Once inside his truck, he turned on the engine. It wasn't more than thirty degrees outside, but that didn't stop him from cranking up the air conditioner. The cold air revived him enough that he was able to back out. He figured he'd feel better once the hospital disappeared from his rearview mirror.

He didn't.

The farther he got from Elizabeth, the worse he felt.

As the mile markers swept past, all Brant could think about was the pain he'd seen in those amber eyes. A pain that actually had him believing that he'd been wrong. Elizabeth did love him. Not because he was her first sexual partner, but for some reason he couldn't explain. The thought of her love had his eyes burning and his throat clogged with emotion. Still, he refused to turn around. She would get over him and, in time, find someone else to love.

Someone who didn't have a dark cloud following him.

The image of Elizabeth being held by someone else made the pain in his chest tighten and his foot press harder on the accelerator. He was going so fast that he passed the old truck that was pulled off on the side of the road before he even noticed it. But it wasn't the truck that had him slamming on his brakes as much as the pair of bootie-covered feet hanging out the open window.

By the time Brant hopped out and ran back to the old Ford pickup, he wondered if he was too late. Moses Tate looked like a corpse stretched out on the cracked leather seat with his gnarled hands crossed over the front buttons of his red long johns. But it only took one shake of his foot to get the old guy's eyes to pop open.

"About time you got here, son," he said. "I'm pert near starvin' to death." He took his time sitting up, his aged bones popping and cracking. "Darn ornery hen kickin' me out of her hospital room after I saved her life. First, she gets mad at me for askin' her to get married, then she gets mad at me for tryin' to take care of her. After survivin' three wives and a live-in girlfriend, I still can't figure women out." He opened the door and eased out. "It ain't the battery, but it might be the fuel pump."

It turned out to be the gas pump. Moses' pickup was completely empty. After figuring out the problem, Brant got back in his truck where Moses was sitting in the passenger's side, sipping from a silver flask.

"Well, I'll be damned," Moses said when Brant told him about the empty tank. "I thought for sure I filled up day before yesterday." His eyes squinted. "Or maybe it was last Wednesday, right before I stopped off at the library to read the paper."

Just the mention of Bramble's library had Brant's chest hurting again. He tried to ease the pain by taking a deep breath, but it didn't seem to help.

"You ever been to the library in Bramble?" Moses continued. "It's got about the most comfortable couches a man would want to sit in—except for Miss Hattie's, of course. And besides the couches, we got us a real sweet librarian." He glanced over at Brant, who now couldn't seem to breathe at all. "You know Ms. Murphy? She looks a little like that fan dancer at Miss Hattie's that you're so taken with."

Brant's gaze swept over to Moses, and the man grinned from ear to ear, revealing his pink gums. "I might not remember what day I put gas in, but I can still see." He shook his head. "I never figured Ms. Murphy for a dancer. Last time I saw her dance was at your brother's weddin' right after she caught that bouquet." He shook his head. "Seein' as she'd always been the old maid, it surprised the entire town. 'Course, nobody wants to be alone. And that little gal has been alone far too long. It's nice to see she finally found someone to love her the way she deserves to be loved."

"I don't—" Brant tried to squeeze the words out, but without air, they stuck in his throat.

While he worried about dying from lack of oxygen, Moses kept right on talking as if nothing was wrong. "'Course, the townsfolk ain't gonna be real happy about it. They were thinkin' it was the other Cates boy who Ms. Murphy fancied, not the one who tried to shut down Dalton Oil. But if you can survive Minnie and the hens, I figure you can survive the town of Bramble." He finally glanced at Brant. "You okay, boy? You look a little peaked."

"I can't marry Elizabeth," Brant gasped out.

Moses looked confused for only a second. "Cold feet? Can't say as I blame you. I had cold feet every time." He held out the silver flask. "Here, take a swig of this. It will help." The fiery whiskey did help, and Brant took more than one swig as Moses continued to ramble. "Marriage is a scary proposition. You're promisin' to cleave to one woman for the rest of your life."

"Then how did you end up with three?" Brant asked.

There was a long stretch of silence while Moses stared out the windshield. "I lost all three. One to influenza. Another to cancer. And the last I just outlived."

"But how did you survive?" he asked. "Didn't you love them?"

"More than my life," Moses said. "But you can't make choices on whether or not it's going to cause you pain down the road. You'll miss a lot of love and joy that way, son." He studied Brant. "So do you love Ms. Murphy, or don't you?"

Brant took another deep drink of whiskey and waited for the burn to fade before he voiced his worst fears. "If something were to happen to her, I wouldn't be able to keep on living."

Moses snorted. "Well, if you can't live without her, what the hell are you doin' sittin' here?"

Brant looked over at the old man. He didn't know if it was the whiskey or the question, but suddenly the light went on. If he couldn't live without Elizabeth, what was he doing sitting there? He didn't know what was going to happen next week, or next month, or next year. But suddenly he realized that it didn't matter. The weeks, months, and years would all be empty without Elizabeth. Without Elizabeth, his life really would be cursed.

Once the realization hit him, Brant only sat there for a second more before he popped the truck into drive and laid rubber, making a U-turn in the middle of the road. Moses, who didn't have on his seatbelt, slid halfway across the seat. But the old guy didn't seem to be too upset by Brant's crazy driving.

"Thatta way, son," he said, as he slapped one saggy knee of his red long johns. "It's time to quit messin' around and take the bull by the horns. And speaking of that, I don't care if Minnie has them nurses throw me out a hundred times. I love that stubborn old hen and have spent way too much time without her. If she don't want to marry me now, I'll just camp out on Miss Hattie's porch until she changes her mind. 'Cause this old man ain't givin' up without a fight."

"Damn straight!" Brant toasted him with the flask before taking another swallow. But he choked on the fiery liquid when he looked in the rearview mirror and noticed the flashing red lights.

Chapter Thirty-one

*Henhouse Rule #6: Don't overlook a fine rooster
just because he has mussed feathers.*

THE LIBRARY WAS QUIET FOR A TUESDAY. There were no
preschool reading programs planned and no Bramble
Elementary field trips. On days like this, Elizabeth usually
ordered new books or did a little cleaning and reorganizing.
But today she just sat at her desk and stared at nothing.

Minnie had been released from the hospital the day
before. Since the hens couldn't return to Miss Hattie's until
the structural damage had been inspected and the house
was deemed safe for occupancy, they were all staying at
Elizabeth's. The small house was filled to the rafters with
Minnie, Sunshine, Baby, Starlet, and Elizabeth's mother,
who used the excuse of wanting to make sure Minnie
didn't corrupt Elizabeth any more than she already had.

But Elizabeth wasn't buying it. After reading Minnie's
journal, her mother had softened toward the old woman.
She was the one who pushed Minnie in the manual wheelchair the hospital had loaned her, the one who helped her
shower and use the bathroom. They still fought like a
couple of hormonal teenagers, but there was an underlying
respect, on both sides, that hadn't been there before.

Thinking about her mother and grandmother had Elizabeth glancing up at the clock. It was only a little after four, a good fifty-two minutes before she could lock up. Still, she couldn't remain in the library a second more.

Since the fire, Elizabeth had come to a decision. She had loved being Bramble's librarian, but it was time to move on. The first thing she wanted to do was make sure that Miss Hattie's was up and running. She looked forward to greeting the first guests and witnessing their reaction to hen hospitality and history.

But as much as she had come to accept and respect her ancestors, she refused to be like them. She didn't want to spend her entire life at Miss Hattie's. She'd already been consumed by one job. She refused to be consumed by another. She wanted to travel. To experience things she'd only read about.

She wanted to live.

And she wanted to love.

As painful as Brant's departure had been, Elizabeth refused to be one of those women who let one bad experience ruin their lives. It wouldn't be easy to forget Brant. Even now, her heart felt as if it had been used for a piñata, but she would do it.

She had to.

It didn't take Elizabeth long to lock up and head down Main Street toward her house. With winter just around the corner, the wind was cold and harsh. She had just stopped to button up her knee-length coat when she was run into from behind and almost knocked to the ground. After catching her balance, she turned to find a large cardboard box with a cowboy hat showing above it and two skinny blue-jeaned legs showing beneath it.

"Beg pardon," Kenny Gene's muffled voice came from behind the box. "But I'm on official business."

"What in the world do you have there, Kenny?" Elizabeth asked.

"Ms. Murphy?" His head appeared at the side of the box, and a bright smile lit his face. "I shore missed you on Saturday. Faith is nice and all, but she don't know the library near as good as you do. She sent me home with two Scooby-doo books that I'd already read. Hey, where were you, anyway?"

"I had some family business to attend to," she said.

"Oh." Kenny seemed to remember the box that he held in his hands. "Well, I've got me some business, too. I need to get this honey from Josephine's to the sheriff and quick."

"Honey?" Elizabeth fell in step next to him. "Why in the world would the sheriff need that much honey?"

He hefted the box up higher as his strides grew longer. "We really wanted tar, but Phil over at Topper Roofs was plumb out due to the fall roofin' special he's been runnin', so the sheriff came up with the honey idea. It won't be hot, or nearly as sticky, but I guess we'll have to make do with what we got. Luckily, Nathan had plenty of chicken feathers. Although he wasn't real happy when we told him what we was plannin' on doin' with them. 'Course, he's always been a gentle-hearted feller. Even when it comes to dealin' with low-down, rotten scoundrels."

Elizabeth stopped in her tracks.

Tar.

Feathers.

Low-down rotten scoundrels.

"Kenny!" she yelled as she raced to catch up with him. "What low-down, rotten scoundrel?"

"The one the sheriff arrested for drunk drivin'." His strides lengthened. "The same scoundrel who wanted to close down Dalton Oil and make Bramble a ghost town." He paused as if waiting for a drum roll. "Branston Cates."

Elizabeth stumbled on a crack in the sidewalk, but Kenny didn't notice and kept right on walking and talking.

"But we're going to show him. Once he's honeyed and hen feathered and rode out of town on a rail—or the back of Lowell's tractor since we couldn't find a rail either—he'll realize that you can't mess with Bramble." He turned suddenly and headed across the street, leaving Elizabeth standing on the curb in shock.

As much as she'd fantasized about Brant being miserable without her, she couldn't stand the thought of him actually being hurt. And while honey and feathers might not physically hurt him, to a man like Brant, the loss of his dignity would be almost as painful as being dipped in hot tar. She started to race after Kenny, but then realized that when the town got something in their heads there was no reasoning with them. There were only a few people who could get the town's attention.

Elizabeth reached into her tote for her cell phone, but then remembered that she'd left it with the hens in case Minnie took a turn for the worse and needed to call the doctor. She hurried across the street to the pharmacy to use their phone, but it was locked up tight. As were all the businesses up and down Main Street. And it only took one glance down the street at the crowd forming in front of the jail to understand why.

For a clumsy girl who had failed physical education three years running, Elizabeth made it home in record time. The gate stuck, and she was forced to climb over it, snagging her hose in the process and landing on one knee in the middle of her garden.

"What in tarnation is goin' on?"

Elizabeth looked up to find Minnie sitting on the porch in her wheelchair wearing Elizabeth's tattered chenille bathrobe.

Ignoring the mud clinging to her shoes and knee, Elizabeth hobbled up the steps. "Where's the phone?"

"Now I realize you're a little crazed over Branston, Lizzie. But you need to pull yourself together and start—"

"The phone, Minnie!"

Minnie's eyes narrowed, but she pulled the phone from the side tote bag that hung on her wheelchair and handed it over. As the librarian, Elizabeth had every person's number in town programmed into her phone so it didn't take long to pull up Shirlene's. Unfortunately, Brody answered and didn't seem to be in any hurry to hand the phone to an adult. It took Elizabeth using her sternest voice to get him to finally yell for his father. Of course, Billy didn't act much better than his three-year-old son. When she told him what was happening, he laughed so hard and so long she was forced to hang up on him. She tried calling Hope and then Faith, but neither were home.

With no one else to call, Elizabeth turned back to Minnie. "Where's your gun?" She expected to get an argument, but instead, Minnie pulled out the small derringer she had insisted on taking with her the night of the fire and slapped it in Elizabeth's palm.

"Be careful what you aim at. You'll only have two shots to hit it."

Two shots seemed like more than enough. Especially since Elizabeth had no intention of shooting anyone. She just needed to scare them long enough to listen to reason. She handed the phone back to Minnie and headed down the steps. As she climbed back over the fence, she heard Minnie call out.

"Come on, you hens! Lizzie's packin'."

By the time Elizabeth reached the corner of Main Street, she glanced behind her to see the hens following. Since they had escaped the fire with only the pajamas on their backs, they all wore something of Elizabeth's—a collection of frumpy suits that would make even a Puritan head for a shopping mall. She barely noticed as her gaze quickly returned to the growing crowd in front of the jail.

Elizabeth had never been the type to be rude, but she had never been this upset before. She elbowed and pushed her way through the crowd like a kid at a carnival freak show. It wasn't easy. People didn't seem to want to give up their spot until they noticed who it was doing the pushing.

"Why, Ms. Murphy," Rachel Dean said. "I didn't think you was into spectatin' sports."

"I need to get through, Rachel," she said. Rachel must've detected the desperation in her voice because she lifted her large hand and thumped Rye Pickett on the back.

"Let Ms. Murphy through, Rye. She's got a hankerin' to see that ornery scoundrel get his just deserts."

"Well, of course, Ms. Murphy." Rye pushed two men out of the way to get her to the front. She arrived just in time to see the glass door of the jail open and Brant step out with his hands cuffed in front of him. He still wore the fireman's t-shirt and the green scrubs. But now there was blood on the scrubs and the collar of the t-shirt was torn. He squinted in the bright afternoon light, his dark hair blowing in the stiff wind. His face had been battered before, but now it looked worse. There was a fresh bump on his chin. But the bump didn't bother her as much as the missing bootie. The sight of his long, bare foot exposed to the cold air made Elizabeth madder than a wet hen. Sheriff Winslow had no more stepped out from behind Brant than Elizabeth started in.

"I would like to have a word with you, Sheriff Winslow," she said as she limped up the pathway.

Brant's eyes widened, and a look that could only be described as relief flooded his face. It made Elizabeth all the madder, and she found herself stepping between him and the sheriff, who looked more than a little baffled.

"Now, I realize I'm a little late gettin' that book on taxidermy back, Ms. Murphy, but I'm still workin' on mountin' that three-foot catfish I caught out at Sutter Springs."

"More like three inches, I'd say, Sam." Moses Tate stepped out of the door in the red long johns he'd worn to the hospital. "'Course, you always were off on measurements."

"Now don't be buttin' in again, Moses," the sheriff said. "That's what landed you in jail in the first place."

"What landed me in jail is a jackass." Moses squinted at Kenny Gene, who stood on the front lawn, emptying bottles of honey into a stainless steel tub. The handles of the tub had a rope tied to them, and the rope was looped over a branch of the maple tree. "But I figure you're in good company. Just what in the blue blazes is goin' on here, anyway?"

"Nothin' that Branston Cates doesn't deserve." Mayor Sutter stepped away from the crowd. "The man wanted to ruin Bramble. And from what I hear still wants to close down Dalton Oil. Now, all of us are more than willin' to forgive and forget a man who owns up to his mistakes. But as far as I can tell, this man don't feel the least bit repentful."

The crowd started grumbling in agreement, which set

Moses to hollering about "blame idiot townsfolk." It took Elizabeth firing the gun up into the air to get everyone to shut up.

"No one is touching this man," Elizabeth stated. She stepped in front of Brant. "I realize Brant has made some stupid mistakes. Not to mention his delusional belief in a silly curse. But everything he's done was to protect his family." She waved the gun around, and people in the front row ducked. "And we all know how important family is."

"If family is so important to him," Rossie Owens yelled, "then why didn't he show up at his own brother's weddin'?"

"Yeah." Kenny Gene slowly raised up the tub of honey by pulling on the rope. "That's about as low as a man can get."

Elizabeth swallowed hard. "Because he was—"

"Don't, Elizabeth," Brant said, but Elizabeth realized that the town finding out about Miss Hattie's didn't matter anymore. All that mattered was saving this man from humiliation.

"Because I own Miss Hattie's," she said. "And when he showed up there looking for answers about his grandfather's death, I handcuffed him to Miss Hattie's bed and wouldn't let him leave."

The shocked, baffled looks on the faces of the townsfolk were almost comical. The silence that followed would've done any librarian proud.

"No, she didn't." Minnie wheeled her way down the sidewalk in front of the jail. "I did."

"Don't even think you're going to get away with that lie, Mama," Harriett Murphy said as she followed behind Minnie. "As the direct heir to Miss Hattie's, I did it."

"No, it was me," Baby cooed. Even in an ugly suit and slippers, the woman caught all the men's attention as she wiggled up the path.

Sunshine breezed after Baby. "But Baby, I was the one who snapped the handcuffs closed."

"I did it! I did it!" Starlet yelled as she trudged up in an ugly gray suit that was busting at the seams. "As the youngest hen, I take full responsibility."

A buzz of confusion went through the crowd before Mayor Sutter hitched up his pants and spoke. "So you're sayin' that y'all are hens from the henhouse? And that the reason Branston Cates didn't show up in town for his brother's weddin'—and to apologize to the townsfolk— was because he was handcuffed to Miss Hattie's bed?"

"That's exactly what we're sayin', Mayor Sutter," Minnie said. "Now why don't you have the sheriff take those handcuffs off Brant before I start remembering a night that a young man with a handlebar mustache came knockin' on my door?"

The mayor's eyes widened before he quickly turned to Sheriff Winslow. "I think we've heard enough, Sam. Take the handcuffs off."

Sheriff Winslow didn't look too happy about it, but he did it. Once Branston was free, Elizabeth leaned in and whispered to him. "While their attention is still on the hens, you need to get out of here as quickly as possible."

"But what if I don't want to get out of here?"

For the first time, she looked at his face. It was battered, but smiling. Not with a slight smile, but a huge smile that showed off perfect white teeth and one dimple.

"This isn't funny, Brant," she said. "These people can turn on a moment's notice. And if you think you feel humiliated now, it will be nothing compared to how you'll feel honeyed and feathered."

"I don't know about that," he said. "Feathers looked

pretty good on you." Before she could stop him, he reached up and grabbed the edge of the tub Kenny had just finished hoisting above his head and dumped the entire contents down over him. Honey dripped from his hair and oozed over his shoulders in huge golden globs.

"What is the matter with you?" she said as she stepped back to avoid the sticky puddle pooling around his feet. "Sheriff Winslow is right. You are drunk."

"On love." He grabbed the bag of feathers on the ground and ripped them open. They attached to the honey like moths to a light and soon he looked like an overgrown chicken. But Brant didn't seem to care. Solemn, stern Brant wasn't the least bit worried about how ridiculous he looked. He just stood there with feathers floating around him, smiling like a simpleton.

"I don't care about being humiliated in front of an entire town. And I don't care about what happened to my grandfather or about a stupid curse." The smile faded as he reached out to smooth the hair away from her face, streaking honey all over her forehead. The eyes that peeked through the feathers held a look that made Elizabeth's breath hitch. "All I care about is you, Beth. And I'm sorry I didn't figure it out sooner. Sorry I was more worried about what I might lose instead of enjoying what I had. But I want to change that. Marry me, Beth."

Elizabeth might've thought it was all a dream if Brant hadn't pulled her into his arms and kissed her.

The kiss tasted of honey.

Hens.

And love.

Epilogue

*Henhouse Rule #50: There are no rules
but hen rules.*

ELIZABETH WOKE TO A PAIR OF FAMILIAR AMBER EYES.

The painting of Miss Hattie looked different in the bright sunshine that flooded in through the windows. Or maybe it was Elizabeth who was different. She no longer looked at her ancestor as a skeleton in the closet. She now looked at her as someone to be proud of. And that pride had her acknowledging the physical traits they shared. Not just the eyes, but the high cheekbones, the stubborn chin, the tilt of the smile. Elizabeth smiled back.

"You look as satisfied as an overweight Texan at a barbeque cook-off."

Since it wasn't exactly the voice Elizabeth had planned on hearing the morning after her wedding night, she quickly sat up and looked over at Minnie sitting in her new battery-operated wheelchair. Minnie searched through the canvas pouch that hung from the side of the chair and pulled out a cherry sucker that she quickly unwrapped and popped in her mouth. Her nose wrinkled.

"Regardless of what that good-lookin' husband of yours says, they ain't even close to being as satisfying as my Camels. And speakin' of smokes, on your way back from Europe, you need to stop by Cuba and get some cigars."

Just the mention of her honeymoon trip had Elizabeth glancing at the clock on the mantel. Her eyes widened as she sprang out of bed. "Why did you let me sleep so late?" She hurried to the bathroom, sidestepping the feather fans she'd used just the night before. Except instead of dancing for a room filled with men, she'd danced for just one. Just one smiling cowboy who showed his appreciation in a way that had Elizabeth blushing to the roots of her hair.

"No need to get all flustered, Lizzie," Minnie said as she followed her into the bathroom. "Branston has been up for the last three hours doing what he does best—takin' over. He sent off that huge family of his, has the helicopter waitin', luggage loaded, and has given us hens a stern lecture about what we can and cannot do while you two are gallivantin' around Europe." She pulled out the lollipop. "It makes me wonder if handcuffin' him to the bed was such a good idea, after all. The man has more rules than Miss Hattie."

As Elizabeth turned on the bathtub faucet, she shot Minnie a skeptical look. "As if you'll pay any attention to Brant's rules."

Minnie cackled. "True. Henhouse Rule #50 clearly states: 'There are no rules but hen rules.'"

Unable to stop herself, Elizabeth walked over and gave Minnie a big kiss right on the forehead.

It shocked the woman so much that the sucker fell out of her mouth onto the lap of her negligee. "What was that for?"

Elizabeth laughed. "Just because, Grandma. Just because."

After she dressed, Elizabeth went in search of Brant. The house was back to its former glory. There had been extensive water damage on the first floor, along with smoke damage to the second, but Branston had spared no expense at getting the henhouse back in shape after the fire. Even The Jungle Room was completely restored to its endearing garishness.

But today Brant wasn't in The Jungle Room. Or in the front salon where Sunshine was practicing her yoga. Or in the library where Starlet was plucking out another song—no doubt about Beau. Nor was he in the kitchen where Baby was busy going over menus for the guests that would start arriving as soon as Brant and Elizabeth returned from their honeymoon. Not just male guests, but also couples. Adults who wanted to enjoy the fun and sensuality of spending the night at the legendary Miss Hattie's.

After searching all the rooms in the house, it finally dawned on Elizabeth where she would find him. Miss Hattie's lilac garden had become Brant's refuge. When he wasn't working in it, he was lying in the hammock under the cottonwood or sitting on one of the chaises enjoying a cigar.

The wedding had been held in the garden and attended by all of Brant's relatives, along with the entire town of Bramble, Texas. The only one who hadn't shown up was Beau. He was running with the bulls in Spain, but planned to meet Brant and Elizabeth in Paris during the second week of their honeymoon.

Elizabeth found Brant in the far northeast corner of the garden, in the spot where Miss Hattie had been laid to rest. But he wasn't standing over the intricate carved headstone with the hen perched on top. Instead, he was standing over the plain tombstone that had just recently been discovered beneath the tangled branches of a lilac bush.

The headstone of one William Frances Cates.

Elizabeth moved up next to Brant, slipping a hand around his waist. Without taking his gaze from the gray limestone marker, he curved an arm over her shoulders and pulled her close. For a moment, they didn't say a word. They just stood there side by side, as close as their ancestors had been buried, thinking about love and death while they breathed in the soft scent of blooming lilacs.

"Do you think they had something to do with us getting together?" Elizabeth asked softly.

Brant glanced down at her and arched a brow. "This coming from a woman who lectured me on fact and fiction."

She tucked her head against his shoulder and smiled. "I know it's silly. But it does seem strange that out of all the people in the world, we ended up together." She looked up at him. "What did your family say when you showed them the letters and your great-grandmother's confession?"

Brant shrugged. "There isn't much to say when you discover that your great-grandfather had an affair with a famous madam, or that your great-grandmother followed him back to Miss Hattie's and shot him down in cold blood." He shook his head. "But what I can't figure out is why your great-grandmother went to such great lengths to keep it a secret. I don't doubt for a second that she was the only one with enough power to keep the truth from coming out. The one who convinced the sheriff and mayor to go along with the false story about him being shot in Bramble."

"Maybe she didn't want anyone else to suffer," Elizabeth said. "And turning your grandmother in to the law would've left a little boy an orphan."

He nodded. "Obviously, Miss Hattie knew what I've only recently learned."

"And what's that?" Elizabeth leaned up and kissed his cheek.

"Revenge is for those who live in the past." Brant turned to her and gave her a deep kiss that left her breathless. "What do you say, Mrs. Cates? Are you ready to leave the past behind and start living in the present?"

Elizabeth hooked her arms around his neck and melted against the strong thump of his heart. "This hen is all yours."

Inside, the other hens gathered at the kitchen window.

"It won't be the same without them," Baby cooed.

Sunshine looked confused. "But I thought they were only going to be gone for a month."

"That's their plan," Minnie said. "But as much as Elizabeth thinks she's too old, I'm bettin' it won't take more than a week for her to be nestin'. And once she's pregnant, I figure they'll spend most of their time in Dogwood." She pulled out another lollipop. "And that's how it should be. Miss Hattie's is no place to raise a child."

"I don't know about that, Mama," Harriett said from behind her. "I think Miss Hattie's has evolved into the perfect place to raise a child."

Minnie smiled before she popped the grape sucker in her mouth. "Well, we'll have nine months to figure it all out. Until then, we've got plenty of other things to worry about." She glanced over at Starlet, who had just sat down at the table with the new laptop Brant had gotten her for her birthday. "Did you locate the hen I've been looking for?"

Starlet shook her head. "Adoption agencies don't give out that kind of information. Luckily, my uncle works for the state and knows how to get around these things." She hit a button and turned the screen to the hens. "I don't know where this chick is living now, but I know where she grew up."

Minnie read the name of the small town and cackled. "Right in our own backyard."

You can take the cowboy out of
Texas but you can't take Texas
out of the cowboy. New York
City doesn't suit rodeo rider
Beauregard Cates. It's time for
him to head on home to Bramble.

Please turn this page
for a preview of

Flirting with Texas

Chapter One

"EXCUSE ME, but aren't you supposed to be naked?"

Beauregard Cates pushed up his Stetson and squinted at the middle-aged woman who stood in the pool of light from the street lamp. She wore one of those touristy t-shirts that vendors hawked on every corner and a bright orange visor that would work real well on an elk hunt. She did seem to be hunting for something. Beau just wasn't quite sure for what. He'd been propositioned before—more times than he could count—just not when the woman's husband stood right next to her. A husband who looked as interested in the answer to the question as his wife seemed to be.

"Maybe you have to pay him to take his clothes off." The man held up his digital camera and clicked off a few pictures, the flash momentarily blinding Beau. "Hell, we've had to pay for everything else in this friggin' town."

The woman shot her husband an annoyed look before holding out her hand. "Give me a twenty, Marty. Joan got a picture with The Naked Cowboy, and I'm not leaving New York City until I get one."

It looked as if Marty might argue, but then he stuffed the camera into the bag hooked over his shoulder and pulled his wallet from the back pocket of his high-waisted, khaki shorts. "I swear, Laurie," he grumbled. "You'd buy a dog turd if that crazy neighbor of ours brought one back from vacation."

Not denying it, his wife snatched the twenty out of his hand and waved it at Beau. "And could you hurry? We want to get to the Empire State Building before it closes."

Beau had done a lot of crazy things in his life, and regretted very few, but somehow he couldn't bring himself to stand in his underwear in the middle of Central Park while a tourist snapped pictures that would no doubt end up on Facebook. And after the incident in New Zealand, Beau's mama had threatened to yank a knot in his tail if he ever ended up naked on the internet again. But before he could decline the offer, the woman that he had been following came out of the bathroom.

Except she didn't look like the same woman who'd gone in. The ponytailed blond hair had been tucked beneath a sleek black wig, and her waitressing outfit had been exchanged for a tiny white top and a skirt that showed off a good ninety percent of her mile-long legs. Not that Beau was a leg man. He was breast fed and proud of it. Still, he couldn't help but enjoy the toned calves and smooth thighs. But it wasn't her legs that gave the woman's disguise away. It was the determined tilt of her chin—and the "Think-Green" tote bag slung over her shoulder.

He tried to remember the name he'd been given. *Janine? Jennifer?*

A thump pulled his attention away from his thoughts,

and he turned in time to see Marty rubbing his chest above the thick black strap of his camera bag.

"What?" He glared at his wife. "You're going to get a picture with some naked guy, and I can't even sneak a peek at a street walker."

"She's not The Naked Cowboy," Laurie huffed.

"About that picture," Beau said as he uncrossed his boots and rolled up from the park bench, "I'm afraid I'm going to have to give you a rain check." His gaze returned to the woman in the black wig who appeared to be having a hard time walking in her sky-high heels. As she headed down the path toward Central Park South, she wobbled more than Beau's one-year-old nephew, Bobby.

"A rain check?" Laurie sounded thoroughly disappointed. "But we're only here until Monday."

Beau turned to her and pinned on his most brilliant smile. A smile that had gotten him out of more bad situations than he could count. "I'll tell you what. Since you're going to be here this weekend, what about if I leave you a couple tickets for the bull-riding competition at the ticket window of Madison Square Garden?" He glanced over at Marty. "Then you can take dozens of pictures of different cowboys—a few who won't mind at all getting naked for you."

"You ride bulls?" Marty asked.

"Yep."

Marty perked up. "No kiddin'? I didn't figure you for a real cowboy. I just figured that you ran around naked in a hat and boots for the money."

"All part of the illusion that's New York City." Beau tipped his hat at them. "Y'all enjoy your vacation now."

It didn't take him long to catch up with the woman.

She moved a lot slower in the heels than she had in the black running shoes she'd worn when she came out of the restaurant. More than a few times, she stopped to catch her balance and adjust the straps of the shoes. Pointy-heeled shoes that made her legs look twice as long.

As he slowed his pace to keep a few yards behind her, Beau had to admit he was a little confused. Why would a waitress walk to Central Park and change clothes in the bathroom? If she was meeting friends after work, why hadn't she changed at the restaurant? Or why hadn't she just gone home like any normal person would've done after working all day on their feet? It would've made Beau's job a lot simpler. If she had gone home, he would now have her address and would be on his way back to his hotel to cuddle up with the sweet little event coordinator he'd met that afternoon. An event coordinator who filled out her western shirt to mouthwatering proportions.

The thought of Peggy Sue and her abundant twins had Beau tiring of his detective work. He hadn't minded sitting in the bar across the street from the restaurant, shooting the shit with the bartender and eating a double cheeseburger, while he waited for "a tall, skinny gal with blond hair down to her butt" to get off work. But he wasn't about to spend the rest of the night playing Dick Tracy when he had a better offer waiting for him back at the hotel. He had promised that he would get the woman's address, and he would, just not at the expense of his sex life. Especially when his sex life wasn't exactly going as well as he would like.

Of course, it was nothing to worry about. Just a little hitch in his giddy-up. A hitch Peggy Sue just might be able to help him with.

On that thought, Beau started to turn around when the waitress suddenly veered off the main path and headed into the thicker foliage.

Well, damn. He didn't know a lot about Central Park, but he didn't think that any park was safe for a lone woman to be wandering around at night. So he mentally said good-bye to Peggy Sue and headed into the trees. The trail was narrow and much darker than the paved path. In fact, he couldn't see more than a few feet in front of him. The waitress was nowhere in sight. He started to get concerned when a tree branch popped out and struck him in the chest. He stumbled back just as something hit him in the calves, knocking his feet out from under him and sending him to the ground. His shoulder hit first. The same shoulder he'd dislocated a few months earlier while kite surfing in Belize. It didn't dislocate again, but it hurt like hell. Gritting his teeth against the pain, he rolled to his back and glared up at the woman who stood over him. From this position, her legs looked like they extended all the way up to the quarter moon that hung in the dark sky.

"Why are you followin' me?" she asked, her Texas twang twice as thick as the stick she poked in his chest. No doubt, the same stick that had his calves throbbing. "Did Alejandro send you to scare me? Well, it's not going to work." She pointed the stick at his nose. "Now you listen and listen carefully, you go back to your boss and tell him that I'm not going to be intimidated. Especially not by some old, gray-haired cowboy who can't even fend off a girl."

Tossing the stick away, she adjusted her tote bag and wobbled back down the trail.

Beau lay there for a few minutes, staring up at the stars.

Old, gray-haired cowboy?

He sat up and rubbed his shoulder. It hurt like a sonofa-bitch, but it was nothing compared to his wounded pride. Not that he had anything to be ashamed of. The woman had caught him off guard is all. Or not a woman as much as some kind of freakish mutant that was a cross between Gwyneth Paltrow and Jean-Claude Van Damme.

It took awhile to locate his Stetson. He slapped it against his leg and placed it back on his head. He walked down the trail with every intention of hailing a cab and heading straight to the hotel and Peggy Sue. As far as he was con-cerned, his detective days were over. But when he reached the paved path, he couldn't help glancing in both directions.

He didn't see the waitress, but a group of kids raced by, four boys in baggy shorts and flip-flops. One passed off a handful of firecrackers to the kid who ran next to him. Beau grinned. Having grown up with four brothers, he knew how much fun firecrackers could be. And how much trouble they could get you into.

Beau's brow knotted. Speaking of trouble, what kind of trouble was the waitress involved in? Who was this Alejandro? And why would he send someone to intimi-date a woman? Her aggressive behavior was more than a little annoying, but that didn't give a man the right to bully her. And maybe that was why she'd been so hostile. She was scared.

The thought had Beau turning in the same direction the waitress had been headed. As he walked, he tried to remember her name.

Joyce? Jeanette? No, it was two j names. Jilly June? Jeannie Joy?

Before he could think of her name, he found her. She

stood by one of the horse-drawn carriages that were parked next to the curb, talking with a driver who wore one of those ridiculous top hats. Or not talking as much as flirting. She was laying it on thick, giggling and touching the man's arm.

Maybe Marty was right. Maybe the woman did a little streetwalking on the side to supplement her waitressing income. It made sense considering the disguise and revealing clothing—and who she was related to.

Beau probably should've left her to her business. It didn't look like the woman was in any kind of imminent danger. Still, he couldn't bring himself to leave until he was sure. He walked around the back of the line of carriages and slipped up on the other side. As he drew closer, he could hear the waitress talking.

"...hope you don't mind if I get a picture of you to show all my friends back home," she said in a voice with no twang whatsoever, "but you're just so cute. And I bet you have to be strong to handle a horse that big."

Beau peeked around the side of the carriage at the man's skinny arms and figured the woman could whip the driver's ass with one hand tied behind her back.

"Well, draft horses are pretty hard to handle." The driver's voice beamed with pride. "And this one is as stubborn as they come. If he doesn't watch himself, he won't be pulling a carriage for much longer."

"Really?" She held the camera higher. If she was taking pictures, she was doing it through video. The red record light was on. "What happens to stubborn horses when they can no longer pull a carriage?"

"They usually find themselves—" The driver stopped and pointed a finger at the camera. "Hey, don't I know you? You're the blonde that was here last week asking questions and taking pictures." He stepped closer, his voice angry. "You almost lost me my job when my boss saw that video on YouTube."

"I don't know what you're talking about." The woman started to back away, but the driver grabbed her arm and pulled off her wig. The blond ponytail spilled out.

"You don't, huh?" He dropped the wig and made a grab for the phone. "Hand over the phone, blondie."

Beau had seen about as much manhandling as he could take. Opening the door of the carriage, he climbed in with the intent of climbing out the other side and helping to even the odds. But before he could do more than open the opposite door, Blondie proved him right. The driver was no match for the skinny girl. She threw an elbow-shot into the man's stomach that had Beau sucking in his breath. The driver released her, but before she could make a run for it, a swarm of other carriage drivers came running. With all exits blocked, most people would've given up. Blondie wasn't even fazed. She vaulted up into the driver's seat of the carriage, took the reins, and shouted a deep-throated "hah!"

Beau braced to be thrown on his ass.

Instead, nothing happened.

"Hah!" Blondie continued to slap the reins. But the only movement it generated from the horse was a flick of its tail.

Her shoulders drooped, and Beau figured she was about to accept defeat when the four boys in baggy shorts raced past. The scent of burning fuses warned Beau, but not quick enough. The staccato pops of firecrackers went off right next to the horse's front hooves. The draft horse reared, and Beau was thrown back against the seat. By the time he sat up, the horse was at a full run. Carefully, Beau made his way to the driver's seat. Blondie wasn't quite as sassy anymore. She had lost the reins and hung on to the side rail for dear life.

Without any guidance, the horse chose his own path. Fortunately for the pedestrians, it was a less populated route. Unfortunately for Beau and Blondie, it wasn't really a route.

Shrubs and low-hanging branches whacked them in the face and scratched their arms as the horse charged down a narrow trail. Figuring that the back was safer than the front, Beau lifted the woman off the seat and pulled her down to the cushioned red leather. It didn't surprise him that she wasn't exactly happy about being protected. She fought worse than a lassoed steer. Still, after being bested earlier, Beau wasn't about to let her get the upper hand again. And since he didn't want to hurt her, it turned into something of a wrestling match.

The woman knew her moves. She tried headlocks, cradles, and half nelsons. But Beau had wrestled in high school, and after only a few moments, he ended up on top with her legs pinned beneath him and her arms held over her head.

The fight fizzled out of her at the same time as the carriage came to a stop.

Beau's hat had come off, and his face was inches from hers. So close, he could see the freckles that sprinkled the bridge of her nose. So close, he could see the starburst of deep blue in her irises. Her hair had come out of the ponytail and framed her face in long, wheat-colored waves. He had always preferred dark-haired girls, but the cloud of gold looked so soft that he couldn't help leaning down to rub his cheek against the silky strands. A scent drifted up. A scent he had no trouble distinguishing.

Cherry pie.

Homemade cherry pie piping hot from the oven.

Suddenly, Beau was hungry.

And not for food.

Like a lightning bolt straight from heaven, desire sizzled through him and settled in a hard knot beneath the fly of his jeans. The unexpected sensation had him pulling back in surprise, and the spitfire didn't waste any time taking advantage of the opportunity. She gave him a hard shove and rolled out from beneath him. Still stunned, he could only watch as she grabbed her bag and jumped down from the carriage.

The slamming door brought Beau out of his daze, and his gaze moved down to the hardened swell beneath his zipper. A smile spread across his face. Not the smile he gave to most folks, but a real smile that came directly from the relief that flooded his body.

Up ahead, he could see the woman hobbling down the path in only one high heel, her golden hair glistening in the moonlight. After an entire night's contemplation, a name popped into his head.

Jenna Jay.

THE DISH

Where authors give you the inside scoop!

From the desk of Katie Lane

Dear Reader,

Have you ever pulled up to a stoplight and looked over to see the person in the car next to you singing like they're auditioning for *American Idol*? They're boppin' their head and thumpin' the steering wheel like some crazy loon. Well, I'm one of those crazy loons. I love to sing. I'm not any good at it, but that doesn't stop me. I sing in the shower. I sing while cooking dinner and cleaning house. And I sing along with the car radio at the top of my lungs. Singing calms my nerves, boosts my energy, and inspires me, which is exactly how my new Deep in the Heart of Texas novel came about.

One morning, I woke up with the theme song to the musical *The Best Little Whorehouse in Texas* rolling around in my head. You know the one I'm talking about: "It's just a little bitty pissant country place..." The song stayed with me for the rest of the day, along with the image of a bunch of fun-loving women singing and dancing about "nothin' dirty going on." A hundred verses later, about the time my husband was ready to pull out the duct tape, I had an exciting idea for my new novel.

My editor wasn't quite as excited.

"A what?" she asked, and she stared at me exactly like the people who catch me singing at a stoplight.

She relaxed when I explained that it wasn't a functioning house of ill repute. The last rooster flew the coop years ago. Now Miss Hattie's Henhouse is nothing more than a dilapidated old mansion with three old women living in it. Three old women who have big plans to bring Miss Hattie's back to its former glory. The only thing that stands in their way is a virginal librarian who holds the deed to the house and a smokin' hot cowboy who is bent on revenge for his great-grandfather's murder.

Yes, there will be singing, dancing, and just a wee bit of "dirty going on." And of course, all the folks of Bramble, Texas, will be back to make sure their librarian gets a happy ending.

I hope you'll join me there!

Best wishes,

Katie Jane

♥ ♥ ♥ ♥ ♥ ♥ ♥ ♥ ♥ ♥ ♥ ♥ ♥ ♥

From the desk of Amanda Scott

Dear Reader,

What happens when a self-reliant Highland lass possessing extraordinary "gifts" meets a huge, shaggy warrior wounded in body and spirit, to whom she is strongly attracted, until she learns that he is immune to her gifts and that her father believes the man is the perfect husband for her?

What if the warrior is a prisoner of her father's worst enemy, who escaped after learning of a dire threat to the young King of Scots, recently returned from years of English captivity and struggling to take command of his unruly realm?

Lady Andrena MacFarlan, heroine of THE LAIRD'S CHOICE, the first book in my Lairds of the Loch trilogy, is just such a lass; and escaped Highland-galley slave and warrior Magnus "Mag" Galbraith is such a man. He is also dutiful and believes that his first duty is to the King.

I decided to set the trilogy in the Highlands west of Loch Lomond and soon realized that I wanted a mythological theme and three heroines with mysterious gifts, none of which was Second Sight. We authors have exploited the Sight for years. In doing so, many of us have endowed our characters with gifts far beyond the original meaning, which to Highlanders was the rare ability of a person to "see" an event while it was happening (usually the death of a loved one in distant battle).

It occurred to me, however, that many of us today possess mysterious "gifts." We can set a time in our heads to waken, and we wake right on time. Others enjoy flawless memories or hearing so acute that they hear sounds above and/or below normal ranges—bats' cries, for example. How about those who, without reason, dream of dangers to loved ones, then learn that such things have happened? Or those who sense in the midst of an event that they have dreamed the whole thing before and know what will happen?

Why do some people seem to communicate easily with animals when others cannot? Many can time baking without a timer, but what about those truly spooky types who walk to the oven door just *before* the timer goes—every time—as if the thing had whispered that it was about to go off?

Warriors develop extraordinary abilities. Their hearing becomes more acute; their sense of smell grows stronger. Prisoners of war find that all their senses increase. Their peripheral vision even widens.

In days of old, certain phenomena that we do not understand today might well have been more common and more closely heeded.

Lady Andrena reads (most) people with uncanny ease and communicates with the birds and beasts of her family's remaining estate. That estate itself holds secrets and seems to protect her family.

Her younger sisters have their own gifts.

And as for Mag Galbraith... Well, let's just say he has "gifts" of his own that make the sparks fly.

I hope you'll enjoy THE LAIRD'S CHOICE. Meantime, *suas Alba!*

Amanda Scott

www.amandascottauthor.com

♥ ♥ ♥ ♥ ♥ ♥ ♥ ♥ ♥ ♥ ♥ ♥ ♥ ♥ ♥ ♥

From the desk of Dee Davis

Dear Reader,

Sometimes we meet someone and there is an instant connection, that indefinable something that creates sparks between two people. And sometimes that leads almost immediately to a happily ever after. Or at least the path taken seems to be straight and true. But sometimes life intervenes. Mistakes are made, secrets are kept, and that light is extinguished. But we rarely ever forget. That magical moment is too rare to dismiss out of turn, and, if given the right opportunity, it always has the potential to spring back to life again.

That's the basis of Simon and Jillian's story. Two people separated by pride and circumstance. Mistakes made that aren't easily undone. But the two of them have been given a second chance. And this time, just maybe they'll get it right. Of course to do that, they'll have to overcome their fears. And they'll have to find a way to confront their past with honesty and compassion. Easily said—not so easily done. But part of reading romance, I think, is the chance to see that in the end, no matter what has happened, it all can come right again.

And at least as far as I'm concerned, Jillian and Simon deserve their happy ending. It's just that they'll have to work together to actually get it.

As always, this book is filled with places that actually exist. I love the Fulton Seaport and have always been fascinated with the helipads along the East River. The buildings along the river that span the FDR highway have always been a pull. How much fun to know that people are whizzing along underneath you as you stare out your window and watch the barges roll by. The brownstone that members of A-Tac use during their investigation is based on a real one near the corner of Sutton Place and 57th Street.

The busy area around Union Square is also one of my favorite hang-outs in the city. And so it seemed appropriate to put Lester's apartment there. His gallery, too, is based on reality—specifically, the old wrought-iron clad buildings in SoHo. As to the harbor warehouses, while I confess to never having actually been in one, I have passed them several times when out on a boat, and they always intrigue me. So it isn't surprising that one should show up in a book.

And I must confess to being an avid Yankees fan. So it wasn't much of a hardship to send the team off to the stadium during a fictional World Series win. I was lucky enough to be there for the ticker-tape parade when they won in 2009. And Boone Logan is indeed a relief pitcher for the Yankees.

I also gave my love of roses to Michael Brecht, deadheading being a very satisfying way to spend a morning. And finally, the train tunnel that the young Jillian and Simon dare to cross in the middle of the night truly does exist, near Hendrix College in Arkansas. (And it was, in fact, great sport to try and make it all the way through!)

Hopefully you'll enjoy reading Jillian and Simon's story as much as I enjoyed writing it.

For insight into both of them, here are some songs I listened to while writing DOUBLE DANGER:

"Stronger," by Kelly Clarkson
"All the Rowboats," by Regina Spektor
"Take My Hand," by Simple Plan

And as always, check out www.deedavis.com for more inside info about my writing and my books.

Happy Reading!

Dee Davis

♥ ♥ ♥ ♥ ♥ ♥ ♥ ♥ ♥ ♥ ♥ ♥ ♥ ♥ ♥

From the desk of Isobel Carr

Dear Reader,

I have an obsession with history. And as a re-enactor, that obsession frequently comes down to a delight in the minutia of day-to-day life and a deep love of true events that seem stranger than fiction. And we all know that real life is stranger than fiction, don't we?

RIPE FOR SEDUCTION grew out of just such a real-life story. Lady Mary, daughter of the Duke of Argyll, married Edward, Viscount Coke (heir to the Earl of Leicester). It was not a happy marriage. He left her alone on their wedding night, imprisoned her at his family estate, and in the end she refused him his marital rights and went to live with her mother again. Lucky for her, the viscount died three years later when she was twenty-six. And while I can see how wonderful it might be to rewrite that story, letting the viscount live and making him come groveling back, it was not the story that inspired me. No, it was what happened after her husband's death. Upon returning to town after her mourning period was over, Lady Mary received a most indecent proposal...and the man who made it was fool enough to put it in writing. Lady Mary's revenge was swift, brutal, and brilliant. I stole it for my heroine, Lady Olivia, who like Lady Mary had suffered a great and public humiliation at the hands of her husband, and who, also like Lady Mary, eventually found herself a widow.

And don't try finding out just what the poor man did or what Lady Mary's response was by Googling it. That story isn't on Wikipedia (though maybe I should add it). You'll have to come let Roland show you what it means to be RIPE FOR SEDUCTION if you want to find out.

Isobel Carr

www.isobelcarr.com